KEEPING
SECRETS

Another spirited novel by the bestselling Amish author!

LINDA BYLER

KEEPING SECRETS

SADIE'S MONTANA
Book 2

Good Books

New York, New York

Copyright © 2015, 2020 by Linda Byler
All rights reserved. No part of this book may be reproduced in any manner
without the express written consent of the publisher, except in the case of
brief excerpts in critical reviews or articles. All inquiries should be addressed
to Good Books, 307 West 36th Street, 11th Floor, New York, NY 10018.

Good Books books may be purchased in bulk at special discounts for sales
promotion, corporate gifts, fund-raising, or educational purposes. Special
editions can also be created to specifications. For details, contact the Special
Sales Department, Good Books, 307 West 36th Street, 11th Floor,
New York, NY 10018 or info@skyhorsepublishing.com.

Good Books is an imprint of Skyhorse Publishing, Inc.®,
a Delaware corporation.

Visit our website at www.goodbooks.com.

10 9 8 7 6 5 4 3 2 1

Library of Congress Cataloging-in-Publication data is available on file.

ISBN: 978-1-68099-611-1
eBook ISBN: 978-1-68099-097-3

Cover design by Koechel Peterson & Associates, Inc.,
Minneapolis, Minnesota

Text design by Cliff Snyder

Printed in Canada

Table of Contents

Chapter 1

Even when you have a firm grip on it, hope can be torn away by the sound of your mother's voice. That's another reason why it's easier to love a horse.

Horses are sympathetic. You can tell by the way they lower their faces, very still, unmoving, when your fingers comb the silky forelock of hair.

Driving horses don't have that forelock. Their Amish owners keep it cleanly cut so that it is easier to put on the bridle. A driving bridle has two bits that must be coaxed between the horse's teeth, and shiny, patent leather blinders attach to the side of it. When the top of the bridle goes up over the ears and the chin strap is secured, the horse looks neat, and, well, Amish.

Sadie Miller's thoughts moved with the steady *ca-chink ca-chink* of the hoe as she chopped resolutely at the stubborn crabgrass between the rows of string beans. The unceasing Montana wind moved the tender garden plants restlessly, their green leaves swaying and bending like funny, green dancers.

Her mother moved ahead of her, bending over to remove the weeds from around the new string-bean plants, her graying hair tossed in the breeze like the bean plants. Her *dichly*, that triangle of blue handkerchief cut diagonally and hemmed on the sewing machine, moved and flapped wildly at the wind's command.

Mam was not overweight. She was not thin, either. She was just right for 50 years old. Her sage green dress whirled around, lifting above her knees, and she grabbed at the pleated skirt impatiently.

"Ach! Will this wind never die down?" she asked Sadie.

Sadie didn't answer, simply because it felt good to let Mam know she was sulking unhappily.

Why? Why did Mam have to come down on her like that? It wasn't fair. She was 21 years old, and Mark was as good as forbidden.

Ah, Mark. That tall, impossibly dark-haired, dark-skinned youth of her dreams. Not really youth. A man, at 31 years old. He was the only person Sadie had ever truly wanted. And now this.

Sadie had opened the subject earlier. She was the only one in the garden with her mother, and she was glad to tell her about meeting Mark on the day when Reuben accompanied her on the quest for a buckboard they had seen advertised in the local paper.

Sadie had been riding Paris, her beloved palomino, while Reuben was on Cody, the small brown mare. They had first thought the horses were from a wild herd. Later they discovered that the animals had been stolen from a wealthy rancher in Hill County. Richard Caldwell, the owner of the ranch where Sadie worked, had contacted the owner of the stolen horses to make things right. Meanwhile, Sadie continued cooking in the huge, commercial kitchen for as many as 25 ranch hands with Dorothy

Sevarr. Dorothy was rotund, and she was aging, but she had a heart of gold despite her fiery personality. Kindness flowed from her in great, healing quantities.

Dorothy's husband, Jim Sevarr, still drove his ancient pickup truck back and forth from Sadie's house, providing her transportation to work. He was an old cowboy, much more comfortable on the back of a faithful horse than driving his cranky pickup, whose gears were never where they were supposed to be.

Sadie and her family lived on the side of a wooded ridge, thick with pines and aspen trees. Their log home had been built by Sadie's father, Jacob, a carpenter and builder.

They had moved to Montana from Ohio about five years earlier, the age-old lure of the west drawing Jacob Miller. The family had settled into the budding new church and community, which the Old Order Amish had started in the beauty of the Montana landscape.

The move, however, had taken its toll on Sadie's mother, Annie, who had slid down a despairing slope of depression, her condition steadily deteriorating into severe mental illness, which Jacob found difficult to acknowledge.

✤ ✫ ✤

Mam's continuing silence made the space between them an uncomfortable irritation that Sadie could not let go. Inside her, disobedience raged while rebellion infuriated her. Tears lodged in her throat.

Yet as Sadie watched her mother's nimble fingers tugging at the stubborn weeds, she did thank God again for the educated doctors and the hospital stay that had enabled Mam to begin her long climb out of the pit of misery that she endured so bravely and silently.

Still. How could she? Did mothers have a right to forbid their daughters from seeing someone?

Life with Mark, or more precisely, the hope of life with Mark, was unthinkable now. Her future rose before her, black, bleak, and windswept. She would turn into a spinster, no matter her beauty or her hair shining like a raven's wing. It shone black actually, depending which way the light settled on it. It nearly matched her blue, blue eyes fringed with thick, black lashes.

Sadie Miller was too pretty for her own good, the old ones said. Beauty could be a curse. Once it got into a young girl's head and puffed up her pride, it became a great, heavy mushroom of vanity that would inevitably take her down every time.

They watched Sadie in church and shook their heads. God was already moving in her life, they whispered. Look what had happened to Ezra. Killed when the buggy went down over the bank on Sloam's Ridge. Sadie almost losing her own life. Ezra would have been the perfect husband for Sadie—loyal, steady, conscientious.

She was just different, that one.

Jacob and Annie had her hands full with three more daughters, one as pretty as the next. Leah, Rebekah, and Anna were all as pleasing to the eye as their oldest sister, but Sadie was the only one gallivanting around on that horse, as far as they knew. She rode around on that palomino horse named Paris, which was downright unladylike. If Jacob and Annie knew what was right and proper, they would rein her in with a firm hand.

They clucked, wise in their years, but they also knew that Jacob Miller's daughters added spice to their lives, mixing some flavor into their work-focused existence.

None of them dating right now either. Not one. Robert Troyer's Junior would be a good one for Rebekah, now wouldn't he? Him being so tall and fair. They clasped their hands and mostly thought these things, but with an occasional slip of the tongue to each other, accompanied by a knowing twinkle in their eyes.

"Mam!"

Mam straightened her back at Reuben's call. She lifted a hand to shade her eyes, searching for her only son, her youngest child.

"Here we are, Reuben. In the garden."

"Can I have a popsicle?"

"How many are left?"

"A whole bunch."

"Okay."

Mam bent to her task, her back turned, and resumed weeding. Sadie cleared her throat, never breaking the hoe's rhythm. The dirt was loosening nicely, although it wasn't the fine loam they were used to in Ohio. The growing season was shorter here in Montana, and having a good, productive garden was much more challenging.

The evening sun began its rapid descent behind Atkin's Ridge. Sadie often thought the sun was like a drop sliding down a tumbler of water. It didn't move very quickly until it neared the base of the glass. Then, in a rush, it was gone. That's how the sun was.

So once it began its descent for the evening, you didn't have much time left in the garden, or to return from a ride, or whatever it was you were doing in the evening.

The silence stretched between the women, until Mam straightened her back, rubbed it with her fist, and groaned. There was no sound from Sadie. Mam turned, watched her eldest daughter's silent hoeing, then stood solidly, her hands on her hips, her eyes narrowing.

"Now Sadie, you can just quit your *poosing* this second. I told you how I feel, and that's the way it is. If you don't want to listen to your father and me, then I suppose you'll have to suffer the consequences."

Sadie stopped her steady hoeing and learned on the handle with the back of the hoe resting on the ground.

"You don't have to say it again, Mam. You already told me once."

Mam watched Sadie lower her eyes and shuffle the hoe back and forth with one hand on the handle.

"Come, Sadie. Let's go sit on the porch swing. Then we can talk. I'll listen awhile and promise to stay quiet this time."

Sadie looked up, blue fire in her eyes.

"What is there to say? If you and Dat forbid me to see Mark at all, then there's nothing to say."

"It would be different if we knew his background. He says he was raised Amish, but where? By whom? Who is his family, if they exist at all? What kind of name is 'Peight'?"

Sadie sighed and lifted her hoe, the skirt of her green dress swirling as she turned and walked decidedly out of the garden.

Mam watched her go, then slowly made her way to the house, her shoulders stooped with dejection.

Sadie put the hoe into the small, log garden shed. She picked up an empty bag that had contained black sunflower seeds for the bird feeders by the window in the dining room. She put it into the trash barrel and wondered why Reuben never picked up anything.

It was the same way with his clothes. He shed his

trousers and shirts beside his bed, both turned inside out. His socks, also turned inside out, remained where he conveniently peeled them off.

No shower for Reuben in the evening. He hated showering before he went to bed. He did it only in the morning, so his hair stayed straight and silky all day, swinging handsomely, the brown and blond strands throwing off the light so that no one knew what color his hair actually was.

Reuben wouldn't talk about girls. He thought they were an unhandy lot, especially in school, bossy know-it-alls who weren't worth a lick at baseball. The only one who came close to being normal was Alma Detweiler, who could bat a ball over the one-room schoolhouse, and often did, making a home run in the process, her long, thin legs churning with admirable speed as she rounded third base, her head turned to watch the ball.

He had taken to dabbing a bit of cologne on his shirt from the wee bottle of Stetson that Leah had given him for Christmas. The practice was a source of knowing winks from his older sisters, who of course never said a word to him.

It was hard enough being 13 and the only guy in the family.

Sadie closed the door, turning the latch firmly, then watched the sky change from blue to orange then lavender, and, finally, purple. The sunsets were nothing short of spectacular here in Montana, and she never tired of them, ever.

She wondered if Mark was seeing the sunset. Was he up on that old barn roof replacing the metal, or had he already finished the job? Was Wolf, his dog, lying at the foundation of the barn? Was Mark whistling under his breath, or was he quiet? More melancholy, morose even, when he was alone?

How did one go about forgetting a person? How could you ever get over the pounding beating of a heart in love?

He had held her against himself three times—once at the mall when she was fainting, spilling her drink all over the shining tile floor. Once at the death of Nevaeh, the beloved black and white paint she had helped nurture back to health at Richard Caldwell's ranch. Once more... When was it? A few weeks ago? A few years? It was hard to tell the difference now.

Mark had gone out of Sadie's life, back to Pennsylvania, after Nevaeh died, saying he was not good enough for her. He had asked to come see her, a genuine Saturday evening date, and then disappeared. Leaving a note saying only that he needed time to make peace with the past. To right wrongs.

What wrongs?

Then there was her dream. Mark as a small boy, a florid-faced man with a whip, the knowing when she woke up. Did she still know?

She thought Mark was her destiny, the man who should be her much sought-after will of God that Mam preached to her girls.

And now this.

Verboten. Forbidden. If she saw Mark, she would be *ungehorsam*, a kind of curse clearly understood among her people. Parents were to be honored and respected. Above all, children were required to be obedient.

But at her age? Wasn't she allowed to make her own choices now?

Her choice was Mark Peight, clear and defined. She loved him and would travel to the ends of the earth for him.

Sadie started when Dat came around the corner of the shed, almost bumping into her. He pushed back his straw hat, ran a hand through his graying beard, and smiled his slow, easy smile.

"Whatcha doin'?" he asked, mimicking Jim Sevarr.

"Oh, just standing here watching the colors change in the sky," she replied easily.

Dat was like that nowadays. Ever since his pride had taken a crushing blow because of his Annie's mental illness, he had only become a better father—more open, mellow, and slow to judge.

"You look a bit poorly around the eyes."

Sadie laughed. "I'm not."

"You sure?"

She poked at a small rock with the toe of her foot. "Well, maybe a bit. It's Mam."

The concern Dat carried in his heart instantly became visible. Sadie saw this look only when Dat's confidence in Mam's health and well-being slipped a bit off center.

"Is she…?"

"No. It's about… Remember Mark Peight?"

Jacob nodded, his mouth a firm line.

"Reuben told me he's back. Said he has a dog named Wolf."

"Yes."

Her father shook his head heavily, burdened, concern clouding his blue eyes.

"I don't know, Sadie. Mam and I talked, and…"

"I know what you talked about. She told me. Twice."

The anger started in her feet and propelled her forward, away from Dat. Then it spread. The tingling adrenaline lent wings to her bare feet, and she ran, racing past the house, down the long, sloping driveway, onto the dusty, country road. Her feet pounded the macadam, her hands pushing down the pleated skirt that flapped in the stiff, summer breeze, her breath coming in quick puffs.

Better to get away. Just run. Keep running.

She ran past the one-room, Amish schoolhouse, the split-rail fence around the schoolyard. She ran past the patch of pines that were forever swallowing the ball from softball games.

She once told Reuben that a dragon lived in those pines and ate the softballs for dessert.

Sadie smiled, thinking of Reuben's indignation and his lecture reminding her that Mam and Dat had taught them not to tell lies. Now here she was, 21 and an old maid. Well, dangerously close to one, anyway, and still telling lies. There was no such thing as dragons.

S'hut kenn dragons.

Sadie laughed out loud. Her laugh became a hiccup, the hiccup caught in her throat and became a sob, and still she ran.

When she saw the moon climbing in the sky, she stopped beside the road, her chest heaving as she caught her breath. That felt better.

The exercise cleared her head, driving the anger away for now, but she knew it would be a constant companion. Yes, Reuben, a dragon of sorts. She would need strength to overcome it.

The unfairness of the situation was staggering. She sank to her knees beside the roadside, plucked long stems of grass, and bent them over and over. Still her eyes remained dry.

She saw Reuben, then. He was running, fast and low, his eyes wild. He was calling her name, and Sadie could tell he was afraid by the whites of his eyes.

Instantly she was up on her feet, waving her hands.

"Here, Reuben, here I am."

Her brother slid to a stop, his fists clenched, his face white. His words tumbled over each other like gravel pouring out of a wheelbarrow.

"I mean it, Sadie. If you ever take off running like that again, I'm going to … going to … I don't know what!"

"I was just…"

"No, you weren't. You big baby. Dat is about nuts. Now get back to the house and stop acting like…"

A shrill, whining rang out. A distant, yet uncomfortably close crack of a rifle, the bullet emitting a deadly whine. Then another.

"Hmmm," Reuben raised an eyebrow, mirroring Sadie's wide eyes and lifted brow.

"Somebody must be practicing their aim."

"It's awfully close."

"Let's get back."

Another shot rang out. The sound was not unusual in the Montana countryside. Ranchers were always on the lookout for predators, or chasing unruly cattle by shooting, or practicing their shots from horseback. "Cowboying around," in Dat's words.

"It's sorta dark for ranchers to be after the coyotes."

"Maybe it's a lion," Sadie said.

Reuben instantly turned his head to search the deeper shadows of the pines, chewing the inside of his cheek the way he did when he was afraid. "Ain't any lions around."

"Jim says there are."

"He don't know everything."

"Almost."

They walked back in silence until they came to the schoolyard. Sadie pointed to the pine woods on the opposite side of the split-rail fence. "How many softballs do you think that woods contains?"

"A bunch." Reuben spoke quickly, his eyes darting from one side of the road to the other.

Suddenly, he turned to Sadie and told her in no uncertain terms that she better not try a stupid trick like this again. He knew it was all because Mark was back, and Mam and Dat didn't like it one tiny bit. Why couldn't she get over Mark and like a normal boy from around here instead?

Sadie nodded, her face devoid of expression. Better to let Reuben have his say. At his age, he didn't understand matters of the heart.

"And, Sadie, not just that. You know when you were up there talking to Mark that day we saw him on the roof? Well, I went down to the barn and let myself into his living place. It's sort of a room he built where he sleeps and eats. Well, that place is totally packed with guns and knives.

He lifted his arm, bringing it down in a swinging arc for emphasis, drawing out the "totally," putting plenty of effort into the word "packed." "I bet he has 50 guns. And 50 knives."

"Mmm," Sadie said, acknowledging this bit of information.

"I don't know about him. He has English clothes lying around. And I don't know what a whiskey bottle looks like, but he has some strange looking bottles in his little refrigerator."

Sadie gasped. "Reuben, why did you go snooping in his refrigerator? That's just awful bad manners."

"I know. I...Well, it bothers me, Sadie. Your eyes turn to...I don't know, stars...or something when he's around. And he isn't a real Amish person, I don't think. I'm afraid of him, sort of. Even his dog is kind of wild-looking, even if he's friendly as all get out. And, I don't know, Sadie, but suppose you would marry this guy against Mam and Dat's wishes, and he'd turn out to be somebody completely different than you think he is?"

There was no answer to this youthful bit of wisdom, spoken in the raw, innocent concern of a person not quite a child and not quite an adult. She knew his words were truthful, without malice or prejudice.

As they neared the house, they heard the sound of the porch swing, a high squeak that turned to a much lower one as the swing went back and forth.

Anna leaped up from the wooden porch rocker, slamming the back of it against the log wall of the house. "Where were you, Reuben?"

"Ask Sadie."

"What in the world got into you, Sadie, taking off down the driveway as if someone's house was on fire?" Anna asked, clearly perturbed.

"I needed the exercise."

Dat cleared his throat from the swing, and Sadie prepared herself for a lecture, but it did not come. The swing kept its steady creaking, Mam's feet sliding comfortably across the wooden floor of the porch.

"That's not why," Anna sputtered, intent on the truth.

"Let it go, Anna," Mam said quietly.

"Well, I will, but they need to know it's too dangerous to be traipsing all over the countryside this time of day. Hey, do we still have those Grandpa Cookies with coconut on the icing?"

"I put the last two in Reuben's lunchbox," Mam replied.

"Of course. Anything for Reuben," Anna said, huffily, sitting down in the rocker again, hard, slamming the back of it against the logs of the house again.

"Pull that rocking chair out from the wall, Anna. You'll knock all the paint off for sure," Dat said sternly.

Sadie sank into the remaining rocker. Maybe she should include Anna in her life more often. Ever since Reuben had learned to ride, Anna's jealousy had become so real, you could almost touch it. It was only natural. Reuben and Anna had been inseparable until he had accompanied Sadie to the ridge to tame the horses. They had tried to persuade Anna to ride, but she refused to even try to get up on a horse's back, flouncing off in a temper every time.

Reuben confided in Sadie a few weeks ago, saying the reason Anna acted like that about riding was because she thought she was fat, and thought she'd look like a big elephant if she went riding.

Reuben had hissed the last bit of information as Anna strolled into the barn, peeling the Saran Wrap from a chocolate whoopie pie. "See? She's always chewing or slurping something, and she's *chunky*."

Anna got up to pull the rocker away from the wall, and Sadie noticed the back of her dress stretched tightly across her shoulders.

"I'm hungry," Anna announced.

"Well, what could we eat?" Mam said softly.

"Those cookies," Anna said, the loss and sadness of not having them in her voice.

"I made fresh shoofly pies this morning."

"Don't like shoofly."

"Oh, that's right. I forgot. You don't. Well, what else could you eat?"

"I know!" Reuben shouted. "Lucky Charms!"

"Lucky Charms!" Anna echoed as she leaped from her chair, slamming it against the wall once more, causing Dat to grimace.

Sadie rocked, the chair's rhythm calming her agitation. She sighed, wishing she was the age when the thought of a dish of cereal accelerated your heartbeat. Her youngest siblings had no serious concerns, no pressing matters, other than achieving passing grades in school or dealing with Mam's refusal to allow you to do some very important thing.

The door to the phone shanty swung open. A small, dark form emerged and walked slowly across the driveway and up to the porch.

"Who were you talking to?" Mam asked.

"Do I have to tell you?" Leah asked, her voice swelling with emotion.

"Kevin Nissley or Kevin Nissley?" Dat asked, teasing, as Mam laughed softly.

Suddenly, Sadie felt very old and very tired, too tired to fight the jealously that reared its ugly head.

Chapter 2

WHEN JIM SEVARR'S RUSTY, OLD PICKUP WOUND its way up the drive, Sadie rose slowly from her kitchen chair, pushing back the untouched English muffin with peanut butter and strawberry jam. She forced herself to swallow a bit of grape juice, then went to the door when the truck stopped.

Mam looked up from the steaming wringer-washer as she lifted the clothes from the soapy water and fed them through the rollers of the wringer. The laundry room smelled of Tide and Downy, the detergent and fabric softener Mam always used. Piles of sorted laundry dotted the floor, Mam plopping them into the sudsy water one by one.

The compressed air, held in a large, round tank, was generated by the slow-running Lister diesel generator in the diesel shanty. When there was laundry to be done, Dat started the diesel so that Mam could fill the washing machine with the hose attached to spigots on the wall. Then she only needed to open the valve on the air line, and, instantly, the up-and-down rhythm of the air motor filled the house.

Some women still preferred a gas engine mounted on brackets beneath their washer, but Mam liked her air motor, so that's what her daughters were used to as well. It was home, it was their way, and it seemed right to use that wringer-washer when they were there.

Down at Aspen East Ranch, Sadie used a large, front-loading, automatic washer run by electricity. Using electricity was as normal as breathing for the Caldwell family. Everything turned on with a flip of a switch or the turn of a dial. Mixers whirred, lights flooded the rooms, dryers turned and blew heat that dried the tumbling clothes, dishwashers hissed and whirred quietly, depending on the cycle. Coffee was ground, brewed, and heated with the flip of a switch. Microwave ovens heated things in a few minutes while the food container stayed cool. There was just no end to the convenience.

But that was at the ranch. The Caldwells were English people, and that was how they lived. It was not wrong for them to use modern conveniences, being born and raised that way. Amish people lived and abided by their *ordnung*. They preferred to stay "behind the world," or to practice living the way they always had, allowing only minor changes in order to be able to compete in the business world.

Sadie loved her job at the large ranch, but she especially loved working with Dorothy Sevarr, Jim's short, buxom wife with a large personality.

Opening the stubborn door of the pickup truck, Sadie grinned her silent "good morning" to Jim, plopped on the seat, and pulled mightily so the rusty door shut completely.

She stopped trying to expect a "good morning" out of Jim shortly after he started picking her up for work.

If she did greet him, the words fell on unfertile ground and withered away, swept under the cracked, vinyl seat by Jim's uncompromising grunt. If she only smiled as she entered the truck instead, he just shifted his toothpick. Sometimes coughed or cleared his throat. But his blue eyes always lit up and the crow's feet at their corners deepened.

It was just Jim's way, and Sadie knew he'd turn the pickup around and begin to talk before they were down the driveway.

"Y' git that there buckboard yet?"

"Not yet."

"Why didn't ya git it?"

"I'm not sure it's worth $500.00."

"Whatsa matter with it?"

"I don't know. The wheels seem sturdy enough, but the floor is rotting through, and Dat will definitely need to build new seats for it."

"Five hundred ain't very much."

"It's enough."

The Montana countryside was green and gold and brown. Sunlight dappled everything so that even the dust shone gold. It was one of those days when the weather was warm but not too warm. It was windy too, but not so windy that it tore at your skirts and grabbed your white covering, pulling your hair horribly and tossing it relentlessly.

The wind never stopped in Montana. It just changed its pace the way horses did. Sometimes it walked, lifting the leaves and the grasses gently. Other times it trotted, swirling skirts and flapping laundry briskly. Still other times it galloped, tearing at your covering, making you bend your head and dash wherever you were going, knowing your skirt was above your knees and knowing it did no good to try and control it.

The wind just blew.

Sadie loved the wind. God was in the wind, she always thought. His power was so visible then. No one could make the wind. No one could start it or stop it. It was God's—that's why.

In church, the ministers spoke of a new birth, comparing it to the wind. Did any man know where the wind stopped or started? God made the wind.

Sadie thought everyone made an awful big fuss about the new birth. The ministers said that God gave people a new birth. The new birth was from God, like the wind was from God. The wind created dancing leaves and swaying branches. The Spirit created good people doing kind deeds. But Sadie knew that sometimes people did kind deeds to be seen by others and not from the genuine goodness coming from a heart flowing with God's love.

People were hard to figure out. Horses were easier to understand and much easier to talk to. Paris always knew how Sadie was feeling. Paris knew when she was silly or light-hearted or angry. Paris was quiet when Sadie was lonely or blue. She would trot over and put her cheek close to Sadie's head, her warm, sweet breath whooshing in and out close to Sadie's shoulder. Then Sadie would cup her hand beneath Paris' nose and tell her everything that caused a dark mood to settle down over her, this cloak of grayness that made her breathe heavily, evenly, not wanting to perish because of it, but feeling as if she might.

Why couldn't she let go of Mark Peight? Here he was again, having bought the small, tumbledown place on the other side of Atkin's Ridge, and there she went riding happily along with Reuben one sunny afternoon, not a care in the world. And who should be up on the roof of the old Zimmerman place but Mark Peight himself?

Then that dry-mouthed, heart-hammering nonsense started all over again simply by the mere sight of him on that roof—the breadth of his shoulders, the way he turned his head, his blue-black hair tousled by the wind, his deep brown eyes looking straight into her heart. Suddenly she couldn't find one word to say.

He came back to Montana because of her, but what good did it do? Dat and Mam stood together as immovable as a rock. A fortress of parents. Staunch, and side by side. She was not allowed to date this mysterious stranger.

Was he a stranger? He had lived within their community for quite a while. He attended church, went to the hymn-singings, and joined the youth. He said he was raised Amish back in Pennsylvania.

But was he raised Amish, really? Who could know if he was telling the truth?

He had a past, that was sure. He was a troubled man, had been troubled in his teen years. But why? He had come so close to telling her his life's story, but then left suddenly to return to Pennsylvania. He sent a brief note to her but with hardly any explanation inside.

Sadie sighed, looked out the dirty window, and wished Mark Peight would get out of her life. But she knew if he did, her world would be completely devoid of meaning, as gray and miserable as the surface of the moon.

She was pulled back to reality when the truck came to a stop.

"There ya go, little lady."

"Thanks, Jim. See you in a little while."

A shifting of the toothpick was her only answer, but

she knew he'd soon be in the kitchen to see Dorothy, the love of his life.

The long, low ranch house was as beautiful as ever that morning, the yellow glow of the morning sun casting it in gold. The yard was immaculate, the shrubs and perennials tended lovingly by the aging gardener, Bertie Orthman.

Bertie rounded the corner of the house, his shoulders sloped and stooped with age, his blue denim shirt hanging loosely on his sparse frame. His hair was as white as snow, and probably just as clean, his mustache trimmed just so, just like the shrubs he kept in perfect form. He stopped when he saw Sadie.

"Now, ain't that a sight for an ol' man's eyes?"

Sadie turned to look behind her.

"What?" she asked, her blue eyes two beautiful pools of innocence.

Bertie grinned, then shook his head.

"Sadie girl, you really are one different person. Don't anybody ever give you no compliment? I meant *you*. You look so pretty wearing that there bluish dress. Just reminds me o' my Matilda, God rest 'er soul."

"Why, thank you, Bertie. I thought you meant someone or something was behind me."

Bertie bent to pluck a weed, then tenderly ran a hand over the top of a boxwood.

"Watch this!"

Sadie watched as he showed her his technique for running the gas-powered trimmer. He was so precise that the shrubs looked like a horticulturist's dream.

"You're good, Bertie. You really are. You have this place looking wonderful."

"Yep, I do."

Bertie grew visibly taller at Sadie's compliment, straightening his shoulders, puffing out his thin chest.

Not much humility in that one, Sadie thought as she smiled at Bertie. Still, he was a dear old man who would never hurt a flea. She felt blessed to work with people who truly were the salt of the earth.

Sadie went around to the side of the house, stepped up on the porch, and let herself into the kitchen. This huge, commercial room was her work place; the room where large meals were planned, cooked, and served to the dozens of hungry ranch hands who worked for Richard Caldwell. Richard was a massive giant of a man with a voice that matched his size, never failing to give Sadie a start when he entered a room.

This morning, there was no one in the kitchen.

Hmm, that's strange, Sadie thought.

She sniffed the air. Biscuits baking. She turned to lift the lid on a large, cast-iron Dutch oven. Sausage on. She pulled on the stainless steel container that held the filter of coffee grounds and found it empty. No coffee made yet.

"Dorothy?" Sadie called tentatively.

There was no answer, the kitchen silent except for the hissing sausage in the Dutch oven.

She bent to retrieve the coffee can and filters from the cupboard below. Measuring a half cup of coffee grounds into the white filter, she placed it into the container and slid it into place. She pushed the "START" button, happy to hear the usual gurgle accompanied by a whirring of sound.

Where was Dorothy?

Sadie walked to the basement door, opened it, and called Dorothy's name again. She was just about to pull on the bathroom door handle when it flew open. A red-faced Dorothy stepped out, wiping her hands on two very wet, brown paper towels.

"Sadie! Can't ya give a person a rest? You just 'Dorothy! Dorothy!' all over this kitchen the minute you can't find me! Can't you just come in quiet-like and figger I'll be around? When nature calls, I have to heed its voice. Can't I get a moment's peace in the bathroom? No!"

"I'm sorry."

"Sorry ain't gonna getcha nowhere. From now on, if'n you come to work and I ain't around, nature has called, and I'm where I should be at such a time."

Sadie looked into the snapping blue eyes below hers, the round face red with exertion, the gray hair electric with fury, and burst out laughing. She laughed until she clung to the counter for support, until tears squeezed between her eyelids, until she gulped and giggled and hiccupped. She peeped at Dorothy sideways, and when she saw Dorothy was still huffy, sitting now on a kitchen chair and eyeing her testily, she laughed some more.

"Ach, my. Oh, my."

Sadie straightened her back and grabbed a paper towel from the roll on the wall to wipe her eyes, apologizing as she did so.

"Dorothy, I won't do it again. I am truly sorry."

Dorothy slurped from her big mug of tea, licked her lips, and eyed Sadie levelly.

"It ain't funny. When you get to be my age, the constitution of your body is an important part of your life. I ain't had my bran muffins in quite some time, an' I'm plumb out o' Metamucil. You know, I told Jim all week, when he gits to town, go to the Rite Aid and git me the biggest bottle of Metamucil that's there. Does he? Does he remember? No siree, he don't. So see what happens? I got to set in the bathroom and here she comes. 'Dorothy. Dorothy. Dorothy!' It's enough to weary a person at this early mornin' hour."

Sadie felt the waves of humor, the beginning of a wonderful, deep-down, belly laugh, but she turned to start another pot of coffee before Dorothy could see her shoulders shaking and her mighty struggle to stay straight-faced.

The kitchen door swung open, and Jim strode purposefully up to Dorothy.

"I'm goin' to town. Ya want me to git ya anything? Boss needs some three-quarter-inch nails."

Sadie watched as Dorothy rose from her chair, all five feet of her. Her chest swelled to even greater proportions as she took a mighty breath. Sadie ducked her head at the coming tirade, watching as Dorothy's eyes narrowed and her lips pursed.

"Now, Mr. Sevarr, what would I possibly want from town? Isn't a thing. Nary a thing."

"But...I recollect there was somethin'. Wasn't there somethin' at the beginnin' of the week? Asprin or somethin'?"

"If you'd give two hoots about yer woman, you'd remember."

Jim looked uncomfortable then, taking off his battered Stetson and twisting it in blackened, gnarled fingers. He searched his wife's face for any sign that would help him out.

"Toothpaste? Shampoo?"

Dorothy harrumphed her disgust, drank more coffee, and spilled it over the front of her dress. Then, she waved to Jim, telling him to go on, git to town, she'd get the item herself if he didn't know what it was.

Sadie knew, then, that all laughing was finished. Dorothy meant serious business, and she had better do her best in the kitchen. And if Jim knew what was good for him, he'd get out of Dorothy's kitchen soon.

Sadie worked efficiently during the following hour, side by side with Dorothy. The silence stretched between them comfortably and with the respect Sadie knew was required of her.

She finished the sausage gravy, and then mixed batter for the hotcakes, pouring perfect yellow orbs of it onto a steaming griddle and flipping the cakes expertly. She and Dorothy cooked mounds of scrambled eggs, shining pots of grits and baked oatmeal, and great square pans of bacon cooked to perfection. Then they carried the vast quantities of food to the beautiful dining room. The steam table sat along one wall, and they slid the pans onto the grids. The steaming water beneath the pans, heated by electricity, kept everything piping hot.

Sadie made sure everything was in order, setting out clean plates, napkins, silverware, mugs, and tumblers. Then she moved swiftly through the swinging doors as the clattering of boots and the rough voices of the jostling ranch hands were heard coming down the hallway from the main entrance.

She was never at ease being in the dining room with the men. Her mother would not let her work here at Aspen East Ranch if she thought Sadie would be among the ranch hands. It was unthinkable. It was bad enough the way she was always talking about horses with her boss, Richard Caldwell.

Mam was too strict, Sadie thought. Most of the men who worked at the ranch were married or had girlfriends. Richard Caldwell told her once that the white covering she wore reminded the men of a nun's habit. It scared them and made them think twice about misbehaving. It was good for them that she was there. It reminded them that there was more to life than running cows and racing trucks and chasing girls they didn't respect anyhow.

Sadie had assured Richard Caldwell that she wasn't any better than those men's wives. They were good women who treated their men well, and she didn't want to be viewed as someone who was better than they. She was certainly only human herself, regardless of her clothes.

Richard Caldwell had only looked at her, levelly, and said nothing. She didn't know whether he took what she said as truth or not.

When she returned to the kitchen, Dorothy had disappeared once again. With one look at the closed bathroom door, Sadie stifled a smile and bent to the task of cleaning up. She soaked pans in hot, soapy water, filled the large, commercial dishwasher, wiped counters, scoured the stove, and then felt dizzy and a bit weak.

She hadn't eaten her breakfast at home, that's what it was. Well, she'd drink some orange juice, then fill a plate after the men were finished eating.

What was that?

She straightened, turned off the hot water, then listened. A knock, although a soft one. There. Another one.

Wiping her hands on her apron, Sadie went to the door and opened it slowly. She didn't see anyone, until she looked down. There was a very dirty, very brown, little boy, clutching the hand of a little girl who must be his sister. She was an exact replica of him, only grimier, if such a thing was possible.

Their hair was impossibly matted, snarled until it stood out from their little heads, stiff with dirt and dust.

There were brown streaks caked onto their faces. The little boy's T-shirt had been orange at one time, but now it was a color somewhere between brown and rust. The girl's skirt was torn, her T-shirt hanging from one shoulder, the neckline completely stretched out of shape. She was carrying a small, leather satchel, not a purse or a duffel bag, but a homemade bag bulging with items that were anyone's guess.

The children stared up at Sadie, their black eyes bright with fear.

Sadie opened the door wider.

"Hi!" she said, smiling brightly, hoping they felt welcome enough to share their names and what they needed.

They didn't answer.

"H ... hello!" Sadie said, trying again.

"I'm Marcellus. This is my brother."

The voice was soft and musical, spoken in perfect English with only a hint of an accent.

"My name is Sadie Miller."

"My brother is named Louis."

"Hello, Louis," Sadie said quickly.

"Good morning."

Sadie was unprepared for the perfectly pronounced greeting, the voice as soft and cultivated as his sister's.

Looking around her, Sadie was undecided what to do. Invite them in? She did not want to get anyone into trouble, but she couldn't let these poor little souls out here by themselves.

Where was that Dorothy?

Taking a deep breath, Sadie asked them to come in. Immediately, the children stepped inside, dropping the satchel on the rug inside the door. Their black eyes opened wide as they took in the vastness of the kitchen area.

"Where ... where did you come from?"

"Our mother set us out of the car. She drove away. Our father went away first. There is a man who comes to our house. Our mother cries. We are not allowed to go with her. She will come back soon."

This was all spoken in perfect English, in the musical voice by the little girl named Marcellus.

There was an audible gasp, and Sadie turned to find Dorothy behind her.

"What in the world is going on here?"

Dorothy for once spoke calmly, in disbelief. Her usual bristling personality quieted at the sight of these little ones.

Sadie heard a sniff, then turned to see Dorothy lower her round, little frame to her knees, holding on to the kitchen chair as she did so. Tears pooled at the corners of her eyes, as she held out her short, heavy arms.

"Angels, that's what they are," she whispered. "Come here," she said, louder, in her usual commanding voice.

The children stepped over obediently, and Dorothy's arms enfolded them to her breast. She smoothed their filthy hair with no thought for the grime. She kissed the dirty little faces, murmuring to herself.

"It's God hisself came to our door. It's a test. These little angels," she kept murmuring.

Sadie bit down on her lower lip, trying to keep her composure.

When Dorothy asked them where they were from, Marcellus repeated what she told Sadie. Dorothy got up, still holding the grimy little hands close, then sank into a chair. Her hand went to her head as if it was almost more than she could bear.

"My little darlings!" she cried, suddenly. "Sadie, go

get Richard Caldwell. Hurry up! He's still eating in the dining room."

"But..."

"Go!" Dorothy thundered, and Sadie went.

A sea of faces looked up as she entered the vast dining room. She found the face of her boss quickly and went to him. He slid back his chair, knowing it was important if Sadie appeared in the dining room when he was eating breakfast with the men.

"Excuse me."

"Yes, Sadie?"

"Dorothy... I... You need to come to the kitchen for a minute."

Richard Caldwell followed her as she made her way through the swinging oak doors, then stopped at Dorothy's side. She watched Richard Caldwell's face as he looked at the children.

He gave a low whistle, then shook his head back and forth. "Likely some drunk threw his kids out," he muttered.

Dorothy's eyes flashed. "Now don't you go sayin' that, Richard Caldwell. These is angels sent from God to see what we're goin' to do with 'em. You ain't turnin' 'em out, so you're not. They ain't no drunk's kids neither. Listen to 'em. Tell the nice man where you come from, Mary. Marcy. Marcelona."

Marcellus looked seriously from Dorothy to Richard Caldwell, then told them the same story as before, with Louis nodding his head beside her.

"There now," Dorothy said triumphantly. "These kids has some upbringing. Can't cha tell?"

Richard Caldwell was speechless. He opened his mouth, then closed it again.

"I'm a goin' to give them a bath, then me and Sadie's gonna feed 'em. You go find your wife. Tell her to come to the kitchen in two hours. About 10 o'clock. You come with her. You an' me an' Sadie an' her gotta decide what to do about these kids. We ain't turnin' 'em out, neither, an' don't even think 'bout calling the police. When Jim gets back, tell 'im to git in here!"

And so Dorothy arranged her soldiers, ready to do battle for her God.

Chapter 3

Dorothy BATHED AND SCRUBBED THE CHILDREN. She brushed their hair and dressed them in clean clothes she borrowed from a few of the ranch hands' kids. She fed them at the kitchen table, heaping their plates with scrambled eggs, toast, bacon, and hotcakes. The children drank thirstily before lifting their forks to eat the food. They had perfect manners, wiping their mouths with the napkins provided.

She huffed upstairs and back down, her face almost the same color as Barbara's purple kimono.

Barbara Caldwell came and watched Dorothy take care of the children. Her heavy, blonde hair was perfectly coiffed, her makeup applied expertly, the luxurious kimono she wore enhancing her elegance. She kept her emotions hidden, but there was no suspicion or judgment in her demeanor. She sat and observed, smiling, glancing at Richard Caldwell, occasionally commenting on the beauty of the children's hair or eyes.

Dorothy sent Sadie to clean the bathroom, dispose of the children's filthy garments, and clean the guest bedroom for them. She sprayed the tub with Tilex, cleaned the heavy mirrors and the ceramic above the sinks, then stopped when she spied an old leather satchel. It was not homemade at all. Rather, there was a tag, also made of leather, with foreign words inscribed on it.

Sadie knew enough about life to know what was affordable and what was not. This most definitely was not affordable, at least for anyone she knew, and it did not come from any store nearby.

But, these destitute little ones? Carrying a bag of finest…?

Glancing over her shoulder, Sadie lifted the flap and peered inside. Another bag. A cloth one. A drawstring. With fumbling fingers, she pulled it open and gasped. Quickly, she tightened the strings, closing the bag.

It couldn't be. Children didn't carry things like this. Who in their right mind would send two little ones, likely no more than five years old, out into the vast world with an expensive satchel containing what appeared to be jewels? Diamonds, maybe?

Sadie had no experience where jewelry was concerned, but she was pretty sure that when objects glittered and sparkled and were that heavy, they were probably real.

She considered opening the drawstring bag again, just to make sure she hadn't imagined what she saw, but decided against it. She shivered and looked at the satchel as if it was coiled and ready to strike.

Sadie cleaned the tile floor on her hands and knees, wringing the cloth well over a bucket of hot, soapy water. She hurried downstairs to dispose of the soiled water, told Dorothy the bathroom was finished, and asked if she needed anything else done in the kitchen before she tackled the bedroom.

"Nah, go on yer way. I'll keep an eye on Louise and Marcelona."

"Louis and Marcellus," Sadie said softly.

"I know. That's what I said."

Sadie didn't respond. She had to find Richard Caldwell. Or Barbara. Someone needed to know about that bag of jewels.

She put the bucket in the closet, then walked resolutely through the dining room and down the wide, oak-lined hallway to Richard Caldwell's study. Taking a deep breath to steady herself, she knocked softly and cringed when she heard that ear-splitting, "Come on in!"

She pushed the heavy, oak door timidly and was relieved to see her boss relaxed. He was tilting back in his great, leather chair. His feet, encased in heavy boots, were propped on his desk. His teeth flashed white in his tanned face as he smiled at her.

"Sadie!"

"Yes. Hello, again. I'm sorry to interrupt your..."

Her voice was drowned out by the shrill ringing of his desk phone. Richard Caldwell motioned for her to sit down, then picked up the receiver and yelled, "Richard Caldwell speaking!"

Sadie grimaced inwardly and imagined the person at the opposite end of the line holding the receiver away from his ear.

She tried not to listen, her eyes roaming the bookshelves and the expensive objects of art. She noticed dust on the wooden blinds and made a mental note to take time to wipe them tomorrow when she cleaned the study.

"Mike? No? Mark? Yeah, got it. What did you say? Paint? Pate? Can you spell that?"

His feet clattered to the oak floor. Tipping his chair forward, he grabbed a notebook and scribbled, yelling the letters as he wrote.

"P...ei... Huh?"

There was a pause before he finished with the "G...
H...T."

"Got it."

Then, "Yeah, come on down. I'll talk to you. Never
enough farriers to go around."

Another pause, then a chuckle.

"All right. See you this afternoon."

Sadie's eyes were two large pools of agitation when
Richard Caldwell turned to her.

"He sure doesn't have a lot to say. A new farmer.
Weird name. Hey, what's wrong with you, Sadie? You
look like you just swallowed your grandma."

"N...nothing. I mean...yes, there is. I... The children?"

Richard Caldwell nodded.

"They... After they had their bath and got cleaned up,
they... I found a bag of...of...I think diamonds or at least
jewels of some kind—in a leather...purse. It was upstairs
in the bathroom. I thought you needed to know about it."

"What? Now come on, Sadie. Kids that dirty and tat-
tered-looking don't carry around bags of jewels."

Sadie's eyes flashed.

"Would I make this stuff up?" she asked.

"No," Richard Caldwell shook his massive head,
laughing, "Not you, Sadie, not you."

He rose and asked her to take him to this leather
satchel.

Sadie walked down the hallway and up the wide stair-
case, acutely conscious of Richard Caldwell's heavy footsteps following her. She paused at the bathroom door
before walking to the well-lit counter and handing the
leather bag to her employer. She watched closely as his
thick fingers tried to undo the flap and then the drawstring. Muttering, he handed it to Sadie.

"You do it."

Her small fingers opened the drawstring efficiently. She held the opened bag out to him, her eyes searching his. Taking the bag, he spilled the contents onto the marble countertop, bent low, and whistled.

"What the...?"

He looked at Sadie, then bent to examine the small mound of glittering jewels, his heavy fingers raking through them.

"Earrings. Necklaces. Rings," he murmured, holding each one up to the light coming from the bathroom mirror.

There was a whisper of movement at the door, and they both turned to see the tall form of Richard Caldwell's wife, Barbara, enter the room.

There was a time when Barbara would have been suspicious, hateful even, of this Amish girl with the unusually beautiful face, her hair as dark as a raven's wing, her great blue eyes fringed with naturally dark lashes.

Sadie's presence had been a threat until Richard Caldwell helped her nurture the sick, broken horse, Nevaeh, back to health. During that time, Barbara's husband came to grips with his past and, as each day unfolded, he grew more loving and tender, especially toward his wife.

Now, seeing them both in the intimacy of the upstairs bathroom, Barbara's old suspicion and mistrust rose like sick bile in her throat.

"I don't suppose..." she began, despair clutching her throat.

"Barbara! Come here!"

Richard Caldwell's voice boomed out, and Barbara hurried to his side. All suspicion disappeared, and the despair fell away as her husband's arm encircled her ample waist, pulling her toward him.

"Look at this, honey."

This new term of endearment brought a thickening to the back of Barbara's throat, the place where tears begin, and she knew she would never be able to hear it enough.

Bending her head, Barbara peered at the jewels in disbelief. "Let me get my glasses."

The purple kimono swished expensively as she sailed from the bathroom, returning almost instantly with her reading glasses perched midway down her nose.

Then, "Wow! Oh wow! Richard! What is this?"

"They belong to the kids, I guess. According to Sadie."

"What?" Barbara was incredulous.

Sadie nodded. "When... when they had their baths, this was left on the countertop," she said, gesturing to the leather purse.

Barbara shook her head. "Are we sure we're not getting ourselves into something dangerous? This is unreal. Perhaps some... mobsters or gang members staged all this. They could be using those innocent children as a prop or something. We should absolutely report this to the police."

"I agree," Richard Caldwell said.

Sadie started to leave. But she turned. "Then I'll let it up to you. I just didn't feel right without at least showing you what I found. I'll return to my cleaning now, if you don't mind."

"Wait, Sadie," Barbara said, reaching out to her. "What do you think we should we do with these two little ones? I don't know... I mean..." she lifted her eyes to her husband.

Richard Caldwell acknowledged the questioning in

his wife's eyes with a very small shake of his head. Then he looked at Sadie, telling her that they didn't feel as if it was the right time for them to be caring for two small children. Did she have any suggestions? If the police were called in, the children would be placed in foster homes unless someone intervened.

"Would your family be able, or willing, to take them in?" he finished.

It was a hard question, one Sadie felt unable to answer. Her mother's mental health had been a real issue in the past. She had found help and resumed a healthy, balanced existence. Aided by her unwavering faith, she was peaceful and happy again. But to require this of her?

Sadie shook her head. "My mother hasn't been well, but there is a possibility. We'll discuss it and I'll let you know."

"Thank you, Sadie."

✽ ✡ ✽

That afternoon, Bertie, the gardener, asked Dorothy if she or Sadie would be available to help him plant the annuals in the garden down by the fishpond.

Dorothy was taking one of her many breaks, forking cheesy clumps of steaming macaroni and cheese into her mouth from the small microwavable dish in her hand. She washed it down with a resounding gulp of sweet tea, the ice clattering against the plastic tumbler as she set it on the kitchen table.

"Now, Bertie, I ain't goin' down there and breaking my back diggin' around in that there mud. It ain't no use. Come September, those plants will be froze stiffer'n my knees, so they will."

Bertie waved a hand in her direction, then snorted derisively.

"Aw, you old grouch. Then stay here in the kitchen and eat your macaroni and cheese. Where's Sadie?"

Sadie peeped out of the pantry door and smiled at Bertie, joy in her eyes. She loved Bertie, but she loved the banter between these two salty individuals even more.

"Sadie girl! You want to help me plant a few annuals down by the fishpond? My old back could sure use some help."

"Your old back? Well, why'd ya think my old back would be any different?" Dorothy spat out.

"I didn't ask for your two cents."

"Well, you got it."

Dorothy chuckled loudly before lifting another great forkful of macaroni to her open mouth.

Surprisingly, Bertie kept his peace and told Sadie he'd be ready in about half an hour.

"I guess, if it's all right with you, Dorothy?" Sadie asked.

"Yeah. May as well help him out if his back can't take it. We're havin' beef stew and rice for dinner this evening, so there's not so much to do. Go on and help him out, the poor, old man."

"You know, if you wouldn't be settin' there eating all that macaroni and cheese, you wouldn't be as…"

"Say it, Bertie! Go ahead and say it!"

Dorothy's eyes were snapping and twinkling at the same time. Bertie smiled, and Sadie suddenly became ravenous for the cheesy concoction Dorothy was enjoying.

"You want a dish of macaroni? Some sweet tea?" Sadie asked Bertie.

Sadie smiled to herself, thinking how English she could sound when imitating the lovely people that she worked with.

She heated more macaroni, punching the buttons of the microwave. At home, she would put her food in a saucepan, add extra milk, and set it on the gas burner of the stove. Then she would wait at least 15 minutes until it was heated through. She cringed at how Reuben burned food every time. He consistently plopped a saucepan on the gas stove, flipped the dial to high, and walked away. Sticking his nose in a magazine, he forgot about the stove until the house filled with the stench of burning food. Then he always blamed the girls for not making him something to eat. Using a microwave in an English person's kitchen was pretty handy.

Bertie settled into a kitchen chair, greatly enjoying his glass of tea and tucking into the dish of macaroni and cheese with as much enthusiasm as a much younger person.

Watching him, Dorothy started on a tirade of the different metabolism rates in people's bodies. Bertie said he didn't know, he never went to school for that. What he did know was this—if you ate too much, you got fat.

"Huh-uh. No. It ain't true. Look at you hoggin' that down. If I ate the way you do, I'd weigh 300 pounds!" Dorothy said testily.

"Is that all you weigh?" Bertie returned, then made a laughing retreat out the door and back to work, leaving Dorothy fussing and fuming and checking the refrigerator for some leftover coleslaw.

✿ ✫ ✿

Sadie found the flats of purple and pink petunias, the hose with the gardener's wand, and a trowel. Bertie wanted the flowers planted beside the brick walkways and on the side of the slope leading to the fishpond, but none in the shade by the trees.

"Petunias don't do well in the shade, you know," he explained. "If you need anything, give me a holler. I'll be mowing by the garage."

Sadie set to work, getting on her knees to dig, plant, and water. She loved the feel of the soil and reveled in the warm sunshine, the beauty of her surroundings, and the drone of bees as they flew busily from different sources of nectar.

Cows bawled, calves answered, horses roamed the paddocks and pastures, dogs barked, and pickup trucks came and went. But Sadie heard very little of these sounds that made up daily life on the ranch. Instead, her thoughts turned to Mark Peight.

Now why would he call Richard Caldwell? Yes, she knew he was looking for work, but... Did he know her parents forbid her to see him? No. How could he? She hadn't told anyone. Even her sisters didn't know. So, he wasn't coming to the ranch as a way to see her.

And now these children. A responsibility for someone. Had the police been here yet?

She was turning away from the dumpster after depositing the used plastic pots, when she spied Louis and Marcellus running toward her. What a difference the soap and shampoo had made! They were beautiful children. They almost seemed adjusted to the ranch, and they'd been here less than a day. Perhaps this was due to Dorothy's assurance that they would definitely be staying, that they had nothing to be afraid of, and that their mother was coming to get them as soon as she possibly could.

Sadie greeted them, and they answered with shy acknowledgement, perfectly worded in soft English.

"Would you like to help me?"

They declined, shaking their heads from side to side. Then Marcellus spoke up. "Gustav, our gardener, says we are too small to help."

Sadie nodded. Our gardener? Ach, my! The children must be from a well-to-do home.

Out of the corner of her eye, Sadie saw the tall form of Mark Peight enter the garden. He came down the brick walkway in his easy, cat-like stride. An electric jolt charged through her body, and, instantly, her hand went to her hair, leaving a dark smudge on her forehead. The children turned to face the tall stranger, keeping their eyes lowered respectfully.

"So there you are," Mark greeted her.

Flustered, Sadie got to her feet. "Hello, Mark."

"How are you, Sadie?"

"I'm doing well. How are you?"

"Good, good. Happy to be back in Montana."

He looped his thumbs in his suspenders and looked around appreciatively. "So this is where you work?"

Sadie laughed, "Not always."

"I didn't think so."

"Bertie, the gardener, asked me to help him out this afternoon."

"These Caldwell's kids?"

Sadie turned to Louis and Marcellus, and then introduced them. "We don't know their last names. They just came today. They..."

Sadie's voice was cut off by Dorothy's agitated yells, asking the children to come up here right now.

Sadie got down on her knees, eye-level with Louis, and told them to be very good. Some men were here to talk to them about coming to the ranch. She told the children

that they should not be afraid. These were good men who
wanted to help them.

Tears crowded her eyes as she watched Louis take
Marcellus' hand protectively. Together they walked obediently up the brick walkway.

"What?" Mark began.

Sadie quietly explained the situation to him, omitting
the jewels, then asked if he wanted to sit down. They
seated themselves on the iron bench by the day lilies, and
Sadie turned a bit sideways, tucking one foot under her
leg.

"But…" Mark was curious.

"I know. It's the most unusual thing. You can tell by
the way they talk that they aren't just some squatters' or
sheepherders' children. Yet their black hair and eyes, their
dark skin, all seem to…"

"They seem foreign."

"Mexican. Latino of some kind. The police are here
now speaking to Richard and Barbara Caldwell. You
know how it is, if no one wants them, they'll enter the
foster system."

Mark looked unseeingly across the fishpond, the pasture in the background.

"Yeah, well, you're not going to let that happen, are
you?"

Sadie shrugged her shoulders.

When she felt Mark's big hands grasp her shoulders
much too tightly and give her a little shake, she snapped
her head up in alarm, her eyes weak with fright.

"How can you sit there with that smug expression
and shrug your shoulders?" he asked, his voice grating
unevenly on the hard words.

His face was inches from hers, his eyes blazing with

raw fury. The force of his emotion drew the air from her lungs like a huge vacuum. She was too powerless to stop it, and her shoulders slid downward away from his grasp.

"Don't," she whispered weakly.

He released her, then abruptly turned to lower his face into his hands. She thought she heard the word "sorry" among the murmurings that followed, but she couldn't be sure.

He stayed in that position until a sick fear began in the pit of Sadie's stomach. What if he was mentally deranged, violent, or dangerous? Why would he become so agitated at the slight shrugging of her shoulders?

Just as suddenly, Mark sat up, brushed back his hair, cleared his throat, and turned to her.

"You have no idea, Sadie. None. If you did, you wouldn't sit there one second longer, knowing those sweet, polite children would be put in foster homes. Believe me, it's not a good place to be."

"How do you know? And how do you expect me to know, living the sheltered Amish life I have always lived?"

"How do I know? Because I was a foster kid," Mark said, emotion causing him to whisper.

Sadie was incredulous. "You were?"

"Yes."

"Why? I mean... How could you have been? Your parents were Amish. Why didn't your relatives keep you? Why in the world were you put in a foster home? Didn't you have any sisters or brothers? No aunts or uncles?"

The questions poured from Sadie, like water rushing and tumbling toward the ocean. Her desperate need to know more about Mark's life crowded out all reason.

"If I tell you why I was a foster kid, you will never look at me again."

The words were stiff, forced between clenched teeth, as if keeping his teeth in that position would keep Mark's past hidden and intact.

Sadie faced him, forced him to look at her. "Try me."

She had never seen eyes change the way his did, going from brown to deep black then back to brown. But it was a hooded, reserved brown. Suspicious even. Mistrusting. Finally, when Sadie's gaze did not waver, his eyes acknowledged her request, but without faith, barren and afraid. Then he took the plunge, baring his soul.

"I found my father. He was drowned. On purpose."

"No!" The word was wrenched from Sadie and she lowered her head, sobs completely controlling her.

"See. I told you. Now I did it. You will never speak to me again."

There were no words from Sadie, only the heaving of her shoulders as he got slowly to his feet.

She felt his presence leaving and was jolted to reality. She raised her tear-streaked face, and in a desperate need to keep him there, blurted out, "Oh Mark, you poor, poor thing! How old were you? I cannot imagine. Please don't say you'll never speak to me again. Don't even think it. I care about you, Mark. I do."

"No, you don't."

"Yes … I do. Please, Mark. You said…"

"Just forget what I said. Go back to work now. Go find yourself a good, normal guy who will make you a good, normal husband. Forget about me and the fact that I came back to Montana."

Suddenly Sadie grasped both of his arms, held on, and said clearly, "I am not going to do that. And neither are you. I'm only going to say this once, and then it's up to you. I love you."

Chapter 4

Mᴀᴍ ᴡᴀꜱ ᴀʟᴀʀᴍᴇᴅ ᴡʜᴇɴ ꜱʜᴇ ꜱᴀᴡ Sᴀᴅɪᴇ ᴀꜰᴛᴇʀ work that day. Her oldest daughter's face was so pale, she looked sick. Her typically sunny, blue eyes looked dark gray, as if thunder had hovered over them all day.

"Sadie? Are you all right?"

It was the tone of her mother's voice, the kindness in her face, that unraveled Sadie completely, a spool of yarn with one end tugged relentlessly.

She threw herself into her mother's arms, and like a six-year-old who felt she was punished unfairly, she hic-cupped and warbled and cried and talked. Her sisters gathered around the kitchen table, clucking and oohing and aahing and sympathizing until the whole day had been laid bare for the entire family to examine. Even Dat caught the tail end of the story when he came home from work an hour later.

They laughed at Dorothy's view of Bertie, exclaimed at the jewels, and became doe-eyed when Sadie described how Mark Peight walked down the garden walkway. They all added their opinions, but grew completely embarrassed at Sadie's announcement of love to him.

Dat caught Mam's eye, and shook his head.

"So there you are. I know I'm not allowed to see Mark, but I also know I want to be with him until the end of my days. I love him. I know my life will not be as easy as some, but I need to be with him. I feel it's my destiny."

After a pause, Dat spoke softly, gravely.

"Well, Sadie, if you believe that it is God's will, would you give Mam and me a few weeks to pray about this? We're not going to forbid it, but we need to be very, very careful. Then we will see what unfolds."

"I can tell you what's unfolding right now, and that's my stomach. Whatever is up with having no supper?" Reuben announced, getting out of the recliner and clutching his empty abdomen.

"Let's get pizza!" Anna shouted.

"Pizza!" Reuben echoed.

"Who has money?"

"Not me."

"I would if we'd just get pizza, but till everyone has their cheesesteaks and ham subs and Pepsi, the bill will come to more than $50.00."

"I'll make a homemade pizza. We have leftover chicken corn soup…"

"No-o-o!" Reuben wailed.

"I'll pay 20," Dat volunteered.

"I'll pay 10!"

"Ten!"

"Who's going to order?"

"Who do you think?" Mam asked, pointing to Sadie.

Sadie laughed and got a scrap of paper and pen, wrote down the order, and went to the phone shanty to call the little rural pizza shop that delivered pizza to the homes spread around the lovely, Montana countryside.

On the way back to the house, Sadie's heart filled with love for her family. Her emotions had run a gauntlet that day, but how wonderfully firm was the foundation under her indecisive feet. The love and devotion of a family was a solid structure that held together through all of life's trials, above any storm that blew in. And how would life ever be manageable without her sisters and Reuben?

When the pizza arrived, the family was prepared with a stack of plates, tall glasses loaded with ice cubes, and Mam's bread knife to cut through the thick crust.

They remembered to bow their heads, their hands folded in their laps while they all prayed in silence. The girls had their own private joke about "putting patties down," the Pennsylvania Dutch version of saying a blessing, when pizza was ordered in. Dat never seemed to pray quite as long, and tonight was no different. Sadie was pretty sure Reuben didn't pray at all, the way he shrugged his shoulders and swung his feet. His head was only bowed halfway, and he watched the pepperoni on the pizza the way a cat watches a mouse nibbling on oats in the forebay of the barn.

When they raised their heads and Mam reached for the knife to cut the pizza, Sadie caught Rebekah's eye. They ducked their heads before Dat could catch their smiles.

It was delicious, as usual, the great slices of thick, crusty pizza dripping with tomato sauce, cheese, pepperoni, and mushrooms.

The subs were made with a special bread recipe, brown and firm, the ham and cheese melted to perfection, the lettuce and tomato still fresh and colorful.

No one said much, as they ate hungrily, then pushed back their plates and relaxed with their drinks.

Sadie watched Anna reaching across the table for one of the last slices, her third. Then she settled back happily on the bench beside Reuben, enthusiastically sinking her teeth into the thick pizza.

Reuben wiped his mouth with a napkin, surveying his hungry sister. "Boy, Anna, you ate a pile of pizza. Must be you were really hungry."

"I was!" Anna said, swallowing and nodding her head.

Reuben eyed her with concern. "You're getting chunky."

"So."

Her answer was about as indifferent as it could be, so Reuben shrugged his shoulders and said he was going to the barn.

"Are you riding?" Sadie asked.

"No. I have to clean my rabbit pens. Dat said."

Sadie figured she had better not persuade him to ride with her. Those rabbit pens were desperately in need of cleaning. Anna had told him that if he didn't clean the rabbit pens more regularly, she was going to call the Humane Society to come get the rabbits, and the animal rights people would put him in jail.

Horrified at the thought of being put in handcuffs, which Anna had explained in full detail, Reuben went crying to Mam. Anna was sent to her room after that. This had all occurred when Reuben was seven or eight, and things had not changed much at all. Reuben still loathed cleaning those pens.

Sadie slipped away from the house, telling Mam she was going for a ride on Paris. Mam nodded absent-mindedly while listening to Leah recount an episode from her day.

Paris and Cody were at the lower end of the pasture, as far away as possible. Usually when Sadie called, they came trotting to the gate, but not always. Depending on their mood, they stayed where they were, tails swishing, teeth crunching as they went on grazing.

Sadie climbed up and sat on the gate.

"Paris! Cody! Come on girls! Come on!"

The slanted evening sunlight brought out the rich gold of Paris' coat. She was the color of honey, the good, rich kind that came straight from the hives. Her mane and tail were a lighter shade of gold, almost off-white, the tone of some people's living room walls.

Paris whinnied, her nostrils making that funny rollicking noise that sounded like laughter. Sadie watched as she swung her head, then turned to make her way delicately across the pasture. Her head bobbed slightly as she walked up to the gate, prodded on by Sadie's gentle coaxing.

Nuzzling her skirt, Paris looked at Sadie as if to ask her how her day was.

"Hello, girl."

Sadie slid off the gate, her arms going around her horse's neck, and she squeezed tightly.

"Good, good girl. You're so beautiful in the springtime, Paris, you know that? You want to go for a ride? Hmm? Let's get some exercise, and I'll tell you about my day."

Paris' ears flicked forward, then back. She lowered her head to look for an apple, sniffed Sadie's palm, and followed her obediently into the barn and through the door of her pen. Her hooves clattered on the concrete as she went to the water trough.

Sadie lifted her saddle off the rack, then set it back down. She forgot the blanket. It was not on its usual rack, so she went to look for it in the harness cupboard.

Turning the wooden latch, she checked the interior. No saddle blanket. Hmm. That was weird.

Reuben came sliding across the gravel, making the sound of screeching brakes, almost colliding into his big sister.

"Reuben, where's my saddle blanket?"

"How would I know?"

"Nobody else uses it."

"I didn't use your saddle blanket. I'd never ride with a pink one, you know that."

"It's not pink."

Reuben turned his head to one side, then said loudly, "Phone!"

Sadie listened, heard the insistent ringing, and dashed to the phone shanty.

The sound of a phone ringing was a bit mysterious. If somebody was fortunate enough to hear the phone in the shanty at all, that person dropped everything and ran to answer it. That's because you never knew if the ring you heard was the first one or the tenth one, and you wanted to grab it before voicemail kicked on.

Breathlessly, Sadie lifted the receiver and said, "Hello!"

"Hey."

There was no mistaking that low, gravelly voice. She steadied herself for the usual plummeting of her heart, and the racing pulse that followed, before saying warily, "Mark."

"Hey, Sadie. I…should have stayed in the barn down at the ranch today instead of coming out to talk to you. I guess the sight of those children… I don't know. I over-reacted. Now you probably won't talk to me again."

Sadie smiled. "Why wouldn't I?"

"Well…I dunno. I guess…"

There was an awkward silence, then, "What are you doing?"

"Getting ready to ride. I was actually looking for my saddle blanket, which evidently sprouted legs and ran off."

"Can you... Come over to my place?"

"I can't." Sadie said the words automatically, without considering whether she could or not. It was late, but...

"Why not?"

"I shouldn't ride clear over there by myself. It'll get dark and it might not be safe for me to ride back."

"I'll meet you halfway."

Sadie bit down on her lower lip with indecision. She was dirty and unkempt from planting flowers in the sun and relentless wind, her stomach was much too full of pizza, and she had the start of a glaring red pimple on her chin.

"No."

There was a silence, dead and cold, before an exasperated sigh finally reached her ears. "Okay."

"Wait. Mark I don't want to be... Well, I don't want to hurt your feelings. Do you want me to be honest?"

She felt the humor rise in her chest and she stifled a giggle. Why not? She had already told him she loved him just this afternoon! "I ate way too much pizza with my family, and I have the start of one very large, very sore pimple on my chin."

There was the space of one heartbeat, then a loud, rolling laugh, pure and real and completely uninhibited.

Finally, "Oh Sadie. That is why I...came back to Montana. It is. I think once we know each other better, so many things are possible."

"I'm not coming over tonight, though," Sadie said firmly.

"Then I'm coming over there. Right now. Would your parents disapprove?"

"No. Yes. I don't know."

"Give me a half hour."

"All right."

Sadie slammed down the receiver and raced across the driveway and into the house while an exasperated Reuben closed the door to the phone shanty, shaking his head.

It was the quickest shower Sadie had ever had, and there was no time for making serious decisions about the color or fabric of her dress, either. At least she was more presentable, she thought, as she dabbed concealing lotion on the hateful protrusion on her chin. She hastily jabbed hairpins into her hair and plopped her covering on top, spraying cologne wildly across her wrists and collar as she heard a truck approaching.

A driver! He had asked someone to bring him over!

Her sisters plied her with questions, Mam looked worried, and Reuben was yelling something about Paris from the barn. But Dat just slept in the recliner, his glasses sliding down his nose, the newspaper spread across his stomach.

Sadie opened the door and was met by Mark coming up on the porch. His hair was disheveled, and he wore a blue denim work shirt.

"Sadie!" Reuben was screeching.

"Hi, Mark. Would you mind going with me to the barn? Reuben is seriously perturbed about something."

"Sure."

"You forgot your horse," Reuben said when they got to the barn.

Sadie had forgotten all about Paris. Her halter was still clipped to the chain by the water trough, and Sadie could tell she was not happy. She was throwing her head up, then back down, rattling the chain in the process.

"Sorry, Reuben."

"Hi, Reuben," Mark said affably. "How are you?"

Reuben was still scrubbing his rabbit pens, but he straightened his back, blew his bangs out of his eyes with an expertly protruding lower lip, and smiled. His eyes danced with mischief.

"I'm good. As soon as these rabbit pens are cleaned, I'll be better yet."

Mark bent to peer inside the hutches.

"Don't you like your rabbits?"

"Not really. I'm getting too old for these guys."

"Do you want to sell them at the livestock auction? I'll take you. Maybe Sadie could come, too. It's every Friday night in Critchfield. They have donkeys, horses, mules, geese, chickens. Everything."

Reuben's face was illuminated with excitement.

"Really?"

"Yep."

"I'll go! I'll sell all these rabbits and buy a donkey instead."

Reuben laughed at the very idea, and Sadie couldn't help but laugh with him, meeting Mark's eyes in the dim interior of the barn.

His eyes were laughing, too, but they contained so much more. It was as if her laughter opened the floodgates of his feelings for her.

That was the danger of being with Mark, Sadie thought later. He didn't say a word, but his eyes contained the depth of his... What was it? Did he love her at unguarded moments? Was he too shy or too proud to say what he felt? All she knew was that when the laughter had fizzled away, they were looking deeply into each other's eyes, a sort of assurance between them.

Reuben looked first at Sadie, then at Mark, shrugged his shoulders and returned to his rabbit cages. Sadie acted so odd when Mark was around, he thought.

They went for a walk, then, after releasing a miffed Paris back to the pasture.

Mark talked about everyday, pleasant subjects. He spoke easily and unhurriedly while Sadie bantered light-heartedly in return. He told her of his plans to remodel the old house and just how much work needed to be done. He worked on it every evening and all day on Saturdays.

Then he turned to her and asked her what sort of house she liked. It was so sudden that Sadie became scatterbrained and said something stupid about Richard and Barbara Caldwell's ranch house. She knew perfectly well that Mark could never afford a house half as big as their ranch. What was she thinking?

He steered her into the empty schoolyard, seated her on the cement porch, and sat very close beside her. He positioned his arm behind her and propped his shoulder on one hand, making her so nervous and confused that she didn't know what to say anymore, so she fell silent.

Then, easily, he began to talk. Really talk.

"Sadie, do you want to hear the beginning of my story? Do you know why I got so upset today? I'm sorry. I went a bit overboard. I'll try and do better from now on."

"It's okay," Sadie whispered.

"My first memory is being carried to a horse and buggy and sitting in the back seat with other children. They must have been my brothers and sisters. They say there were five of us.

"My father was a farmer, of sorts. I remember my parents milking cows by hand. I remember the sound of the milk hitting the steel pail, then watching the foam rise up as the pail filled. I remember cats drinking from a dish that my mother filled with the warm milk.

"The milk was stored in milk cans. You know, those big steel ones with handles? We stored them in cold water and then took them to the cheese house."

Sadie shook her head. "I wouldn't know. Dat was never a farmer. I think the farmers in Ohio, at least in our church, had milking machines and bulk tanks."

"Oh. Well, I told you I was raised in a very plain sect."

"Yes."

"Our house had no running water. We went to the wash house to pump our water, and then carried it to the iron kettle and heated it on a wood fire. My job was to carry the wood. We were poor, Sadie, painfully poor."

He stopped, shifted his position, and ran his hand through his black hair. Sadie watched the veins in his large, brown, perfect hands. She wanted to trace them with her fingers, just touch them to see if they were as secure and strong as they looked.

"My mother was a beautiful woman. They said she looked like an Indian from the southwest."

"She must have been," Sadie murmured.

"I remember her hair. When she washed it, it hung way down her back and was thick and sort of coarse. It was straight as a straw broom and swung back and forth when she walked.

"Her name was Amelia, but they called her Meely.

"I was the oldest, then Beulah."

"Beulah!" Sadie said, astounded. "That's not an Amish name."

"I know. I think my mother was a bit of...maybe rebellious toward the strict laws of the church. She named her children Beulah, Timothy, Diana, Rachel Mae, and Jackson."

"But that's six children counting you, Mark."

"But...I was told there were five. Well, whatever. Those were the names of my siblings."

"Why do you say 'were'? Where are they? Are they all...dead? What happened to them, Mark?"

"I don't know."

"You don't know?"

"Wait, Sadie. Let me go on. We must have been trouble for the church. I remember my mother asking my father many questions. She wanted out of the church. She wanted to move. She wasn't afraid of *bann and meidung*. I always thought she said "bone" or "bean," and I could never understand what a bean had to do with leaving the church and moving away somewhere.

"My father must have become despondent. Despairing, whatever. Our cupboards contained less and less. One time I was so hungry that I ate cornmeal from a white paper sack and drank water to wash it down. I shared it with Beulah and Timothy. Diana cried and cried. Her bottle was empty, so I put water in it to keep her quiet. She cried anyway, and I couldn't find my mother.

"I remember the smell of soiled diapers. I quickly learned how to open the large safety pins on the cloth diapers and change them. Sadie, this is one of the most painful things about my childhood. There weren't always clean diapers available, so my little brothers and sisters had to go without. I would watch, though, and clean up after them the best I could. I used a rag that I washed out over and over."

Sadie bowed her head, the knowledge of Mark's child-hood pressing down on her very soul.

"I still don't know where my mother went. I just know she wasn't there for long periods of time, and neither was my father.

"I learned to keep the house fairly warm by adding wood to the range in the kitchen. I would get a piece of wood and lay it carefully on a chair. Then I would climb up on the chair, remove the heavy lid on the top of the range, and put the stick of wood into the firebox.

"Sometimes some women would come, and they'd be angry. Their black skirts swished all over the house while they cleaned with Clorox. I guess it was Clorox. It smelled very strong. The women used the wringer washer all day long and filled our cupboards with bread and cheese and cookies and apples. My mother usually cried when they did that. I don't know if it made her happy or angry or if she just felt ashamed of the way we lived."

"Well, where was your mother, Mark? Did she have to go to work, or was she out running around, doing things she shouldn't have been doing?"

"You know, I can't tell you, because I really don't know. She just sort of came and went. I was six or seven, so how much would I really know at that age?"

"But surely she could have explained and hired a babysitter?"

Mark shrugged his shoulders. "My father became increasingly quiet. Actually, he was sort of like a shadow in my life that came and went. I don't remember very much about my father. Only once…no, it's too awful to say."

Sadie lifted her head, found his gaze. "Trust me."

"No. That can stay buried. I think my father was a man with no hope. Men of the church tried to help him, they must have. They would drive in with their horses and buggies and wide black hats, and stand in the barn for hours. They would talk and wave their hands to emphasize the force behind their words. My mother hated them."

Sadie drew in a quick breath. "Not hated."

"Yes. She hated them. She spat out the door once. It was a horrible sound, one I will always remember. I guess a little boy can absorb lots of things that seem evil, and it never really goes away. It's... I don't know."

Mark shook his head slowly, his eyes burning.

Sadie sighed, a quick intake of breath, then laid a hand on his arm as softly and gently as she could.

"There's healing, Mark. There is."

Chapter 5

THE WHOLE RANCH WAS BUZZING WHEN SADIE walked into the kitchen the following morning.

The television set in Richard Caldwell's study was turned up louder than normal as ranch hands huddled around the desk, sitting on the arms of the sofas and standing at the door. They shifted uncomfortably when Sadie walked into the dining room, casting furtive glances in her direction, shifting their snuff, tucking in shirttails, and clearing their throats nervously.

She wondered what was going on, but of course, she would never ask the men. The important thing at this point was to get the steam table ready for the large, square containers of hot breakfast food. She would drop the pans into the grids so the hot water underneath would keep the food warm, even for the latecomers.

Setting her plastic bucket of soapy water on the table, she added a dash of Clorox and went to work washing the sides and bottom of the table's long, shining enclosure. She wiped down the grids, the top, and the front, rinsing the rag every few swipes.

She stopped, her hearing strained, as she heard a yell of disbelief followed by exclamations of anger or dismay from a few of the most verbal ranch hands. Richard Caldwell was yelling too, his thundering voice bellowing above all the others.

"Aww! It ain't right! This is an outrage. Who in his right mind would do something like that?"

Sadie stood positively motionless.

"He's dead! A magnificent animal! I saw them load him in the truck. He was absolutely huge. Aw! It ain't right."

Sadie heard every word.

What? Which animal? It was all she could do to pick up the plastic bucket and return to the kitchen. She lingered reluctantly before opening the swinging oak doors.

Dorothy looked up from her post at the stove, viciously stirring a large pan of scrambled eggs. She was wearing an electric pink shirt over a brown, pleated skirt. The skirt rode up on her ample hips, leaving a few inches of her white, nylon slip exposed beneath the hem. Her hair was in a state of static profusion, held back by two very pink barrettes. Her eyes flashed blue amid all the pink surrounding her.

"It took you long enough!"

"I was listening. The men are all piled around the TV. Something about a dead animal on the news. Richard Caldwell was really yelling this time."

Without a word, Dorothy marched over to the small television set perched on a stand in the corner and turned it on, expertly pushing buttons on the remote control until she found the channel she wanted.

Sadie picked up the forgotten spatula and stirred the eggs, turning sideways to watch the flickering screen.

Dorothy positioned herself directly in front of the TV, obliterating any action from Sadie's view. Muttering to herself, Dorothy clicked the button, then turned around as the television screen went black.

"Nothin' much I can see. Some crazy person shot a horse. What's so strange about that? Horse likely had a bone broke. Those animal-rights people is plumb nuts. You ain't even allowed to dispose of a stray cat. You know what kills a cat so fast it ain't funny?"

Sadie lifted the heavy pan with both hands, and a golden yellow avalanche of scrambled eggs tumbled out of it and into the square container on the counter. She shook her head at Dorothy's question, biting down on her lower lip with the effort of lifting the heavy pan.

"I ain't gonna tell you."

"All right," Sadie said, shrugging her shoulders non-committally.

"You know why I ain't gonna tell you? 'Cause you'd tell everybody else, and next thing I know, I got those animal fanatics on my tail. I got enough to worry about now. Those kids. Those two precious souls, God love 'em. I can't imagine what's gonna happen to 'em. The cops has all the information they could get. They fingerprinted 'em, poor babies. Just like common animals, and what did they do wrong? Not one thing. Innocent as newborn babes."

Dorothy stopped for breath, her cheeks flaming. "I'm takin' 'em in! I am. I told my Jim, and this is what I said. I says, 'Now Jim, honeybun, you lookie here. We ain't never had no children of our own 'cause the Lord didn't see fit to give us any. I may be old and fat and half wore out, but as long as the Lord gives me the strength, I'm keepin' these young 'uns, sure as shootin'. They's sent straight from heaven.'"

She mopped her shining nose with the dishrag that lay beside the stove, then took a deep breath and launched into a vivid account of the room they were going to fix up for them.

Sadie buttered toast, nodded in agreement, smiling, nodding her head, whenever a question abbreviated the sentences.

"You know, pink for Marcelona. She should have pink walls, but that would never work for Louise. He needs blue or green. So what I'm going to do is paint one side of the room pink, about the color of my shirt, and the other side blue, probably about like your dress. Then... Oh Sadie!"

Dorothy clasped her hands tightly, gazing at the ceiling, pure joy stamped on her round features.

"At the Dollar Tree? In town? They have decals to paste on the ceiling that glow in the dark! They glow. I bought a package to test them before I knew about the children, mind you. Now that was straight from the Lord, too. He knew why I bought them stars. He knew! Two blessed children were coming into our lives. Me and Jim's."

She sighed ecstatically.

Sadie glanced uneasily at the clock.

"It's going past eight."

Dorothy looked, then fairly ran to the refrigerator, bouncing off the cabinets as she whirled toward the dining room.

"Lord have mercy, Sadie! Why'd you let me ramble on thataway? Git the bacon!"

Sadie never failed to marvel at Dorothy's speed. She was such a rotund little being, her feet clad in the questionable shoes from the Dollar General Store, moving with the grace and speed of an antelope, only rounder.

Barking orders, she swung the oak doors, her arms laden with heavy pans of steaming food, Sadie holding her breath more than once as she careened haphazardly between kitchen and dining room.

When everything was laid out to her satisfaction, she whizzed through the doors one last time, dumped steaming black coffee into her large mug, and flopped into a wide kitchen chair, reaching for a napkin to wipe her face.

"Whew! That was close!"

Sadie carried a plate stacked with hotcakes to the table, then went to the pantry for syrup, finally sitting across from Dorothy as she buttered the hotcakes liberally. Dorothy dumped cream into her coffee, stirred, then slurped the steaming hot liquid appreciatively.

"You better watch that butter, young lady."

Sadie laughed.

"I'm hungry. I love pancakes, melted butter all over them."

The door opened slowly.

Two small faces appeared, entering so timidly they seemed to slide against the wall, clearly uncomfortable in this vast kitchen so strange and unusual.

Dorothy's mug clattered to the tabletop as she leapt to her feet.

"There you are! Did Jim bring you in the truck?"

She was on her knees in front of them, brushing back their long, thick, black hair, adjusting T-shirts, tying shoelaces, clucking and fussing like a bantam hen with new chicks.

The children nodded, their eyes round with apprehension.

"My mother is coming to get us today," Marcellus announced, her eyes filling with unshed tears.

Louis nodded, speaking in his impeccable manner.

"She promised she would come soon. I think she will."

"Of course, she will. She'll be back as soon as she possibly can," Dorothy assured them, gathering them to her ample bosom, stroking their hair, murmuring endearments.

Straightening, Dorothy told Sadie to take them to the dining room and let them fill their plates. She did as she was told, a small brown hand in each of her own, swung through the doors, and looked straight into the brown eyes of Mark Peight.

"Good morning, Sadie," he said in his low gravely voice, the gladness in his eyes catching her unaware.

She felt the color rising in her face, lowered her eyes, and mumbled a good morning before checking the room for occupants who stared at them both. Clearly flustered, she bent to address Louis, handing the heavy white plates to the children.

Mark watched Sadie, the gladness leaving his eyes, brown turning to a very dark shade, and he turned brusquely on his heel and walked away.

"There you are!" Richard Caldwell boomed. "Come here!"

Sadie walked over to his table, after helping the children with their food and directing them to a small table along the kitchen wall.

"Good morning!"

"How are you, Sadie?"

"I'm doing okay."

"Hey, you need to hear this. On the news this morning, there's a story about the mysterious death of Black Thunder. Remember the horse?"

"What?" Sadie asked, incredulous.

"Yeah. Apparently, there's a guy, or a group of guys, I don't know, shooting horses just for the fun of it. He ain't the only one dead. It's the most disgusting thing. I mean, shooting a horse is just wrong. Especially a valuable one like that. His owner is heartsick. I called him this morning."

Sadie was aghast, the color draining from her face, as Richard Caldwell explained the situation in Lorado County. Ranchers keeping their horses inside, or the cowhands guarding the corrals, no horses allowed to be in pastures, and certainly not in the open range.

Sadie listened closely, thinking of Paris, grazing happily in the large, secluded pasture with Cody, Reuben's brown mare.

Surely the killers were not in this area. They couldn't be.

She launched into animated conversation with Richard Caldwell, spreading her hands for emphasis, the love for her beloved horse so apparent. Richard Caldwell watched her face, the expression changing from despair to panic then sadness as she remembered Nevaeh, the black and white paint that had broken his leg when she tried to clear a high fence.

Mark Peight had filled his plate, found a place to eat at the long table crowded with cowhands, and bent to his food, before looking up and seeing Sadie talk animatedly, with Richard Caldwell watching her face so closely.

The food-laden fork went slowly into his mouth, then out as he swallowed forcefully, never taking his eyes off the two at an adjoining table.

His eyes narrowed, his nostrils flared slightly as he slowly laid down his fork, color rising in his face. Putting both hands on the table's edge, he pushed back his chair, turned on his heel, and strode past Sadie and her boss, closing the door with a resounding "thwack" as he made his decided exit.

Her first instinct was to go after him, grab his sleeve, hang on, and ask him why he left so suddenly without acknowledging her presence.

Richard Caldwell watched Sadie, saw the distraction as Mark strode past, watched her turn sideways in her chair to watch him leave. Silently he took a sip of his coffee.

Sadie was clearly agitated now, but she sighed and met Richard Caldwell's eyes, resignation stamped all over her lovely features.

"You know him?"

"Yes."

"How well do you know him?"

Sadie shrugged her shoulders, pushed her dark hair back, bit down on her lower lip, and would not look at him.

"He's the best farrier I ever watched, and I've seen a bunch of 'em in my time. He shod Sage, that big gray brute, but ended up throwing him with the twitch to do it."

Sadie's eyes flamed.

"That's just cruel. You don't have to hurt a horse's mouth to restrain him."

With that, she got up, bid him a good day, and marched into the kitchen.

Richard Caldwell sipped his coffee, speculating, before a slow grin spread across his face, and he shook his head.

✿ ☆ ✿

Sadie and Reuben went riding that evening after the dishes were washed, Paris and Cody eager to run.

They held them in, with the horses chomping down on their bits, prancing to the side, even rearing in the air, balking a bit, as if they couldn't bear to be held back.

They went down the winding driveway and turned right, riding single file along the macadam road before coming to the field lane that turned to the high pasture along the ridge.

Sadie tightened her knees, leaned forward, and loosened the reins, grinning back at Reuben the instant Paris gathered her legs beneath her and catapulted up the lane.

There was no reason to hold them back. Just pasture grasses and wildflowers for at least a mile, so Sadie let Paris go.

The blond mane whipped across Paris' neck, her head pumped up and down, the dull, muffled sound of her hooves striking the earth sounding like pure music to Sadie's ears.

The wind tossed Sadie's dark hair, tore at her *dichly*, and still Paris pounded on. The grasses swayed, the trees blurred by, and she rode on, the enjoyment of allowing Paris to run free unfettering her own spirits, the worries about Mark Peight streaming behind her, lost on the wind, for now.

Out of the corner of her eye, a dark object crept into her vision. Turning her head, she yelled, goading Paris, who responded with a lowering of her head and an outstretched neck as her muscles renewed their strength, knowing Cody was gaining on her.

Reuben was bent low over Cody's neck, laughing. His hair was a shade lighter than his horse's mane, but they flowed together, rippling in the speed of the wind.

Sadie realized Cody might actually beat Paris, so she leaned forward, urging Paris on, talking, talking, and was rewarded by the sight of Cody and Reuben falling back, but only for a second.

As they leaned into the turn, Cody somehow got the inside, and Reuben yelled at Sadie as they inched closer.

On she came, Cody stretched out, running as Sadie had never seen the horse run. She was determined, all by herself, to beat Paris, Sadie could tell. There was a focus in her eyes, a determination in her bearing, and no matter how much Sadie urged Paris on, Cody and Reuben kept gaining.

"No!" Sadie screamed.

They were neck and neck now, coming down the stretch of pasture that led to the lane, so Sadie knew she had to pull Paris in, or they would run downhill at that speed. Sitting up, she pulled back slightly, turning Paris in a circle, back to the wildflowers.

Reuben was standing up in his stirrups, pumping his fist into the air, yelling at the top of his lungs, exultant, completely caught up in the moment.

"Cody did it, Sadie! She did! I don't care what you say! Cody beat Paris!"

Sadie was laughing, shaking her head, panting, as she pulled Paris to a stop. Cody came prancing up beside them, her nostrils moving rapidly, but clearly not finished running.

Paris was blowing hard.

"You did not beat me, Reuben!" Sadie gasped.

"I did! I'm sure I did. Cody's nose was ahead of Paris. I saw it!"

Reuben's tanned face was alight with victory, his hair disheveled, no Amish straw hat in sight. He decided long ago that there was no use wearing a hat to go riding. It wouldn't stay on his head longer than 10 seconds.

"All right! All right!" Sadie conceded, watching Reuben and glad he won, for his sake, although she didn't seriously think Cody had actually done it.

"Hey, I bet if I was English, I could race Cody at the rodeos!"

Sadie nodded, "I bet too you could! And you'd win!"

"Aw, I can't imagine! Think about it, Sadie. Riding like that in front of thousands of people, winning a bunch of money. Wouldn't it be unreal?"

"Yeah. But we aren't allowed to race like that. We don't go to rodeos and stuff either."

"Why ever not? That's so dumb. Who said?"

Reuben dismounted, threw the reins expertly over Cody's head, then stretched out in the grass. "Who said?" he repeated.

"Well, you know how it is, Reuben. We have rules. It's too worldly to be competitive with our horses. I mean, think about it. If you're born Amish, you grow up sort of knowing what's allowed and what isn't. It's no big deal."

Reuben grabbed the stem of a tall wildflower, peeled off the leaves and stuck it in his mouth. He pushed it to the side, as expertly as Jim Sevarr with his toothpick. "I'm going to go English, he said.

"Now, Reuben," Sadie said mildly.

"I mean it."

"You'd break Mam's and Dat's hearts."

Reuben nodded soberly, then spat out the stem.

"I know. I'm Dat's only boy."

"That's right. The least you can do for your parents is love and obey them. You know that."

Reuben nodded soberly, then sat up.

"I like Dat."

"Well, good for you, Reuben. Dat's not a hard person to get along with."

"I like you, too. Sadie, you're my best sister."

That was quite a stretch, Reuben saying that, Sadie knew. She reached out with genuine affection to touch her brother's hair.

"You're my best brother, too."

"I'm the only one you have," Reuben grinned.

"But my best one, anyway."

It happened so suddenly, the only thing Sadie heard was a high whining sound, sort of like a whistle, but more deadly. She didn't hear a crack. Not the way you're supposed to when you tell someone you heard a gunshot. It wasn't really the hard sound of a gun, the sort that makes you wince every time you hear it.

She knew only one thing: Cody was down. She hit the ground with a sort of grace, the way an accordion folds and produces a beautiful sound from the air pumped into its bellows. One moment she was grazing with Paris; the next, her legs folded beneath her as she made a short, groaning sound, sort of a whoosh. Her head bent back as her legs flailed, she made one pitiful attempt to right herself, then fell. She never took another breath.

Paris snorted, jerked the reins from Sadie's hands, then galloped off a short distance, her ears flicking, her head held high, watching the tree line.

Reuben cried out, a youth's cry of alarm, innocent in its raw terror. There was no anger in the sound, only the consternation of not being able to understand.

"Lie down! Reuben, lie flat in the tallest grass!" Sadie hissed.

He obeyed immediately, and they lay with their ears pressed to the ground.

Sadie was terrified.

Who would have done this? Surely not the same people Richard Caldwell talked about. That was in Laredo County at least a hundred miles away. It couldn't be. Likely a hunter, mistaking Cody's brown coat for a mule deer or an elk. But hunting season wasn't until the fall. It had to be someone shooting illegally. A poacher.

Her ear pressed to the ground, Sadie heard nothing except her own heart thumping wildly, seemingly tripping over itself, the blood rushing into her ears with each thump.

"Reuben?" she whispered.

"Hmm?"

"Do you hear anything? See anything?"

"No."

"We need to get out of here as fast as possible."

"I'm not leaving Cody."

Slowly they raised their heads, peering through the grasses.

When there was no movement anywhere, Sadie hoped they'd be able to make a run for it. She had never been so afraid. She was completely panicked now, her mouth so dry she could not swallow.

"Reuben, you have to go with me. We need to go, NOW! What if...that man with a gun was waiting in the trees or..."

"He probably left. I'm not leaving Cody."

Then he was up, walking to his beloved horse, dropping to his knees, stroking her neck, pushing the heavy mane aside with his hands.

Sadie crawled over on her stomach, much too frightened to stand.

Reuben didn't cry. He just hunkered beside his horse, his eyes flat with the truth of it. Someone had shot Cody.

Sadie couldn't bear his quietness. She put a hand on his shoulder.

Reuben shrugged it off.

"Don't."

"Reuben, listen. We'll get you another one. I will take this blame. We never should have gone riding. I knew there was trouble, but I just... well, figured they were in Laredo County."

"You mean those men who shot Black Thunder?"

Sadie nodded.

Still Reuben stayed, stroking Cody's neck, her face. When he turned to look at Sadie, the disbelief, the inability to comprehend such evil, turned his eyes a darker color, the corners drooping with the weight of his sadness. His mouth trembled, but no words followed.

"We have to go. Please."

"Not yet."

There was a dark pool of blood seeping out beneath Cody's chest. Sadie watched Reuben carefully, willing him away from the sight of it.

Suddenly, he drew a sharp breath.

"C... Cody is bleeding."

Sadie nodded.

"She's really dead."

He bent his head then, put both hands over his face to hide it, as great sobs shook his thin frame. Sadie gathered him in her arms and cried with him, wetting his shoulder with her tears.

She cried for Cody, for Reuben's pain, for life when it turned cruel, and for the fact that she didn't understand everything.

Did she understand anything?

Why was Mark angry? Surely he would not have become so upset that he would shoot a horse? But Reuben said his home was filled with guns.

He wouldn't.

Sadie stroked Reuben's back, the only way she knew to comfort him, and when he stepped back, dug out a rumpled red handkerchief and blew his nose, he looked at her and took a deep breath.

"I'll be okay," was all he said.

Chapter 6

IN THE DAYS THAT FOLLOWED, THE WHOLE FAMILY rallied around Reuben.

Anna bought him his favorite candy bars, baseball cards, and red licorice from the store in town.

Rebekah let him drive Charlie when she went to visit Aunt Elma who lived about eight miles away. Mam baked pumpkin whoopie pies and chocolate ones, filled with thick, creamy frosting and wrapped in Saran Wrap individually.

Dat called the hide and tanning company. He traveled with the truck up the field lane to the field of wildflowers, where they loaded the carcass. He never said a word about any of it to Reuben, which had to be the best, leaving him to remember his horse as he loved her, alive and well, running fast.

There was a huge controversy going on down at the ranch. Sadie busily pieced together snatches here and there, unable to come to a conclusion of her own. It was difficult pondering why any person or group of people would aim a rifle and shoot an innocent, unassuming horse in its own pasture.

There were no tracks, no leads for the police. A few days of discussion on the news, then nothing.

The Miller family did not report Cody's death; it was their way of staying out of the public eye. They looked on the incident as something God allowed to happen. Whether it was evil or not, it had occurred. The family accepted it, mourned the horse, then everyone moved on, including Reuben.

Only Sadie understood his pain. Really understood it.

When he flopped on the recliner and stared into space, then picked up a hunting magazine to hide his face, Sadie knew he was biting down on his lower lip, blinking madly as he vowed not to cry.

One evening, when dusk was settling over the back porch like a soft, gray blanket of comfort, promising rest to the tired occupants of the porch swing, Dat broke the silence. He was building a screened-in deck for a man who had an old buckboard he'd give to someone who would restore it.

Instantly Anna sprang up, clapping Reuben's shoulder.

"There you go, Reuben!"

Reuben snorted.

"What would I want with a buckboard? I don't know how to fix it up, and besides, I have no horse."

"Paris," Anna countered quickly.

"She's not broke to drive."

"Charlie!"

That was met with an unenthused snort.

"Would you restore it, Dat?" Sadie asked.

"I don't know. It's not really my thing."

"Who does that?"

"I have no idea. Plenty of people in Ohio, but here... I don't know of anyone Amish, anyway."

"Would you do it, Dat?" Sadie asked.

"I don't really want to."

"If Reuben and I help? If we get a horse that matches Paris, we could really have something neat. Maybe even drive them at horse sales."

"Or shows! Or rodeos!" Reuben shouted.

"Now!" Mam said.

That long drawn out "now" was always Mam's way of reprimanding gently but firmly, sort of like pulling back the reins on a horse. You knew you had to stop and consider, not go so fast; there might be an obstacle along the way, and you needed to be aware of it.

Still it was an idea.

For one thing, it might help Anna. She desperately wanted to feel needed and to rebuild a kinship with Reuben, the way it was when they were younger. Sadie often felt guilty for taking Reuben from Anna the way she did. But unlike Reuben, Anna was not a rider. She was becoming quite chubby, her cheeks round and rosy with good health and lots of good food, and absolutely not a care in the world about it.

Her face was very pretty and tanned, with greenish-gray eyes that looked blue when she wore a blue dress and gray when she wore anything else. She was going on 15 now and looking forward to being finished with school. Anna was as happy and easy to get along with as any of her sisters.

Sadie sat up, adrenaline filling her body with energy.

"Dat! If you bring the buckboard home, we'll fix it up, and we'll keep watching for a horse for Reuben, and we'll teach that horse and Paris to be hitched double. Anna can help."

Anna was chewing on a hard pretzel, sounding very

much like a horse crunching an ear of corn. Reuben watched her out of the corner of his eye.

"Do you have to crunch that pretzel so hard?" he asked, his eyes narrowing.

"What's it to you? Maybe my pretzel's good!"

Mam got up, yawning, gathering her housecoat about her, saying it was time all decent, hardworking people went to bed.

Sadie caught a whiff of Mam's talcum powder as she neared her chair, the same warm, silky scent she always wore, sort of like fresh baked bread mixed with a flowery odor of roses. She had just washed her graying hair; it hung down her back, held fast by a black, elastic ponytail holder. The long, thin ponytail made her seem as vulnerable as a child.

Mam always had her hair up in a bun, a white covering obscuring most of it. She appeared neat, clean, and in charge of her life and her family. Somehow, at moments like this, Sadie knew Mam was a tender sort of person, though still dependent on medication. Her mental condition had greatly improved but was still delicate.

Mam despised the fact that she was on "nerve pills," but she never wanted to return to the abyss of breakdowns she had earlier slid into.

Thankful now, Sadie said goodnight. She took a cool shower and tumbled into bed. She was too sleepy to read. It was too warm to be very comfortable, so she lay on her back, her hands propped behind her head, and stared wide-eyed at the ceiling, thinking.

The giggles from Rebekah's room irked her. It irked her more when the giggles rose to shrieks of glee and Leah dashed across the hall to the bathroom, slamming the door.

Sadie harrumphed inwardly. They acted so childish these days. Both of them were very interested in their guys and acted as if it was the only subject worth thinking about. Likely they'd soon be dating.

Sadie felt old and a bit useless, except for Paris and the ranch. If that Mark Peight insisted on acting so *bupplich,* then she'd just ignore him, and he could go fly a kite for all she cared. She was getting thoroughly sick of his strange ways. Besides, anyone with a childhood like that was bound to have some dysfunctional issues, and she wasn't going to marry anyone like that.

She had felt so sure that God was leading them together, that this was her destiny. Well, no more. She was done. She rolled on her side, punched her pillow, and sighed.

So that was how it was going to be. Mark Peight would just have to live in Montana if he wanted to; it didn't mean she had to be his wife anytime soon. Or... anytime at all.

Suddenly, a train of nostalgia rolled over her heart, its mournful whistle causing her to wince with remembering Ezra.

He was so good. So kind, uncomplicated, and easy to figure out. Life with Ezra would have been like calm waters, serene, her days floating by with no turbulence.

It was unreal, at times. He was no longer here on earth. If anyone deserved a home in heaven, it was surely Ezra. Maybe she was meant to be alone, then reunited with him once she got to heaven. Who knew?

Pi-i-ng!

The sound was only heard in her subconscious mind. The second time she heard it, she figured the temperature must have been higher than usual this afternoon, the way the house was creaking and snapping.

She heard another pinging noise, this time against glass.

What?

She sat straight up, kicked the sheet off, and headed to the window.

Crack!

Sadie recoiled, taking a few steps backward.

Someone was throwing a small, hard object against her window, above the screen.

Clutching her throat in horror, she stood in the middle of the room in total darkness, wondering what to do. Grab her robe and make a dash for the stairs? Get Leah and Rebekah? Wake Reuben?

She heard her name, a hissing sound.

Someone was out there. Someone who knew her and knew which room was hers.

"Sadie! It's me!"

A hoarse whisper. "It's me! Mark!"

Mark Peight! Throwing pebbles at her window like some lovelorn hero of the past. What a loser!

Anger gripped her, its claws tightening her senses, until she realized it would never work to go to the window and tell him exactly what she thought of him. Storming out of the ranch house because of who knew why, then showing up at her window in the middle of the night almost.

She had a notion to stay exactly where she was until he went away.

"Sadie! It's me. Mark!"

Again, she heard the urging in his voice.

"Sadie!"

Pushing her face against the screen, she looked down at his tall dark form, his face lifted as he eagerly awaited her answer.

"What do you want?"

She didn't mean to sound as grouchy as she did. She wished the words, or rather, her tone of voice, would stick in the screen and stay there, or dust the night breeze without harming anyone.

"What do you think I want?" he hissed in return. There was so much anger in his tone, Sadie took a step back, her eyes opening wide.

"I have no idea."

"I need to ask you something."

"Ask away."

What possessed her? Why did she answer with barbs emphasizing every word? She wanted to hurt him, like he'd hurt her by storming out of the Caldwell dining room, then ignoring her, and leaving her to wander a desert of insecurity.

How could she ever have felt he was her destiny? He was too hard to understand.

"Come downstairs."

The words were a curt order.

She pursed her lips, considering her answer. She no longer felt that panicky heartbeat in his presence, which uncomplicated things a lot. Folding her arms, she took her time in giving him an answer.

"Well, I need to get dressed."

"No, you don't. Just grab a robe."

"Hush! You'll wake Mam!"

Sadie knew Mam was a very light sleeper, as alert as the mouser in the barn. There was no way she could creep down the stairs without Mam knowing. Dat would go right on sleeping, the proverbial log. If Mam caught her sneaking outside in her night clothes, she would be in some very serious trouble.

"Hang on!"

She dressed quickly and crept down the stairs, her heart pounding now, which puzzled her. She thought she had surely moved on from that childish emotion. But by the time she reached the kitchen door, it was hammering against her ribs, drying her mouth until her tongue felt like cotton. She was still trying to be angry, but she couldn't keep the anger if the excitement of seeing Mark again drove it away.

Rounding the side of the house, she found him sitting on the lawn, his back to a tree, looking as if he had been there all evening. It was dark, but not so dark that she couldn't see his features or the shape of his head, the slope of his shoulders.

Dropping to her knees, breathless now, she said, "This is a weird time for you to come talk to me."

"Yeah, well…"

There was a silence, swelling with question marks.

Then, "Sadie, I have to know. What does Richard Caldwell mean to you?"

"Mean to me? What are you talking about?"

"I…was eating breakfast, and… You have never talked to me like that. Never. Your whole face lit up. You moved your hands. You pushed back your dark hair. It was like…suddenly you had a great reason to care about life. Almost like… I don't know."

He leaned forward, his elbows propped on his knees, the picture of misery. The great shoulders slumped in dejection.

Sadie sat down, pulled her skirt over her knees, and said nothing.

How could he? Surmise, presume, suspect, whatever. It was all the same. She could not believe him.

"Mark, he's my boss. I work for him. That's all."

"It didn't look that way."

"He's old enough to be my father!"

"So? That doesn't mean anything in the English world."

"It does, too."

"Look, Sadie, I know a lot more about that world than you do. A man like him, with his wealth, his status..."

"What about me? You think I would actually encourage him to...to...? So that's what you think I am?"

There was no answer.

Sadie's chin lifted. She felt the anger literally course through her veins. Scrambling to her feet, she stalked across the lawn, through the darkness, glad for its cover as the heat rose in her face.

She felt no tears, she was far too angry.

"Wait!"

Sadie did not wait. She walked as fast as she could, past the shrubs, up onto the porch. She had just reached for the door handle when she was caught, a hand on her waist. She was forcibly whirled around to face a very tall, ominous Mark.

"I didn't say that."

"You meant that!"

The screen door opened, and they were both caught in the blue glare of a blinding LED flashlight.

The deep, sleepy voice of Jacob Miller boomed, "*Vass geht au?*"

Dat!

Mark smiled sheepishly, then stuck out his hand.

"Hello, Jacob Miller. I'm just...here to talk to Sadie about something."

"You that Peight guy?"

"Yes, I am."

"Well, if you have something to talk about, I suppose the porch swing would be a proper place to sit, and since I doubt if you want me to hear what you're saying, I'll go back to bed again."

With that, the flashlight clicked off, the darkness covered them, soft and merciful, the screen door closed softly, and he was gone.

Mark cleared his throat, shuffled his feet.

"Can we sit down?"

The last thing Sadie wanted to do was share the intimacy of the porch swing with him, but she said stiffly, "We can."

Like robots they were now, turning and sitting down as if on cue. Sadie sort of hit the edge of the swing, miscalculating its position in the dark. Then she sat back too far and almost slid off, causing the swing to lurch like a boat hitting waves. She had to brake with her feet. Then the whole ridiculous situation hit her, and she burst out laughing, a sort of unladylike snort that caught her totally unaware.

They were both laughing now. With great swells of relief, the tension between them evaporated, welcome as summer showers on a parched earth.

Laughter was like that. A smile worked the same magic. It eased tension, opened the way for friendly conversation; it lowered a drawbridge for large ships that had to arrive at their destinations on time.

"You just about sat on the porch floor," Mark said finally.

"Hard, too!" Sadie laughed.

"What was I going to say?"

"You were talking about my boss. Mr. Richard Caldwell, himself."

"Yes, I was. And I plan on finishing my questions. What were you talking about?"

"Didn't you hear the men's conversation? It's all over the ranch. Someone is going around killing horses. Like a sniper. It started in Laredo County, sort of ... well, I think the area where the horse thieves were. You know those thieves were never caught and brought to justice. Black Thunder, the leader of the wild horses—he's dead. His owner is devastated. It's awful, Mark. You surely heard about Reuben's horse?"

"What?"

"Reuben's horse. He was shot. Up on the field of wild-flowers where we caught Paris and Cody."

"You can't be serious!"

"Yes. It was horrible. Reuben is being brave, but he'll never forget it. He's so young. I mean, I was what, 18 when Nevaeh died? I'll always remember that day."

"I will, too. Certainly. That was the day I finally held you in my arms. I could have died there. On that wagon. My life was fulfilled then. I knew what heaven feels like."

Sadie did not know what to say, so she said nothing. The chain attached to the heavy steel hook creaked with each moment of the swing, and Sadie could sense Mark's agitation.

"That's why I get so ... I don't know."

Suddenly he burst out, "I am so jealous of you, it's scary. When I saw you talking to your boss, I felt like a great black beast that wanted to ... punch him, drag him away from you. It's shameful and awful, but I don't know what to do about it."

"What hurts me most, is that you would even think I would be ... having an affair with him or something? How could you?"

His answer, a lowered head, moving back and forth, was his denial. "I'm like a colt that's been mistreated. I don't trust anyone. Not one single person. I want to, but…"

"I would never do anything as out of…just plain unheard of…" She was cut short.

"It's not unheard of!" he shouted.

Instinctively she put a hand over his mouth, like she would to try and shush a small boy.

"Shhh!"

"Sorry," he said quietly. "My mother, my lovely, beautiful mother, had a horrible affair with a real estate man. They slunk around the house like deceiving liars. Snakes. That's what they reminded me of. You know the kinds of snakes that are the exact same color as the grass and twigs and leaves?"

Sadie nodded.

"That's how it was. His car would drive in, my father would be in the fields, dragging that rusty, ancient, screeching harrow across his rocky soil with two skinny brown mules that looked as if they'd fall over any minute. He'd knock at the front door…and, well, I was only a kid, but I wasn't dumb. I knew. I think finally, that was the end of everything. The farm was sort of put up for sale, I guess, and that's when my father…wanted to stop living."

"But…did your mother run away with the real estate man?"

"Yes. There was an awful fight."

"But…I don't understand. If your parents were of the Amish faith, why did they act like that? Wouldn't they…I mean, surely they knew they did wrong?"

"My father did nothing wrong! Not one thing. He was a good man. He tried his best. I think he married way out of his league, if you know what I mean. Dat was sort of ordinary looking, a bit thin, and didn't have the... I don't know. Mam was beautiful, probably could've had any guy she wanted."

He paused, then turned and looked Sadie in the eye, and said, "Like you."

"Not me," Sadie whispered.

Mark bent over and caught both of her hands in his. He held them, securely, warmly, and kept them. The swing creaked, the night sounds shrilled and warbled and hooted, a symphony of nature resplendent in its variety.

"Yes, yes. Sadie, listen to me. It's why I ran off to Pennsylvania after I held you in my arms. I figured if I let myself love you, if I went falling headlong over a cliff without any thought to my past, of who I am, look what could happen. And when I saw you at that table with Mr. Caldwell... I... well, I went a little crazy. Can you blame me? You're so beautiful, Sadie, and how do I know that inside you there's not a promiscuous heart, like my mother's?"

"But, Mark, your mother was one in a million! That doesn't happen among our people. We are raised and kept to a commitment to God. The church, our marriage vows, all are taken very seriously. I have never heard of anyone... I mean, your mother was... Whew!"

Sadie had no words to describe her disbelief.

"I think she joined the church and wanted to do what was right in the beginning. She bore five children in five years, the way the church wanted it, doing nothing to prevent it. And perhaps, she simply couldn't handle the drudgery, the sleepless nights, the endless work, I don't know."

Sadie nodded, quiet now. She pulled her hands free,

hesitated one second, then brought her hands to his forearms, slid them up to his shoulders, and pulled him close, laying her head on his hard, muscled chest.

"Mark?" she whispered.

He groaned softly before crushing her to himself, his head lowering.

"I want you to know you can trust me. I can only say that, and the rest is up to you. I'll try and be someone you can place... I mean, for you to tell me these things, is just amazing. Where have you learned to confide in someone? So often, troubled children aren't able to do that."

"You are the only person who knows. Well, the counselor, but..."

She nodded, and stayed quiet.

"Sadie, do you believe in distant courtship? Are your parents very strict about these things?"

"I think that's pretty much up to us. I can't imagine... I don't know."

Clearly, she was becoming quite flustered, floundering with her words.

He chuckled softly. "I think I know what you mean, Sadie."

He kissed her softly, then soundly, and Sadie knew she had never felt closer to anyone in all her life. The will of God was so clear she could almost hold it in her hands, like a bouquet of wildflowers on the ridge, their fragrance enveloping them both, promising a future that was not smooth and untroubled. Rocky and steep at times, stormy at other times, their love was a vessel of strength that would bind them together, like two souls in a fortress of might.

And she'd be very careful how she talked to Richard Caldwell.

Chapter 7

I N CHURCH A FEW WEEKS LATER, THE *KESSLE-HAUS*, where the single girls stood, waiting to be called in and seated on the benches assigned for them, was abuzz with the shootings.

Erma Keim, a garrulous, big-boned girl of 28, who had never bothered about boyfriends or marriage, her white organdy cape and apron wrinkled and limp, her hands pumping the air for emphasis, expounded loud and long about this latest atrocity.

"I don't believe it," she was saying in a voice not meant for the quiet of a pre-service *kessle-haus*.

"I mean, this is ridiculous. Finally, we got those wild horses out of here, and now they claim someone is shooting horses on purpose. I refuse to believe it."

She tucked a strand of wavy, red hair beneath her covering, which sprang back out in defiance, looking wavier and redder than before. Her covering was limp and out of line, like her hair. She socked herself back against the counter, her green eyes bulging as she folded her arms across her skinny waist.

"It's true. Reuben's Cody is dead," Sadie said bluntly.

"What? Your brother? Is Cody his horse? What do you mean?"

Erma was fairly shouting now, her eyes looking as if they could leave the sockets of her face, were they not attached by strong muscles.

"Yes, yes, and yes," Sadie said, nodding soberly.

"But shot? I mean, just plain out of the clear, blue sky?" Erma shouted.

Sadie nodded, then told the attentive listeners the story of the race, the shot, the fear that followed.

"*Upp*!" Erma said, nodding in the direction of the kitchen door, where Maria Bontrager, the lady of the house, stood, motioning them to come to the service.

Erma always went first, being the oldest by more than a few years. Today was no exception, with Sadie following on her heels, and then Leah and Rebekah. The group of girls fell in line as they wound their way to the living room to be seated with the remainder of the congregation.

The open windows promised a breath of air in the already stuffy room. Sadie knew all too well how warm it would become before the three-hour service ended.

Her heart jangled a bit when Mark Peight led the row of single boys. He was so tall! So dark. How could she ever remain the same when she saw him? She was so glad no one could tell how her heart jumped and skipped a beat at the sight of him.

She sighed, a small expulsion of air, when she saw the boys being seated in the kitchen, out of their sight. She couldn't see him at all during the service, but maybe it was just as well; she'd keep her mind on the sermon.

When the strains of the first song began, she opened the small black *Ausbund*, the old German hymnbook

written by the forefathers in prison. She turned to share
it with Leah, who shook her head slightly as she busily unwrapped a red and white striped candy, which she
popped into her mouth. She rolled the cellophane wrapper into a small bundle and tossed it below the bench
ahead of her.

Sadie stuck her elbow out, punching Leah's arm. She
turned to look at her sister with bewilderment in her
innocent blue eyes.

Sadie drew down her eyebrows, pointed with her chin
at the cellophane wrapper below the bench and mouthed,
"Pick up your paper."

Leah shrugged, enjoyed her peppermint, and opened
her mouth to help with the singing, its volume building
by the minute.

Sadie leaned over. "Give me one, please," she whispered.

"Don't have another one," Leah answered.

Sadie answered by tapping on the pocket of Leah's
dress below the apron, where the presence of a few candy-
sized lumps resulted in a meaningful stare from Sadie and
an upturned hand.

"Give me."

Leah frowned but lifted her apron, producing a candy
obediently before settling back to help with the singing.

Sadie unwrapped the peppermint discreetly, bent her
head to pop it into her mouth, folded the wrapper, and
put it in her pocket along with the ironed handkerchief.

Leah watched from the corner of her eye and mouthed,
"Goody."

Sadie grinned, then ducked her head when she felt the
grin spreading.

The girls knew they were to behave with circumspec-
tion in the church at all times. But on a warm summer

morning, a bit of sisterly fun helped ease the boredom of sitting on the hard benches for three hours, less alluring today than it ever was.

The slow rhythm of the singing swirled around her. The wave of tradition and comfortable Sunday-morning sounds were as much a foundation for every Amish young person as the regularity of the services.

It was a form of worship they could adhere to, be content with, and grow in grace and spirituality without asking hows and whys. Lots of people chose to question, though. They became contentious, berating the ministers and their sermons, and sometimes taking their families to "go higher," which meant they joined another church that allowed them more worldly things, like cars and electricity.

Parents shushed their crying babies. Fathers with crying two-year-olds looked to give the children to their mothers, who may have been upstairs with other tiny siblings. So an aunt or grandmother scrambled to relieve the father of his unhappy offspring. After questioning the child closely, she'd offer a drink of cold water or a small container of pretzels or fruit snacks.

When the minister rose to begin the sermon, the congregation grew quiet, eagerly awaiting his words. He did not disappoint. The graying patriarch expounded on the word of God in a dynamic, undulating voice that gripped his listeners.

Sadie noticed a disturbance on the bench where the younger girls sat, a few rows ahead. Anna was extremely restless, her head turning first one way, then another, fixing her cape, then her covering.

Sadie became uncomfortable. What was wrong with Anna? It seemed as if she could not sit still for a minute.

Her face was pale, and she kept grimacing in the most unattractive manner.

Just when Sadie could stand it no longer, Anna rose and made her way carefully between the rows of girls, making a hasty exit up the stairs.

Sadie thought no more about it, guessing that Anna went to the bathroom, and resumed singing. When they stood to hear the Scripture, after kneeling in prayer, Sadie went to the *kessle-haus* for a drink of cold water and noticed that Anna was not among the girls her age. As she turned to go upstairs through the kitchen, she lowered her eyes demurely. She did not want to meet Mark's eyes, already feeling flushed as she walked past him.

She closed the door firmly, went softly up the stairs, and turned the knob of the bathroom door. It was locked. She stood back, her arms crossed, waiting until the bathroom was unoccupied.

She heard the water running, a pause, then Anna, very pale, opened the door. Sadie looked at her closely, noticing the swelling of her eyes. Was it just the warm summer weather?

"You okay?" she asked.

"Course, why wouldn't I be all right?" Anna said, her voice strained. Hoarse? Had she been crying?

Erma Keim thumped her way upstairs, and Anna pushed past Sadie, quickly disappearing down the stairway.

Sadie and Erma entered the bathroom together, Erma saying quite loudly, "Something smells bad! Eww! Someone threw up or something!"

Sadie winced, never knowing Erma to be tactful. She sniffed, then pushed aside the lace curtains to open the window wider.

"How can you tell?" she asked.

"I just can. Hey, my job at the produce market is coming to an end in September. Do they need someone down at Aspen East, where you work? I need to get serious about a job."

Sadie smiled to herself, knowing they were not supposed to discuss business or monetary concerns on a Sunday. But typical Erma, speaking loudly what was on her mind, no matter the day or the circumstances.

"I can check for you."

At the thought of Erma Keim and Dorothy Sevarr together in one kitchen, Sadie resigned herself to culinary war, with Dorothy defending her kingdom as queen of the domain, and the invading Erma trying to steal the crown in the first week.

The room was becoming quite warm. Women groped in their pockets for a square of folded, white handkerchief, lowering their faces to wipe discreetly at the perspiration beading their foreheads.

Little boys sat patiently beside their fathers, their bare feet swinging, their bangs dark with sweat, as the fathers swiped at their collars, loosening them slightly. The tired and restless babies grew too uncomfortable to sleep, while mothers patiently held them, their eyes a picture of submission.

The second speaker, a shy young minister who had only been ordained a few years ago, droned on. His monotone voice led the older men down a ramp slick with sleepiness, lassitude, then sleep, until they jerked back to consciousness—and embarrassment.

The minister did the best he could, Dat said. The Lord had chosen him, and someday, he'd overcome his quietness and shyness. Dat always had a soft spot for Phares Schlabach, who Dat said was truly humble, a good servant in the Lord's vineyard. And don't you kid yourself; if you paid attention, he said some profoundly interesting things, pointing out bits of Scripture no one else thought about.

Dat was like that. He respected and admired the quiet ones. The simple men of the community who struggled to make a living were often overlooked. They stayed in the background, smiling, and thoroughly enjoying the more talented storytellers who drew all the attention.

Dat said his girls would do well to marry a man like Phares.

After services, Sadie helped set the long tables with the Sunday dinner they always ate at church. The women spread long, snowy white tablecloths on benches elevated by wooden racks to form tables. For each place setting, they supplied a small plate for pie, a cup, knife and fork, and a water glass. Along with plates of sliced, homemade bread, the women served butter, jam, cheese, peanut-butter spread, pies, pickles, sweetened little red beets, and plates of ham.

It was the traditional meal at every church service, and so delicious each time. It was more like a snack or a hurried lunch. There were no elaborate dishes. They did no cooking, except to make a large pot of coffee. But it was a church dinner, a taste of home and community, a meal shared after services, as talk and laughter moved among the good food. Everyone ate hungrily and revived their spirits.

Sadie and her sisters washed dishes, filled water glasses, served coffee, whatever was necessary. They talked with their friends as they held fussy babies so mothers could sit down to eat in peace.

Erma Keim dashed among the tables, every movement

well calculated, the picture of efficiency. Sadie couldn't help but wonder what that presence would accomplish down at the ranch. But she dismissed the notion quickly at the thought of Dorothy's snapping eyes and her unladylike snort.

"They need pie on the men's table," Erma said, whisking past with an empty water pitcher held aloft.

Sadie turned to the pie rack to extricate one, then slid out another before turning to head for the men's table, where she found Reuben enthusiastically spreading a huge glob of the peanut-butter spread on a thick slice of whole wheat bread. She held her breath as he lifted it to his mouth, then grinned when he gave her a thumbs-up sign, peanut butter spread all over his fingers, the knife, and his face.

Sadie chose to walk home in spite of the heat. It would be worse, packed in the surrey with her sisters, Reuben yelling and complaining as always. Rebekah said she would accompany her and invited her friend Clara and, of all people, Erma Keim.

"Why Erma?" Sadie hissed behind a horizontal palm.

"She gets lonely on Sunday afternoon," Rebekah said quietly. "Besides, you're almost the same age. Both entering spinsterhood."

There was no time for an answer. Erma caught up from the rear in long, purposeful strides, her face alight with the prospect of spending an afternoon at the Miller home.

"Boy, that pie was nasty!" she bellowed into Sadie's ear. "Must be Ketty was baking again!"

Sadie shrank from the grating sound of Erma's raucous laugh, but smiled politely.

"Poor Fred Ketty."

The whole afternoon was spent in the kitchen, making popcorn loaded with melted butter. They tried all different kinds of seasoning, laughing uproariously when Reuben sprinkled hot pepper sauce on top of his dish, then raced for the water faucet, his tongue on fire.

Mam even joined in the fun, and Dat read *The Budget*, grinning behind it, sometimes lowering the paper to peer over his glasses when Erma said something exceptionally peculiar.

There was no doubt that she eyed the world in a different light and with strangely colored lenses. Men were a huge bother, not worth the ground they walked on, except for Moses in the Bible, Abraham Lincoln, and maybe John F. Kennedy, although he was a Democrat and they were a bit liberal for her taste. She thought the locals all looked alike in their cowboy hats, though the hats vastly improved their faces, which, the way they spent all their time outdoors, resembled the surface of the moon.

Not one boy had ever asked her out. Not one. She was as uncaring about that fact as she was about her looks, though Sadie wondered if this was really true.

She made a homemade pizza from scratch that tasted better than anyone's, she assured them airily. She ate four square slices of it, belched, wiped her mouth, excused herself, and decided it was time to go home.

"I know we're not supposed to call a driver, but I don't have a horse and buggy, so how else am I supposed to get home?"

With that, she marched to the phone shanty and called her neighbor lady, then sat on the porch swing to wait for her.

"Why don't you go along to the supper and singing at Melvin Troyer's?" Leah asked.

"Me? You want me to? Nah. People would say I'm setting my hat for Yoni's Crist. He's 40 now, did you know that? Everybody thinks he should ask me for a date, then, you know, marry me. I wouldn't take him. He has no ambition. You can tell by the way he walks that he doesn't like to get up in the morning. Not for me, no sir."

Sadie laughed. "Come on, Erma. I'm going to set up a blind date for you."

Erma leaped out of the porch swing, coming down squarely on both feet, her hands in the air, her mouth open wide.

"No!"

"Why not?"

"Because."

"Come on, Erma. Please? We'll get a driver and go to Critchfield. You pick your favorite restaurant, okay?"

"No. Absolutely not. I do not want a man. Certainly not Crist."

"Why not?"

"I told you why not."

"If I ask Mark Peight to go?"

Erma's eyes narrowed. She plopped back on the swing.

"Sadie Miller, you are crazy for hanging out with that guy. If anyone is shooting horses around here, it's him. He's not really right, is he? Good-looking, yes, but he scares me.

"*Upp*, here's my driver coming. Hey, thanks for the popcorn. I had fun. Come see me sometime. I live behind my Dad's house now. In a trailer."

"Do you really? We'll come see it," Leah assured her as Erma was off in a cloud of dust.

The supper and singing proved uneventful. Mark Peight was absent again. He never came to the suppers

and singings anymore, which irked Sadie more than she
cared to admit.

What did he do on Sunday? Why didn't he ask for an
ordinary date like normal people? He probably had some
deep, dark secret of his own, like Erma Keim thought.

Sadie played volleyball. At supper with her friends,
she sat at the singing table and sang with everyone else,
her thoughts far away.

Was she crazy, the way Erma Keim said?

She watched Yoni's Crist Weaver. He was tall, wide in
his shoulders, dressed nice enough, with a receding hair-
line. Actually, his hair, what there was of it, was thin and
brown. His eyes were pleasant, not too close to his nose,
which was large and took up a lot of room on his face.
He seemed shy, quiet, not very comfortable in the girls'
presence. Sadie thought he'd make a wonderful companion for the boisterous, colorful Erma. She would fill his
days with her never ending viewpoints, and her unique
take on life would completely change him. Wasn't there
an old saying about opposites attracting?

Later that evening, Sadie sat at the kitchen table
with Rebekah, drinking a Diet Pepsi, munching on "old
maids," the leftover unpopped kernels of popcorn that
remained in the bottom of the bowl.

"You should somehow get her fixed up a little. How
would you go about telling her those limp coverings are
simply a disaster?" Leah giggled, covering her mouth
with her hand.

"Her hair is worse. Hasn't she ever heard of hair
spray?"

"She has a nice figure, she's thin, at least, but her feet
are so scarily big. I bet she wears a size 11 or 12."

"That's okay. Crist is bald almost, and 40."

"They'd be so cute together."

"I don't believe her one bit about men."

"I don't either."

Sadie looked at the clock.

"Shoot. Midnight," she said, yawning.

"Where's Leah?"

"I have no idea. She was talking to a group when we left."

They drained their Pepsis, wiped the table, and were just ready to go upstairs to bed when headlights came slowly up the drive.

"Hmm, Leah," Rebekah said, watching as the buggy approached.

Then, "Oh, my goodness! The... They're going to the barn. I bet you anything Kevin... Oh, my!"

Catching Sadie's sleeve, she tugged, and said, "Come on, Sadie! He's coming in! Quick!"

Together they dashed up the stairs, flung open the door of Sadie's room, and collapsed on the bed, giggling like school girls. They heard Kevin's deep voice and Leah's nervous laughter.

The girls whispered about the lack of cookies or bars in the house, anything Leah could serve to him on that first, much-anticipated date.

"There are chocolate whoopie pies in the freezer," Sadie said.

"He doesn't want a frozen whoopie pie."

"They're best that way."

"Well, go down and set one on the table for him."

They dissolved into giggles imagining Leah's anger if they did something so completely senseless on her very first date.

They were both sound asleep when Leah finally came upstairs. She had managed well on her own, asking him politely if he wanted a snack, which he declined, saying he ate a big helping of cheese and pretzels at the singing. Really, he was far too nervous to eat anything after working up the nerve to ask Leah if he could take her home.

✡ ✡ ✡

Sadie arrived at work the following morning in a state of melancholy. Not only had her younger sister been on a date, but she seemed to be back to square one with Mark.

When Dorothy fussed and fumed, Sadie became more irritated than usual and told Dorothy she needed to get more kitchen help or retire. One or the other, take your pick. She meant every word she said, and when Dorothy sat down on a kitchen chair and ignored her the whole forenoon, Sadie didn't care.

Marcellus and Louis came to the kitchen with Jim. The kids were sweet and clean, with only a hint of the usual anxiety in their eyes. Sadie turned on her heel and started savagely stacking dishes in the commercial dishwasher. She resented the way Dorothy turned into another person the minute the children made an appearance.

She felt old and dissatisfied with her life. She was bitter about Mark and his strange ways. She was tired of it now. She wanted a home of her own, a husband to love and cherish. She wanted to quit slaving away at this ranch. She wanted, well... Mark.

When Jim came in, she barely acknowledged his jovial smile.

"We're a bit sour this morning?" he asked her, chuckling.

"A bit."

"Want to ride with me to town?"

"Yeah, take her with you. Dry cleaning needs picked up," Dorothy said flatly.

So that was how Sadie found herself in Jim's pickup with a list of groceries in her hand. Her foul mood lifted as the truck wound its way along country roads, dust flying from under the tires.

She rolled her window down, flung an elbow out the side of the door, watched the scenery roll away, and listened to Jim's good-natured conversation.

They picked up the dry cleaning, zipped it carefully in a navy-blue garment bag, and laid it on the truck bed. They bought groceries and picked up salt blocks at the feed store. Then they stopped for a cup of coffee.

It was pleasant sitting in the truck, watching the hustle and bustle of the people. Everyone seemed intent on their own personal business. They were all a variety of achievers but working together to make the town a place that was busy and industrious.

A shining, 15-passenger van came slowly down the street, the driver and the occupant of the front seat straining to read the street signs. The women's coverings were heart-shaped and their hair combed back severely, shining and sleek. Another group of Amish from Lancaster County, Pennsylvania, visiting the west.

Sadie turned her head, hoping they wouldn't see her. She simply was not in the mood to talk to strangers. When the van stopped, she willed herself to be invisible to them.

Just when she thought they had moved on, she heard a rich masculine voice say, "Excuse me."

She turned her head, and her gaze found the bluest eyes she had ever seen. He had a mop of streaked blondish-brown hair, a square jaw, and a very nice smile.

She was going to say "Hello" or "Hi," but nothing came out of her mouth. Nothing.

When she finally got her bearings, she stuttered a bit, became flustered, yanked open the door of the pickup, and stood on the street. Later she wondered why in the world she did that when she could have given him directions from her seat in the pickup just as easily.

"I'm looking for Bozeman Avenue."

She gave him halting directions as he watched her face intently. She wished he'd ask her name, but he didn't. The group was from Lancaster County, as Sadie had suspected. They were staying for a month or so. He said his mother was in ill health, and Sadie said she was sorry to hear it.

Then they simply stood there for several moments and looked at each other. He turned to go, then stopped and asked her name. When she told him, he smiled and said, "See you around."

Sadie felt as if a smile like that made anything possible. He left her standing in the street beside the old pickup, but twice he looked back.

Chapter 8

Eventually, Sadie persuaded Dat to hire a driver and get the buckboard she wanted. She said she would pay for it and do all the painting herself if he would build new seats and replace the floor. They had an extra pair of fiberglass shafts, although Reuben airily informed his father they weren't worth much if they were going to hitch Paris double.

Dat lifted his eyebrows, then lowered them, took off his straw hat and scratched his head. His graying hair was in disarray, but it didn't matter because his hat would cover it anyway.

"Thought you weren't going to get another horse," he said slowly.

"If we find one that looks like Paris, I will."

"Good."

Sadie made a phone call and told Dat that John Arnold would be here at two to pick him up. Then she swept the buggy shed, picked up baler twine, swept the forebay, washed her saddle and bridle with saddle soap and wax, then, to pass the time, she swiped at cobwebs hanging around the barn.

She called Paris. The horse was grazing at the lower end of the pasture with Charlie. Paris answered with a lazy lift of the head. She pricked her ears forward and lowered her head, her tail swishing steadily.

Charlie, however, decided it might be worth a try for some feed. He came obediently, his brown head bobbing in easy rhythm with every step, his shoes clicking against the small stones on the path.

"Come, Paris! Come on!"

Sadie coaxed the horse with her hands cupped around her mouth, but Paris refused to budge, staying under the shade of the large oak tree, her head lowered sleepily.

Sadie shook her head and turned to go when she heard the truck returning in a spray of gravel and a cloud of dust. Dat and the driver leapt from the truck, losing no time in unhitching the trailer, before John Arnold sped off down the driveway in a great swirl of rolling dust.

"What is up with him?" Sadie asked.

"There's been another shooting. Poor sheep farmer over in Oaken Valley. Name of Ben Ching. He had two champion quarter horses. The only thing he owned worth anything. Both shot this morning, early."

Sadie stared at her father, her eyes filling with tears.

"But who...?"

Dat shrugged. "His wife works at the dry cleaners in town. They're Chinese, or Japanese, foreign something. Their daughter is a barrel racer."

Sadie crossed her arms and shivered, then looked off across the valley. Dat turned to loosen the straps that held the buckboard, which looked more like a decrepit old wreck with each passing moment.

"It's like a bad omen, Dat. Those horse thieves on the loose, the wild horses scaring us, and now this. It's almost as if someone is determined to... I don't know, make us all afraid of something unknown."

Dat unhooked another strap, straightened, and said wisely, "Well, I wouldn't say that. I think it's unsuccessful horse thieves who are still mad and taking revenge on their failure. They won't get away with it."

Sadie nodded. "How did they know the spot on the ridge where Cody was shot? You know, sometimes I wonder if it's not someone closer than we think. Who else but us knows of that field of wildflowers?"

"The people you work with down at the ranch?"

Sadie shook her head. "I doubt it. I mean, there is not one single person down there who seems even vaguely suspicious. Well, these two children..."

"What two children?"

"You know, Marcellus and Louis."

"Who?"

Dat stopped working, straightened, and looked at Sadie, switching the piece of hay in his mouth to the other side.

"Those... dark-skinned Latinos, Mexicans... whatever they are. Beautiful children. I told you."

"No, you didn't. I heard nothing of this."

"Well, you must not have been home when I told the rest of the family."

She told her father the whole story down to their impeccable manners, Dorothy's total devotion to them, and the jewels in the drawstring bag.

"Hmmm."

That was all Dat said before Reuben came out of the house holding one cheek and with a sour expression on his face.

"Reuben!" Sadie called, "Look what arrived!"

Reuben looked, snorted, then said, "Piece of junk."

Dat smiled and Sadie stifled a laugh.

"What's wrong with you?"

"Toothache."

"A serious one?"

Reuben nodded. "Hurts plenty. Mam's taking me to the dentist at 4:30."

✼ ✡ ✼

Sadie cooked supper that evening with Anna's help. Rebekah and Leah were working late at the produce market, so it was an ideal time for Sadie to spend time with her youngest sister.

As Sadie peeled potatoes, Anna shredded cabbage on a hand-held grater, her head bent to the task. She answered the questions Sadie asked, but the usual youthful chatter was completely absent.

"Now, for coleslaw. Fix the dressing. A few table-spoons of mayonnaise, some sugar…"

"Not mayonnaise," Anna said sharply.

"Why not mayonnaise?"

"Miracle Whip. Half the calories and fat."

"Anna! Seriously? When did you start worrying about calories?"

Immediately Anna became flustered, nervously tugging at a covering string, refusing to look at Sadie.

"I'm not. I…just…like the taste of Miracle Whip so much better. That's all."

"Just so you know, you aren't fat, Anna."

"Yes, I am. I'm grossly overweight. I'm obese."

Sadie leaned against the counter, pursed her lips, and watched a red-faced Anna mixing sugar into the shredded cabbage.

"Whatever gave you that idea?"

"The scales."

"You don't weigh more than me, Anna."

"I weigh a lot more."

"How much do you weigh?"

"I'm not saying."

No amount of coaxing would persuade Anna to reveal the troubling number. Sadie detected a note of genuine sadness in her sister's voice, so she let it go. No use prompting and upsetting her younger sister more than she was.

They ate at 6:00. Leah and Rebekah did dishes together while Sadie tidied the kitchen. She put magazines and newspapers in the basket beside Dat's recliner, then wandered aimlessly from the porch swing to the living room and back. Finally, when she realized the hour was quite late, she became concerned.

Where were Mam and Reuben? His appointment had been at 4:30, and it was getting close to eight. Oh, well, likely they had gone to buy groceries.

She wandered out to the barn, having heard hammering noises coming from that direction. Dat was tearing up the floor of the buckboard. Sadie was clearly delighted, unable to believe he was already starting on a project he didn't want to do in the first place.

She watched from a distance, then decided not to approach him or praise him for his work. Sometimes when you did that, Dat turned gruff, downplaying his emotions, even walking away.

Sadie went into the phone shanty and sat on the cracked plastic chair at the counter. Flies buzzed at the screen, half dead or still trying in vain to escape. If they would only turn around and look in another direction, they'd be able to fly straight out the door to the great, wide, freedom outside.

Flies were like that. Idiotic, annoying little insects that drove you crazy in the summertime, hibernating in the cracks of the windows in winter, making a brand new appearance in spring. So far, Sadie could find no purpose for flies, other than making life miserable for humans and beasts alike. Horses swished their tails endlessly all summer long, cows swatted, stamped their feet, swung their heads, and still the flies tormented them. Housewives swatted flies, hung fly paper, yelled at children to close the screen doors, and still the flies found a way in.

She picked up the phone and heard the familiar "beep, beep, beep" that indicated someone had left a message. But there was none, so she replaced the receiver and swatted aimlessly at a pesky fly. As she turned to leave, the shrill vibration of the phone pierced her consciousness and made her jump.

Instantly, her thoughts, as always, turned to Mark Peight. As sure as the sun came up every morning, whenever the phone rang, her heart leaped within her, and Mark came to mind.

She picked up the receiver. "Hello?"

No answer.

Sadie waited a few seconds and decided to try once more. "Hello?"

She heard raspy breathing. But only that. No words.

The silence now turned ominous.

Quickly she replaced the receiver, then stood watching the phone as if it might turn into some dangerous object if she wasn't careful. It rang again, that shrill sound, and shivers went up her spine.

Should she pick it up? What if someone was playing a

joke? Mark Peight? Would he do something like that? What about Mam and Reuben? Maybe there was an accident? That thought goaded her as she immediately picked it up.

"Hello?"

Only the same raspy breathing, almost the way a snake sounded as it slithered across a rock.

Once, when she was walking with her friends on the way home from school, a snake had made its way up the side of a rocky cliff. It seemingly made no sound at all, and yet, it was there, just like this breathing.

She hung up firmly, resolved not to pick up the receiver again, and walked out of the phone shanty. She was determined to put it from her mind. It was nothing. Just a wrong number.

She was grateful to see headlights winding their way up the hill in the deepening twilight. Mam and Reuben! Fear and uncertainty faded away at the thought of Mam coming up the hill with a grouchy Reuben in the backseat. Mam was her anchor at times like this.

The car stopped and the interior light came on. Mam paid the driver, then emerged from the vehicle and opened the back door for Reuben.

Sadie and Anna helped unload groceries, scattering the bags across the kitchen table and countertops.

Mam threw her bonnet on the counter, her face colored slightly, her blue eyes snapping.

"Now that's the last time I'm doing something like that!" she announced firmly.

Oh, here we go again, Sadie thought wryly.

"I absolutely hate it when a driver does that to me!" Mam fairly shouted.

"I called him first. Yes, he can go. Fine. He comes to pick up me and Reuben, and once we're in the van he says he hopes we don't mind taking Dave Detweiler, Sally, and guess who else? That Fred Ketty, of all people! Oh, I was about nuts. Here I had an appointment, and he still had to pick up these other two women. And you know Fred Ketty? She's as slow as molasses in January, never ready when the driver comes. When she finally came lumbering out the sidewalk so slow, I had a notion to tell her to go back and change her apron. She had food all over it. Talked the whole way to town in Dutch, of course, picking her teeth with a toothpick. Oh...!!"

There were no other words to describe her trip to town except for that final exasperated "Oh!" Mam wiped her face with a paper towel, then rummaged through the plastic grocery bags muttering about her ice cream being nothing but milk.

"Now, Mam," Sadie said soberly. But her heart was full of joy and thanksgiving. The old Mam was truly back. Her spirit. Her passion. It was all there, a banner of well-being.

Mam liked going to town by herself. She would rather pay twice the amount than split the cost with other riders. It was more convenient to go her own way to the stores where she wanted to shop, and then have the space to load everything in the small van, rather than crowding in more people who, in Mam's words, "stopped at every fencepost."

"Then Reuben's tooth was infected and the dentist pulled it, saying he thinks he has him numbed up, but here was Reuben in all this pain and misery, and Dan Detweiler's wife had an appointment at that quack chiropractor, what's his name? Bissle or something. I wouldn't take my cat to him, but Sally goes every week. Says he helps her sciatica, or however you say that. Well, there we sat, Fred Ketty talking my ear off, still shoving that toothpick around."

Suddenly she stopped, turned to Sadie, and said, "Did you know about those quarter horses being shot?"

"I heard," Sadie said, opening a box of Raisin Bran Crunch, pouring a liberal amount into a bowl.

"It's a bad omen. Fred Ketty said there's no way anyone would find her sitting in a buggy. It's downright dangerous. I had a notion to tell Ketty she don't have to worry, as tight as Fred is with his horse feed. That poor, hairy creature they drive is too pitiful to shoot."

Sadie laughed, then put her arms around her mother, laid her head on her shoulder, and held her close.

"Mam, I love you so much. You are back to being my Mam again."

"Ach, Sadie. Ach, my."

Mam's voice sounded choked with emotion. When Sadie stepped back, Mam held her at arm's length, her eyes soft and watery.

"Let's give God the credit."

"I will."

It was more than the gas light that cast the kitchen in a warm yellow glow that evening. The love of God was so near, Sadie could touch it.

Mam hummed softly, then laughed.

"You know, I'll probably never be able to share my town trips well. Isn't that awful? I should be ashamed of myself."

"No. You are so my Mam," Sadie answered, as she poured cold milk on her dish of cereal and headed for the porch swing.

The view from the porch was magnificent. The navy blue night competed with the disappearing blaze of the sun, casting the clouds in burgundy, magenta, and powder blue. The pines were black and pointed, like a silhouette of soldiers standing at perfect attention, the glory of the sunset their leader.

A mockingbird sang his plaintive evening cry, its warble a drumroll for the pine trees to begin their march. After that he imitated a robin, chirping shrilly, on and on, stopping only when the car bearing Leah and Rebekah wound its way up the drive.

The sisters tumbled out, saying goodnight, then plopped on the porch swing.

"Slide over, fatty. Whatcha eating? Mm! Give me a bite."

Leah grabbed the bowl, while Rebekah lifted a spoonful to her mouth.

"Mmm. Did Mam get a fresh box of Raisin Bran Crunch?"

"Yep!" Sadie said happily.

Home was like this. A place where everything came together. All the anxieties of jobs, insecurities, the whole wide perplexing world and its difficulties were put to rest the minute you opened the kitchen door and met your sisters or Mam.

Not one person on earth understood you the way a mother or a sister did. They could see straight through you. So there was no use trying to be cheerful when you really weren't, or pleased when you were horribly disappointed, or anything that made you out to be something you weren't.

"Hey, don't eat all that cereal. It's mine, remember?" Sadie said.

"I'll get you some more. Hey, did you hear about that poor family whose quarter horses were shot? Everyone is talking about it down at the market. It's just pathetic. The parents were hoping their daughter would take first place in the barrel race at the end of August."

Reuben came out and flopped down on the concrete steps, one hand held delicately to his swollen cheek. He sighed loudly. Then he rolled his eyes in the most pitiful way, sighing deeply again. When that didn't get much of a response, he said loudly, "My tooth was infected."

Leah had just launched into a vivid account of the tragedy and the beauty of the reddish quarter horses. Sadie and Rebekah listened wide-eyed.

"My tooth was infected," he repeated, much louder.

Leah stopped, turned to Reuben, and asked if it hurt.

"Oh, yes. I think the dentist used a digging iron and a crowbar to loosen it."

"Reuben!"

"It felt like my whole jaw was coming apart. I'm never going back to that dentist ever again."

The girls clucked sufficiently, pitying him until he was satisfied that he had impressed them with his bravery. He sat back against the porch post, listening as the girls talked of the sheep farmer and his daughter.

Reuben sat up, listened intently, then began waving his hands.

"This is odd. This is really odd. Listen to this."

He had his sister's full attention now, so he leaped up from the steps, his aching mouth forgotten, took a deep breath, and proceeded to tell them about the character at the dentist's office.

"He was skinny, greasy, his hair in a ponytail, tattoos all over his forearms, and I guess I was staring 'cause Mam told me I'm not allowed to. He was... Well, I'd hate to meet him in the dark."

"What's so odd about him?"

"I'm not done yet. His cell phone rang. You know, people with manners usually go outside to talk, or else they talk quietly. Boy, not him. He stayed right there and talked in the oddest way."

He hesitated, then asked, "What's a chink?"

Sadie looked at Leah. "Isn't that a slang word for a Chinese person?"

"I don't know. You're the reader, not me," Leah answered.

Reuben continued, "He said a lot of swear words. Mam's mouth got tighter and tighter. He said something about those chinks. And talked about a target, then got really angry about some messed up operation."

"It couldn't be."

"Who knows?"

"Was it someone who knows something about the quarter horses?"

"Oh, dear, Reuben, you should have gone out to the parking lot and got his license number."

That brought a solid snort from Reuben.

"How could I? I didn't know which vehicle he was driving. And besides, I don't know if he's connected with that quarter-horse deal."

As darkness fell, the girls made plans for a chicken barbecue dinner. Dat joined them on the porch and offered some advice. Mam contentedly sipped a tall glass of sweet tea on the wooden rocker.

Sadie noticed Mam's covering was crooked and that she had a pinched look around the corners of her mouth. Sadie could only imagine the restraint it required to accept the long wait at the chiropractor's office and then endure her distaste for Fred Ketty's toothpick.

They decided to organize a bake sale and give all the

proceeds to Ben Ching and his family, the quarter horses being such a terrible loss. They'd make chicken corn soup, barbecued chicken, and whatever else the Amish folks could think of. All the food would be donated. Mam suggested a consignment auction, which the girls thought was a great idea, but Dat said they'd need some of the settlement's active leaders to give the "go-ahead."

In the days that followed, the girls wrote letters and made phone calls while Dat organized a meeting the following Thursday evening. The men who attended solemnly planned the event and voted unanimously to hold it at the Orvie Bontrager farm on the second Saturday in September. As they drank coffee and ate chocolate whoopie pies, they chose Dat to speak to Ben. They asked the women to plan the bake sale.

Sadie offered to give spring wagon rides with Paris—for the English people who turned up for the benefit. Reuben snorted so loudly at the suggestion that Old Emery Weaver turned the whole way around to see where the noise came from. Reuben slid way down on the recliner behind his book so no one could see his face. Anna giggled out loud, and her face turned bright red as she ran out on the porch to finish laughing.

Sadie rose straight to the challenge. Let them laugh. She knew she could do anything she wanted with Paris, so she'd show them.

She coaxed Dat into putting temporary seats on the old buckboard. She painted it a glossy black and put an old piece of carpet on the floor, and it was just fine. Rebekah pronounced it a mighty chariot of goodwill. Sadie couldn't have agreed more.

Reuben refused to participate. No amount of wheedling or promised sums of money made a difference. He sat on the fence like an obstinate little owl, blinking his eyes wisely, chewing on a long piece of hay. He mostly snorted or made cutting remarks. When Sadie told Dat, Reuben was taken down a notch by having to stack firewood on the north side of the barn.

Anna loitered on the outskirts of the pasture, but when Sadie gestured for her to help, Anna disappeared into the house. Finally, in exasperation, as Paris sidestepped and tossed her head trying to get rid of the blinders, Sadie tied the horse to the fence and went to find someone to help.

Reuben was slowly stacking firewood, so angry that he threw a sizable stick at her. Sadie marched up and pulled his ear as hard as she could, and he began yowling in earnest until Dat appeared around the corner of the barn.

Sadie found Anna at the kitchen table, her head in her hands, blinking back tears. She swatted savagely when Sadie asked her what was wrong.

"Sadie... I would love to help you, but..."

She stopped, her plump shoulders slumping dejectedly as she whispered, "I'm too fat to help you give buggy rides."

Instantly, Sadie slid into a chair opposite her sister, reached across the table, and took one of Anna's soft, brown hands.

"Anna, look at me. You are the perfect one to help. We'll wear the same color dress the day of the sale, and you can drive. Help me, Anna. I can't do this by myself."

"Reuben would be better."

"Not for this. He's a wonderful rider, but driving is better for you. You genuinely like people, and you'll be friendlier. Reuben would be so... so... snorty all the time."

Anna wiped her eyes, a flash of self-confidence in her shaky smile.

Chapter 9

T HE COMMUNITY WAS ABUZZ WITH PLANS FOR the consignment sale. There were always new messages on the phone and people donating things they thought would sell well: sofas, kitchen chairs, lawn mowers, bedding, old quilts, anything they didn't need and would help to form a lively auction.

The old buckboard was sort of a do-it-yourself job, Sadie knew, but it looked clean and glossy. The wheels were solid, and the new pair of fiberglass shafts fit perfectly. Paris was a picture of regal beauty once she was fitted between them.

Sadie and Anna had two weeks to work with Paris. It wasn't as long as Sadie would have liked, but it would have to do. The first time Sadie put a harness on Paris, she pranced and snorted at the unaccustomed attachment on her back. Anna held her steady, walking behind her with the reins while Sadie spoke gently to the horse as they walked and then trotted around the pasture. Paris pranced and tossed her head, but Anna was consistent, holding the reins steady as Sadie led her around the pasture.

"Stop throwing your head," she admonished her horse. "You know you're not acting like a good horse should."

They stopped, and Sadie stroked her neck, adjusted the collar, then stepped back. She had an idea.

"Anna, take her by yourself. I don't think she likes me hanging onto her bit. You try."

Anna bit her lip and shook her head.

"I can't."

"Try. Just lift the reins a bit and cluck, the way Dat does with Charlie."

"I can't. I'm not you. She won't listen."

"Anna, please. Just try."

Sadie could see the resolve in her sister's face as Anna straightened her back, lifted her chin, and nervously said, "*Komm*, Paris."

For one split second, Sadie was afraid Paris would not obey, then, her head lowered only slightly, she leaned into the collar and pulled, the buckboard rolling smoothly after her.

"Turn her in a big circle," Sadie called, and when Paris lifted her head and stepped out with a fancy gait, Sadie got goose bumps. She felt like crying, then laughing, clasping her hands together so hard her knuckles hurt.

Look at her! A genuine show-off, she thought. A real one. Oh, Paris, you gorgeous creature. You look like a horse in a show ring. Her light mane and tail streamed in the stiff, evening breeze. She made a perfect circle, trotting slowly, then stopped obediently when Anna pulled in on the reins.

"Whoa."

"Oh, Anna! That was perfect! Absolutely! You are simply a natural driving Paris. I wouldn't even have to be there!"

Anna drew in a deep breath, sat up very straight, her eyes shining, and said, “Do you really mean it, Sadie, or are you just saying that for *goot-manich*?”

“No, no, I’m not just being kind. You did a wonderful job.”

From that day on, Anna flourished. Her confidence in her ability to drive Paris steadied both horse and driver. And when Anna finally took Paris down the drive, the horse flicked her ears only when Anna slammed the lever forward and the old brakes screeched.

They trotted Paris down the road, passersby waving and turning to watch. Anna sat straight, waved, and smiled. Sadie knew the buggy rides would be a hit with the sale patrons. And they’d do wonders for Anna’s confidence.

✡ ✡ ✡

The day of the consignment sale turned out to be cloudy in the morning. Sadie ran to the window countless times to see if the gray clouds were churning with darker ones that promised rain. Finally, she walked outside, licked her forefinger, and held it up to the breeze, which was very slight. But she could still feel the difference, the side to the west drying quicker.

Yes! It would not rain today. A few sprinkles or scattered showers, perhaps, but not a pelting rain with no let up.

She dressed quickly. The new pale-blue dress shimmered over her shoulders as she put it on. It was a beautiful color, a happy one, if there was such a thing, she thought. She pinned her apron quickly and gave her appearance a final check in the mirror. She grabbed her purse off the oak clothes tree in her room and hurried down the stairs.

She was alarmed to meet Anna, who averted her tear-stained face as she busily tied her shoes, sniffing quietly. Mam was wrapping chocolate shoofly pies in Saran Wrap, thoroughly flustered. Dat hitched Charlie to the sparkling clean surrey outside.

Ach, my, Anna, Sadie thought.

"What's wrong with Anna?" she whispered to Mam.

Mam turned to look, saw Anna's face and asked, "Anna, why are you crying?"

"I'm not."

Mam shrugged her shoulders, wrapped another pie, and quickly slid it into the pie rack, a homemade tower with 12 shells surrounded by screen, with a door and a handle on top. It was the easiest way to transport 12 pies in a buggy, or any vehicle for that matter.

After they left, Sadie caught Anna's eye and raised her eyebrows in a silent invitation to spill her sadness. Immediately, Anna's chin quivered.

"My dress is too tight, Sadie. I look so awful. It's... I look like a pale blue elephant!"

The last word was drawn out on a wail of despair, the self-hatred so evident you could taste it, a horrible metallic taste of untruth wrapped around Anna's conscience until it eliminated all rational thinking.

How? How did a person go about correcting this?

Sadie put one arm around Anna's soft shoulders and slid two fingers inside the belt of her apron. She assured Anna that there was room to spare, and whatever made her think the dress was too tight?

"Everything I wear is too tight," Anna said, shrugging Sadie's hand off her shoulder.

Standing before the bathroom mirror, Anna burst out in another long, drawn-out exclamation of disgust.

"My hair! I hate my hair."

"Anna, stop."

Sadie was firm, standing behind her, finding her gaze in the mirror.

"No! Look at me! I'm a fat ugly ... toad. My hair isn't right."

"Anna, come. Sit down."

Sadie told her God made her unique, according to His will, and it was wrong to think of yourself in such a harmful way. These thoughts were of the devil, and eventually, she would believe them, which could cause harmful behavior, like anorexia or bulimia.

"What's that?" Anna asked, wide-eyed.

"I'll explain it sometime. Driver's here!"

The Orvie Bontrager farm was a kaleidoscope of color and movement. Vehicles crept along the driveway and parked in fields and ditches. Children ran about in bright colors, constantly changing the scenery—a red dress here, a green shirt there, yellow straw hats bobbing along on little heads, sticky little fingers clutching colorful candy.

The auctioneer's cry rose and fell as he sold horses and surreys, ponies, sheep, goats, pigeons in cages, a litter of kittens. The crowd pressed close, eager to hear the bidding.

Sadie and Anna went to find Paris. They had decided to bring the horse down the evening before to familiarize her with the throng of people, vehicles, and other animals. When she saw Anna and Sadie, she nickered a good morning, shoving her nose into Anna's palm for her usual treat of an apple, a carrot, or a few sugar cubes.

"How was your night? You didn't like it down here, did you?" Sadie whispered.

Anna nudged Sadie's elbow. "Look who's here!"

Mark Peight was striding purposefully in her direction, a broad grin on his handsome face.

"Hello! What are you doing with Paris here?" he asked.

Sadie struggled to keep the anger from taking control of her tongue. If you'd date me the way normal guys do instead of storming out of a dining room and then coming to throw those silly pebbles at my window, you'd know what I'm doing here.

"Buggy rides," she said, and none too friendly.

The broad grin folded in on itself, the white teeth obliterated by fine lips that gave no hint of a smile.

"I see."

Sadie busied herself with the currycomb, brushing much faster and harder than normal, until Anna cleared her throat nervously.

Mark shoved his one foot against a bale of hay to reposition it, then sat down, loosely, easily, with that cat-like grace he possessed. He pulled out a piece of hay and chewed it. Patting the bale beside him, he smiled at Anna and asked if she wanted to sit there. Anna, gazing at him with adoring eyes, obliged him immediately.

"I'm sure Paris is brushed well enough," he said slowly.

She didn't give him the satisfaction of a reply, just yanked the black harness off the hook and threw it savagely onto Paris' back.

"Whoa!" she said, when Paris sidestepped.

"We're a bit testy today," Mark said, his deep brown eyes teasing her.

Sadie faced him, her hands on her hips.

"No, we aren't. I mean, no, I'm not testy. I just have work to do, unlike you, who does only what he pleases all the time."

"You look awful pretty when you're mad."

With that, he got up and strode purposefully out of the barn. Sadie watched in disbelief, then remorse, as he strode up to the doughnut stand. Lillian Yoder, in a beautiful lime-green dress, hurried over to take his order, bowing and dipping, her blond hair shining with every toss of her head.

As Mark became drawn into a serious conversation with her, it was all Sadie could do to turn away from watching the scene at the doughnut stand as she picked up Paris' bridle.

Anna giggled, "He bought six doughnuts."

"Hmmph."

Anna shrugged her shoulders, convinced Sadie would be an old maid forever, the way she acted about Mark Peight.

Sadie led Paris to the fence near a big handmade sign: "Buggy Rides, $2.00."

Sadie backed Paris between the shafts, as Anna held them aloft.

Sadie loosened the britchment straps, making sure the collar was not pinching her neck, and polished the bridle with a clean rag. A crowd was already forming, holding out the dollar bills required.

Sadie smiled, accepted the money, and helped the first six people into the spring wagon. Then she drove off with Paris acting like a perfect lady. She let Anna take the next six people, secretly gloating at the thought of having already accumulated $24. All the angry thoughts of Mark Peight slipped away.

The barbecued chicken smelled wonderful, the thick gray smoke rising from the pits as it rolled over the crowd. Sausage sandwiches, doughnuts, funnel cakes, and burritos—there was so much food Sadie wondered how to decide what she wanted most.

As she pulled Paris to a stop, she saw a middle-aged Asian couple climb up on the auctioneer's platform, followed by a boy about Reuben's age and a petite young girl dressed in traditional western garb.

The barrel racer and her family! The auctioneer introduced them as the Ching family. He told of the shooting, of the loss of their beloved animals, to a crowd hushed with sympathy. When he announced that the proceeds of the sale would go to help them buy more horses, hats went sailing into the air, and the crowd erupted in a cheer of goodwill and charity.

The Amish men kept their hats on their heads, stoic and quiet, as was their way. More than one straw hat was bent, white coverings alongside, as they wiped furtive tears.

Mr. Ching took the microphone and spoke in halting English of his deep gratitude. The crowd was completely quiet, listening reverently. He spoke from the heart with the good manners of the old Chinese, his arm at his waist as he bowed deeply, his wife nodding her assent at his side.

"For all the world like two beautiful little birds," Dorothy would say later, shaking her head in wonder.

Mr. Ching introduced his daughter, Callie, who would be the real recipient of this day of unselfishness. She stepped up to the microphone and spoke in a low, musical voice about her loss, the heartbreak of finding the two quarter horses dead in the pasture, the bullet holes, and the investigation that followed.

"Last, I wish to thank all my friends of the Amish for this day."

She bowed, waved, and stepped down, her black hair swinging down her back, her boots clicking on the wooden platform.

The auctioneer announced that no one would want to miss the making of egg rolls, wontons, and Chinese chicken and vegetables under the blue and white tent, all made by the relatives of the Ching family who had come from Indiana for the benefit.

Sadie stepped down from the spring wagon, and Anna took over. Sadie went to find a cold drink of lemonade, her throat parched by the sun and the dust.

Mark Peight stood by the lemonade stand in lively conversation with Callie Ching and appeared to be quite taken with her.

Had he no shame? The nerve of him! What a flirt! And she being English and all.

Sadie took two deep breaths to steady herself. Common sense finally settled in. He was a grown single man and could hold a conversation with whomever he wished. It was none of her concern. They were not dating, and she had no right to these ugly little monsters of jealousy that cropped up every time she saw him with another female. It was ridiculous.

But when Callie put a hand on his arm, and he bent his head toward hers, Sadie's emotions skyrocketed into the wild blue sky.

Why did she care so much? He made her stomping mad with his ... his ease and his grace and his smile and his pitiful past. Why wouldn't he ask her for a decent date and stop being so secretive? She was just going to forget about him, and the next time he wanted to confide in her, she'd suggest he tell Lillian Yoder or Callie Ching. But she knew she couldn't say that, because what if he did?

She felt all mixed up and evil inside, so she prayed hard for help right then and there. I need you, I am not being who I should be, she prayed.

Was love supposed to be like this—a standoff between feelings of wonderful heights and valleys so low they were unbearable, with the unexpected avalanche of emotions she could not understand thrown in randomly?

Well, she definitely was not thirsty for lemonade anymore.

She bought an ice-cold Pepsi from Reuben and his rambunctious friends at the drink counter. He threw a handful of ice at her, and she told him he'd better behave or she'd tell Dat. But Dat wasn't there, Reuben reminded her, because he went to town for more ice.

Sipping her Pepsi, Sadie made her way through the crowd, smiling to herself at the sight of Fred Ketty leaning intently over a counter watching an aging Chinese woman making egg rolls.

"Oh, for sure, for sure," she heard Ketty say, and hoped she didn't have that ever-present toothpick dangling from her teeth.

"Oh! Oh, I'm sorry!" Sadie said.

She had bumped solidly into a broad chest and spilled her Pepsi all over a striped blue shirt. She stepped back and looked directly into the same blue eyes she had met in town.

"Sadie Miller, right?" he said.

She could feel the heat in her face and knew the blush quickly spreading across it was a telltale sign of … of what? Remembering him?

"How are you?" he asked, seeming confident in his ability to win her.

"I...I'm okay. I...I was on my way..." She jerked her thumb toward Anna on the spring wagon.

"Don't let me keep you," he said smiling.

"I'm...That's my horse, Paris. I'm giving buggy rides for $2."

"Will you take me for a buggy ride?"

"But you're Amish. You've been on a buggy plenty of times."

"Will you take me anyway?"

"I will."

"Just me?"

Sadie lifted her chin.

"Yes."

She persuaded Anna to let her take her turn driving. She climbed up on the driver's side and took the reins. He hit the seat beside her with a solid thump, his shoulder landing squarely against hers.

"This your horse? Named Paris? That's awesome."

He turned to look at her, and their eyes met. They both grinned a happy smile of recognition and shared admiration.

"I don't even know your name," Sadie said.

"Guess."

"Hmm. You're from Lancaster. Isn't everyone named Stoltzfus or...um...Zook? Strictly guessing!" she said, laughing.

"I love how you say Lancaster. LAN-caster. We say LANK-ister, sort of the...well, whatever."

"You still didn't tell me your name."

"Guess. Hey, how come you're circling around? We don't want to go back yet. My name is Daniel."

"Just Daniel?"

"Daniel King."

"Oh. Hi, Daniel."

He stuck out his hand and she grasped it warmly, a good solid hand, smooth and strong. She did not want to let go but did so reluctantly, the current between them so strong that they fell silent immediately.

Paris was tiring, her steps becoming slower as they made their way out Orvie's driveway and past parked vehicles, the sound of the auctioneer's sing-song voice fading rapidly.

"It's so unreal out here in Montana. I've never seen anything like it. I don't want to go home ever again."

"We like it here, although we've definitely had our trials."

Paris was walking uphill now, her head nodding with each step. Sadie told Daniel about the wild horses, Mam's illness, the ranch, everything. Words came so easily, they were nearly unstoppable, a brook bubbling in a rich stream of memories and feelings.

Daniel spoke of his home, the hustle and bustle of Lancaster County, the tourism, the pace, while Sadie nodded her head in understanding. Holmes County, Ohio, was no different. They both agreed that bit by bit, in small devious ways, the world slowly encroached on the old traditions, threatening Amish culture.

Suddenly, Sadie took notice of their whereabouts, spying a sign that said,

Atkins Ridge, 3 miles.

"Oh, my goodness, we've come too far. We have to get back. Anna will wonder what has become of us."

"Let her wonder. She'll be okay. Your parents are there."

But Sadie felt uneasy now. Anna wanted to give more buggy rides, she felt sure, and she did not want to disappoint her sister this way.

A pickup truck came over a rise, and Sadie pulled slightly on the right rein, making sure she was on her side of the road. When she glanced at the truck, Mark Peight's bewildered brown eyes looked directly into hers. She lifted her chin, set her shoulders, and did not answer his wave as the pickup moved past.

We're not dating. You are not my boyfriend. You sneak around enough to keep me on a string, and I'm resisting you now. If I choose to live this way and be with someone else, I have the right. It's up to you to honor my companionship, and you have not been doing that. I'm moving on.

She became stronger with each thought.

"Someone you know?"

"Yes."

"Boyfriend?"

"No."

No, just someone who has the ability to tie my heart in knots. Someone who loves me, then hurts me. Someone I don't think I'll ever understand fully.

"We're leaving next week."

He cleared his throat, then turned sideways on the seat. "Sadie, I can't remember when I felt so... I don't know. I feel as if I've known you all my life. If you don't... If you aren't seeing anyone, could I take you out to dinner on Saturday evening? I know that's not our typical way, but I'm not from around here, and I don't have much choice. I would like to spend some time with you before I go."

Only the space of a second passed, a butterfly movement of hesitation, before she turned to meet his gaze.

"I would like that, yes."

He had said, "Go out to dinner." Just like classy English people do. They had dinner in the evening and lunch for lunch.

His hand reached up to touch her hair.

"I can hardly believe your hair is real. It's so black, it shines blue. I love the way you comb it. I'd love to see you without your covering."

Sadie did not know how to respond, so she said nothing, just shook the reins across Paris' back to urge her toward the auction where her safety lay.

"I didn't count on ... you. I mean, I hadn't planned on meeting someone like you. Now I don't want to leave."

Her conscience jabbed her. She had told Mark she loved him, she wanted him to ask her for a real date, the way normal guys did. But he refused. Was it wrong to go on a date with this Lancaster-County Daniel? Surely she was not doing anything wrong. She could not wait on Mark Peight forever. She wasn't getting any younger. Besides, someone with a past like his was risky.

So, no, she was not doing anything wrong. Yes, she would go out with Daniel. It was just dinner.

Suddenly, without warning, Paris lowered her haunches, then lunged into her collar. She took off running, her ears flicking back and staying that way.

Grimly, Sadie gripped the reins with all her strength as a pickup truck passed at a dangerous speed, the diesel engine revving, black smoke pouring from two silver pipes, gravel spitting from the broad tires.

The same color! It looked like the same pickup containing Mark Peight!

Sadie fought to control Paris, calling out to her in a strong voice, trying to still the panic rising in her own chest.

Daniel leaned forward, gripping the seat, watching quietly, letting Sadie take control of her own horse.

When Paris slowed, he grinned and put a hand on her shoulder. "Good job. I can tell you're one with this horse. It's awesome."

Then, a high, whining, deadly sound.

The reins snaked out of Sadie's grasp as Paris went up, up, and came down, hitting the macadam at a dead run.

Someone was screaming and screaming, a volume of sound that made her throat hurt. Who was it? Daniel? Herself?

Paris was galloping in a complete frenzy. She had no one to guide her, no rein to hold her back, all her instincts goading her away from the sound of that gunshot. She ran at full speed.

Sadie remembered. The dark night. Captain. Ezra. The ridge. The black beast running, running, gaining on them. Was this how it would all end? She had been spared before. This time, instead of snow, the sun was shining and the cornflowers were blooming. Yet once again, the specter of death loomed before her.

Chapter 10

GRIPPING THE SEAT WITH ONE HAND, SADIE CLUNG to Daniel with the other. The spring wagon swayed and bounced, and the dusty air made breathing difficult. The black reins slapped the surface of the road, then flew away, as out of control as everything else.

"Should we jump?" she screamed, falling onto her knees as the spring wagon lurched.

Daniel shook his head. "Call Paris! Keep talking to her!"

When he saw Sadie's whitening face, he screamed, "Sadie! Stay with me! Talk to your horse!"

She was so frightfully dizzy. How could she get up and call Paris if the whole world was out of control? Bile rose in her throat.

"Sadie!"

Daniel reached out and slapped her, hard. Her head flew back, then up, and back to reality. Sadie called and called.

"Paris! Come on. Whoa, whoa, good, good girl. Stop, Paris. The bullets are gone. It was only one. Slow down, babe. Slow down, Paris. Stop running now. You're going to upset us."

Was Paris tiring? Was she responding?

Without warning, Daniel got up and stood on the shafts, steadying himself on the dash of the spring wagon. His face was white, his mouth set in concentration as he calculated the distance.

Oh, those flailing hooves. Sure death if he fell! The steel wheels! If they rolled over him, he would never survive.

"Don't scream, Sadie! Keep talking."

She had never been called on to muster all the reserves of courage she had. With extraordinary effort, she continued talking, pleading with Paris.

Daniel crouched, then sprang, a released tension, propelling himself forward by sheer force of will, until his legs grasped Paris' haunches. Searching and finding the reins, hauling them back, he eased Paris into a controlled run.

They came to a stop beneath an overhang of pine branches. Paris was a deep brown color, soaked with her own sweat, her sides heaving, her nostrils moving in and out by the force of her panting.

Daniel slid off her back, went to her head, put his hand on her mane, and slowly lowered his forehead against hers.

Sadie fainted, evidently, and awoke lying by the roadside under the pine boughs, heaving and gagging, as she threw up like a little child who had become thoroughly carsick. Daniel held her head, rubbed her back, and offered her a clean, white handkerchief. She thought she would surely never look at him again, gripped in a fit of nausea.

"I'm so sorry. Please forgive me."

"It's all right. You did an awesome job."

Sadie wiped her mouth, blew her nose. There was that word *awesome* again. It must be his favorite word.

"I have to go to Paris," she said.

He quietly helped her up, supporting her as she clung to Paris' neck, weeping softly, whispering heartbroken endearments.

"I couldn't live without you, Paris. You are the best horse ever. Thank God we're alive," she murmured, over and over.

A car passed, the driver watching them, presuming their horse got a bit overheated and they'd be fine, waved, and moved on down the road.

Daniel remained quiet as Sadie wiped her face, kissed Paris' nose, and laughed shakily.

"Sorry. I love my horse. Oh, Daniel, who is shooting these bullets? Who is endangering these lives? I'm so afraid."

He looked into her eyes. "We need to report this when we get back."

"No! Not to the whole crowd. I'll do it later from our phone shanty at home. Please? I don't want the ... fuss, the publicity."

"Whatever you want."

His quiet strength was hers now. Calmly, he helped her into the spring wagon, a hand on her back to support her.

They decided it would be best to drop Daniel off at the sale. He would tell Anna and her family what happened while Sadie took Paris on home.

"Aren't you afraid to drive home alone?" he asked.

"No. They won't be back. It's only a mile or so."

She desperately needed time alone to clear her head. The staggering thought that Mark Peight could be the sniper completely did her in. It had to be the same truck.

It was, wasn't it? How could she even begin to understand this complex person, this result of two terribly dysfunctional parents? Or was even this a fabrication, a lie, told in the most convincing manner?

She prayed, "Dear Lord, you're going to have to show me the way. I'm in a maze, lost, can't make any sense out of this. I felt your leading, I did. Now I don't know anymore."

She needed space, she needed her family. She needed, above all, the calming presence of her Lord and Savior. Hadn't he said his yoke was easy, his burden light?

As Paris plodded up the driveway, her neck stretched out in weariness, Sadie sang softly,

> *His yoke is easy. His burden is light.*
> *I've found it so. I've found it so.*
> *His service is my sweetest delight*
> *His blessings overflow.*

Peace wrapped her in its loving arms. She cried with joy and thanksgiving as she bathed her beloved Paris, wiped the harness and put it away, then fed the horse a double portion of oats and corn and a block of the best hay. Sadie kissed Paris' nose and told her goodnight, walked into the house, and collapsed on the sofa, where her family found her a few hours later.

✿ ✡ ✿

"I don't care what you say," Dorothy said forcefully, steam enveloping her face and shoulders as she unloaded the commercial dishwasher. "You're going to keep on messing around with them horses until you get yerself kilt, and I mean it."

It was Monday morning after the lavish breakfast had been served. Sadie cleaned the floor, swishing the foam mop across the ceramic tile, cleaning corners longer than necessary just to hide her smile.

"But..." Sadie began.

Dorothy turned, a stack of clear plates in her hands, and shook her head from side to side, her eyes snapping.

"Hm-mm. Don't 'but' me. I ain't listening. If'n yer parents had a lick of common sense, they'd take that crazy gold horse and sell her for ... for dog food. She ain't safe! Now a well-trained horse would not have bolted like that. What n' na world was you thinking in the first place, hitchin' 'er up like that?"

Sadie kept mopping back and forth, scrubbing at a stubborn spot on the tile. Then she straightened, pushed back a stray lock of hair, and faced Dorothy with her hands on her hips.

"Paris *is* well trained. Any horse would bolt with that sound of a rifle, gun, whatever it was, being fired. It was an ... an accident, a weird thing that happened."

Dorothy's eyes flashed.

"An act of God, you mean. That's what you get for prancing around with a stranger from ... oh, wherever. Did you ever think for one moment about what Mark thought when he saw you?"

Rebellion rose in Sadie's throat, a sort of thickening, causing her voice to become harsh.

"I don't care what he thought. I'm not seeing Mark Peight. I don't ever want to date him either. He's a coward and a ... a ... Oh, he makes me so mad! Why can't he come to the house and ask me out for an official Saturday night date? Huh? Answer that, Dorothy!"

Dorothy didn't answer, her lips set in a firm line.

She put a large stockpot on the shelf, yanked her apron down, smoothed it across her stomach, and reached for her large, purple mug.

"Sit down!" she barked.

"No! I'm not finished mopping."

So Dorothy sat and slid off her shoes, putting her feet up on a low bench, revealing the nylons she cut off at the knee, rolled, and twisted to a firm knot. She never bought knee-high nylons, never, saying they slid down your legs, and then what did you have? A sloppy-looking ring around your shoes, which did no honor to them pretty shoes from the Dollar General in town.

Dorothy dashed an extravagant amount of cream in her empty mug.

"Fill this for me, Sadie. Please."

Sadie propped the handle of her mop against the refrigerator. She turned and filled Dorothy's mug at the coffee maker, resisting the urge to set the mug down on the table with a severity that was unnecessary.

"You know if you put your cream in the cup first, then pour the coffee on top of it, you don't need a spoon?" Dorothy asked.

Sadie took her revenge by remaining silent. It was a sweet sort of gratification. Dorothy had no right talking about Paris that way.

"So now you're mad. Well, you got reason to be. Shouldn't'a said that, I guess. But you, young lady, need a talkin' to."

"About what?"

"Your horse, for one. And your guy."

Sadie leaned forward, her hands propped on her knees, her eyes bright with the force of her words as she looked straight at Dorothy. "He's not my guy."

"If you did the right thing, he would be."

"What's that supposed to mean?"

"Just what you think."

Sadie shook her head back and forth, a pendulum of denial. Dorothy got up heavily, her face the picture of frustration. She went to the pantry and returned with two cold, leftover biscuits. She slammed them into the microwave, punched the buttons solidly, then turned to face Sadie.

Yanking open the door of the microwave, Dorothy slapped the biscuits on a plate and spread an alarming amount of butter on top of each, then sank her teeth into one.

Sadie wished she'd stop eating biscuits or slurping that disgusting coffee in between each gigantic bite.

"I don't know where your parents are. You should not have been allowed to take that... What's his name?"

"Daniel."

"Whatever. You shouldn't have taken him on that horse and buggy ride alone. Where was your mom and dad? Now you have all these fancy-dancy notions in your head about a stranger from... wherever, Canada, Iraq, Iran. Who knows?"

"He's from Lancaster, Pennsylvania," Sadie said dryly.

"Lancaster? That great Amish place everyone talks about?"

Sadie nodded.

"Hmm. Well, maybe he could turn out all right, but you are committed to someone else, you know you are. You love him."

When Sadie began her denial, Dorothy lifted her chin and held up one finger. "App! *Upp*! Stop that! Anyone that gets mad when someone doesn't ask them for a date wants to be with that person. Look at me and Jim. My James. He waited. Took his good old time. I persuaded myself that he made me angry and I didn't want him, but in truth, I did. I sure did. I got me a good man. The salt of the earth, he is."

Sadie took half of a biscuit, spread it with a thin layer of butter, then turned the plastic honey bear upside down and squeezed. Holding the bread carefully above the plate, she answered, "But Jim likely had a normal childhood, not like Mark's."

She bit into the sweet, buttery biscuit, watching Dorothy's face.

"I don't know what you call normal, unless gettin' up at four a.m. to milk 30 cows when you're nine years old is normal. His parents divorced when he was in third grade, too. Had a paper route to help keep his family going until his mom remarried, but his stepdad kicked him out when he was 15. Made his own way, so he did."

"But that's still not quite as bad as Mark's childhood, and I have a feeling I only know the tip of the iceberg. Aren't people like Mark seriously damaged their whole life long?"

"Some of 'em."

"I don't know him that well. What if Mark is seriously disturbed?"

"That's where you come in at."

"What do you mean?"

"You need to be there for your man. He…"

"He's not my man."

"As I was saying, you need to be there for your man. He needs a good woman behind him, one that comes from a firm family structure. If ever anyone had a good family life, you do. You need to…"

Before Dorothy could finish, Bertie Orthman, the aging gardener, made a grand entrance, holding a gigantic bouquet of orange, yellow, and peach-colored daylilies. He got down on one knee and closed his eyes, one arm sweeping the air in time to his humming.

> *"Flowers for my lady fa-a-ir.*
> *My beautiful lady fa-air!"*

Dorothy drew herself up to her full height, lowered her eyebrows, and let out the biggest snort Sadie had ever heard.

"Bert! For Pete's sake, don't you think you're layin' it on a bit thick?"

Bertie dipped and bowed, then swept his arm in an arc, presenting Dorothy with the beautiful bouquet. "There you go, Dot. Beauty presented to the beauty of my life!"

Another snort. "You know I ain't beautiful. Give 'em to Sadie."

Sadie laughed and accepted the gorgeous display. Bertie laughed with Sadie, then told her it was all in fun, to brighten their day.

These two, dear, old souls. What a joy to be with them! English people were just more open, more at ease to create a scene like this. They lifted her bogged-down spirits on this humorless morning, when the whole world seemed serious and dangerous and dreadful.

"You jes' can't take a joke, can ya, Dot?"

Dorothy threw him a nasty look. "You know, Bertie, if you ever let that cat of yours over into my yard again, I'm gonna shoot the flea-infested thing. She gits on my bird feeder, and then she sits, lickin' her lips, just waitin' to latch onto one of my birds.

Bertie's mouth closed in on itself. The sparkle left his

eyes, his eyebrows lowered, and he glared at Dorothy.

Shoving his face up to hers, he said, "If you … ever, ever shoot my cat, I'll have the law on you."

"Then keep her over there."

Sadie burst out laughing.

"It ain't funny."

"Sure, it's funny," Bertie said. "You know, Sadie, she sits on her front porch, rockin' and rockin', watchin' her birds, and I'm right across the road, lookin' out the same direction on my back porch, rockin' and rockin', holdin' my cat. We're like two people on a bus, facing the same direction, never communicatin' 'cept here at work. Never give each other the time of day at home."

"You know why? 'Cause I'm afraid if'n I get too friendly, you'll think I don't mind about that cat of yours, and I do."

"Aw, Caesar Augustus ain't gittin' yer birds."

Dorothy's mouth fell open in disbelief. "That yer cat's name?"

Suddenly the door ripped open with such force that the conversation came to a halt. They all turned to see who would fly into the kitchen in such a hurry, surprised to find Richard Caldwell himself, looking weary and shaken, but with a light in his eyes that no one had ever seen before.

"Her name is Sadie Elizabeth Rose."

Dorothy was the first one to find her voice. "Who?"

"Our daughter was born at 5:15 this morning!"

Sadie sputtered but could form no words at all. She just stared at Richard Caldwell, eyes wide, mouth agape.

"She ain't yours," Dorothy said brusquely.

"She's ours. Barbara's and mine!"

"But why? How come no one said anything about it?"

"We kept it a secret."

Dorothy's eyes became cunning, and she nodded her head, pursing her lips.

"I knew there was somethin' in the works, so I did," she said matter-of-factly.

Richard Caldwell walked over to Sadie, who was still speechless, and put both of his big hands on her shoulders, looking into her face with the most tender expression she thought he was capable of.

"Your namesake. We want our daughter to be just like you, Sadie."

Sadie opened her mouth to say thank you, to be polite and gracious and classy and grown up, but her mouth wobbled and her nose burned and she burst into the most embarrassing tears of her life.

Instantly, Richard's huge arms went around her. He was sniffing and wiping his eyes and laughing. Dorothy joined in hugging them both, and Bertie clapped his old, worn hand on Richard Caldwell's shoulder, congratulating him in very colorful language.

The tiny, six-pound, 14-ounce Sadie Elizabeth Rose caused quite a stir at Aspen East Ranch. Everyone said they knew something suspicious was going on, especially when the boss started eating breakfast upstairs with his wife. Sadie didn't think anyone guessed the Caldwells were anticipating a baby. Barbara was a big woman, so her clothes easily concealed the pregnancy. Even so, it was a remarkable feat for both of them to keep it secret.

No baby showers, no nursery, no nothing, Sadie thought. But the minute the birth was announced, the house became a beehive of activity. The painter, the interior decorator, the carpet cleaner, had all been on standby.

Within a few days, the bedroom adjacent to the master suite had been turned into a nursery a mother could only dream of: pink and green rocking horses on the curtains, the crib set, the rugs. Even the new swivel rocker had a shawl with the same horses across the back. Little horse shoes adorned the walls, and luxurious pillows were strewn everywhere.

Sadie dusted and vacuumed, scoured the bathrooms, cleaned the mirrors, and scrubbed the floors. Bertie brought in great armfuls of lilies for every room, while Dorothy ran in circles and cackled and fussed and wore herself out completely.

When Richard Caldwell brought Barbara home from the hospital, everyone at the ranch saw the change in her. She was wan but absolutely elated, and she looked 20 years younger, as if this was the crowning moment of her privileged life—a precious daughter of her own.

Sadie was in awe of Barbara. Being Amish, she had seen lots of babies, even helped out as a *maud*, but never had she seen such devotion and unabashed joy as this. The Caldwells considered their beloved child a miracle, pure and simple.

Even Richard Caldwell's booming voice had quieted. He talked softly, walked lightly, even closed doors gently. He carried his tiny daughter in the crook of one arm, showing her to all the ranch hands as if he, alone, had thought up the whole idea of the human race.

When the days turned shorter, the evenings cooler, the Caldwells decided to throw a huge cookout for all the help at the ranch to celebrate their daughter's birth.

At first, Dat frowned on it, saying it would be no place for Sadie. She explained how Dorothy needed her. He sighed and said he guessed she could go if she wanted to.

Sadie wanted to go, more out of curiosity than anything else. She would help with the preparation of the
food, then find a quiet corner to watch everyone else.

Maybe with Mark? Where was he? It had been almost
a month since the shooting on the day of the consignment
sale. She had been convinced it was Mark shooting from
that truck. Killing. All those guns were evidence, weren't
they? She could tell Reuben thought about it, too.

She tried to distance her heart. She tried thinking
only of Daniel, but she couldn't forget about Mark. Not
entirely.

The evening before Daniel had left to return to Pennsylvania, he came to say goodbye. He had been so kind
and so sweet, just as he'd been on their dinner date. They
had gone to an expensive steakhouse with dim lighting
and delicious food she never knew existed. Daniel was
handsome, talkative, always laughing. He told her about
his family, which sounded very much like her own, only
with 10 children. They had their everyday spats and ordinary disagreements, but no argument stayed serious for
long. He loved his mam and got along great with his dat,
except during the time when he wanted to get a car and
join the wilder group of youth. His dat put his foot down,
and Daniel didn't have the heart to hurt his father, which
touched Sadie deeply.

Here was a normal, happy, well-adjusted young man,
who was so good-natured it bordered on disbelief. Was
he really so kind to everyone?

He had not kissed her. Sadie wanted him to, then felt
guilty for thinking about it.

She had been swept completely off her feet and began
a long-distance romance that would be kept alive through
letters and phone calls.

Had Mark caused her to be this way? Was it wrong? She knew attitudes about distant courtship varied greatly from one Amish community to the next. She agreed that it was not good to touch each other before marriage.

Or was it? Mam didn't think so. In fact, she was quite serious about this subject and adamant about her views on dating. She was strict about flirting shamelessly, staying pure and chaste, but didn't everyone need to know who their partner really was before marrying?

Sadie knew what Mam meant, without her saying much at all. She did not like the new trend of thinking that you could be above reproach, better than your peers, free of all temptation.

Still, Sadie wished Daniel had kissed her, to see if she liked him. He hadn't hugged her; he only shook her hand and looked deeply into her eyes when he said goodbye.

She had his address and phone number. They promised to write and call each other every week.

As always, she tried not to think of Mark. Who could she trust, ever?

Daniel likely had every girl in Lancaster "setting her hat" for him, as Mam used to say. Could she depend on a husband from Lancaster County? The distance was so great. Oh, he said he loved it out here, but did he really? As close as he was to his family, especially his brothers?

This business of finding a husband was just not her thing. She was no good at it. And yet, when she held little Sadie Elizabeth, she knew with complete certainty that she wanted a darling baby girl of her own someday. She wanted a house and a kind husband, someone who was easier to understand, easier to love, than that Mark Peight and his strange and strong silences.

Chapter 11

THE CALDWELLS HIRED EXTRA HELP THE WEEK before the cookout, or "shindig," as Dorothy put it. She was taking extra vitamin B-12s all week. Her nerves would plain get the best of her if she wasn't careful.

Barbara Caldwell had spent entirely too much time in the kitchen, and Sadie knew it made Dorothy uncomfortable. But Barbara had planned the menu and stuck around to make sure everything was done to perfection.

The Caldwells asked Reuben to come to work with Sadie and help with the vast amount of yard work that needed to be done around the large house. Bertie always kept the plants and shrubs looking their best, but this was a special evening, and he had more work than usual to do. Besides the ranch hands, all the wealthy ranchers and their wives, the Caldwell's business associates, and even the physicians from the hospital were to be together as friends for one special evening.

When she saw the large, red riding mower whizzing along at an alarming rate, Sadie wondered what in the world had come over Bertie. Taking a closer look, she was horrified to find Reuben hunched low over the steering wheel, his elbows lifted, clearly pretending he was driving something other than a lawn mower.

Now he was coming into the homestretch, zipping around a low lying willow tree. He straightened his back as he jammed on the brakes, slammed to a stop, and took a long drink from the red-and-white Igloo thermos Mam had filled with his favorite fruit punch.

Back on the mower, Reuben lurched off at high speed, and to Sadie's chagrin, loud singing ensued.

> *Shall we gather at the river?*
> *The beautiful, the beautiful river!*

Sadie held her breath as he sped around a tall blue spruce, leaning way over to steady himself. She dropped the dish towel she was holding and ran outside to talk to her brother about his lack of driving skills.

Her pink dress rode up as she ran, an annoyance to every Amish girl who wore a dress with a pleated skirt. She slowed to a walk and pushed down the unruly skirt, waving her hand. She gasped as he spun around the pillars at the entrance, narrowly missing the famed roses climbing the trellis beside it.

"Reuben! Hey!"

She hoped he'd hear her before he overturned the mower and pinned himself beneath it. Her shoulders slumped as he took off in the opposite direction, leaving her standing at the edge of the lawn with nothing to do but watch him go.

A tall form emerged from the barn, closing the distance between them in long strides. Now who was being nosy enough to come and help her out? She didn't need help. This wasn't exactly a dilemma; Reuben just needed to be warned a bit.

"Need some help?" a familiar voice called.

Sadie turned, a cool answer on her lips, to find a hat-less Mark Peight, his hair disheveled, his short-sleeved white shirt stuck to his body with perspiration, and a streak of dirt across his tanned face.

The cool answer fizzled away into despair, the feeling when you know you were wrong and there's not one thing you can do about it. She despaired of seeing him and not being able to catch her breath, leaving her thoughts completely scrambled, nerveless fingers fumbling at an apron that had been straight in the first place. She marveled at his deep brown eyes that crinkled at the corners, and his mouth so perfect she could only stare at it, wondering why she had ever thought another person existed.

She lifted her hands in a helpless gesture. "Looks like it."

Reuben was in his own world of imagination. The mower buzzed up an incline. At the top Reuben leaned over, twisting mightily on the steering wheel, then racing back down, practically airborne.

"He's going to throw that thing over," Sadie said between clenched teeth.

She began walking quickly toward him. Mark laughed as he watched Reuben's antics. Just as Reuben went whirling around a yellow bush, his song caught Mark's ears, and he bent over double, laughing even harder.

"He will be gathered at the river!" he gasped.

Sadie glanced at Mark before spasms of her own laughter overtook her. The longer they watched, the funnier and more absurd the whole situation became, until they were caught in a helpless tide of laughter.

Finally, Sadie caught her breath. "Richard Caldwell would not be happy. We have to stop him."

They both walked quickly toward Reuben. When he finally saw them, he shut the mower off, sat back, and beamed, clearly pleased with himself and happy to show off his expertise as a lawn-mower driver.

"Hi, Mark! How are you?"

"Good. I'm good. Looks like you're enjoying yourself."

"I sure am. This is totally cool."

Sadie cringed at Reuben's *rumspringa* language. She glanced sideways at Mark, who was clearly enjoying Reuben's company.

"Reuben, you have to slow down. You're going to flip that lawn mower."

Reuben leaned way back in his seat, turned his face to the side and yelled, "No way! These things don't flip over."

"Reuben, they do. All you know is pushing our reel mower. You have never driven one of these, ever. You have to slow down, please."

Sadie was serious. She was afraid for Reuben's safety, although she assured him he was doing a good job and that Bertie would be pleased about how soon the mowing was done. Reuben grinned, waved, and was off without reducing his speed one bit. He zipped around the corner of the corral and lurched across the cement walkway with a clatter.

Mark began laughing again.

"It's not funny."

They walked together across the lawn, and Mark asked Sadie if she wanted to see the horse he was shoeing at the stable.

Sadie stopped, looked wistfully in the direction of the barn, but said she should help Dorothy, since she was all in a stew about the coming cookout.

"You going?" he asked nonchalantly.

"Dat doesn't really want me to go. He says it's no place for me."

"It probably isn't."

She looked up at him, surprised. That sounded rather strict, coming from Mark. However, when their eyes met, everything else vanished. His dark brown eyes were warm, caring, wanting, a conveyor of his longing, an insecurity bigger than the ability to speak of his love. She could not look away.

A thousand questions crowded her mind until she felt caught up in a whirlwind of emotions that shook her entire being. This was her Mark Peight, the one she met on that snowy road with Nevaeh so long ago. Before the questions. Before the partial telling of his life's story. Was he just shy? Or was he hiding something?

"Don't go," he murmured, his voice catching.

"I have to help Dorothy with the food."

"Is there no one else?"

"No."

He nodded and looked off across the corral.

"Well, come in and see this horse. It won't take long."

He was a magnificent animal, no question. Gray, with dapples across his rump, he stood tall and regal, heavy in the shoulders, his mane and tail a shimmer of light, grayish-white hair.

"Wow."

"One of the best horses I've ever seen." Then, "How's Paris?"

"She's doing well."

"Even after the runaway?"

"What do you know of the…that day?" she asked with accusation dripping from every word.

"I passed you. Remember?"

She whirled, her eyes flashing with anger and disbelief. He caught her arm and held onto her with a vise-like grip.

"It wasn't me. I didn't shoot."

"How can I know that for sure? You disappear for months at a time. You ... you ... "

There was a scraping of boots as a small, swarthy figure burst into the shoeing area. He held a whip aloft, ready to bring it down on Mark's head, or rather, up, as it would seem to be the case with this short person.

He stood behind Mark, his feet planted squarely, his heavy shoulders stretching the fabric of his shirt. He was a picture of righteous indignation and chivalry, rescuing the damsel in distress.

"You!" he yelled in thunderous tones. "Let her go. Release the lady!"

Mark stepped back, his face registering surprise.

"Sorry. I didn't mean anything. We were..."

"You let the lady go. I am Lothario. My name is Lothario Bean. You do not treat ladies this way. You Americans are such ... such baboons. You must learn to take care of your women. They need protection. They need your devotion and aid at all times. My Lita. I do not grasp her arm or talk harshly to her. Now you go back to shoeing your horse, and *I* will assist the beautiful lady back to her kitchen."

He drew himself up to his full height, emphasizing *I* with great pride and dignity. Then stepping up to Sadie with his head held high, he offered his arm and bowed his head.

"Come," he said, in a heavy Latino accent.

Sadie smiled with a quick glance at Mark. Lothario escorted her out of the barn, across the drive, and to the kitchen door.

"Now, if you ever have any problem with that man who shoes horses, you just call on me, Lothario. I do not stand by and let any lady become a victim of bad treatment. No. No."

"Thank you, Lothario. I appreciate your help. Give my regards to Lita and the girls."

His dark face shone with love for his family.

"God has blessed me. God has been good. I thank him all the time. I sing to Jesus in praise. Someday, I play my guitar for you. Not him. Not him." He jerked his short dark thumb in the direction of the barn.

✿ ✡ ✿

Sadie was ill at ease the remainder of the day. She constantly ran to the windows to check on Reuben's lawn-mowing progress. Dorothy was impossible to deal with, so Sadie stayed out of her way as much as possible. When Barbara came into the kitchen yet again, Sadie was afraid for her, knowing Dorothy's temperament was a pressure cooker of suppressed frustration.

"Why them fancy kabobs? Why not hot dogs and hamburgers and homemade beans? Fiddle falutin' people!"

Sadie thought as she read over the menu. Shortcakes. Peaches. Real whipped cream. Tamales. Shish kabobs. No wonder everyone was in a tizzy.

Sadie and Dorothy worked together quite well preparing for the cookout. Dorothy miraculously calmed down, becoming efficient and making every step count until the evening of the cookout. The mound of food that was prepared was remarkable. Richard Caldwell—jovial, wearing a tall white chef's hat, talking in his usual stentorian tones, waving his spatula wildly—handled the grill by himself, producing perfect strip steaks.

Dorothy and Sadie carried out tray after tray of delicious sides. The cabbage slaw was crisp and chilled, the thick rolls warm and crusty. There were mounds of twice-baked potatoes that had almost been Dorothy's undoing, mixing the cheese, bacon, and chives to the right consistency.

Dat had asked Sadie to come home after the food was served, which she planned on doing. Lita Bean would help Dorothy finish up. As Sadie untied her apron in the kitchen, Mark Peight appeared at the door.

"Do you have a way home?"

Oh, Mark! She shook her head, unable to speak one word.

"Could we walk? I know it's … four miles?"

"More like five."

"Then I'll get someone to take us."

"No. No. We can walk. We have all night."

They thanked their hosts and wished everyone good night. The warm feeling of belonging to a large family of workers and friends followed them.

Their footsteps were the only sound, except for a dog barking somewhere in the night. The stars hung low over Montana, like a black dish of night with holes punched in it, the stars a beautiful wonder.

"You tired?"

"I'm okay. The stress was almost worse than the actual work. Cooking for ranch hands and dumping the food onto a steam table is entirely different from cooking for the … well, wealthy people who are used to chefs and unusual food."

"It was delicious, Sadie. I've never had better cabbage slaw."

"Thank you."

Their steps were the only sound for a length of time until Mark cleared his throat.

"So, did Mr. Bean escort you to the house okay?"

Sadie laughed. "Isn't he something? You know, many Latinos are staunch Catholics. A very strong, dedicated faith. He's a good man."

"Isn't that the church we supposedly came from?"

"I guess. Hundreds of years ago."

"You think we're better than they are now?"

Mark's words were heavy with bitterness, hatred almost. Sadie stopped involuntarily and turned to face him. She wanted to question him, but thinking better of it, she turned to walk on.

"What?" Mark asked.

"Nothing."

"Yes. What did I say that upset you?"

"It's just the way you said it. You don't like plain people, do you? Why did you join the Amish faith if that's how you feel? You don't even like us much, let alone have faith in a group of people to help you travel through life."

Mark sighed, a long, deep sound expelling from his chest.

"I guess I'll always carry the burden of my past on my back, waiting to explode at the slightest opportunity."

Sadie did not speak. What he said was true. He was a walking tinderbox of buried hatred. Why did she keep trying?

Her thoughts whirled. Suddenly, she became weary, her head heavy, her feet dragging. It was no use. This man was scarred for life. She felt trapped in a situation she had very little control over. The only way out was to stay completely away from him.

Before she could follow her weary thoughts, he caught her hand in his.

"Come, let's sit down. I want to talk."

And he did. He talked for hours, as Sadie listened, crying at times, amazed at others.

His mother was excommunicated for her sins, the promiscuous *ungehorsam* life she led. His last memory of his mother was her waving out the window of a red car, her hair streaming behind her, wearing heavy black sunglasses, leaving with that real estate man. His father cried and cried and cried.

"You know, Sadie, his crying seemed so…final. The depth of his loss is stamped on my heart forever. He was so…so pitiful. I held the baby. I remember the smell of her filthy dress that hadn't been washed for who knows how long? Dat never recovered. To this day, it haunts me. Why didn't I do more? Maybe I could have prevented his death."

"No, Mark…," Sadie began.

She was silenced by his harsh words, torn from his tortured mind. "Yes! I could have. I was so busy with the children. If I would have kept closer watch, he wouldn't have died."

He sighed, and a torrent of words followed. "The men, the elders of the church, they came often. They blamed Dat. They said he was going to hell. Anyone who couldn't keep his family in line was not worthy. What did they mean? Worthy of what? Heaven? God? So is my father suffering in eternal flames for the wrong my mother did to him?

"I hate my mother. I hate her so much I can't tell you. If I would see her again, so help me, I don't know what I'd do.

"Why didn't any of the church members take us children? They could have tried. Nobody did anything. We were basically cast out.

"Dat must have gone to look for my mother. I remember him dressing in English clothes, cutting his hair, shaving his beard. He would go English for her. He left me alone at night with the little ones.

"The baby would cry and I'd get up to fill her bottle with water. There was no milk. She screamed and cried. I flavored the water with strawberry Jell-o. That hushed her for awhile. Good thing we had strawberry Jell-o.

"Dat gave up then. He stopped searching for Mam. His hair and beard grew back. He got a job at a welding shop. We had milk. I learned to make soup with beans and tomato juice and hamburger. The only thing I couldn't do was sew. Our clothes were torn and much too tight.

"I thought my father was doing better. He read his Bible a lot. He sang to us. One time his parents came. They cried. Mommy Peight brought us food, clothes. She hugged us. I think they weren't allowed to be there and came in secret because I didn't see them until last year when I went back.

"That day…" he began, then hung his head.

A shudder passed through him. His head stayed bent. Sadie put a hand on his shoulder and kept it there.

"Dat didn't come home. I made soup for the little ones. We slept alone. The next morning, I searched the barn, the woods."

There was a long pause. Sadie stroked his shoulder as if comforting a small child. Or Paris.

"He was half sunk in the water, half out of it. He was covered with algae. That's why I didn't see him right away. There were dragonflies on his back. Flies."

"But, Mark, if he was half out of the water, maybe he was trying to get out. Maybe it wasn't a suicide at all. Maybe he had an accident."

"No. He didn't want to live. He couldn't handle all of us children. We were the ones that should have never been born. The counselor tried to tell me differently, but I know how it was. We were a mistake, born to two people who would have been so much better off without us.

"I imagine my mother was a free spirit, liberal, always rebellious. She gave birth one year after another, the way the church required. Dat was too simple to see it, or too much in love, whatever it was. I spent my whole life wishing they hadn't had any of us."

"Mark, you can't think that way. There is a purpose for every soul brought into this world. I truly believe that. God wants you here on earth or you wouldn't be here. He loves you as much as he loves anybody else. Likely more, even."

"No, he doesn't."

"Mark!"

"He can't. Not after what I did. After Dat drowned himself, the church had nothing to do with us. We were tainted children then. So the authorities put us into the foster system. We were all separated. I was eight.

"We became English. I went to a public school. The kids were nice enough; so were my foster parents. They drank a lot of beer. Keith became drunk a lot, but not angry drunk, just...stupid drunk. Sharon gave me good things to eat. I found out what pizza was. And cookies.

"I don't understand what happened then, but I was suddenly placed in another home. I lived in fear of their 17-year-old son. He...well, I won't go into detail, but when I was 12, I ran away, alone, at night. I found my

way to an Amish home in another community. Betsy, the
family's mother, took pity on me and allowed me to stay.
I worked in their produce fields all my teenage years. The
Amish man, I think, was bipolar, schizophrenic, whatever.
He had vile temper fits. Blamed Betsy for everything, but
he never touched her. Never. It was always me. He beat
me regularly. Either with a whip or a hammer. The hammer was the worst.

"The whip would hiss through the air, catch my legs,
then my back. It burned like fire. After awhile, though, I
got used to it, if such a thing is possible. I can still hear the
tomato plants being whacked off by the force of his whip.
I picked the tomatoes too green. Too rotten. Filled the
hampers too full or not full enough. Everything wrong
was my fault.

"But what he did to me was better than what the
17-year-old did to me. Sadie, I'm a ruined person, basically. I've seen just about everything there is to see.

"Betsy was a saint. She even baked like an angel. She
lived with that man to the best of her ability, and I bet to
this day their community has no idea who he is or what
he did.

"The night he broke my ribs with the hammer, that
was the night I left. I just walked away, no extra clothes,
no nothing. The dog barked, but I didn't care. I'd be better off dead, I thought, so I just walked. My ribs burned
in my body. I couldn't lie down, it hurt too bad, so I kept
walking. Some guys picked me up. Told them I fell off a
wagon. The took me to the hospital. I stayed there for
two days.

"My life after the hospital was basically English.
I worked odd jobs in construction, at McDonalds,
anywhere I could make a bit of money to save for an

apartment. I started drinking, and I can't tell you what alcohol meant to me at that point. It was the wonderful substance that eased all my pain. It bolstered my self-confidence, it made me happy, it made me laugh, it made me forget, at least for a time. It was like a god that finally had mercy on my torment.

"You see, Sadie, I hated myself. I still blamed myself for my Dat. And that Wyle, that 17-year-old, I guess I felt that was my fault, too. I was a mess, and I don't know why I even try to persuade you that I'll be okay.

"Do you understand, now? Why I went back home to get away from you? I spent a whole year in rehab, a facility to help people get away from drugs and alcohol."

Sadie gasped, "Drugs?"

Mark nodded. "I tried it all. Anything to make it all go away.

"The counselors at the rehab were wonderful. Trained professionals who are used to dealing with people who are … well, like me. Or, like I was. I came out clean, sober, and healed, to an extent, I guess.

"I always leaned toward the Amish, though. I guess they were my roots. When I left rehab, I found out that my parents' church had sort of fizzled out. It was a bunch of radicals who had lost the *frieda* with the real Amish of that area. I visited my Grandfather Peight. My Daddy. He is the single source of my greatest healing."

"Besides God," Sadie said softly.

Chapter 12

Mark continued, "No, God was in my grandfather in the form of forgiveness, love, tears, and a kindness so huge I couldn't wrap my warped mind around it. He even looked like God. His hair and beard were white, his face unmarked, his eyes…"

Mark's voice dropped to a whisper. "Sadie, if I ever get to heaven, I imagine God's eyes will look exactly like my grandfather's. Pools of kindness without end.

"He told me how their church fell apart, fueled by evil hatred and harsh unbiblical practices. They had no communion for years. They were being led by a group of… Well, I won't say it. But thankfully they moved away. The rest of the church saw the error of their ways and became better people.

"My grandfather told me, if there was anyone to blame, it was him. He should not have believed these ministers. He was so glad to see me. He taught me my love of horses, how to shoe them. I stayed with him after rehab until I heard of Montana. I had some money. I just wanted to see what it was like here, you know? A young man's yearning for adventure and all that. So I came out here by Amtrak. I was here two weeks and was taking a horse to Richard Caldwell's ranch. It was snowing, there was a dark form on the road, a young girl waving her arms, clearly scared out of her wits, which she must not have had too many of, being out on a slippery road with a dead horse…"

"He wasn't dead!"

Mark's laugh rang out, his arms went around her, and he held her so close she could feel the fabric of his shirt stamped against her cheek.

"That was when my real problems began. I almost returned to alcohol. Sadie, I loved you the first minute I saw you. I did. I don't care what people say about love. For me, it was love at first sight, and God was in that snow, too. He was pure and white and… Well, he was there.

"But since… I dunno, Sadie. It seems as if my enemy is my past and the way it makes me feel about myself. When I think of you and your family, your perfect little life, I hardly have the audacity, the daring to be with you. Or your family."

He stopped, shook his head, his hair falling darkly over his eyes.

"Mark, don't be sarcastic when you say, 'your perfect little life.'"

She was hurt beyond words. As if he was mocking her for being who she was, which was grossly unfair. Her first attempt at dealing with the belittling comment was sort of soothing, assuring him they were far from perfect, to make him feel better about himself. But then she caught herself. He could not shift the blame on her.

"I wasn't."

"Yes, you were."

"Oh, okay. I was. You know better."

"Mark, perhaps I do. You carry the blame for the sordid things in your life, but you are much too eager to shift it onto someone else's shoulders, or you would not have spoken to me that way. You drag yourself down constantly and want to drag others down with you."

Now the sarcasm came thick and fast.

"So where did you go to college?" he asked. "You sound exactly like some trained counselor. You think you're smarter than me?"

It was a whiplash of words, ruthless and stinging. It goaded Sadie into action. She sprang up and started running toward home. She ran blindly, uncaring, just to put great distance between them. She ran until her breath came in hard puffs, her chest hurt, and her legs felt as if the bones and tendons had liquefied.

She saw the silhouette of her home on the hillside, the driveway a winding ribbon of silver. It all swam together in the film of her tears.

She had never seen him look as handsome as he did tonight. He wore a brown, short-sleeved shirt of some rough-looking fabric, almost like homespun. His dark brown eyes matched his shirt, his black broadfall trousers were neat and clean. When he took off his straw hat and tousled his dark hair, Sadie could not tear her eyes away. There was simply no use.

Was it all because he was so handsome? Was she so shallow?

He was impossible. She replayed his words, the story tumbling through her senses. What agonies! So young!

She cried the whole way up to the driveway—for him, for the father of those children, for life's unfairness. But mostly she cried because he did not bother to run after her. Where was he now?

When she heard a car coming, she quickened her steps. If she hurried, she'd reach the safety of the driveway before the lights approached. Reaching the mailbox and paper holder, she relaxed, slowing her pace. She turned to the right, more out of habit than anything else, to see if she recognized the car.

The headlights went out. Only the glistening of the silver on the mirrors and the bumper were visible. The steady brrm, brrm, brrm of the engine was plainly audible, and the sound indicated it was a diesel. A pickup. It was barely moving, as if it was in slow motion.

Wait!

Two smokestacks! It was the same truck! The one that had passed her with Daniel.

Fear washed over Sadie's body in powerful chills. It sent her up the embankment where she pressed flat against a pine tree. The needles scratched her face and arms, the sticky resin stuck to the palms of her outstretched fingers.

The truck beat a loud staccato, her ears pulsed with the beating of it. Then it stopped. The motor was off.

Sadie turned, grabbed a low branch, and scrambled up the pine. The branches of a pine tree were just like a ladder, only pricklier. The branches were close together and straight so that you could climb easily.

She climbed up about 10 or 12 feet and settled herself on some thick branches. She remained as still as possible and listened. There was no sound at all.

She craned her neck, peering around the trunk of the pine tree, but there was only an incomprehensible blackness. She could see nothing, not even the silver of the mirrors.

Had she imagined it all?

Wait. Voices.

A truck door opened. As Sadie watched, the tall form of a man emerged, then turned back to help two small ... what was it? She squinted her eyes and peered into the darkness. If she moved anymore, she was sure to slide sideways out of the pine tree. Shifting her weight, she leaned back, holding onto a branch above her. There. Two children.

The tall man helped them out. One of them disappeared in the thicket beside the road. He stooped to speak to the other one.

Suddenly the lights were back on, a brilliant bluishwhite. They startled Sadie so much that her fingers convulsed and she lost her grip. The last thought she had before she fell was the realization that the wicked inhabitants of that pickup truck would kidnap her as soon as she hit the ground.

The thing was, she never hit the ground. Instead, she became sandwiched between two branches like a hot dog in a roll, her body doubled-up quite painfully, her breath constricted.

The truck's engine started, revved, pulled out onto the road, and moved slowly past. Someone laughed, a voice spoke.

Now the shot, Sadie thought. I'll be shot just like the horses.

The truck moved on around the bend in the road, disappearing into the warm night.

She had to get out of this tree. Every muscle of her body was cramped. She twisted first one way and then the other, the rough pine bark digging red brushburns into her arms and legs.

Redoubling her efforts, she twisted, turned, and wriggled, but with no luck. Her arms were becoming quite painful, her hips wedged tightly.

She needed to stop panicking, think clearly.

Okay. If no amount of twisting would get her out of here, her best bet would be to find a firm handle somewhere, anywhere. Then using her hands as a lever, perhaps she could pull herself up and out.

Flailing her arms on both sides, her fingers found a branch to the left, but was it too far away? She twisted her upper body again as hard as she could and was rewarded by the feeling of a good, solid, pine bough. She grasped it firmly and heaved with every ounce of strength she possessed.

There was a ripping sound as her skirt caught on a broken knob, but slowly she pulled herself upright.

Glory, Hallelujah! She was out.

Still shaking, she climbed down from the tree, branch by branch, until her feet hit the soft, spongy, pine-needle-laden soil beneath the tree. She felt like kissing the ground, like weary sea voyagers of old had done.

She assessed her situation. Her muscles groaned and her back hurt, but she could move both legs without too much pain. She scrambled down the embankment and began the walk up the seemingly endless driveway.

What if the truck returned? What if it was filled with those horse-killers?

Her feet pummeled the earth now, as she raced up the driveway. Clattering onto the porch, she flung herself on the swing, her breath coming in hard, short whooshes of air. She imagined that this was how Paris felt after a race with Cody through the field of wildflowers.

No wonder she was so grouchy at work the following day. Her back hurt, her head hurt, her arms had bruises on them, stinging horribly when she lowered them into the dishwater.

She was sure she had torn a ligament in the calf of one leg. She hobbled all day about the kitchen, her eyebrows lowered, speaking to no one unless absolutely necessary.

Dorothy hid her smiles of enjoyment as she ate one leftover dish after another. That was the thing that really irked Sadie to start with: the sight of Dorothy at the kitchen table with a dish of cabbage slaw, a slice of carrot cake, and a large mug of coffee at six o'clock in the morning. Watching Dorothy nauseated Sadie. No wonder Dorothy had trouble with her constitution.

Finally, when the tension in the kitchen became so thick it was unbearable, Dorothy clapped a hand on Sadie's aching shoulder, lifted her chin, closed her eyes for emphasis, and said, "Sit down!"

"Ouch!" Sadie said, rubbing her sore shoulder.

"Sit down, I said, Sadie darlin'."

"Why would I sit down? Can't you see this place is a horrible mess? And all you do is eat all morning."

Dorothy's answer was a tilted head and a great guffaw of sound.

"Sit down, Sadie. Either a bear got ahold of you, or you fell out of a tree, or I'd say you got heart problems. And them heart problems ain't the physical kind, now is they?"

Sadie lowered her head into her arms and groaned. Dorothy went to the coffeepot, filled a mug, and set it firmly on the tabletop in front of Sadie.

"Drink this. And here."

She went to the cupboard, came back with a bottle of Advil, and shook out two pills.

"Not with coffee," Sadie said, peering out of her arms with one eye.

"Oh, take 'em. Go on. Won't hurtcha.

"Now, tell me what happened. For one thing, if'n you'd wear better shoes, 'stead of traipsin' around in them there sneakers of yours, if you'd go to the Dollar General and get a pair like mine, you wouldn't be hob-blin' the way you are. You go for looks instead of good, solid quality. I have a hunch you're doin' the same thing with that heart o' yours. Ain't nothin' gonna match good, solid, down-to-earth men. Same as shoes."

Dorothy paused. "Ain't you gonna tell me what hap-pened?"

Sadie lifted her head, swallowed the pills with coffee, and grimaced.

"No."

"An' why ever not?"

"It's none of your business."

"Has nothin' to do with that Mark guy, now does it?"

"No. Yes. I don't know."

Sadie stared miserably into the distance.

"He's quite a looker," Dorothy continued. "Even Bar-bara commented on it. Caught that doctor's wife checkin' him out, so I did. Jes' shook my head to myself and thought, he can't be easy. He's got that brooding look about him. Too quiet. Never smiles right. Just one of them there plastic smiles he hides behind. You love him, don't you?"

"I did."

"You don't now? You want some more of that carrot cake? I'm havin' me another slice. I run my feet off last night. Not that I minded it, not that I minded it. Not with my Dollar General shoes, mind you."

She cut herself a generous slice of cake, scraping the cream-cheese frosting from the wide knife with her tongue as Sadie watched, swallowing her nausea.

"So, what happened?"

"Nothing."

"Now don't give me that. You come to work looking like you got run over by a truck, and you say nothing happened."

Sadie eyed her warily, sighed, then told her everything, ending with her stay in the pine tree.

"I mean, suppose Mark is the shooter, going around killing horses? And what about Louis and Marcellus? It could have been them, all these mysterious goings-on. We don't have any idea where they come from either. For all we know, they're little spies or something, planted here to find out where the horses are."

Dorothy snorted so loudly, Sadie jumped.

"You ain't got a grain of common sense, girl. Now don't you go belittling my Marcelona or Louise. Them kids is definitely victims of domestic abuse. Rich kids. Their parents likely involved in some illegal mess. We know their names now. Police contacted 'em, or tried to. Couldn't come up with nothin'. They evidently skipped the country. No, that pickup you saw. Likely some dad cartin' his kids around and one of 'em had to go potty. Your mind blows everything way outta line."

"Huh-uh, Dorothy."

"Oh, yes it does. Even with Mark, it does."

"What do you know about Mark Peight?"

"Probably more than you think."

Sadie blinked and looked away. Now she was curious. But she was too proud to ask Dorothy what she meant by that remark, so she dropped the subject.

They served leftover steak and fried eggs for breakfast. They made toast with store-bought bread and pancakes from the big commercial box of mix. Since everyone had overeaten the night before, they figured breakfast could be scant. Besides, they had the whole flagstone patio to hose down and chairs and tables to wash and put away. The work loomed before them.

Jim brought Marcellus and Louis, who were each set to work with a plastic bucket of hot soapy water and a rag, and promises of a swim in the pool as soon as the job was completed.

The children were blossoming under Dorothy's care. They loved to help around the ranch when they could. Jim hovered over them, seeing to it that the job was done properly. Bertie came to the patio, engaging Jim in a long, heated conversation about politics, which made Dorothy hiss beneath her breath until she was fairly steaming. She told Sadie if that old coot would get off the porch and let Jim go, he'd get more work done.

An hour later, the men were still standing at the exact same spot, and Dorothy'd had her fill. Marching up to the grizzled old gardener, she placed her fists on her hips and told him if he'd shut his trap, her James could get something accomplished, but she guessed people who worked for the government didn't need to worry about working to earn their money.

Bertie waved his arms and yelled. Then he stomped off the porch and went to find garbage bags, while Dorothy turned on her heel and marched self-righteously back to her domain, the kitchen.

Sadie turned the garden-hose pressure nozzle on high and washed down the flagstones from the previous night's party. She was sleepy, the flies were pesky, and her leg hurt worse as the forenoon wore on. She had never felt quite so depressed in her whole life.

What was the point of hanging on to Mark Peight? He obviously was not an easy person to understand.

What made him say those unkind things one minute, then become one of the nicest people anyone could ever hope to meet in the next?

Her mind was a million miles away until she saw Richard and Barbara Caldwell come out of the house, walking purposefully toward her. Sadie let go of the lever that powered the water spray and turned to greet them with the respect a boss required.

"Good morning," she said evenly.

"Yes, it is a good one. How are you?" Richard Caldwell boomed, his wife smiling at Sadie.

"You have dark circles under your eyes," Barbara observed.

"Do I?"

"We're being too hard on you, right? You're overworked."

"No, no," Sadie demurred.

They told Sadie what was on their minds. More horses had been killed the evening before. There was a serious threat in the area, and the local police needed telephone numbers to leave messages and warn the Amish.

This time, a full-blooded Tennessee Walker, the pride of the Lewis Ranch, the LWR, had been gunned down in broad daylight, along with a prize mare. And as an afterthought, three miniature ponies had been killed also, all in a drive-by shooting. They had, however, one vague clue. There was a truck, a blue diesel, seen in the vicinity, driving by slowly about the time of the shooting.

Sadie's shoulders slumped as color drained from her face. She plucked at a dead geranium without thinking, trying to bide her time before lifting her face to meet the piercing gaze of Richard Caldwell.

"Sadie? Do you know anything at all?"

Sadie sank weakly into a lawn chair, then met their questioning gazes. She told them honestly everything she knew, including the shot ringing out when she was with Daniel King and the truck the evening before.

Richard Caldwell fairly shouted at her, the veins protruding in his thick neck. What she was doing, traipsing along the road in the dark like that? Barbara placed a well-manicured hand on his arm and patted it a few times to calm him.

"The police have to know this," Richard Caldwell bellowed.

"They do," Barbara agreed.

"Everything? Even last night's incident?"

"No. There's more than one diesel truck in this area. Likely a kid needed to go to the bathroom, as Dorothy said."

✿ ✡ ✿

As the Amish people listened to the phone messages from the police, fear settled over the community like a cloak of heaviness. Parents feared for their children's safety. They kept their horses in barns, and children no longer rode on carts hitched to ponies. Local drivers took them to school in vans.

Families walked whenever possible. When distances were too great, they drove their teams cautiously, glancing furtively to the left and right, never relaxed, goading their horses to a fast trot.

Dat shook his head and said Fred Ketty may be on to something when she said the end of the world was nigh with so much evil in rural Montana.

Then two of Dave Detweiler's Belgians were found below their pasture. The fence had been cut with wire cutters, and the great horses had been chased out, then gunned down. There were no footprints or any trace of the killers left behind.

The Amish people were shaken but took the news stoically, as is their way. No use crying over spilled milk, they could have been struck by lightning, and God would not be mocked. These men would be brought to justice.

Sadie was afraid for Paris, so she kept her inside the barn. Dat said he wasn't keeping Charlie off that good pasture. He guessed if they got the horse, they would. That comment made Sadie so angry she felt like telling Dat a thing or two, but she knew she shouldn't.

Paris hung her head over the door and whinnied all day, while Charlie stood in the pasture and whinnied back. Reuben got so tired of it he brought Charlie into the barn and closed the gate. The whinnying stopped, and Dat never did anything to change it.

Reuben claimed aliens were hovering over the pastures in green flying ships and shooting horses for revenge. Mam scolded him thoroughly. She said there's no such thing as aliens, and he better watch it or he'd have to go work in John Troyer's truck patch, helping to clean it up as fall approached.

That shut Reuben up.

Sadie was afraid to ride. Still, when summer breezes turned into the biting winds of autumn, when the frost lay heavy in the hollows and the brown leaves swirled among the golden ones from the aspens, she could no longer hold back.

She asked Reuben to accompany her on Charlie. He looked up from his word-search booklet, his eyes round with fear.

"If you think for one minute that I'm going riding with you, you're nuts. Charlie isn't a riding horse. It's like riding a camel. He trots, and you bounce up and down, rattling all your teeth loose. I'm not going."

"Reuben!" Sadie wailed.

"Nope. Go by yourself."

"Okay. I will."

"You're crazy."

With that, Reuben went back to his word search, shaking his head wisely.

Mam was down in the basement, rearranging jars of canned goods. Sadie contemplated asking for permission, but she knew the answer would be a dead no. So she just left, though she felt a bit guilty.

Dat was at a school meeting and wouldn't be home until later. But she met Anna coming down the stairs from the haymow, holding a black cat who was struggling mightily, clearly displeased at being removed from the warm, sweet-smelling hay.

"Whatcha doing?" she asked innocently.

"Riding."

Anna shrugged her shoulders, hanging on grimly to the cat struggling to be free.

Sadie laughed, then whistled happily as she caught Paris' chin, kissed her nose, and began brushing the sleek, golden coat.

"We're going riding, Sweetheart, for better or for worse. Here we go!"

Chapter 13

THE FEELING OF BEING ON HORSEBACK AGAIN WAS one of jubilation. Sadie loved seeing Paris throw her head high, her ears swiveling forward then back, tuned in to Sadie's commands. Of course, there were no commands, and there wouldn't be. All Sadie had to do was give Paris a slight squeeze on the ribs or lay the reins easily on her neck. The communication between the two was so complete as to be almost imperceptible. But Paris knew, and so did Sadie.

Paris wanted to run. Should Sadie take her to the field of wildflowers? Sadie shivered. Taming Paris and Cody among the wildflowers had been so beautiful, but now a dark sort of foreboding hung over the field, turning it gray with her own apprehension. Could she ever ride there again?

She would never forget Reuben's sobs and the despair that shook his young body. He still had no horse. He wanted nothing to do with another one.

She held Paris in until the road wound uphill, then she let the horse run. She would let her stretch out, let her gather her feet beneath her, lunge with those powerful haunches, her heavy shoulders, feel the wind in her face just up this ridge. Then she'd turn around and go back.

Paris lowered her head. Power surged through her body as she raced up the winding road of Atkin's Ridge. Sadie leaned forward, sitting low in the saddle, savoring the wind that rushed in her ears.

They were almost at the top of the ridge. The light was darker here, the trees dense. There was a high embankment to her right, a heavy growth of trees and another steep incline to her left. It would be best to turn around and let Paris go slowly back down the way they had come.

A mockingbird dipped in the air ahead of her, his silly calls following him. First a cardinal's call, then a thrush, and finally a seagull. Had this saucy bird no shame, mocking these beautiful birds of the air? She turned her head, following his whereabouts until she located him high up in a scraggly pine.

She guessed that was why she didn't see the pickup truck until it was directly in front of her.

The throbbing, pulsating diesel sound pierced her awareness. A shot of raw fear surged through her with the power of a streak of lightning.

No! Not now! Remorse followed on fear's heels. Why had she been so foolish?

The truck was coming steadily, slowly. The blue color gleamed in the twilight.

There was only one way out. Up the embankment. Paris could do it.

Turning the horse, Sadie laid the reins on the left side of Paris' neck.

"Up, Paris! Up, girl." Sadie leaned forward, preparing herself for the powerful gathering of her hooves, the leaping.

Paris obeyed to perfection. Oh, wonderful horse! Her feet were sure, her hooves ringing on the rocks as she scrambled up, up, sideways up the incline. Sadie leaned over her neck, speaking softly, goading her on.

The occupants of the pickup yelled something. Sadie heard their harsh anger. But what did they say? Would they follow her?

The forest was green and brown, yellow and red with autumn, decked out in its final show before winter winds would howl through it, turning everything stark and white.

"Dear God, keep me safe. Stay with me, protect me, and keep me from harm," she prayed like a little child.

Paris took one last leap up the incline before pushing her way through the thicket, brushing nervously past two trees. Sadie pulled in the reins, sat up, listened, her heart racing.

There. She could still hear that truck idling. They had not moved on!

What was their motive? Who were they looking for? How could they terrorize a peace-loving, sleepy, little Montana community this way? Sadie was convinced the blue diesel truck held the shooter—or shooters.

Suddenly, anger overtook her common sense, and she turned Paris to the left. If she could get close enough, she might be able to see the license plate through the trees.

Should she tie Paris or stay on her back?

The truck was still idling, and Sadie was afraid to look and see if its occupants were inside or out.

Better stay on the horse.

"Shhh, Paris," Sadie whispered.

They moved quietly through the trees until the rear of the pickup was in sight. But it was too far away now. She leaned to the right, her eyes straining to see the figures on the metal rectangle. All she needed was that license plate number.

Was that a six? Or an eight?

She screamed then, a sound of pure terror, as two heads appeared coming up over the embankment. Paris lifted her head. Sadie loosened the reins and screamed again.

"Go, Paris! Go!"

She bent low and let Paris take control. Horses could always find their way home, and Sadie trusted Paris more than anything. They raced through the forest, zig-zagging first uphill, then sideways downhill, over rocks, between trees. Sadie looked back, her eyes wide with fear.

What would happen once Paris broke out of the woods? She couldn't go back on the road. Did those men know where she lived?

A feeling of despair enveloped her, threatened to choke her. She couldn't go home. Besides, Paris wasn't going home. She was running downhill in the opposite direction, away from home. She slowed, her ears pricked forward, before wheeling, veering sharply to the right and running diagonally down the side of the forested hill.

The sun was getting very low in the west, dust-laden streaks of light slanting between the trees. The browns and reds turned into stripes of flaming color.

A fence!

Instinctively, Sadie pulled back, but Paris had seen it and was slowing of her own accord.

"Whoop. Watch it, Paris. There's a fence."

Horses! This was someone's pasture.

Well, they'd have to find their way around it.

Paris picked her way carefully now. The horses in the pasture lifted their heads, whinnied. Paris answered with a high cry of her own.

The biggest horse lifted his head farther, then trotted over.

Hadn't she seen him somewhere before? He was so massive in the shoulders. And that color. So distinct. The grayish-oatmeal color of an Appaloosa mixture.

Sadie rode carefully as the horse trotted up to the fence, tossing his head, his mane whipping in the brisk wind.

The fence dipped into a culvert, then went almost straight up a steep hill. Sadie rode easily, but she was tense, her fear a support that kept her vigilant.

She remained alert for any unusual sound, the sight of a human being, the rumbling of traffic, anything that could mean she was being followed. As she crested the hill, she saw the rooftops of a barn, shed, then more outbuildings.

This, too, seemed vaguely familiar. But, no. She wasn't far enough out to be on Mark Peight's property, was she?

The fence stopped at a corner, then turned straight across the hayfield to the barn. She stopped Paris, indecision making her falter.

As if on cue, she heard the low rumbling of traffic. Was it the diesel truck? Well, if it was, they could just drive straight on past Mark Peight's place and be gone. She was safe for now.

Suddenly she became rigid with anger. Who in the world did they think they were? Riding around like cowards, wreaking havoc on people's lives, wrecking livelihoods, creating heartache.

The police were doing what they could, but there was no evidence, so they weren't making much progress. That made her mad, too.

Something had to be done. Someone had to take charge. If Mark was any sort of man, he'd stand by her and help out.

Besides, if he truly was innocent of ever having anything to do with these twisted individuals, who seemed to receive some sort of nameless thrill by killing innocent animals, this would be his chance to prove it.

Over and over he had assured her that this thing was way over his head. He couldn't fathom it, this senseless killing. In typical Mark-fashion, he had pouted and ignored her, his way of letting her know she had hurt his feelings by refusing to place her trust in him.

Hadn't he pledged his word the night of the cookout? That long magical evening when their words flowed, an artesian well of entwined emotions, a night she would never forget.

Kicking the stirrups and yanking on the reins, she startled Paris into a gallop across the hayfield and into the barnyard. She hauled back on the reins, then waited.

When she heard no one, she called his name.

Mark rounded the corner of a building wearing a nail pouch, his sleeves rolled up, hatless, surprise written all over his face from his wide-open eyes to his open mouth.

"Sadie Miller! What on earth...?"

She dismounted, led Paris into the forebay, and said, "Shut the door."

He obeyed immediately, latching it securely.

"Mark, I want you to listen to me. I need your help. These men are shooting horses again. I went for a ride, and they..." She caught her breath. "They saw me."

"Who are they?"

"How would I know? It's that blue diesel pickup. They have the gall...the...the...indecency to ride around wrecking people's lives as if a horse, a beautiful creature, was a...a *stump* used for target practice. And listen, I think they're after Paris. For a long time I didn't want to believe that, but now I'm sure Paris has something to do with it.

"Remember the black?"

Mark nodded.

"Well, he was shot. So was Cody. I still think there's a connection between the horse thieves and these shootings. Now they must be after Paris. I think she's a valuable horse in some way I don't even know.

"Mark, let's get close to the road, maybe put a road-block across it. They're in the area. We need to get that license-plate number. I'm tired of everything. The fear. The not knowing. If no one else does anything, I will."

In the dim interior of the barn, Mark could see this was no lady in distress. He watched her face intently and saw her honest resolve. She meant business, and she meant it now.

He smiled at her. "You really mean it?"

"Yes, I do. Now hurry. Can Paris have a drink? Some hay? She's been ridden hard."

Snapping a neck rope around Paris, Mark loosened her bridle, then took it off, hanging it on a nail nearby. Paris dipped her head as if to acknowledge the kind gesture, then drank deeply, her nostrils quivering.

Sadie laughed. "That's funny. She never drinks out of water troughs she's not used to."

Mark lifted his eyebrows suggestively. "A good omen for us," he teased.

Sadie blushed and kicked at some loose straw, as if her concentration could push his teasing away.

They tied Paris in a stall, gave her a block of fragrant hay, and turned to go. The sun was setting behind a distant ridge, and Sadie's heart sank along with it.

Sadie had to let Dat and Mam know where she was.

Bewildered, she asked Mark what she should do. He steered her into the implement shed where a black phone hung on the wall.

She picked up the receiver, dialed the number, and, of course, no one answered. She left a quick message, saying she was at Mark Peight's house with Paris, and they were not to worry. She couldn't tell them how she'd get home because she didn't know. Darkness was fast approaching.

When she hung up, she looked at Mark.

"Can we put a roadblock across the road?"

"I don't think that's legal."

"Can we stop them somehow? Can you flag them down? What reason could we give for trying to stop them?"

"Don't worry. I'll think of something."

He strode off toward the barn, returning with a heavy Stihl weed whacker.

"I'll work at the weeds around these buildings. You sit behind that row of pine trees."

Sadie assessed the trees, and then nodded her head.

"I'll climb up. They're easy."

They parted ways, Mark going to his designated area, Sadie to hers.

There was plenty of light. Good.

Mark pulled at the weed-wacker rope again and again until it sputtered to life, then moved it back and forth in long, sweeping motions.

Sadie listened, wondering if they would hear the sound of the diesel truck above the whining of the weed wacker.

Sadie watched Mark, the play of his shoulders, the ease with which he handled the heavy equipment.

Why did he have to be so complicated?

A little while later, Mark laid down the weed wacker and looked in the direction of the pine tree.

"You still up there, Sadie?"

"Yep!" she answered.

"I think your buddies went home the other way."

"I guess so."

When had their friendship turned into this? They were both more relaxed this evening than ever. It was an easy, natural feeling. It seemed as if she had known Mark all her life, and this was an evening where everything would go right. He had come to the end of his driveway with her. Not once had he laughed at her or made sarcastic remarks about the Amish. And that was something. Perhaps it was the circumstances, the danger, or maybe it was Paris, or something other than themselves to worry about.

Uh-oh. There they came.

At first she thought it might be a tractor; they were moving so slowly. Then she saw the gleaming silver smokestacks and heard the rumbling of that diesel engine. Her heart beat faster with the realization that they might be stopping.

Were they dangerous, armed men? Or was this all a figment of her imagination? Maybe this truck had absolutely nothing to do with the drive-by shootings.

The truck came slowly—slowly—over a low rise. She could see three men in the vehicle, all wearing hats pulled low. The driver was a big man; the other two were smaller. They were watching the road and the fields intently for any movement.

Oh! There was Mark. He just stood there with the weed wacker. Sadie shifted so she would be able to see the rear of the pickup. The truck slowed even more when the driver spied Mark.

Sadie could see the license plate. The numbers! She could see them!

Just as Mark stepped forward and Sadie thought the truck would stop, the driver accelerated. The tires screeched as the truck seemed to lift in the front. It fish-tailed as the driver gunned the motor, and they were off down the road at a dangerous speed.

Mark stood by the side of the road, scratching his head in bewilderment, while Sadie scrambled out of the tree and ran to his side. She was breathless when she reached him.

"I could see the license plate as plain as day!"

"Definitely something odd with that bunch."

"They're smart. Oh, Mark, I know they're the ones doing this. I just have this feeling. An intuition or something."

"I bet you anything this is the end of the diesel truck," Mark said shaking his head.

"Why?"

"They'll use another vehicle now. They didn't trust me at all, or they wouldn't have taken off like that."

"Oh."

"Well, there's not much we can do now," he said. "So? You want to come in? See where I'm staying? I don't have a house yet, you know."

Sadie looked around at the fast-approaching night.

"How am I going to get home? I can't ride Paris."

"What were you doing on the road riding that horse to begin with? Don't you know it simply is not safe right now?"

"I do now."

"I'll take you home. Paris can stay here."

He laughed in a low, gravelly sound. "You could stay here all night as well."

"Mark!"

"Just teasing."

As it was, she stayed far too long anyway. He showed her the room he had done up for his living quarters. It was surprisingly tidy and neat. His bed was made with a brightly-colored Indian blanket. A huge gun cabinet contained many guns of all sorts, and there were racks of guns on the wall. A glass-fronted cabinet held almost as many hunting knives.

His dog, Wolf, rose from the floor in front of the brown leather sofa. He was a magnificent animal, but fearful-looking. The wolf in him was so apparent he didn't really seem like a dog at all.

"The color of his eyes!" Sadie exclaimed.

"Isn't he beautiful?"

"He is. But, oh my, Mark, I'd hate to meet him in the dark."

"That's why I have him. I met too many ghosts in the dark as a child."

"You mean you had him when you were little?"

"Fifteen."

"Seriously?"

"About the age I learned to protect myself, yes."

Sadie sat down as Mark continued to speak. She sat quietly, her hands in her lap, watching his face. He never looked at her when he talked this way, which was all right if that made it easier to bare his soul.

She hung onto every word, knowing that understanding his aching past is what would play the most powerful part in understanding this man.

"See, before I started with ... the substance abuse, oh ... Did I tell you about my uncle? He was Amish. A member of my parents' church. I don't know how old I was, but we ... my brother and I were there for a time to help in his produce fields. That's when my whole world flipped upside down and I felt as if I had nothing ... no gravity, even, to keep me upright, centered. I was basically floating around in a misery of having nothing to hold onto.

"You couldn't trust English people, but neither could you trust Amish. My uncle, anyway. I often wonder how much he had to do with my mother's leaving."

"Is this uncle the same man you told me about before? What was his wife's name? Betsy?"

Mark nodded.

"Why didn't you tell me he was your uncle?"

He shrugged his shoulders. "Embarrassment. Afraid you'd never look at me again. Never date me...or marry me."

Sadie remained quiet.

What had he just said? Marry me? She bit her lip, hard.

"When I worked for my uncle, I realized that Amish people, men of faith, were lower in nature than even the foster system. That's really when the pins were knocked out from under me. Every person needs something they can believe in, and often, for children especially, God is not that real. So children depend on good people to give them food and clean clothes and love. But when you live without the love of your parents, you're like a stray dog. You have to scrounge through trash cans to get whatever you can. A smile here, some food there. You look for any tiny bit of kindness and grasp it with greedy, hungry fingers, and you never forget it.

"So my parents were gone, but the hardest part of my life was when even my uncle betrayed me. At first, I looked up to him. I wanted so desperately to believe he was good, that he was someone I could finally trust. Even the first beating, Sadie, I thought I deserved. My self-blame made him seem like a better person.

"So I tried even harder. I checked every tomato, every cucumber, and placed it carefully in the basket. When he tied me in the silo chute overnight for accidentally knocking over a stack of plastic tomato hampers, I gave up. There was no goodness, no mercy in this vile man. Recognizing that was a sort of freedom, but that's when I could no longer keep my feet on the ground. I free-floated in a world of hatred.

"The hate bit into my wrists that night I was tied to the steps of the silo. Those ropes became the hate in me, and that hate gave me strength to pull free. I almost lost my one hand to infection."

"Not hate, Mark. God helped you become free."

Mark shook his head. "No, Sadie. There was no room for God in that silo chute. It was filled with rage, my silent screams, my determination to kill that man."

"No, Mark! Please don't say those things."

"So now you see. Now you know why I'm not good enough for you."

"It's in the past."

"Never totally. I guess finding God is harder for a person who has hated the way I have. The alcohol was a sort of haven for awhile. So were the drugs. But I couldn't go on. Once I was so messed up, I almost died one night. I guess…that was probably the first time I could recognize God in my life. It must have been him, or else I'd be dead.

"But God acts like a missing parent sometimes. He's often hard to find. At first, you have to survive on bits and pieces. A sunset, for instance. Or a sunrise. Little things sort of pierce your armor of hardness, but it's elusive. God is terribly hard to understand. Why does he allow a life like mine? Why?"

"Your life is good, now, Mark," Sadie said quietly.

"By all outward appearances, yes. But I struggle. It's tough. I want to be free of my past, completely, but…I can't."

"Is that … is that …?"

"What?"

"I can't say it."

"Come on, Sadie. Out with it."

"Is that why we don't date like normal young people in an Amish community do?"

"Yes."

She was silent at that. Mark paused.

"You see, Sadie, I'll hurt you. My jealousy, my anger, it's not fair to you. I hurt you now, and we're not dating."

Like a star falling across the night sky, the knowledge awakened her. She almost gasped audibly. She clasped her hands firmly around her knee to keep them from going around Mark's shoulders.

She knew then. She knew that she was the link, the gravity, the conduit of God's love to Mark. He needed her. Her love was from God. She was only a vessel he had prepared, and would continue to prepare, as long as Mark needed her.

What did it matter? Her life would not always be safe or secure. She would, no doubt, suffer at times. But only at times. They would have their good days, and many of them. If the bad times came, God would be there for her. Yes, he would. Oh, how he would!

She drew in a soft breath. Turning to him, she laid a hand on his arm.

"Mark, can we have a date on Saturday evening?" she asked.

Her arms slid around his shoulders when he bent his head toward hers, not knowing if the tears of joy between them were his or hers.

Chapter 14

SADIE LAID IN HER BED FULLY AWAKE. WHAT WAS that sound? Was it the creaking of the siding, the snapping of wooden floorboards? She heard it again. A hoarse sort of sound.

Retching. Someone was being sick.

She swung her legs over the side of the bed, tiptoed quietly across the hall to the bathroom door, and turned the knob. It was locked securely.

"Reuben?"

Her answer was another tearing sound. Someone was really sick.

Knocking, she called again, "Reuben?"

There was no answer, only the sound of the bathroom tissue being unrolled.

"Anna?"

"Go away." The words were garbled, almost indistinct.

"Anna, let me in. Are you sick?"

"I'm all right. Go back to bed."

"No."

Sadie leaned against the wall outside the bathroom, crossed her arms, and waited.

Finally, the door opened a tiny crack, a thin sliver of yellow light from the kerosene lamp showing through. Anna appeared, carrying the lamp. At first, Sadie shrank back against the wall, then gave up and stepped forward.

She was shocked to see Anna's face. It was so pale, with red splotches on her cheeks. Her lips were ballooned to twice their normal size, tear streaks in jagged, glistening paths down her swollen cheeks.

"Anna!"

"Go away!" Anna hissed, pushing past her.

The lamp chimney rocked unsteadily as Anna turned to enter her room. Her hands outstretched, Sadie followed her.

"Anna, stop! I'm going to wake Rebekah and Leah if you don't act normal. Why are you so angry? Do you have the flu?"

"Course I have the flu! What does it look like? You think I *want* to throw up, or what?"

Sadie stepped up and took the kerosene lamp from Anna's nervous hands, guided her back into the bedroom, and closed the door noiselessly.

"Yes. I think you want to throw up," Sadie ground out, pushing her face very close to Anna's, watching as her pupils dilated with fear.

Sadie set the lamp on the small dresser. Turning, she said, "Sit down."

Anna obeyed, hanging her head in shame. It touched Sadie's heart. So young and still obeying her elders in her innocent way as she was trained to do. At 16 years old, when she started her years of *rumspringa*, she would be given more freedom to make her own choices. But for now, she still obeyed the voice of her parents or older sisters.

"Anna, listen to me. You don't have a stomach virus, do you? You want to throw up to get rid of food you ate because you feel fat. Am I right?"

Anna shook her head from side to side, her eyes downcast, picking at her white T-shirt with fingers that never stopped moving. Sadie said nothing until the back-and-forth movement stopped.

"Have you been making yourself vomit for a long time?"

"I don't...do that. I feel sick."

"Then we have to take you to a doctor. You may have a serious disease that causes the nausea."

"No!"

"Why not?"

"I hate doctors. They...they weigh you."

"You've been losing weight, Anna."

"I am?"

Anna lifted her head, hope shining from her swollen eyes. Sadie watched quietly as Anna pulled her T-shirt tightly across her stomach, then released it abruptly.

"Anna, it's okay if you want to lose weight, but you can't do it like this."

"Like what?"

"Purging. Making yourself throw up."

"I don't."

"Yes, you do."

Confronted with the truth, Anna began to cry. It was a pitiful mewling sound at first, then deeper, hoarse sobs. She twisted her body and threw herself face-first into her pillows.

Sadie sat down on the twin-size bed, her hands in her lap. Instinctively, she knew it would be better to let Anna's misery boil over for awhile.

Her eyes roamed the small room. She noticed the poster of dogs, the cheap Wal-Mart candle that didn't match any color in the room, the clothes in a heap by the closet door, a cellophane wrapper by her bed.

The furniture was mismatched hand-me-downs of dressers that had been used by her sisters as they grew through their early teens. When Anna reached 16, she'd have a larger room filled with new furniture, beautiful things, art on the walls, a room that stated her own tastes.

A wave of pity washed over her Sadie. Poor Anna was stuck back here at the end of the hall, in a room that was almost an afterthought, unimportant, forgotten—too much like Anna herself. As the youngest daughter, she sat in on her older sisters' conversations, listening in awe to their vivid accounts of weekends with girlfriends and interesting boys, all of it a faraway, scary place for Anna to imagine.

The *youngie*. As she approached *rumspringa*, her own inadequacies quadrupled in size, her apprehension mounting into inconsolable proportions. She filled that worried place with food, the source of her comfort and happiness.

Anna was quiet now, only an occasional hiccup reminding Sadie of the sobs, the onslaught of her despair. Slowly, she placed a hand on Anna's shoulder.

"Anna, you aren't fat."

There was no answer, only a long, drawn-out shudder.

"Do you know how much I weighed when I was 15?"

Silence.

"140."

Anna sat straight up, staring at Sadie.

"You did not!"

"Yes, I did."

"I only weigh a little more than that," Anna whispered, the corner of her lips lifting.

"Of course, you do."

Anna pulled up her pajama-clad knees, wrapped her arms around her legs, and talked. She told Sadie she had been perfectly content to be who she was until some friends had a sleepover at Sarah Ann's house. There they compared skin problems, hair color, sizes and weight. Jeanie told Anna that she was the heaviest by 10 whole pounds, and why was she so much bigger than her sisters? Why was her hair lighter?

After that, Anna had sat in the sun all summer spraying vinegar-water in her hair, then lemon-juice water, then baking-soda water, anything to change the color. She had even tried spraying it with mosquito repellent, but all she got was an itching, flaky scalp.

She was always hungry, that was the thing. She could eat all day long, every day. Doughnuts, peanut butter crackers, chicken corn soup with saltine crackers, applesauce, hot dogs with sauerkraut, and potato chips. She loved Mam's snickerdoodle cookies and Subway's sandwiches. Everything in the whole world was delicious, except brussels sprouts. They tasted like spoiled cabbage.

At the dentist's office, she watched a lady on the television eat spaghetti. It made her so hungry for spaghetti that she asked Mam to make it for supper, and she ate it for days and days with dried Parmesan cheese sprinkled all over it, and homemade bread with butter and garlic powder, oregano, and more cheese. She put it in the broiler of the oven, and it was the best thing ever.

At the produce stand where she worked with Leah, she loved to eat a garden-fresh tomato, sliced thick and sprinkled with salt and pepper. She ate great sections of cantaloupes and oranges and blueberries, as well.

"Then I gained over 25 pounds," she said sadly.

Sadie laughed, a sound of genuine understanding.

"It's all right to eat. You're hungry, you're growing, and you're healthy."

Anna shook her head. "I'm fat!"

Sadie looked at her steadily, unflinchingly. "You are not fat."

"According to Sarah Ann and Jeanie, I am."

Sadie nodded. "Girls can be so cruel. So terribly, unthinkingly, crushingly cruel. So mean. But you know what, Anna? The reason they say those things is because of their own insecurities. They don't feel good about themselves, or they wouldn't put other girls down.

"Every 14- or 15-year-old girl has her own struggles with feeling adequate, secure, able to move among her peers with ease and confidence. It's tough out there. We have a close circle of people being raised in the Amish way, but we're only human beings, and we suffer in the early teen years same as everyone else."

"I can't believe that you did."

"I sure did. Sometimes I wished the end of the world would come so I wouldn't have to be 16. I was terribly hurt by the loss of Paris and by moving to Montana. I hated it."

Anna told Sadie about how she felt left out by her and Reuben, with their tremendous riding skills and their way with horses. She felt as if she had no talent at all. She couldn't even sew a decent dress on the sewing machine.

Sadie listened quietly and felt some remorse. A plan formed in her mind.

"I'll tell you what, Anna. If you cross your heart and promise that you will never, ever, as long as you live, make yourself *cuts* again, then I will get a horse for you. Reuben won't ride with me anymore, so you can. I'll teach you."

"No."

"Why not?"

"I'm too *blottchich*."

It was then that Sadie realized that the brick wall Anna had built around herself was impossible to breach in one heartfelt talk. How deep was her problem?

Oh, dear God, Sadie prayed silently. Bless Anna, look upon her with grace. She's so young and so mixed up about what's important in life.

She yawned and stretched.

"Well, if you think you're so *blottchich*, then we'll drop it."

She stood up, gathered her robe around her, shivering.

"Winter's coming," she said sleepily.

Anna watched her wearily.

"I...I can't ride a horse. I'm scared of them. I'm not like you. You just look at a horse and it likes you. They don't like me. They bite me."

Sadie laughed. "You know that's not true."

"It is."

"Goodnight, Anna. Sleep well. No *cutsing*, okay?"

"Okay."

The wind was moaning among the eaves, a sad sort of harmony with the night, as if they had put their heads together and written this symphony for the approaching winter.

Sadie heard very little of it, falling asleep the minute her head touched the soft pillow.

✣ ✡ ✣

In the morning, Dat sat at the table poring over the newspaper as Mam expertly flipped the sizzling golden rectangles of cornmeal mush in the cast-iron frying pan. Each year when the leaves turned color and the air carried a frosty nip, Dat wanted fried mush for breakfast. It was an item of food that had been passed down for many generations. He liked it cut in thick slices, then fried in oil for at least half an hour. He ate it with two eggs sunny-side up and a glass of orange juice. Then he had oatmeal as a sort of breakfast dessert, often accompanied by shoofly pie.

Sadie wondered whether to tell them about Anna's problems.

Mam put the mush on a platter, then cracked the eggs into the same pan. Sadie poured the juice, looking up as Leah walked into the kitchen.

"Morning."

"Mm-hm."

"Cleaning today?"

Leah nodded.

"Can someone make toast?" Mam asked.

Sadie sliced thick slices of homemade white bread, raising her eyebrows at the lack of whole wheat flour.

"Out of it," Mam said, observant as always.

"That's unusual."

"Well, I called Johnny Sollenberger yesterday to take me to town. He's my least favorite driver, but no one else could go, and guess who he had going to town with him?"

Sadie pushed the broiler closed with a squeaky bang and looked at Mam.

"Fred Ketty."

"Ach, my."

"So I just didn't go. Figured we could eat white bread."

Dat chuckled. "Ach, Fred Ketty. She means well."

"I'd go into hiding if I was called Fred Ketty," Leah observed sourly, pulling up her chair.

Reuben slumped in his chair, rubbing his eyes with his fists.

"Where's Anna?"

"Let her sleep. She was up late."

They bowed their heads, asking a silent blessing on the morning meal. When they raised their heads, Sadie decided to bring up the subject of Anna's purging.

Mam listened wide-eyed while Dat shook his head in disbelief. Reuben promptly stated that nobody noticed Anna, same as him, and she was just doing it for attention. A generous portion of egg and fried mush churned in his mouth as he spoke, until Dat told him to swallow his food first, then finish speaking. This sent Reuben into a dark silence, and he shoveled food into his mouth at twice the speed.

Mam said it was more than just ordinary teenage angst, which Sadie agreed was true. Leah nodded her head in acknowledgment as well.

"She needs a horse," Sadie said.

"You think that would help her snap out of it?" Dat asked.

"Anything to build some confidence."

Reuben snorted. "Well, what about me? I still don't have a horse. If it would help, I can start throwing up."

Dat explained patiently to Reuben that he had shown absolutely no interest in another horse, so they figured he'd have to be ready for one first.

"I hate horses," Reuben said quite abruptly.

He left the table, hurried into the living room, and threw himself on the couch, burying his face in his arms. Mam opened her mouth to call him back, but Dat waved his hand to quiet her.

"He'll be okay. This thing with Cody will take time."

It was Saturday, so there was no hurry, except for Leah going to her housecleaning job. Sadie lingered with her parents, discussing the issues of the day, then told them that Mark would be coming to the house that evening.

Dat drank his coffee to hide his smile, but Mam lifted her eyebrows in concern.

"He's sure given you the runaround already," she observed dryly.

Sadie nodded in agreement, deciding not to try and prove a point. She'd have one date and see what occurred. She giggled to herself, wondering what her very proper mother would say if she knew that Sadie had asked for the date, instead of the other way around. But Sadie knew it was all right. At this point, they were closer than many couples who had been dating for some time.

She cleaned the refrigerator and defrosted the freezer while Mam baked shoofly pies, discussing Anna and Reuben all the while.

Mam poured water on the mixture for the pie crust, felt it with her fingertips, then poured on a bit more. She pushed the mound to the middle of the stainless steel bowl and molded it into a perfect pile of moist pie dough.

She went to the flour canister and scooped some into a bowl. She scattered a generous amount of the snowy white flour onto the countertop. Pinching off the right amount of dough, she sprinkled more flour on top. Then she grabbed the rolling pin and began an expert circular motion until she had a perfect orb of evenly rolled dough.

Folding it in half, she pressed it into the tin pie plate, then took a table knife and cut off the extra, overhanging dough.

She made six pie crusts, ladling the brown sugar, egg, water, molasses, and soda mixture into it, measuring the amounts carefully. Mam said if there was too much liquid, the pies ran over in the oven; too little and you had a dry shoofly pie.

Next she took up a handful of crumbs made from flour, brown sugar, and shortening, sprinkling large handfuls of them on top. It never failed to amaze Sadie how the liquid and crumbs merged to create the three perfect parts that made a shoofly pie: the "goo," the cake, and the crumbs on top.

Mam was an expert, her shooflies always turning out with the deepest amount of goo, the softest cake, and just a sprinkling of crumbs. She said it was from doing it over and over for years.

"Well, if you have a date, perhaps I had better make a ho-ho cake," Mam said, her smile wide and warm as she watched Sadie clean the shelves of the refrigerator.

"A what?"

"A ho-ho cake. A chocolate cake with creamy white filling topped with fudge sauce. You eat it with ice cream. Or without."

"Oh, yes. They're a lot of trouble, aren't they?"

"Well…yes."

"Then don't."

"Of course, I will. You have a date!"

Sadie grinned, then her nose stung as she tried to hold back the tears. She would never forget the anxiety of passing through the dark valley of her mother's mental illness. She hoped she'd also never forgot to thank God for her mother's ordinary, everyday awareness and love for life.

There were still times when she would catch her mother gazing out the window with tears gathering in her eyes. On those days Sadie's heart would plummet to her stomach as she wondered if the depression would return. But it never did as long as she faithfully followed her doctor's orders, with Dat's full support.

Sadie sincerely hoped Anna was not following in her mother's footsteps. Sadie knew depression could be hereditary sometimes, and she wondered if Anna was showing signs of it.

As Sadie cleaned the rest of the house with Rebekah's help, she noticed it was close to dinnertime. What time might Mark show up? Had he made plans with anyone else?

"Isn't Kevin coming over this evening?"

"No. He has church tomorrow."

Reuben brought the mail, thumping it down on the kitchen table as loudly as he possibly could. Letters rained down on the freshly scrubbed linoleum, squeezed out from between the magazines and catalogs.

"Letter for you! Looks like a guy's handwriting!" Reuben said, chortling.

"No, it's not," Sadie said automatically, before examining the handwriting.

She held very still as she gripped the blue envelope with both hands. She felt a slight tremor as the handwriting leaped at her.

Reuben was right!

Oh, had Mark done the same thing again?

Her breath came in quick gasps that she struggled to hide from Mam and Reuben. Rebekah peered over her shoulders.

Oh, please God, no. Not now.

With shaking hands, she tore open the envelope, unfolded the single white sheet of writing paper, flipped it over, and read the signature.

Daniel King.

She sagged in the recliner in pure relief, her limbs folding as if the joints were liquid.

> *Dear Sadie,*
>
> *I am miserable. I cannot forget you. I'm almost 2,000 miles away, and all I want to do is go back to Montana. I think I love you. Why don't you write to me?*

Sadie's fist went to her forehead, and she thumped it without thinking.

I didn't write because Mark became a very important part of my life, that's why, she thought wryly.

His letter was full of his praise for Sadie and reproach for the terrible distance between them and his aching heart. Sadie folded the letter slowly, then shoved it back into the envelope, her eyes unseeing.

He was one of the nicest people she had ever met. She knew he would be an easy person to love, to marry. He was so normal, with such a good heart, a grounded attitude, a wonderful appetite for life and love.

Suddenly, she was unsure about seeing Mark that night. She felt waves of doubt lift and bear her away, floating up and out, dipping low as a wave dropped her, and then rising up when the next one came. She drifted in an ocean of restlessness that never ceased movement.

Daniel. His hair streaked blond. His laughing eyes. Always smiling. So easy to understand and ... well, get along with. Her life would be so easy.

Reuben peered at her. His intense gaze brought her back to earth.

"Well, who was it? Mark skipping out on you again?"

As if in a trance, Sadie shook her head.

"No, not this time."

Perhaps he should. Perhaps he should go back to Pennsylvania and find his English mother and all his siblings and leave her entirely out of his complicated life. He'd never be normal.

"Mam, I think I'll go to my room. I need to sort through some of my clothes and organize them."

Mam looked up from her dishwashing.

"You sure it's your closet you need to organize?"

"Now you sound like Dorothy."

Mam laughed.

"May I read his letter? It's from that Lancaster boy, right?"

Sadie smiled at her mother. "Someday," she whispered.

Mam shook her head as she sprinkled detergent on a kettle and resumed her scrubbing.

Chapter 15

SADIE PULLED THE HEAVY, PURPLE HAIRBRUSH through the wet, thick strands of her hair. She winced as she thought how nice it would be if her hair were not quite as thick and heavy.

Mam said in the older days, it was strictly forbidden to cut women's hair, no matter how long it became. She remembered seeing her aunt with hair hanging to the back of her knees. She would wind it around the palm of her hand over and over, securing it with nearly two dozen hair pins.

Now, Sadie and her sisters kept their hair trimmed to below the shoulders, making it easier to wash and dry. Even the coverings fit better, although she knew it was still a controversial subject. Some of the more conservative mothers absolutely forbid their girls to cut their hair.

With a fine-tooth comb Sadie drew her hair up and back, securing it with barrettes.

That didn't look right. The whole top of her head looked horribly lopsided. She unclipped the barrettes and started over, leaning as close to the mirror as she could, drawing the comb slowly and carefully through her thick tresses.

Still not right, she thought grimly.

She ground her teeth in frustration at the sound of loud, thumping footsteps. It could only be Reuben. Now what did he want, the nosy little beggar?

"What?" she said to the mirror, as his beanie-encased head appeared in the doorway.

"Mark's here!"

"No, he's not."

"I know he's not!"

Yelps of glee accompanied his retreat as Sadie shook her head and snorted. Now her nerves were on edge for sure.

She sat on the bed, one side of her hair combed and held with clips, the other side hanging heavily down the side of her face. As she looked in the mirror, it struck her that her appearance matched the state of her heart. Unfinished. Two-sided. One side so different from the other.

She wished Daniel King lived in Montana. Perhaps if she saw him again, she would know if he was the one God meant for her.

How could you tell?

She had no time to feel alone after Daniel left. Mark had reappeared immediately. He was at the ranch, in church on Sunday, involved with the incident with the blue diesel truck and Paris. They had talked of his past again, which was very meaningful to their relationship.

But surely if she loved Daniel, she wouldn't be so content to stay here in Montana and love Mark. Hadn't she felt so clearly once more that he was the one?

Getting up, she fixed her hair again and decided it looked all right this time. She had already planned what to wear, so there was no hesitation at the closet. She slipped the paprika-colored dress over her head. It was a dark burnt, but muted orange color.

Orange and yellow were considered much too flamboyant for plain girls. Pink was frowned upon but tolerated for some occasions. This color, Sadie was sure, would cause a stir if worn in church. But this was a Saturday evening date, so she could push the envelope a bit.

She loved the fabric, the way the pleats hung in luxurious folds from her waist. The sleeves were just below the elbow and fit perfectly. Yes, she liked this dress.

She put on her covering with confidence, pinned it, then sprayed cologne from her collection in the drawer.

Mmm. That certainly was the most wonderful smell.

She straightened the comforter on her bed, adjusted the shams, picked up a pair of hose that had a run in them. Mam said she would go to the poorhouse buying stockings for her girls if they didn't try to be more careful, so Sadie felt a bit guilty as she stuffed them in her brown wicker wastebasket.

There. She was ready for her first genuine date with Mark Peight.

He arrived on time, his horse and buggy spotless. He looked so good, Sadie felt weak just walking toward him. His hair was black, so thick and dark, combed just right. Was it carelessly or carefully? Whatever it was, he took her breath away, as usual.

His eyes never left hers as she walked toward him, one elbow leaning on the shoulder of his horse. He was wearing a white, short-sleeved shirt, which only made his complexion appear darker, his perfect mouth widening into a smile of welcome.

"You look like a leaf still hanging on a birch tree in that color!"

Sadie laughed. "It's not yellow!"

"It's pretty, whatever color it is."

His elbow dropped, and he glanced toward the house.
"No hugging, right?"

"Better not."

He nodded. "You want to drive to town for ice cream?"

"I'll get my coat."

The ice cream was wonderful. They ate it while seated at a small table on the porch of the little shop, the wind just nippy enough to add color to their cheeks. They talked easily about everyday, uncomplicated subjects, careful to keep the serious things hidden. Sadie learned he liked coffee ice cream, also her favorite. She took that as a good omen rather than a coincidence.

Daniel King wasn't in her thoughts at all. She studied Mark as she ate her ice cream, admiring his hands once more. She felt as if she would never doubt her love for him ever again.

That is, until she saw a man leaning against his white pickup truck. He looked so much like Daniel, for a second Sadie thought it was him. That smile! Her hand went to her chest as her breath left her body, making a soft whooshing sound.

"What's wrong with you?" Mark asked watching the color leave her face.

Sadie waved a hand reassuringly. "Oh, it's nothing. I just thought…"

She stopped, knowing she had gone too far, like trying to park a car and hitting the curb. She should just stop, not telling him what she thought.

"What?"

"Oh, it's nothing Mark. Just someone I thought I knew."

"That guy leaning against his truck?"

Sadie said nothing.

"Okay. Be that way. Don't talk. You thought it was that guy from Lancaster. That Daniel King. Your knight in shining armor who rescued you from the evildoers who shot at Paris."

His words dripped with sarcasm. Like acid they ate away at her sense of well-being, destroying her confidence by the second.

"No, no, it wasn't him."

"'Course not, but you thought it was. Your face turned white as a ghost."

"No, no, it didn't. I mean, he's... It's nothing."

Their ice cream finished, they walked toward the horse and buggy. It was tied to a sturdy hitching rail provided by the store owners for the Amish to use, but it was behind the store, and they had to walk through an alley between two brick buildings.

Suddenly, Mark stopped and lowered his dark head. Sadie instinctively backed away. She felt the porous texture of the brick with her hands as she shrank farther from him. He had suddenly turned ominous, his features slated with gray, his shoulders hulking.

"That is precisely why I don't date," he said in a tone Sadie had never heard before.

He stalked off as a man possessed. She followed him slowly, shocked and afraid. She never once thought he would leave. Not once. The rasp of the wheels against the concrete of the hitching rack proved her wrong.

She ran, her hand outstretched. "Wait! Mark! Please wait!"

The horse lunged against its collar. The buggy swung at a dangerous level as it careened around a bend, spraying gravel. Then, around the next set of buildings, it disappeared.

Darkness had fallen. The only light was from the yellow street lamps and the bluish-white lights from the storefronts. She stood in the middle of the alley, biting down on her lower lip. No matter how hard she tried not to cry, she cried anyway. She cried for the hopelessness of their love and their relationship, which was as delicate as dominoes standing in a line, ready to topple at the slightest touch. Like the dominoes, their relationship had no foundation at all. It was all because he was handsome, and she was a hopeless flirt.

Self-hatred infused her being until she sagged down on the concrete around the hitching rail and let the blame overtake her. It was all her fault.

She should have shut Daniel firmly out of her life, and she hadn't. His attention had soothed her and puffed up her vanity. Now she had lost Mark because of it.

Sadie lifted her head and assessed her situation. She was alone in town. She needed to call someone to come get her, but who? If she called an Amish driver, the whole community would know what happened. There was no such thing as asking them to keep a secret; they spread gossip to every Amish person they drove.

Did Mark really leave her? Surely he'd be back. This was simply unreal.

She considered walking home, but decided against that as soon as she heard booming rock music in a low-riding car that crept past, the occupants yelling at her as they drove by.

No way.

She was still crying, so that had to be taken care of first. She dug into her purse, grabbed a wad of tissues, and honked her nose into them. Then she dabbed at her eyes and cheeks and drew a long, steadying breath.

What about James Sevarr. Dorothy's Jim. She had his phone number in her purse. All she needed was a phone.

Summoning all her courage, Sadie re-entered the brightly lit shop and stood in line. When she got to the counter, she timidly asked if she could use the phone to make a local call. The proprietor was very kind, simply falling over himself in his eagerness to help her, which almost made Sadie cry again.

Jim answered the phone, said he was laid up with gout, but Dorothy would come get her.

She had never felt quite as alone as she did waiting for Dorothy. She sat at the very same table she had shared with Mark earlier, trying to keep from crying again.

When Dorothy appeared in her rusted orange Honda, her head not nearly as far above the steering wheel as it should have been, Sadie didn't know whether to laugh or cry. As it was, she did a lot of both, first blubbering and sniffing and blowing her nose, then shaking and laughing hysterically when Dorothy said she would go after that Mark Peight in his horse and buggy and run him off the road.

Dorothy turned the wheel abruptly when they came to the first stoplight, saying she was hungry for Wendy's chili.

So they sat in a blue booth beneath an orange light, ate chili and french fries, sipped Cokes, and talked.

Sadie was belittled. She took the blame for the whole incident and told Dorothy so, which immediately set her off like a rocket.

"Now see here, Sadie, you're gettin' yerself into a dangerous position you are. It's like them abusers. They slam their wife or whatever and git 'em so befuddled, they actually think it's their own fault. It happens over and over, and you're too thick in the head to see it.

"He ain't to be trusted. You mark my words, Sadie Miller."

Dorothy was angry to the point where she seriously wanted to go to Mark's house, confront him, and make him apologize. Sadie shook her head adamantly, of course.

The thing was, Sadie knew that Mark's past drove him to act the way he did. Dorothy didn't know much about Mark's difficult childhood. For all she knew, Mark was perfectly normal. But Sadie could not, in good conscience, betray Mark's trust and tell Dorothy the secrets of his past. No, she was the only one to blame.

Between gigantic spoonfuls of chili, Dorothy said more than once, "You deserve better, my love. You deserve better."

"You want a vanilla frosty?"

Sadie shook her head.

Dorothy heaved herself out of the booth, her green polyester slacks catching on the table. She tucked her red plaid shirt securely into the elastic waistband, pulling the pants up as high as they would go. The bottom of the pant legs barely reached her beige-colored ladies shoes from the Dollar General, but she strode purposefully up to the counter, returning in short order with a large vanilla frosty.

"Mmm, these are the best thing ever! Don't know how they git 'em so creamy."

Dorothy shoveled great mouthfuls of the creamy milkshake into her mouth, then she suddenly leaned back and clapped a palm to her forehead.

"Oh, shoot! Brain freeze. Ate too fast."

She leaned over the table, moaning in agony, saying, "Whew!" over and over, until a kindly old gentleman came to their table and asked if there was anything he could do to help. His only answer was a glare of pain from Dorothy and a tart reply about hadn't he ever seen anyone with a brain freeze? So he shuffled off bewildered.

Sadie slumped over the table, her shoulders rounded with dejection.

"So now you know, Sadie. He ain't for you," Dorothy concluded, carefully tilting the paper frosty container as she scraped out the last of the ice cream. "No, sir, he ain't."

Then she put down the empty cup and reached over and held both of Sadie's hands as gently and softly as the touch of an angel.

"I know this ain't your way, Sadie, but I'm prayin' for you right here this minute. You need it, honeybun."

And she prayed in a beautiful singsong voice, the most compassionate prayer Sadie had ever heard.

"Heavenly Father, I know you're watching over my Sadie girl. You really need to get serious and show her the way. Right now her future is in the balance. Thank you for providing everything she needs to get through this difficult time. Continue to bless her with your strength and your wisdom. Amen."

"Thank you," Sadie whispered, her voice choked with emotion.

"Now don't you go thinkin' I prayed that to be seen and heard of men. I didn't. God just needs to hear some serious prayin' going on right now. That Mark don't trust you right, and you so in love with him. You're like a love-sick little puppy, so you are."

The ride home was quiet, except for Dorothy's occasional "rifting," as she called it. She rubbed her ample stomach and complained of indigestion, saying she hadn't taken her usual dose of Gas-X yet today, and here it was almost bedtime.

Sadie was numb to any kind of emotion. She answered when she was expected to do so, laughed when it was required of her.

When the orange Honda wheezed to a stop at the back porch of the Miller house, Sadie pushed a 20-dollar bill in Dorothy's direction, which she declined furiously, saying that's what was the matter with this world—no one did anything for anyone anymore unless they expected to be paid.

Sadie went inside to find her parents in their usual recliners. They looked up with concern when she came in.

"You're home early? With a vehicle?" Mam asked, her eyes round with concern.

"Something came up. Mark had to leave early," Sadie said, averting her eyes as she made her way up the stairs.

"Goodnight," Mam said, quietly, then raised her eyebrows and rolled her eyes in Dat's direction.

Dat shook his head and resumed his reading.

✿ ✿ ✿

Sadie woke with a groan, punching her pillow in frustration when she thought of the events of the night before.

Reuben worked on a jigsaw puzzle, humming the same tune under his breath the whole entire morning until Sadie thought she might lose her good sense and sound mind.

She wandered out to the barn, but Paris was at the far end of the pasture. Sadie didn't feel like calling her, so she let her go. Besides, there was no use calling the horse if she couldn't go riding.

Uncle Samuel's came for supper, but Sadie was in no mood to visit with his loud and jovial family.

So she sat in her room instead. She wanted to answer Daniel King's letter, but was too numb to think of anything to say. Picking up a book, she read halfheartedly, wishing the whole time that she had never met Mark Peight.

She was getting terribly hungry when Anna opened the door very quietly, slipped inside, and sat down on the beige-colored loveseat. Her eyes were large and round with concern. Sadie noticed a definite jutting of her collarbones and a thinness around her neck.

"What happened, Sadie?"

"I'd rather not talk about it."

"Seriously?"

"Yes."

"I need to talk about the vomiting."

Sadie looked at Anna, really looked.

"Have you done it again?"

"No."

Anna's eyes were downcast, averted, and she was completely unable to raise them to meet Sadie's gaze.

"You're telling a *schnitza*."

"I didn't feel good."

"Did you force yourself to throw up?"

"No."

"I don't believe you."

"I don't have to force myself anymore. My stuff comes up real easy."

"Anna!"

Sadie was horrified. All the thoughts of Mark and his sordid behavior flew from her mind, replaced by a concern much more immediate and serious.

Things like this only happened to English people with serious body issues. Not her own little sister! Where had it started? Were they all so concerned about their appearances, their weight, their figures, who was cute and who was not? Was it God punishing them for being too worldly?

All these thoughts crowded into Sadie's mind like a rampage of fear and anxiety, until she remembered Dorothy's prayer. It rose in its power and light, pushing back the onslaught of fear and panic.

Yes, God, please help us, bless us with wisdom and understanding for each other. For Mark, for Anna, for us all.

To get at the reason she hated her body, Anna would need compassion and understanding, but she would also need a firm hand. Should Mam be the one to deal with Anna?

So many problems, so many decisions.

✿ ✡ ✿

It was only at work the following week that Sadie found a measure of peace. It came by way of Bertie Orthman, of all people, the aging gardener and veteran of a troubled life.

She was emptying a large dishpan of potato peelings into the compost bin beside the lily bed, when Bertie's balding head protruded from the window, followed by his arm holding a steaming mug of tea. He was chortling with glee.

"Come here, Sadie girl. Lookee what I got. My old bones is starting to ache about this time of the year, and nothing helps like a hot cup of tea with milk and sugar. Join me?"

Sadie looked over her shoulder, wondering if Dorothy was expecting her.

Bertie saw and hissed, "Come on. That old bat don't need to watch every move you make. She ain't the boss. Richard Caldwell is, and a right good one he is, too. Can't really put my finger on it, but he's made the biggest change in his life I ever seen. His heart's in the right place. It is. I ain't much for talkin' about the Lord, but he's not the way he used to be. One of life's mysteries. You don't always understand the way things work, so you just take the good with the bad, sorta sift through it."

He paused, waving his hand toward the door. "Come on."

Sadie entered the garden shed, her eyes adjusting to the dim interior. It was as clean as Dorothy's kitchen, every tool on its own hook, every insecticide and fertilizer in its own container labeled with blue tape. An electric hot plate took up one side of a small counter where a red teakettle bubbled merrily.

"This is so cute, Bertie!"

He beamed with Sadie's praise as they each sipped a mug of thick, fragrant tea. When the subject turned to Dorothy, Bertie smiled and declared confidently that if Dorothy ever became a widow, he would marry her in no time flat.

"A heart of gold, that's what she has. You know, people aren't always the way they seem. She's had a rough life. Her past is likely one of the most pitiful stories ever. She came through with flying colors, that girl did. Her dad was the town drunk, and she was beaten nearly every night. But she's smart enough to know that you can't blame other people for your past. You gotta make the best of it. She's feisty, and so she came through, so she did."

Is that how it was? Could people turn out all right, no

matter how mistreated they were?

She wanted to tell Bertie everything about Mark, then decided against it. It wasn't fair to Mark. He had confided solely in her, and she would not betray his trust.

But why did she care? Why? Especially after that abominable display of immaturity? It was all his foolish jealousy, his … his… She didn't know what.

Her miserable train of thought was derailed by Bertie's soothing voice.

"Yes, life ain't all roses. But them blessings, the good stuff, is all you need to take with you. You can get all tangled up in the thorns if you want to. Wallow in 'em for a little while, and all you do is hurt yourself. Jes' look at them two kids Dorothy took in. They don't understand what happened with their mama. They don't try and figger it out neither. They cried awhile, but they know that right now, Dorothy's their mama. Ain't it amazing, Sadie?"

Sadie nodded, smiling a smile that was less than genuine.

Bertie saw and nodded his head.

"You got troubles of your own, Sadie girl. That smile is playin' with shadows, as Mum used to say. It'll work out, it'll work out. The Man Above works it out. All you gotta do is wait. It'll be okay in the end."

Sadie thanked him for the tea. Her spirits definitely lifted as she made her way up the flagstone path to the kitchen. Patience. She would wait on the Lord, who would renew her strength, as the Bible said.

Chapter 16

THE FIRST SNOW OF THE SEASON DROVE IN HARD, icy little pellets that made pinging noises against the windows to the north. The lowered sky was gray-white, the air filled with the whirling iciness.

Inside the Miller house, the wood stove in the living room cracked and popped, the good, dry oak logs burning cheerily, the flames dancing against the glass front. The braided rug in front of the stove was charred in places where a hot coal had fallen out as Dat was loading up the stove with logs. He always muttered under his breath and stomped on the burning coal when it fell. Mam said it was better to ruin a rug than her hardwood floor. Mam kept the wide floorboards polished and varnished to perfection. She mopped that floor with a dry mop and furniture polish and got down on her hands and knees to wash it gently with vinegar water. Mam even had rules about moving furniture across it: the furniture had to be put on a thick rug that slid smoothly across the floorboards, so there'd be no scratch marks left behind. That hardwood floor was the one thing in which she admitted having pride.

Sadie sat in the big, brown recliner, a cotton throw across her knees, a box of tissues on the propane light stand with a few crumpled ones strewn across it. She had just come home from work at the ranch, putting in a whole day of overtime by working on Saturday. Her head cold made the day drag on and on. Dorothy was nursing a sore hip, so there had been very little love lost between them: Sadie coughing, sneezing, and blowing her nose, Dorothy limping and complaining the whole day long.

The only bright spot of the day had been listening to Marcellus and Louis conversing in Spanish as they sat on the kitchen floor sorting through yard after yard of white Christmas lights. The children coiled them carefully in separate containers so that Bertie could hang them from the eaves, doors, and windows, and even drape them across shrubs and pines.

The children's voices were always low with a wonderful lilt, a sort of singsong to their sentences that flowed and rippled in a sweet cadence. Sadie never tired of the sound.

Dorothy believed the children had lived in a mansion rather than an ordinary home. They had talked of gold faucets, sunken bathtubs, and servants. Cooking, cleaning, ironing, and laundry was all done by someone who was not their mother.

Richard Caldwell had spoken wisely, saying the jewels had to be shown to the police. Meanwhile, he had taken them to his personal safe-deposit box at the bank. First of all, he said, there was the danger of receiving stolen goods, and secondly, if the children did come from a wealthy home, there was a chance they may have been kidnapped for ransom.

All of these uncertainties had made Dat and Mam cautious and skeptical, stoic in their reluctance to becoming involved. It was not their way. The wealthy children were of the English, and what future could they possibly have among the Amish? What if they did agree to give them a home, and then the children grew to adulthood, found their biological parents, and became torn between two cultures?

Dat and Mam assured Sadie they would never leave them out in the cold. If no one else offered to take them, they would, but only temporarily. Sadie was distraught, her face pale, showing the strain of events on the ranch.

"But Dat, think about it. We're supposed to be the Christians, full of charity, love, and all that good stuff. And here we are refusing them.

"You have a point, Sadie. You really do. We won't leave them abandoned."

Sadie lifted her tear-filled eyes. "I don't think they were abandoned. I think… I still wonder if someone didn't just… I don't know. It's just a big mystery, and it drives me crazy. They talk of a huge lawn, golf, servants, pools. Why would they appear at the ranch in dirty, pitiful clothes, with a small drawstring bag of jewels?"

Mam put a hand on Sadie's shoulder. "Sadie, it's good you're concerned. But you must be careful. Listen to your father. He's right. I still think the perfect arrangement is to let Dorothy have them. Dat said that's all Jim talked about when he took him to the horse sale last week."

Sadie nodded. As usual, she could place her trust in her parents' decision. When they were side by side like that, when God had a hand in Dat's and Mam stood beside him, you just had to reach out your own hand and place it in Mam's. They were so rock-solid.

So the mystery of the children remained a large question mark. Dorothy said "them jewels in the pouch" would stay in the vault at the bank, and if she died, it all went back to Marcelona and Louise, as she called the children. The jewels sure weren't hers, and she wanted no part of them. All she needed was that piece of paper that made her and Jim legal foster parents of those precious angels sent straight from God.

Sadie often marveled at the perfect way God had taken care of those adorable children, who, without a doubt, came from a very troubled background.

Sadie laid back in the recliner and closed her eyes. Her head was throbbing. As soon as the Tylenol began working effectively she would have to write to Daniel King. She had not replied to his letter, struggling with indecision, and she could not put it off any longer.

The thought of that whole situation increased the pain in her temple, and she groaned silently.

She had just drifted into that blissful state between waking and sleeping, when you are only half-aware of your surroundings, when everything is soft and warm and safe.

Suddenly, the door opened with a bang, followed by a much louder one as it was flung shut. Then an agitated, "Mam!"

Sadie grimaced, rolled her head to the side, and said hoarsely, "Mam's not here, Reuben."

"Where's Dat?"

"They went to an auction at the fire hall. Why didn't you go along?"

Reuben did not bother answering.

"It's just that... Oh, Sadie!"

That was all he could say before his white face crumpled and he began to cry little-boy tears. He rubbed his eyes, gulping and making a desperate attempt to stop the tears.

Sadie pulled on the lever at the side of the recliner and sat up with a thump. Concern for Reuben made her forget her headache for the moment.

"Reuben! What is it?"

He twisted his body to hide his face in a throw pillow on the couch, then sat up abruptly, tears streaking his cheeks with a brown smudges where his fists had rubbed them.

"Sadie! It's so awful! I…I had my BB gun. I was shooting sparrows. You know Mam doesn't want those sparrows at the feeder?"

Sadie nodded, "Go on."

"Well, a flock of starlings flew behind the barn, and I guess I lost track of where I was, and before I realized it, I was in the horse pasture.

"I let Charlie out this afternoon because he kept carrying on so bad in his stall, and I thought he might settle down if he got some exercise. I got down to the lower pasture, and… Sadie! He's dead! Just exactly like Cody."

The last words were a sort of despairing scream, hoarse with fear and disbelief.

"I heard the shot. I saw them. They saw me. As soon as they saw me, they took off, but their car got stuck in a ravine. A little ditch.

"Sadie, I was never so scared in all my life. I had to take that chance. It was too late for poor Charlie, but I had to try to catch that license-plate number."

"Reuben, you didn't!"

"I did. I ran without thinking, taking the chance that they wouldn't shoot people. Boys.

"I was running so fast, the snow hurt my face. It's all a blur. They sat there, spinning their tires, revving the motor, but nothing happened. I kept running. One of the men jumped out, swearing and yelling, waving his arms. Then he leaned all his weight against the car. He was big and fat. Really heavy."

"The car? Wasn't it a blue pickup?"

Reuben shook his head.

"It was a low black car. One of those crazy ones. The fat man saw me then, got back in the car. The wheels spun and spun and spun. Blue smoke came out, and that's when I thought I wouldn't be able to get the license number. Because of the smoke. Then I saw it. As plain as day."

He paused, his face a mixture of painful fear and accomplishment.

"You're not going to believe this. It was one of those license plates that has words, whatever you call them. Special ones, where people spell names or nicknames."

Sadie nodded, leaned forward, her eyes intently on Reuben's face.

"What is it?"

"If I have it right, it's T-R-A-D-R, then a space, and J-O."

"Trader Joe?" Sadie asked.

"That's what it said."

"Oh, my goodness. Oh, my, Reuben. We have to get Dat. We have to contact the authorities. The police have to find these men. I'll call a driver, okay?"

She got out of the recliner in spite of a pounding headache and another fit of coughing. Catching her breath, she asked Reuben to go out to the pasture and make sure Charlie really was dead and not suffering alone in the snow.

Reuben shook his head, but obeyed without another word.

✿ ✿ ✿

The driver came quickly and took Sadie and Reuben to the fire hall where a lively quilt auction was being held. They found Dat without any trouble, and the news spread like wildfire.

The police arrived and questioned Reuben, who stood with his beanie pulled low on his forehead and his blue denim coat hanging open, the collar of his green shirt frayed and crooked.

Even so, his face was clean, his blue eyes direct and honest, and for a young Amish boy, he was very well-spoken. He stood by Dat and Sadie, explaining exactly what had happened in great detail. He politely addressed the uniformed police officers with a quiet, "No, sir" or "Yes, sir."

Sadie was impressed by her brother's fortitude and composure in the face of such a shocking event. Reuben was clear, articulate, and highly believable in his forth-right manner. He did not hide anything; neither was there any grandiose embellishment. It was a simple, truthful story explained clearly by a young boy. The police had no reason to doubt his honesty.

The police drove Dat, Sadie, and Reuben to the scene of the crime in the back of the police car. Reuben's eyes darted constantly from the leather holsters containing gleaming pistols, to the computer and the electronic gadgets on the dashboard, to the hats and gold wrist-watches they wore. He missed nothing at all.

True to Reuben's words, they found Charlie lying on his side, stretched out in the cold snow, his faithful life as a buggy horse over.

A huge lump welled in Sadie's throat as she remembered another time, another place, with Jim and Nevaeh—and seeing Mark Peight for the first time.

She swallowed her tears and felt sorry for Dat, who was struggling with his emotions as well. A driving horse was a close companion, that was the thing. There was a bond between horse and driver that didn't break easily. When the horse died, it was like losing a dear and close pet.

Charlie had been especially faithful with his plodding, steady gait. He started running and stopped readily when commanded. He never balked and seldom shied away from 18-wheelers or trucks with flapping canvas tarps or obnoxious motorcycles. He just took it all in stride and trotted right along.

Even in winter, Charlie was as sure-footed as a mule or a donkey. You could close both buggy windows, fasten them securely, and hold loosely to the reins through the small rectangular openings.

With Charlie, a buggy ride was relaxing. You could put your feet up on the dashboard, let the reins hang loose, and sing along to the steady clapping of his hooves. You could eat an ice cream cone with one hand and drive with the other, or if the ice cream dripped, you could hold the reins between your knees while you cleaned up the mess with a napkin.

If ever there was a horse you could describe as good, Charlie was it.

Sadie got down on her knees and stroked Charlie's neck, arranging the coarse black hair of his mane just so. The icy pellets of snow were already accumulating in the heavy brown hairs of his side, their staying a stark reminder of the lack of warmth, of life, within his body.

"Goodbye, Charlie. Thanks for all the good times," she whispered brokenly.

She looked up to see Reuben and Dat shaking hands with the policemen. She got up, and all three stood together, the silence a comfort that needed no words.

They turned to go in unison, their heads bent, shuffling softly through the snow. Their heads were bent with acceptance of another act of God in their lives. It didn't make sense, but they accepted it and bore it stoically.

A high whinny brought them back to reality.

Paris! Sadie had almost forgotten about her. Now Paris would be terribly lonely. She would whinny and whinny all day long, a relentless cry for Charlie to come back to her.

"Hear that, Dat? She's going nuts!" Sadie said, anxiety in her voice.

Dat nodded. "We have to get another horse immediately. Can't go to church on Sunday if we don't."

"Where will you get one?"

"They have that sale in Bath every month. Don't trust them, though. Too many drugged horses there."

That was how they found themselves at the livestock auction in Critchfield the following Friday evening. Jesse Troyer told Dat there were going to be a few of Owen Weaver's drivers there.

Clapping his shoulder the way he always did, laughing along with his words, Jesse had told Dat the local hearsay was that Owen was as honest as the day was long, only his days were just a bit shorter than most.

Dat had shaken his head at Jesse's generosity of spirit.

"You know, Jake, at the end of the day, we all have to make a living, and if Owen wants to tweak a few ends here or there, that's his choice. He's a horse-dealer, Amish or not."

There were as many Amish folks as English at the auction, Sadie decided. Or almost.

The acrid smell of the sawdust mingled with horse smells, dust, and burning charcoal-broiled burgers from the cheaply paneled kitchen, along with the sounds of squawking chickens and bleating sheep. It was all the part of the quintessential country auction.

Sadie loved a lively animal auction. Being seated high up on the elevated rows of built-in chairs was the closest she would ever come to sitting in the bleachers of a ball game, an event strictly forbidden by their *ordnung*. Amish usually did not attend organized sports, whether as viewers or as participants. The auction, however, was permitted as necessary to buy a good driving horse.

Many of the older men came to the auction barn in Critchfield almost every week. It was their source of entertainment, something to look forward to after a week on the job. They ate their cheeseburgers and french fries, drank strong coffee, and visited with the grizzled old farmers and ranchers. They watched the sales of various animals, listened to the local gossip, then returned home to their wives who clucked in consternation over their quilts or embroidery as their husbands related all the good stories to them.

Small children hid shyly behind their fathers' trouser legs, but older ones ran loose, clinging to gates like little squirrels in their agility, running across corridors, laughing and shouting, their faces sticky with the lolli-pops, Nerds, and packets of Skittles they consumed.

Sadie knew their mothers, who prided themselves on their housekeeping and child-rearing abilities, would be shocked to see their faces sticky with the sugary treats they bought at the counter, their hands dirty from holding yet another baby lamb or goat. The indulging fathers, on the other hand, took no notice, often busily engaged in conversations with friends.

The auctioneer's voice rose and fell, amplified to crash-ing proportions by the loudspeakers on the wall. He sold baby rabbits, roosters, hens, geese, and ducks, followed by hordes of frightened, bleating sheep and goats.

That was the part Sadie did not like. The men who herded them into the sales ring cracked their heavy whips above the terrified animals' heads, creating a sort of panic in them. Their eyes became wide with fright as they tried to scale the wooden walls.

Why did they have to crack a whip at all? Simply to show their inhumane authority, that was all. She often felt like going down there and yanking that beastly whip out of their hands and flinging it on them to see how they liked it. The whip should not be allowed. A good border collie or a simple herding stick would do the job just as well, she felt sure. She sighed with relief when the last baby lamb disappeared through the steel gate.

The auctioneer took a hefty swig of his warm Moun-tain Dew and began to talk about horses. The horse auc-tion began with a team of magnificent Belgians, led by Owen Weaver himself. His portly frame looked shorter than ever, dwarfed by the huge beasts on either side of him.

He took the microphone and expounded expertly on the unequaled merits of these fine horses. His flowery descriptions of the animals showed he was obviously a veteran horse-seller. As his words flowed, Sadie grinned to herself, remembering Jesse Troyer's comment to her father. Surely Owen's day wasn't very long at this auction.

The team was sold for $6,000, but no one could tell if Owen was pleased or not. No emotion showed on his blank face. A true professional, that one.

A black Percheron was sold after that, followed by a string of driving horses. Sadie caught Dat's eye, and he gave her a thumbs-up signal accompanied by a hearty wink. She raised her eyes with a questioning look. Dat answered by jutting his chin toward the gate. Sadie turned in time to see Mark Peight riding Chester.

The whole auction barn seemed to tilt at an angle, and everything went black, but only for a moment. She was unaware of Dat's bidding, of the auctioneer's voice, of Anna and Reuben bouncing up and down with glee when Dat bought the black gelding they wanted him to buy.

Why was Mark selling Chester?

When the gate opened, Chester pranced out. Mark held him back. He looked relaxed, leaning back on the horse, one hand on his thigh. He eased him into a perfect canter, then a trot, moving as one with his horse.

The bidding escalated. The auctioneer's helpers stepped out, stretched their arms, and yelled piercing cries of "Ye-ep!" each time a bidder nodded his head. When the sum reached $5,000 the crowd erupted into whistles and applause. Sadie felt goose bumps on her arms and tears pricking her eyes.

Oh, Mark!

She knew then that she had to talk to him. At the very least, she had to let him see her and watch the reaction on his face. It would be easier to know if he hated her than to not know how he felt at all. If he rejected her, it would be her final answer. Then she could reply to Daniel King's letter.

On shaking, unsteady legs, she got up and excused herself as she wedged past the crowd of bidders. Biting down hard on her lower lip, she ran down the remaining stairs, hurried to the right and up the steep wooden steps lending to the horse pens.

She didn't notice the smell of hay or the rancid odor of fresh manure. She only knew she had to see Mark.

He was leading Chester, a girl in jeans with blond hair hanging to her waist following him. He listened to what she was saying, a smile on his face, as he tied Chester in a pen with two other horses.

Sadie hung back, afraid. She twisted her burgundy-colored apron in her hand. She smoothed her hair, lifted her chin, and stepped out.

"Mark!" Her voice cracked, and she hastily cleared her throat. She called him again.

"Mark!"

He stopped and looked in her direction. As if in a dream, his eyes found hers. What was the expression in them? Yes. It was anger. He hated her, wanted nothing to do with her.

Then…oh…then…his brown eyes lightened, and he came toward her. His mouth widened into a soft grin of welcome. The light in his eyes was not hatred; it wasn't even annoyance or disappointment. But, oh, wonder of wonders, he was overjoyed to see her!

He didn't stop until he had wrapped her firmly in his arms, bent over her, murmuring words of endearment into her ear. Her ribs hurt with the pressure of his hugs, and she suddenly became aware of her surroundings.

"Mark. Mark! Someone will see."

"Let them."

"Mark, please, let me go."

He did, then stepped back, looked deeply into her eyes and said, "I'm sorry."

That was all, but it was enough. It was more than enough. It was a treasure chest filled to overflowing with precious gold coins worth much more than anything Sadie had ever owned. She was rich, wealthy beyond measure. God had provided the answer she so desperately sought.

He was only human. His apology was his way of taking responsibility for his own actions. He did not blame his mother or his father, his past, anyone, or anything. He had done wrong, he knew it, and he repented. The coins in the treasure chest of this love glittered and sparkled.

The blond-haired girl stood awkwardly at the gate, annoyance written all over her face. She cleared her throat, a nasty twang to her voice as she said, "Excuse me?"

Mark apologized, politely showed her out, then returned to Sadie's side.

"We need to talk."

"You want a greasy, sloppy, burned cheeseburger?" she asked.

He laughed. Oh, that beautiful sound! Then he caught her hand in his and took her to a stained table at the top of the stairs, in the smoky, plastic-paneled dining room of the food stand.

They took huge bites from the cheeseburgers, that were slathered with heavy mayonnaise, thick slices of tomato, dill pickle, onion, and lettuce, and served on cheap white rolls. They shared an order of greasy steak fries loaded with salt, pepper, and ketchup, wiping the excess off their faces with lots of thin paper napkins from the smudged holder against the wall.

He talked a lot. More than she had ever heard him. It seemed as if that one, solitary "I'm sorry" had opened a floodgate of goodness. But he confessed he still had a difficult time with trust.

"I just go a bit crazy when I think you are attracted to someone else, even if you say you love me. I'm sure my mother told my father that she loved him many times, and he believed her. That's what terrifies me. I'm afraid that I will give my heart to you, and that you'll hurt me, just like I've always been hurt. I trust no one, least of all, you. It's awful having to tell you these things, but I hope you understand why I overreacted to situations that normal guys can just shrug off."

Sadie nodded.

Later he would tell her that he had never loved her more than at that moment when she nodded, quietly understanding and accepting his insecurities, his *bupplich* attitude. Her love was the strongest chain he had ever had to hang onto, especially when the quicksand of his past threatened to submerge him yet again.

People of every kind came up to their table to talk to them. They smiled politely, endured the needless chatter, but were eager for everyone to let them alone.

It was Owen Weaver himself who told them that Fred Ketty had spread the rumor that they had broken up. She was in town and saw them eating ice cream together.

On her way home again, Sadie was sitting by herself at the same table. She figured they had an argument and stopped the friendship. So Owen had to look twice to see if it was Jake's Sadie sitting there with Mark.

Mark was at a loss for words, but Sadie rescued him smoothly, saying Mark had to move his horse from the hitching rack, which was the truth.

Owen shifted the toothpick in his mouth, scratched his rotund stomach, and laughed good-naturedly.

"Ah, that Fred Ketty. She's a sharp one. You have to give her that. Between yard sales and the Laundromat in town, she sees a'plenty, now, don't she?"

He clapped a thick hand on Mark's shoulder, rattling the ice in his glass of Coke. Mark grabbed his glass, held on to it firmly, not daring to take another sip with the affable Owen ready to pound his shoulder at any moment.

"So why are you selling that horse of yours, Mark? He's a beauty."

Mark grimaced, then slid over in the booth, turning his upper body to see Owen better. Also, Sadie guessed, to get out from under the descending, good-natured hand clapping on his shoulder at regular intervals.

"I have too many. It's turning into a habit. I come to the horse sale and think I have to buy one."

Owen's toothpick fell out when he grinned widely, nodding his head until his hat slid sideways. "I can see it. I can see it! Young man like you, a paycheck and no wife to spend it. Ah, enjoy your horses. Soon enough you won't be able to afford it with a good wife and a buggy-load of youngsters to take care of that paycheck."

He gave Sadie a meaningful wink. She would gladly have slid under the table and stayed there.

Mark and Sadie continued to talk into the evening. It was only when a seriously worried Anna came through the door, her face pale and her eyes burning with unshed tears, that Sadie remembered the rest of her family. She clapped a hand to her mouth and gasped.

"Anna! Over here!"

Anna was so relieved, she sagged into the booth beside Sadie and laid her head on her shoulder.

"Where in the world did you go? Dat is frantic!"

"She's with me," Mark said, smiling. "She's with her boyfriend."

Anna sat straight up, clearly flustered.

"You guys are just different. One day you're happy, and the next day you're ... whatever."

Mark laughed, and Sadie put her arm warmly around Anna's shoulders, hugging her close.

Chapter 17

SADIE WROTE TO DANIEL KING ON A PLAIN WHITE sheet of notebook paper, telling him in the kindest way she could about her relationship with Mark. She felt quite sure Lancaster County was full of girls he could date. He was close to his family, so it was likely best for him to stay and move on with his life.

That winter proved to be the turning point in her relationship with Mark. They went to hymn singings and supper crowds where the youth would assemble and visit. They spent Saturday evenings with other couples, most often Kevin and Leah. And when they went on dates alone, they stayed up and talked for hours.

Sadie slowly adjusted to Mark's personality. There were times when he withdrew into a dark place inside himself, and he didn't speak unless she spoke first. Even then, his answers were curt, accusing, as if she had done something to make him feel so down. No amount of questioning or pleading made any difference. These times were when he felt lowest about himself, and if she tried to talk him out of it, he only pulled her down with him. So she learned to leave him alone at such moments.

He had never promised her the relationship would be easy, but was it always going to be this way?

Anna lost weight all winter long, a strange flush in her cheeks every evening. She was taller than Rebekah now and nearly as tall as Sadie. None of her dresses fit anymore, so the girls helped Mam to sew new ones for her.

Sadie spent hours discussing Anna's problem with Mam and her sisters, but everyone had a different opinion, so nothing was ever resolved.

Mam maintained her stance that as long as Anna kept a reasonable weight, ate good, healthy food, what was the harm? Everyone ate the occasional doughnut and wished they hadn't.

Leah tended to side with Mam. Rebekah thought she should be taken to the same doctor that had made such a wonderful difference in Mam's life.

Too much money. No insurance.

What about the money they received for finding the stolen horses?

Mam's hospital bill.

What about the rest of it?

It was Sadie's.

And on and on, with no real conclusion.

Sadie still felt the same. Anna needed a horse. So did Reuben. If Dat didn't do anything by springtime, then she would take matters into her own hands.

Sadie noticed the change in Anna just as spring arrived. The reason she remembered was because it was the same day that she first heard the Chinook.

Dat called it that. It was the first warm air of spring, blowing from the south so softly it was barely noticeable. The light sighing sound was nature's way of breaking down the long icicles that hung from the eaves. It would still take weeks and weeks for the Chinook to wear down the snowdrifts.

Sadie did not sleep well the night she heard the Chinook. Mark had gone home early from their date, but that wasn't what kept her awake. It was the steady dripping of the melting icicles that kept her up all night.

She would have loved to burrow into her pillows, pull the comforter up over her head, and sleep until dinnertime. She was tired, cold, and in no mood to sit on a hard bench for three hours or be stuffed in the surrey with all her sisters and Reuben.

She burned her fingers on the broiler pan when she retrieved the toast and snarled at Anna because of it. Mam scolded her in clipped tones, telling her to stop taking out her foul mood on Anna.

Her dippy egg was undercooked, and Sadie swallowed her nausea as she pushed the plate away. Mam never finished a dippy egg properly. More nausea pushed at her throat as she watched Mam dip a corner of her toast into a glob of swimming egg white. Maybe she should make her own eggs from now on.

Dat slurped his coffee in the most annoying way, and Reuben dumped almost the whole plastic container of strawberry jam on his toast. He laid the sticky knife on the tablecloth and promptly set his elbow on top of it. He devoured almost half the toast in one bite. That was the last straw.

"This family has the most indecent table manners," Sadie said tartly, wincing at the sour taste of orange juice in her mouth.

Dat and Mam looked at her with surprise, Anna ducked her head in embarrassment, but Reuben shoved the remainder of his toast in his mouth and blurted, "Sour old maid!"

"I am not an old maid," she fired back.

"Why doesn't Mark marry you then?" Reuben asked, victory shining from his eyes.

Sadie swallowed her anger, gathered all her common sense and Christian virtue—it was Sunday morning, after all—and told Reuben that he'd better get ready for church.

✶ ✡ ✶

Her mood lifted when she entered the *kessle-haus* and her friends greeted her with warm hugs and girl talk. This was a part of her world that she so often forgot to appreciate, she knew.

The girls walked to their seats, and a few minutes later, the boys came in and sat on the opposite side of the shop, facing the girls.

The singing began, the voices ebbing and flowing as they always did. Out of the corner of her eye, Sadie noticed Emery Hershberger's Leon leaning a bit to the left, looking at something, then correcting his posture again.

At 15, he was turning into quite an attractive young man, with a tall, easy gait, wide shoulders, and auburn hair. He used to be a heavy-set red-haired boy with a spattering of freckles and a loud, obnoxious voice. Now, his hair had turned darker and his complexion settled into a smooth, healthy color. He certainly was not the boy he used to be. Why hadn't she noticed that before?

Leon leaned over again, and this time Sadie leaned forward ever so slightly to see the object of his attention. Her eyes traveled Leon's line of vision, and she nearly gasped aloud.

Anna!

Her head was bowed demurely, the way it should have been, but there was a decided blush coloring her wan cheeks. Her thick lashes swept them as she kept her eyes downcast, her brown hair swept up in a thick, shining mass below her white covering. Her dress was the color of the ferns that grew beneath the pines on the ridge, a woodland color that complemented Anna's complexion.

Oh, my Anna! My dear little insecure sister. You are growing up, blossoming into a maiden of the forest, right beneath our eyes. A beautiful young girl, unnoticed for so long, with all the attention going to your older sisters.

Sadie could barely look at Leon. She was an intruder, an outsider who had no business looking for any sign between them, and yet, she couldn't help but see what was so painfully evident.

Ah, Anna. You're not yet 16. So innocent and unspoiled, so pitifully sure you're overweight and ugly.

What was best?

Sadie felt old and a bit careworn at that moment. It seemed as if she and Mark were an outdated grocery item to be taken off the shelf and replaced with a fresh one.

She grinned, then bent her head. Boy, wouldn't that get Mark all fired up when she told him?

✿ ✡ ✿

That afternoon, when Mark stopped at the porch to pick up Sadie, his horse and buggy as immaculate as always, she greeted him lightheartedly. It was a wondrous thing to be so happy and confident in their relationship. She marveled at the natural way they could be together, even at the simple act of climbing into the buggy and sitting beside him. That intimacy was a privilege. They talked easily now, with no self-consciousness—words, expressions, smiles, a familiar part of their lives.

The first thing she told him was about Leon Hershberger and Anna. Mark raised his eyebrows, smiling. Sadie never tired of his smile. When they were 80 years old, that smile would still amaze her. However, it didn't stay. The horse plodded on gaily, but a sort of coldness crept over the buggy's interior.

Sadie talked on, then watched him a bit uncomfortably before blurting out, "Is there … something wrong?"

He said nothing.

Then after wiping the wooden dashboard of the buggy with his handkerchief, he cleared his throat.

"My mother wrote me a letter."

His words had the impact of a sledgehammer. Sadie went cold all over. She became numb, then senseless, blinded by blackness for a second, before her heart began to beat again, but harder.

Oh, no. Now what?

They'd come so far. Would it all be stripped away now?

She knew there would be no easy way out of this. Dread in all its forms hovered over her. His whole past would be flung in his face yet again, this time in physical form.

Oh, dear God, look upon us with mercy. *Barmherzikeit*.

Her voice was very small when she said, "And? What did she write?"

Mark's hand reached over and pulled at the handle of the small wooden door built into the dashboard. It was a place in the buggy to put lighters, small flashlights, clean handkerchiefs, or tissues. It was the catchall for necessities, like a vehicle's glove compartment. Sadie thought it could rightfully be called a glove compartment, as there was almost always a pair of gloves in the back of it. You had to wear gloves to drive a horse in cold weather, especially if it was an unruly one, opening the window for better control.

He handed her a plain white envelope, saying nothing, his jaw set in that firm line.

She looked at him, questioning.

"Go ahead. Read it."

With shaking hands, she removed the letter from the envelope and unfolded it. Just an ordinary sheet of writing paper. There was no date or return address. The handwriting was cursive, neat, the type many Amish teachers teach their pupils.

> *Mark,*
>
> *I got wind of where you live through the Internet, an object of the devil for you, but a necessity for me. IIA.*

Sadie's eyebrows turned down. She looked at Mark. "Wow."

Mark remained still, a statue of control.

> *I'm still out in the world and I plan on staying here. My kids are scattered all over. They know who I am, but they don't care about me. I guess I deserve that, I don't know. You're the only one I can't find. You are the oldest of the pack.*
>
> *What a bunch of kids I had! Have had almost as many husbands. I'm on number four. Married this guy for his money. Can't stand him. I can't sleep at night, have to take all kinds of junk to put me to sleep.*

I want to see you. Sure hope you're not Amish. Are you married? If you are, bring your wife.

This is my home phone number. Please call soon.

I still do love you, you know. At least I wrote now, to let you know I care.

Your mother,
Amelia Van Syoc

Sadie folded the letter slowly and put it neatly into the envelope. She smoothed the dust blanket over her knees before daring to look at Mark. His expression remained unreadable.

Carefully, she laid a hand on his arm, then slid it underneath his arm and laid her head on his shoulder, tears forming beneath her eyelids.

She just could not imagine. How could his own mother, his flesh and blood, be so callous?

Slowly, Mark put down the reins, turned, and crushed her to him. He held her as if she was his only hope of rescue, the single life preserver in a swollen sea, where dark troughs of rolling water threatened to take him down into the awful abyss of his past.

Sadie slid her arms around his wide shoulders, willing him to know that she would remain by his side where she belonged. She would help him to keep his head above water during the rough times.

He groaned, a broken cry, then kissed her with a new intensity.

"I love you so much, Sadie," he said hoarsely as tears fell on the shoulder of her black woolen coat.

"I love you, too, Mark. I love you more with each passing day."

He gathered up the reins, then laughed quietly as he wiped his face.

"Good thing Eclipse keeps trotting right along, isn't it?"

"He's a good horse," Sadie replied, slipping her hand into his. She loved holding Mark's hand. He had perfect hands, she thought.

"So now, what will you do?" she asked quietly.

"Nothing for now. I want to pray about it, think about it. I have no clue where she is. If I go see her and she sees I'm Amish, she might shut the door in my face."

"I'll go with you," Sadie said instantly.

"You will?"

"Yes."

Yes, she would go. He needed her beside him every step of the way to support and encourage him. She would follow him to the ends of the earth.

He kissed her passionately again, and Sadie realized their love had reached a new level that brought another whole set of concerns. She must talk to Mark about their physical interactions, but she hardly knew how to open the subject without causing serious damage to his feelings—and his ego.

Dat and Mam had talked to her about their concerns, knowing Sadie and Mark did not hold to the strict code of distant courtship. Sadie was the oldest daughter, and they trusted her conscience, but dating is dating. They, too, had been through those years and knew the intimacy of late nights together. Like many couples, they struggled to remain pure until the day they married.

"Things are changing, Sadie," Mam began on the day she and Dat sat down with their oldest daughter. "Over a hundred years ago, we held with the practice of 'bundling,' or sharing a bed fully clothed, under a comforter or quilt, to stay warm on cold winter evenings. This practice stayed in one form or another in some communities, even in some families. Some groups of concerned parents worked hard to eliminate it altogether; others adhered strictly to the old ways.

"There's a lot of pressure in our community to practice complete distant courtship, the way the higher churches do. Some of the New Orders have a much stricter dating code than we do. And it's worrisome to me. Even though we drive horses and buggies, our moral standards are more like the English than some of the people who leave our community and choose to drive cars. Some who leave for the New Orders have higher morality than we do, yet we're the so-called conservatives."

Dat nodded in agreement as Sadie listened carefully to Mam's words.

Sadie could only be perfectly honest about her feelings. "Do you both agree that absolutely no touching, not even holding hands, is what God intends?" she asked.

Her parents were clearly uncomfortable with that question.

Finally, Dat spoke up. "I can't imagine it."

Mam quickly broke in, "It's what everyone says they want now. It's the new, better way of dating."

Sadie bent her head. She was embarrassed to speak the truth to her parents, but she told them that she and Mark kissed and held each other but did nothing further. Her face flamed with the confession.

Her parents were full of understanding. And in Dat's eyes, was that a twinkle of knowing?

"Then let your conscience be your guide," Mam said. "You know when it's time to stop. Probably the perfect way would be to remain distant."

"I disagree," Sadie said firmly.

Mam was taken aback and watched Sadie's face intently.

"I do. I don't feel guilty for the things we've done, but I know I will soon if it goes any further."

Dat threw his shoulders back and laughed, releasing the tension. Now they were just Mam and Dat and Sadie. Honest. Completely comfortable. Not false or competing to see who could be the best Christian.

"We are who we are, and each man must answer for what he allows himself to do," Dat said. "It's between you and Mark and God."

Sadie knew she had to approach Mark about this subject, but she also knew that now was not the time, not after the letter from his mother he had just shown her. He was so delicate with things pertaining to his ego, his sense of well-being.

She held his hand and entwined her fingers in his. Their love was a wonderful gift from God and the single best thing that had ever happened to her.

✼ ✪ ✼

The police department's search for the snipers had come to a dead end. The license plate led to a stolen car. There were no fingerprints, no leads to pursue, only the same brick wall they always came up against.

For the rest of the winter, there had been no shootings. Most of the Amish argued that it was too cold to be out and too dangerous to make a getaway on the slippery roads. At any rate, a sense of safety pervaded the community, and people relaxed as they got out their horses and buggies to go to town, visit, or travel to church. Would that change now that spring was on the way?

Richard Caldwell shook his gray head, his neatly trimmed mustache bobbing as he warned everyone it was a lull in the storm, that the worst was yet to come.

"They're mad. They're out for revenge, and they're not giving up any time soon, you mark my words," he told anyone who would listen.

The kitchen work at the ranch had been almost more than Dorothy and Sadie could handle, especially last Christmas. There had been parties, showers, and dinners all winter long, with little Sadie Elizabeth the center of her doting parents' extravagances.

Dorothy was not happy with all the plans Barbara Caldwell was making but knew that if she wanted to keep her job, she better keep her mouth shut.

Richard Caldwell expanded the ranch. He hired an additional five men to build bigger pole barns for hay and equipment. He increased the size of the cattle herd, and he added sheep to his financial ventures, which brought in every relative Lothario Bean could find to work at the ranch.

They cooked large meals for all the ranch hands and work crews, until one day Dorothy threw her hands in the air, marched into Richard Caldwell's office, and told him that they needed another person in the kitchen, and if he didn't get one, she was going to up and quit right there.

While Dorothy argued with the boss, Sadie remained in the kitchen, peeling potatoes and keeping a low profile. She smiled to herself and wondered how it was going in the office. Dorothy really lost her temper this time.

Sadie looked up as they came through the swinging doors of the kitchen. Dorothy's face was the color of salami, her eyes spitting blue sparks. Richard Caldwell looked somber, every inch the gentleman. He was holding Sadie Elizabeth, who was wearing a little pair of Levi's with a plaid shirt, already dressing for a life on the ranch.

The look in Richard Caldwell's eyes gave Sadie goose bumps. What a father this oversized, noisy, uncouth man had become. Little Sadie had molded him into a gentle, devoted daddy.

She had her own puppy already, a little brown dust mop that shed hair over everything, which made more housework for Sadie. It was the sad story of the stray dog that Richard Caldwell had buried when he was a boy that brought the little brown puppy. He was striving to be a good father in every respect, not wanting to make the same mistakes his father had made in the past.

Barbara Caldwell wasn't fond of Isabel, as the dog was named, but she didn't complain as long as Sadie kept the rooms vacuumed. That was part of the reason Dorothy had marched into his office.

"Dorothy says she's quitting."

"Is she?" Sadie asked, laughing as she put down a wet potato and paring knife. After drying her hands on her apron, she reached for little Sadie Elizabeth.

"She says so. Unless I get more help. You know of any Amish girls looking for a job? One of your sisters?"

"Anna. But she works at the farmer's market."

"No friends either?"

"Uh...I think...there's Erma Keim. She's almost 30, never married, a real workhorse. She was looking for more a little while ago."

So that was how Erma Keim began working at the ranch, opening a whole new chapter in the kitchen for Sadie and Dorothy.

Erma was a diesel engine of hard work. Her large, freckled hands flew, her long, sturdy limbs simply catapulted her from kitchen to dining room and back again. Even so, Erma had a rough start, not fitting in with the kitchen responsibilities—or with Dorothy—as Sadie had hoped. It might have been smoother for Erma if she had started off quietly, perhaps with a smidgen of humility. But no, Erma knew how to do everything and do it better than Dorothy, which was like setting fire to a long fuse that sizzled and crackled slowly. Sadie came to work everyday eyeing the burning fuse with caution, completely uncomfortable with Erma's loud voice.

On her second day, Erma said Dorothy's sausage gravy could be much improved, although she'd never eaten a better biscuit. On the third day, she asked why they never served breakfast pizza. It was a huge favorite at Erma's house.

Dorothy had been making frequent trips to the restroom all morning. Sadie knew her constitution was way off, which spelled serious trouble for Erma if she kept on talking about Dorothy's food.

Suddenly, Dorothy had enough. She threw her balled fists on her hips and said loudly, "I've been here for 30-some years, and you've barely been here that many hours. I know what the men like and what they don't, and I highly doubt that your newfangled pizza would be appreciated."

That shut Erma up. She started scrubbing the wall behind the stove, muttering to herself and casting poisonous looks in Dorothy's direction. But now she knew where she stood in the pecking order, though she contested it every chance she got.

"Why don't you ever serve dinner rolls?"

"Men don't want them little bitty rolls. They want a thick slice of bread they can latch onto."

When she suggested changing the pancake recipe, Sadie put a warning finger to her lips and sighed with relief when Erma let it go.

When Erma wasn't around, Dorothy complained to Sadie. "She ain't normal, that girl. Ain't no wonder she ain't got a husband. I wouldn't marry her either if I was an Amish man."

However, Erma made a friend for life when she struck up a conversation with swarthy little Lothario Bean and began discussing the merits of keeping eggs and the best way to build a good henhouse.

Sadie decided the human race was full of surprises and unlikely friendships at every turn.

Chapter 18

AND THEN, JUST LIKE THAT, REUBEN BONDED WITH another horse.

Reuben began suggesting he call a driver to go to Critchfield on Friday nights. Dat would grin behind his paper and ask Reuben what he wanted there. Reuben would say an ice cream cone at the food stand or a chicken at the animal sale. His answer never failed to bring a genuine laugh from Dat and a smile out of Reuben.

The horse was brown with a black mane and tail, just like Cody. The ears were small with a curve, giving him an intelligent look.

Reuben named this horse Moon. There was no particular reason for the name. He just liked to say "Giddup, Moon" or "Whoa, Moon." Reuben said it sounded professional.

The girls had a conversation about the merits of naming a horse Moon, but they agreed to keep quiet and never once mention anything to Reuben.

Reuben spent hours in the barn brushing, cutting and trimming the mane, and washing his saddle with the pungent saddle soap, humming under his breath all the while.

He spent a whole day cleaning the pens, getting fresh shavings from the feed man, throwing down hay, and sweeping every bit of it carefully into Moon's stall.

Sadie had never seen a horse as spoiled as Moon. He quickly became overfed and used to having his own way. When Moon had a mind to stay inside, Reuben could not get him out of the barn no matter how hard he tried.

He sidestepped and crow-hopped, snorted and lunged, until Sadie felt like using a riding whip on him, something she thoroughly disliked. Sadie clasped her hands until her knuckles were white.

Reuben usually handled a horse easily, but he had to be cautious when Moon was putting on a show like this. Reuben was clearly frustrated. His navy blue beanie slid around on his head, completely covering one eye. His nose was red from the stiff March breeze, and the snow wasn't helping matters at all.

"Just stop him," Sadie called out. Her commands were like throwing kerosene on a small fire.

Reuben hopped off the horse, grabbed the reins, and stalked over to Sadie, his eyes spitting his anger. "There you go, Miss Professional, you do it if you think you're better than me."

Sadie raised one hand, as if to take back her advice.

"Go! Get up on him and see what you can do!" he yelled, swiping angrily at a dripping icicle.

Sadie caught her breath as the icicle clattered to the concrete, shattering into a thousand fragments. Moon jerked his head, wheeled around, and tore the reins from Reuben's hand. He took off down the driveway at a gallop, his haunches gathering beneath him as he gained momentum.

Oh, no, Sadie thought.

"Now, look what you did!" Reuben shouted, clearly too upset to talk sense.

How would they catch this horse? He hadn't been here long enough to call this home. Where would he go?

"Reuben, come," Sadie called, already heading for the barn. "You can ride double with me. Come quickly. Hurry."

Sadie slipped the bridle over Paris' ears and swung herself up. Reuben followed without further urging, his arms sliding around her middle.

"You dressed warm enough?" Sadie asked over her shoulder.

"Yeah."

Paris was eager, needing little urging to run. There was no sight of Moon on the road. Sadie pulled back on the reins, then decided to go right. She urged Paris into an easy gallop, keeping her eyes on the road ahead for any sign of Moon tearing along.

As Paris' head bobbed, her mane flowed back in a cream-colored mass. Sadie always loved the sound of her pounding hooves on the macadam, that strong, rhythmic sound of power.

They searched open fields, woods, and ravines. Cars passed, curious drivers peered out at them, but they could find no sign of Moon.

As twilight deepened, Sadie realized they had traveled much farther than they should have. She reined Paris in.

"Reuben, I don't know if Moon turned in this direction. Should we turn around and try the other direction? Toward Atkin's Ridge?"

Reuben swiped at his running nose with the back of a gloved hand and shrugged his shoulders miserably.

"We'll try," Sadie said, hoping her voice sounded more

encouraging than she felt.

"If we don't find him, someone will. Likely he'll run into someone's barnyard," Sadie said, squeezing Reuben's knee reassuringly.

She laid the rein expertly across the right side of Paris' neck, which turned her around. She was eager to run again.

"Why are you holding her back?" Reuben yelled.

"Hang on!" Sadie called, loosening the reins as she did so.

Paris gathered her hooves beneath her, stretched out, and ran. She ran joyously, with that deep, easy stride that was so characteristic of her. Sadie relaxed, not particularly watching for Moon in the joy of the ride.

She and Reuben were both laughing when the car passed them on the left, then stopped in front of them. Their laughter stopped immediately, the sound corked in their throats as two men emerged at the same moment. They stepped forward, holding their arms out as if to form a human fence, a barrier to halt the horse and riders.

Sadie realized the danger of the situation. The men may be armed. If she stopped, they could force her off Paris, and if she didn't, they might shoot.

Indecision crowded out her fear, but only for a moment. She compressed her lips, leveled her eyes, and focused on the road behind the two men.

"Stay low, Reuben. Here we go."

She loosened the reins, kicked Paris' sides, startling her into an instant full gallop. The men's faces were covered with ski masks of black stretch fabric, with only the horrible whites of their rolling eyes showing.

Bent low, she goaded Paris toward the middle, where there was only a small opening she could break through without hurting anyone.

Would Paris do it?

She called out with all the power she could gather from her unsteady heart. "Go, Paris!"

She heard the men yelling obscenities. With a powerful leap, Parish crushed through the obstacle they had made.

"Go, go, go," Sadie whispered.

Out of the corner of her eye, she saw that low black car creeping up beside them, slowly crowding them farther off the road. They rode desperately now, bent low, their breath coming in gasps. Around the next corner, up this last grade, and their house would be in view. But never had the distance seemed so long.

The car was coming closer, the windows down, the men leaning out. Would this be the end of her life then? Had God spared her when he took Ezra, only to have it end this way?

"Stop! Stop!" one of them yelled.

Her answer was another kick in Paris' stomach. She could almost make out the schoolhouse fence in the snow.

The motor revved, the car crowding them off the side of the road and toward the ditch. Now there was no alternative. She had to stop Paris very suddenly.

"Reuben, I'm stopping."

She could feel him bracing as she hauled in on the reins with every ounce of her strength. Paris responded immediately, almost sitting down in her desire to perform for Sadie.

The car flew past, then braked. The men in the car looked back in bewilderment. That was when Sadie leaned forward and begged Paris to take them past the car yet again.

"Go, go. Oh, Paris, you can do this!"

The hulking black vehicle was a blur as they hurled past.

The driveway!

If they could just make it to the end of the driveway, they would have outwitted these men. Sadie was convinced they were not armed, but why?

Paris ran low and fast, her feet pounding the macadam. They were on the wrong side of the road, the car closing in fast. But they were still ahead.

Oh, no! A truck was coming!

"Reuben! Stay with me!" she screamed, breathless now.

Sadie whipped the reins so that Paris veered to the left, never slowing her pace. The truck driver turned the wheel desperately to the right, narrowly missing Paris, almost scraping the black car, the driver shaking his fist and pumping the horn with the palm of his hand.

Sadie saw the mailbox and the paper holder. Oh, thank you, God.

They raced around the boxes, gravel and soil flying from beneath Paris' hooves as they hit the driveway. The ringing of hooves on macadam is very different from the sound of them on dirt and stone. It was a sound so sweet, it was almost Sadie's undoing. She knew they had made it. She became limp, without strength, like a rag thrown about. She rode numbly, looking over her shoulder for the shape of that dark vehicle.

Sadie's eyesight was blurred by her tears, but she saw the slowly moving hulk of a car. Its hoarse cries assailed her senses, a foreboding so thick it was impenetrable. A sound so violent, the only suitable word to cover it was evil. What did these men want from her?

Paris kept up her desperate pace, lunging up the driveway, running low past the house. Leah was just stepping out of the phone shanty, Mam's old sweater wrapped tightly around her shivering body. She jumped back as the horse went sailing past, then shook her head and walked after them as Paris slid to a halt.

"Sadie, what is going on? You scared us so badly. What were we supposed to think when Co...I mean, Moon, came running fast up the drive without a rider! One of these days you guys are seriously going to get hurt with your *ga-mach*."

Leah's face was white, her words cutting, her anger barely controlled. Mam and Rebekah entered the forebay, breathless, old sweaters wrapped around their shoulders as if they had grabbed them off the hooks and raced out the door.

"Sadie!" Mam's word was sharp, her relief evident.

"You're just crazy!" Rebekah said, loudly, accusingly.

Reuben slid off Paris and opened his mouth to answer when he saw Moon's face hanging over the gate of his stall. Charging along the forebay, he grabbed his horse's face with both hands and planted a loud kiss on his nose.

"Aw, Moon, my Moon," he crooned. Then he turned, his face alight, and said, "Hey, he ran home. He knows where he belongs!"

Sadie smiled, her dimples deep with genuine warmth and admiration. That Reuben could ride!

As Paris drank deeply from the trough, Sadie told them what happened. She tried not to elaborate, knowing Mam would become too upset. As it was, Mam crossed her arms and said there was no way they were allowed to ride until the law got to the bottom of this.

Dat and Anna entered the barn, wiping slivers of wood from their work coats. They had been piling wood in the basement all evening. They listened as Sadie related the incident yet again. Dat glared with disapproval, admonishing their behavior with sharp words. Anna stood at his side, her eyes large with fear.

"It's Paris!" she said finally. "They want her. She's the only one left from those wild horses. She's a beautiful horse. She likely has an expensive bloodline in her or something."

Leah and Rebekah nodded solemnly.

"If you know what's good for you, you'll stay off the road with her."

"Better yet, don't ride her at all."

Sadie stared at her family in disbelief. The incident wasn't her fault.

Dat looked at her.

"The encounters you've had recently tell me that they must be watching this place quite regularly. You better listen, Sadie."

"They don't want me and Moon, do they?" Reuben asked innocently.

"Probably not. But you better not take any chances," Dat replied.

As the family walked back to the house, Sadie stayed to rub down Paris, then gave her a small amount of oats. She brushed her mane and tail, stroked her neck, crooning her words of admiration, before closing the gate. Sadie could still see Dat's head bowed soberly, his hat a silhouette in the disappearing light.

❋ ✡ ❋

The incident caused quite a stir down at the ranch. Richard Caldwell called the police, giving Sadie no chance to back out. He put a hand on her back and escorted her into his office.

The officers intimidated her, and she felt as if, somehow, she had broken the law and that they would haul her off to jail and make her pay a stiff fine.

The younger of the two was obese, stuffed into his clothes, the belt under his ample stomach tucked away from view, which caused the black holster at his side to jut out awkwardly. He had a sandy crew cut, drooping moustache, and red freckles dotting his nose.

The older officer was more mature in his ways. Somehow Sadie couldn't take her eyes off of his large, bobbing teeth. They were long and yellow, just like Paris'. She couldn't help wondering if his toothbrush was still in the plastic packet it had come in.

She greeted them politely, with a bowed head, and answered their questions as precisely as she could.

No, no facial features were visible.

Black ski masks, yes.

No, she didn't know the make of the car. She wasn't familiar with vehicle types.

The men were silent as they wrote on yellow legal pads. Their radios crackled. Richard Caldwell looked stern, and Sadie pleated her apron over and over, trying to remain calm and composed.

When they looked up, they told Richard Caldwell that they would do what they could, but so far, they had not been able to accomplish much. All they had were leads leading to a dead end. This, however, had been the most serious incident, and they warned Sadie to stay off the road.

Sadie nodded, said, "Yes, sir," then returned to the kitchen, a cloud of humility over her head.

Erma Keim accosted Sadie before she even reached the large granite-topped worktable. Erma's red hair was static with curiosity, but Sadie was in no mood to explain or let her in on one single secret.

"Well?" Erma asked, her knife stopping midair.

Sadie shook her head, offering nothing, her mouth a serious, straight line. Erma laid the knife down carefully, took up a stalk of celery and bit down on it as if her life depended on how large a chomp she would take. Glancing sideways at Sadie, she tried again, "Well?"

"They were talking to Richard Caldwell."

Another gargantuan bite, followed by a snort of epic proportions.

"I'm not dumb, Sadie. There was a reason why he so politely escorted you into his office with those policemen. Look, I won't tell, but I can't stand the suspense. You have to tell me what happened. Did you steal something from the ranch, or were you caught with something illegal, or..."

Sadie raised her eyebrows. "You think I'd do that?"

"No, of course not, but if you don't tell me, I'll make up my own reasons why you were in with those police."

Sadie laughed, and then related the incident as minimally as possible. Even so, she had to endure Erma's popping eyes, her clucks, her shrieks of alarm, and her dramatic warnings and finger-shakings.

Dorothy entered the kitchen carrying a huge piece of beef in paper wrapping, her breath coming in fits and gasps. Flinging it on the worktable, she grabbed her side, leaned forward, and grimaced.

"Ow! Pulled a muscle!"

"You should have let me help you," Erma offered kindly.

"I can carry a beef roast up them steps as good as anybody else. Thank you," Dorothy said formally.

Sadie turned her head to hide her grin. This was the merry-go-round the ranch kitchen had become: Dorothy desperately seeking control over every aspect of the cooking, Erma muttering under her breath or complaining about the way things were done, and Sadie caught in the middle, forever attempting to find common ground between the two.

The menu for the meal that evening was beef stew with dumplings, baked beans, a lettuce salad, pickled beets, and homemade bread with apple butter.

The lettuce salad had been Erma's idea. It wasn't an ordinary salad with a mixture of vegetables, but rather a salad of lettuce, thin slices of onion, and sliced, hard-boiled eggs. Dorothy grudgingly allowing it, and Sadie wondering what the men would say.

To go with the salad, Erma cooked a wonderful hot bacon dressing with plenty of bacon chips in the creamy mayonnaise-based concoction. Sadie filled a small dish with the salad and ate it while they cooked. It was delicious. Dorothy hovered in the background, not saying a word no matter how hard Sadie tried to pull her into the conversation.

The lettuce salad was a huge hit, and many of the men complimented the cook, as Dorothy was called. She bowed her head, batted her eyelashes, and put on a show of humility as she accepted the praise, never mentioning Erma or her recipes.

Richard Caldwell noticed the change in recipes as well and came into the kitchen with a broad smile softening his granite features.

Erma was still in the same stage Sadie had been in a few years ago, when the sound of Richard Caldwell's voice made her drop the Pledge furniture polish. Erma tried to pass it off as nothing, but Sadie could tell he unnerved her by the way her speed increased when he entered the room.

Richard Caldwell clapped a hand on Dorothy's rounded shoulder and congratulated her on another outstanding meal.

"That dressing was the greatest thing I ever poured on lettuce!" he boomed, causing Erma to scrub the pans with a new intensity.

Dorothy nodded, the deep pink color in her apple cheeks turning to crimson. She said nothing, turning to look apprehensively in the direction of Erma, who was slathering a roaster with dish detergent, squeezing the soap bottle so hard Sadie was afraid they'd never get rid of all the leftover suds.

"So who gets the credit for the recipe?" he yelled.

There was more furious scrubbing in Erma's corner while Dorothy drew herself up to her full height. She pursed her lips and narrowed her eyes in concentration.

"My grandmother had a recipe like that," she said.

It wasn't a lie. It was the truth.

And it was all Richard Caldwell needed to know. Assuming the recipe came from Dorothy, he smiled and thanked her again. Then he left the kitchen, picking up a biscuit on his way out and winking at Sadie, who smiled back.

Oh, boy, Sadie thought.

Erma kept scrubbing for a full minute before turning and wiping her forehead with the back of her hand, leaving a white shelf of suds across her eyebrows.

Slowly, much too sweetly, she said, "I didn't know we used your grandmother's recipe."

"We didn't."

"I guess that's a useless bit of information Richard Caldwell doesn't need to know."

"'Course not."

The kitchen was a beehive of tension after that. Erma scurried back and forth, her eyes popping, her hair standing on end with resentment. Dorothy's expression indicated no good either, in that haughty state where she became unapproachable.

Sadie's own mood hovered between irritation and resentment. Work just wasn't the same with Erma in the kitchen. The mounting tension had steadily increased all week. She was exhausted.

For the first time she could remember, she did not want to come back to work in the morning, Oh, she had her sleepy Monday-morning blues like everyone else, but nothing that blackened her entire day the way these two did with their silly squabbles.

Sadie finished boiling the potatoes for the morning's home fries, washed her hands, then said she was going to find Jim. It was time to go home. She tiredly stuck her arms into her coat sleeves, shrugging the coat over her shoulders.

"The floor ain't done," Dorothy said evenly.

"I'll get it," Erma said, stepping forward. "You can go."

Dorothy's eyebrows shot straight up, and she watched without comment as Erma filled a bucket, added soap, and bent to begin her task.

"You sure you can handle it?" Dorothy asked.

"What?"

"The floor?"

"It's not a big floor," Erma answered, swiping furiously.

Dorothy shook her head, smiled, and winked at Sadie. Then she bent to find Erma's gaze.

"You piling coals of fire on my head, or what?"

"No, I'm washing the floor with soapy water. I have no plans to pile coals on your head."

Dorothy burst out laughing, and after a pause, Erma sat back and laughed with her.

"No stupid ol' lettuce salad gonna ruin us, now, is it?" she chortled, wiping her eyes.

Erma nodded, a hint of tears glistening in her own eyes.

Chapter 19

P<small>ERHAPS THE UNBALANCED RELATIONSHIP BETWEEN</small>
Erma and Dorothy was a good thing. Mark told Sadie
that his mother had sent another letter stating her des-
peration to see him. He would go this time. Sadie didn't
hesitate to tell him that she would accompany him on the
trip to visit her.

The ranch could be run smoothly without her, even if
Dorothy and Erma were like a team of horses that jerked
on the singletree, one lunging forward while the other
held back.

They planned a trip by train on Amtrak. Their destina-
tion was almost 600 miles to a town in North Dakota. As
they made arrangements, Mark became reserved, offering only a minimal amount of information, his eyes dark
pools of restraint. Sadie wondered if he wanted her to go
along at all. So a few days before they left, she voiced her
concerns, haltingly.

"Mark, I'm not sure how you feel about taking me
with you."

"Why do you say that?"

"You're… It's tough… I guess I'm scared. She doesn't

want you to be... Amish. What will happen when she sees me? You could go alone and dress English, and she'd never know the difference."

Mark looked at her coldly, his expression unreadable. Then he bent his head, hiding his eyes in his hands.

"I wasn't going to tell you, Sadie. My mother is very, very ill. She's dying, I think. I wasn't going to tell you," he repeated.

"Oh, Mark!"

"We actually spoke on the phone a few times, and, Sadie, she's so bitter. I'm still reeling from those calls. Her voice so weak..." He paused, then, "What can I do? I don't feel as if I'll be able to help her. I have so much baggage of my own to carry. It'll be like the blind leading the blind, two mixed-up, bitter people."

"Your baggage is lighter than it was."

"You think so?" His tone was mocking. Then, "You have no idea."

✡ ✡ ✡

Sadie prayed as she packed her things that night. She prayed as she showered, dressed, and said goodbye to her family the next morning. She begged God to stay with them, impart his wisdom, and erase all the old hatred that lingered in both Mark and his mother. Somehow, she knew that hatred was the only thing keeping Mark and his mother from true happiness and peace.

Reuben took Sadie aside and told her not to worry about Paris. He'd take good care of her. Besides, he was planning to teach Anna to ride, now that she had lost so much weight. Sadie told him she would depend on him, but to be very careful with the snipers still on the loose.

Reuben was almost as tall as Sadie now, their eyes almost level. The sudden knowledge of this surprised her.

Dear Reuben.

When Mark pulled up to the porch with a driver, Sadie was ready to go. She turned to say goodbye to her family, but the lump in her throat made it difficult.

Mam smelled of frying corn mush and laundry detergent. Sadie breathed in deeply as she hugged her tightly.

Dat's expression was gruff, but his eyes were liquid with love. Sadie's sisters handed her a packet of tissues and a pack of Juicy Fruit chewing gum. Reuben smiled, then dipped his head to hide his tears.

In the van, Mark tried to keep the conversation light. He bantered with Adam Glassman, the driver, telling him they were eloping, which caused heat to infuse Sadie's cheeks. But when the train pulled in and they were settled in their seats, a cloud settled over Mark. His features darkened until he turned away from her and pretended to be asleep.

Sadie sat still and watched the other passengers. She smiled at a baby no older than six months. The harried mother acknowledged her smile gratefully, glad to have a friendly person sitting so close.

"Are you used to babies?" she asked timidly.

"Not in my immediate family, but yes, there are lots of babies in our community," Sadie answered.

"I'm so nervous about taking Braxton on a trip this way. What if he cries and I can't make him stop?"

"You'll be fine. He looks perfectly happy," Sadie answered.

She picked up her magazine, flipped through it, and began to read an article about training a horse to drive. It absorbed her interest completely until her stomach began to rumble.

She was surprised to find it was almost lunchtime. When her glances at Mark's back did nothing to rouse him, she picked up another magazine and read one boring article after another.

The baby fell asleep, the mother noticeably relaxed now. The train's wheels hummed beneath them, taking them farther and farther from home.

The Juicy Fruit gum took the edge off her rumbling stomach, but she was still hungry and then grew irritable. She had not eaten breakfast but only drank two cups of coffee, which she definitely should not have done. Why hadn't she packed a few sandwiches? When would Mark wake up?

Finally, he sat up and turned to talk to her. Sadie could tell by his eyes that he hadn't slept at all. He just shut her out of that deep, dark place he went to at certain times. No amount of prodding ever uncovered the reason why.

He said nothing about food. In fact, he didn't talk at all for the next hour. Sadie attempted short spurts of conversation, but she felt as ineffective as a housefly bothering a horse, getting only grunts for answers.

The lack of food and support from Mark drew her spirits down until she was in one of the worst moods possible. First, she wished she hadn't come; then she wished she had never met Mark Peight at all.

She was blinking back tears when an announcement came over the speaker saying they'd be stopping in the next town for approximately an hour and a half.

She glanced at Mark and was rewarded by his gaze.

"Hungry?"

She nodded happily.

He returned to her then, attentive, polite, and kind as always. He told her to order whatever she wanted and not to worry about the cost. This was sort of a vacation for them both.

She decided to try something new from the menu, a pasta dish consisting of a flat spaghetti. It was a word she could not pronounce: linguini. It was covered with sauce called marinara, another word she had never heard of, and topped with little shrimp and the most heavenly tasting cheese. There were slivers of thin garlic toast, and a salad made of fresh lettuce, dark spinach, croutons, cheese, and a spicy dressing. It was wonderful.

"Definitely not Amish food!" she laughed.

"Nope. No mashed potatoes and chicken gravy here," Mark replied.

For the remainder of the journey, he remained attentive, talkative, almost lighthearted. He emerged from his swamp of hopelessness as if it had never occurred.

There was no one to meet them in the town of Ashton, of course. The station was small, the old building consisting of crumbling bricks, an aging wooden cornice, and battered window frames. A remnant of white paint clung stubbornly to the graying wood of the exterior, weathered by hot winds and freezing blizzards.

Even in the light of early spring, a gray despondency hovered over the flat little town. There was nothing except scrubby emptiness that went on and on and on in all directions. Dirty tumbleweeds, covered with the dust that rusty pickup trucks agitated, clung to buildings as if hoping to escape their journey into oblivion.

Sadie shivered, glancing at the hovering water tower in the sky, a sort of peeling, steel sentry, crumbling along with the brick buildings and the windowpanes.

The wind blew constantly, just like at home, pulling at her skirt and ruffling Mark's hair.

Sadie crossed her arms and looked around a dusty waiting room with a filthy carpet, a cow skull on the wall, and dusty chairs. She decided right then and there that Mark was the only safe thing in this town.

He talked to the girl behind the desk, asking if there was any taxi service available, handing her the address from his pocket.

She chewed a huge wad of gum, snapping and popping it at regular intervals. She nodded her head in recognition.

"Ya see there," the girl said, pointing out the window with an index finger, the nail polished to a crimson hue.

"Cross the street. Jeff don't have a sign over his store, but go in through that open door, and he'll give ya a ride. If yer folks are on Killdeer Road, Jeff can find 'em."

She fixed Sadie with a frank, curious stare.

"Ya Mennonite? No, lemme guess, yer Mormons, right?"

She batted her lashes, those thick heavy spiders of mascara, and grinned up at Mark. He laughed, clearly enjoying her open approach to their different way of dressing.

"None of those. We're Amish."

"What kind of animal is that?" she asked, her penciled eyebrows drawn down.

She burst into laughter so loud, she almost lost the enormous wad of gum.

"It's sort of Mennonite," Sadie offered, seeing this girl was clearly baffled. No use trying to explain.

"Well, you're awful good-looking, whatever you are. You said yer mother lives out on Killdeer Road? Ain't never seen anybody wearin' those kinda clothes, so she must have left the fold."

Mark nodded. "She did."

"Nice yer goin' to see 'er. She'll be glad. That's good."

Sadie felt the goose bumps begin on her arms, and quick tears sprang to her eyes. Those words from this person with no guile somehow seemed prophetic, a good omen.

This worldly girl helped them cheerfully and sincerely wished them well. She was the sort of person who would have helped the poor man in the Bible who was assaulted and beaten, lying in the culvert by the side of the road.

The Spirit of the Lord was like the wind. You saw what it did, but you couldn't tell where it came from.

"Hey, tell you what. If'n it don't suit Jeff, jes' come back. I'll call my mom to fill in for me, an' I'll take ya."

Mark thanked her, and as they turned to go the girl waved her hand and told them to leave their luggage. It wasn't in anyone's road, no how.

Jeff was a portly individual, his overalls grimy with grease and mud. The clasps at his shoulders the only clean thing about him, except for his teeth, which were long and surprisingly white.

He greeted them with a curious grin, quiet eyes, and a hearty, "Ya lost?"

Mark smiled back and told him that perhaps they were. He told Jeff about his mother's residence on Kill-deer Road, and Jeff pondered the length of it in his mind.

"The only place I know out there is that... Naw, that ain't yer ma. She's crazier 'n a coyote with fleas. Tain't her."

Mark froze, a statue of indecision. The panic and fore-boding in his face was almost Sadie's undoing.

Why had they come? They knew nothing of this strange woman. She meant nothing to Mark. Would they regret this wild-goose chase? Would it hurt rather than help Mark?

"If'n this woman's yer ma, you gotta be prepared. Talk has it, she ain't right in the head. Haven't seen her in a while, huh?"

Mark shook his head.

"Sorry, I don't mean to be a' gossipin'. Lord knows there's way too mucha that goin' on. An, besides, she's yer ma."

Jeff called over the half-door to his wife, telling her that he was leaving for a little while. Then he went to get his keys.

Sadie slid her hand into Mark's. He tightened his hand and gave her a grateful look. But the pallor of his face gave away the fact that he was in turmoil, finding Jeff's words to be fiercely disturbing.

They made their way to the aging, white pickup, the running board rusted so badly, Sadie stepped over it entirely.

Apologizing, Jeff pushed aside the trash: empty tea bottles, sticky orange-juice cartons, screwdrivers, duct tape, dirty little receipts, crumbling newspaper, an assortment of junk that must not have been disturbed for months.

"Don't nobody ride in my truck hardly ever," Jeff said laughing good-naturedly. "Shoulda taken Lila's car. She keeps it a sight cleaner."

They eased out of town, Jeff waving at each person on the sidewalk, pressing down hard on the horn when three dogs crossed the street in front of them. A mangy-looking sheep dog, a German shepherd that looked less than friendly, followed by a large dog of various descents, ambled across.

"Ol' Bertha's got her dogs loose again. What this town needs is a dog warden. Mayor, such as he is, says we can't afford one. Well, we can't afford the accidents these big bruisers cause, trotting all over town as if they own it."

Jeff shook his head, pushed back his cap, glanced in the rearview mirror, and made a hard left.

"Trouble is, ain't enough of us. Work's not so good anymore. Most of us worked for the wheat farmers or the big gas company, only the gas ain't producin' the way it used ta."

Jeff rambled in his friendly manner. The truck swerved around potholes and bounced across skips in the macadam. Jeff turned the steering wheel first one way, then another, grimacing as the right front wheel hit an especially large pothole.

He pointed to tall grain bins, their sides coated with rust, sienna-colored messengers of time and neglect.

"See them?"

Mark craned his neck.

"Part of the ranch we're headed to. Nothin' left hardly. It's yer typical sad story. Good man, that Scout. Scout's his nickname. His real name is Bill Van Syoc. Hard-working. Owned half the county in acreage. Wheat farmer. Cattle. Married that... Well, I can't say in front of you people what I normally would. Excuse me, but she ran everything into the ground. The town people saw him go from a proud, ambitious person to a wreck in no time flat. Took to alcohol. It's a shame."

Mark sat beside Sadie tight-lipped, so she said nothing and just looked out the window at the landscape.

North Dakota was literally as flat as a pancake. There were no rolling hills, no dips, just long stretches of prairie. The roads were as straight and flat as the land.

Weather-beaten grain bins seemed to cling to the earth.
Occasionally one appeared slanted, almost as if the wind
had pushed at it steadily until, inch by inch, the building had leaned in the direction the wind wanted it to go.
Rusted sign posts stood like rail-thin, starving people.
There were no fences, which made everything seem loose
and free.

An occasional meadowlark warbled from the top of
a wooden mailbox post while smaller birds dipped and
whirled across the sky. The grasses were showing hints
of green, although the entire landscape still showed its
brown winter hue. This land seemed foreign, somehow.
The vastness of it made Sadie feel like she was in another
country.

Jeff looked to the right, squinting beneath the visor,
then pointed with a gnarled finger.

"See them buildings?"

They nodded their acknowledgment.

"That's where we're headed."

As they drew closer, Mark's eyes folded into slits. The
mailbox sagged on a post hanging on by a thread. The
post stood haphazardly in an opening much too large to
hold it upright.

The house was unconventional for the area, built by
someone with oversized dreams, as if the builder attempted a sort of mini-castle, then found his funds depleted and
stopped all the work, finishing it as cheaply as possible.

The roofline had no sense of balance due to the gable
ends, turrets, and balconies. Parts of the house had beautiful gingerbread cornices, but the rest was plain and finished with ordinary vinyl siding. Some of the windows
had black shutters, but most of them had nothing at all,
making them appear unprotected and unfinished. There

was a large front porch with expensive urns that were filled with weeds. Weeds climbed the house too, their sadness spilling over the windows and door frames in brown destitution.

Poison ivy covered the chimney, the massive sandstone apparatus that consumed almost the entire south side of the house.

Jeff drove slowly, trying to avoid the deep washes in the unkempt driveway. Beneath a towering tree were the remains of a water fountain, a hammock, roses growing wild.

When Sadie saw an elaborate statue of a little girl holding a basket of flowers, her skirt blowing in the wind, almost buried beneath wild ivy, she thought her heart would break. Once, there had been a beautiful garden, but time and neglect had turned it into a forlorn picture of sorrow.

Oh, the complete desolation!

Jeff stopped the truck, then looked at them levelly.

"Now are you sure you don't want me to wait? Let's just say I'll set right here until you go knock on that door, all right?"

"I'd be obliged, but we'll try and make it short. I'm sure you have work to do at home," Mark said.

"I'll be fine."

Sadie smiled at Jeff and was rewarded with a look of sincere warmth. Then she looked up at Mark. He would not meet her gaze, his face having lost most of its color, his mouth set in a grim line.

The sidewalk had been beautiful sandstone laid to precision, but it was covered over now by an assortment of weeds and vines.

Surely no one lived here. Certainly no one visited anymore.

She followed Mark up the steps of the front porch, her heart hammering against her ribs. When he knocked on the large oak door, still wondrous in spite of the neglect, she bit her lip and clenched her fingers.

There was a chorus of barks, howls, and yips, and then the door swung slowly inward.

At first Sadie thought the woman could not possibly be a real person, only a caricature someone rigged to the door to frighten intruders. She was so thin! Way too tall, too white, the cheeks sunken, the black hair hanging in dirty tendrils around her shoulders.

The woman threw them an angry glance, a black look of suspicion. The look was so that Sadie clutched desperately at Mark's sleeve, but he shook off her trembling hands.

"Whadda ya want?"

The voice was only a thin rasp, barely audible above the chorus from the dogs. She slapped halfheartedly at the largest, a white Siberian husky, with blue eyes and the dark brows so often seen in that breed.

"I am... I am Mark Peight. This is my girlfriend, Sadie Miller."

He could not say more or less. It was straightforward, mincing nothing. His family of origin, his marital status, and the Amish religion was all there for her to comprehend and absorb.

The dogs quieted when one thin, white hand went to the husky's head. The other hand went to her throat, clutched at the black satin robe, then fell to her side. A long, thin breath whistled through her dry, white lips.

Suddenly, she lowered her head and the lank hair fell over her face. Sadie thought she was going to fall and moved forward to catch her, when the woman put one hand on the door frame, swayed slightly, then steadied herself.

"Aaah." It was a hoarse, broken cry.

Then her head came up, the eyes large and black with defiance. She took a step back.

"You're... A-Amish!" she whispered hoarsely.

"Yes. I am also your oldest son."

"Just... just go. Leave me alone. You'll condemn me to hell. It's where I'm going soon enough anyway."

"Don't, Mam."

"What did you call me?"

Her voice was painfully raw. If a voice could bleed, it would sound like this.

"I called you Mam. You are my mother. You asked to see me, so I came."

"But... you can't come into my house."

"Why not?"

"You... you have to shun me. I am *im bann*."

"I know."

"Just go." The words were tired, broken, so weary they left a trail of complete exhaustion across Sadie's heart. But she ignored it, stepping forward bravely.

"No, we're going to stay here with you for a little while," she said.

She met Sadie's eyes, saw the innocence, the guile-lessness, and wavered. Her indecision was so apparent, flickering in her large dark eyes.

"Why would you?"

"We traveled all this way to be with you, and we'd love to stay, talk, and..."

"I'm ill. I won't live long. You don't want to be here."

"We'll just bring in our luggage, if that's all right," Sadie answered.

They bade Jeff goodbye. He gave them his cell phone number, shaking his head in worried disbelief that they were actually staying there.

When Mark and Sadie walked through the front door, the dogs rose to greet them. They were quiet now, and Mark bent to stroke them all, fondling their ears like a true dog-lover.

His mother stood by the wall, supporting herself on the back of a red wing-chair, watching with an expression that had no name.

Chapter 20

SADIE NEVER THOUGHT THE WORD "DESPAIR" would be suitable to describe a home, but it was the only word that fit the place where Amelia Van Syoc lived. It wasn't the dust and grime as much as the atmosphere of a person living without hope.

The house had been full of beauty at one time but now held only decay. The carpet, the hardwood floors, and the ceramic tiles were covered in years of dust and dog hair. Every window was covered with insulated drapes, dark blinds, or simply with fabric. Even the sunshine and fresh air were trapped outside.

There were boxes piled everywhere, as if she had tried to fill the emptiness by purchasing things. Over time she accumulated huge containers filled with all kinds of useless items. There was a path between the boxes through the living room, kitchen, and dining room. Otherwise, they had to set things aside to be able to reach the bedrooms where Amelia had told them to put their suitcases.

They had each sleepless nights on lumpy mattresses. In the morning they sat across from each other at the kitchen table with nothing to say. There was no food in the cupboards, and they found the refrigerator almost empty, so Sadie made coffee and drank it black.

Mark was in that dark place, answering Sadie's questions through averted eyes. He glanced at the bedroom door his mother had entered the evening before, gasping for breath as she did so, telling them she was tired and going to bed.

Was she still alive? Would she allow them to stay?

Sadie longed to get started on cleaning the house, but Mark had not yet given her permission. So she sat, drank the awful coffee, and gave up trying to engage Mark in any further conversation.

Sunlight filtered through the lone uncovered window, creating a bright patch of light on the ceramic floor. Sadie placed her foot on it, as if it would beat back the darkness creeping into her body and mind as she contemplated this lonely woman's life.

The heavy oak door creaked on its hinges as Mark's mother slowly pulled it open from the inside. Sadie looked away from the white face and piercing dark eyes that were creating a sort of panic in her chest.

She never said a word, only shuffled to the bathroom, her black satin robe clutched to her skeletal frame.

The dogs had been sleeping at Mark's feet calmly, as if they knew help had arrived and were glad of it. Obediently, the dogs rose as if she had called them. They followed her down the hallway and laid outside the bathroom door.

Sadie tried desperately to met Mark's eyes, but he had shut her out. His face was like cut granite, his eyes flat and black.

There was a hoarse cry, a shattering of glass, and a thump from behind the closed door. Instantly, Mark was on his fee with Sadie at his heels.

"Are you all right?" he called.

When there was no answer, he turned the knob, then went in. Sadie gasped when she saw the pathetic figure huddled by the commode, a glass shattered beside her and a bottle of pills scattered around her, absorbing the puddles of water on the floor.

Mark knelt beside his mother and called her name.

"Meely! Mam!"

The face was even more colorless now, the eyes closed.

Mark felt for a pulse, put his ear to the thin chest, then scooped her up in his arms like a child. He carried her from the bathroom to the living room, folding her long, thin body on the cluttered, brown sofa.

Out of habit, Sadie quickly returned to the bathroom to pick up the shards of glass and mop up the water. When she returned to the living room, Mark was calling his mother's name yet again.

When she finally responded, he was so visibly relieved it was heartbreaking. Meely cried in low moaning sounds, her thin lips drawn back in agony. She turned her face away, a gesture to save her withering pride.

"I'm...," she whispered.

Mark bent, then went on his knees beside the sofa, his hands hanging awkwardly by his side as if afraid to touch her.

"I'm...," Meely tried again.

A long, broken breath.

"I'm ... going to die."

"Not yet, Mam. We're here. Sadie and I."

She nodded, struggled to sit up, then fell back on the sofa, closing her eyes. Her hands fluttered restlessly over the satin robe.

Sadie reached out, pulled up the heavy fabric of the robe, and laid it gently across her stomach.

"Meely." The word was new, but she said it quietly, bravely. "We're here to stay. We're going to take good care of you. Is it okay for me to clean and buy some food?"

Another weary nod, then she twisted her body as she strained and heaved, completely sick to her stomach.

Sadie glided noiselessly to the kitchen, found a container, and returned to the living room, stroking Meely's back as she strained.

"It's okay. We're here. You'll be all right," she crooned.

Mark watched her and remembered. The snow, the cold, the horse so thin, so evidently dying. Sadie kneeling by the horse, holding its head, stroking the mane, whispering words of endearment in Pennsylvania Dutch. It was then he had fallen in love with her, and that love had only grown stronger with time.

He was suddenly overwhelmed with emotion and put a hand reassuringly on Sadie's shoulder. He did not look away when she turned to meet his gaze, burning now with intensity.

Meely wiped her mouth with a crumpled tissue, then moaned softly, waving her hand in dismissal. Slowly she turned to face the wall.

Sadie watched as Meely's eyes closed, then turned and headed for the kitchen. Mark was suddenly behind her. He slid his arms around her and held her as if she was the anchor that grounded him to his very life.

"I love you so much," he whispered in her ear.

"And I love you, Mark. Always," she returned.

Anything was possible with Mark's love. Her spirit lifted to new heights.

They cleaned all morning. They carried boxes to one designated room, swept, pushed aside the drapes, cleaned windows, scoured bathrooms, emptied waste cans, and moved furniture. By mid-afternoon they were absolutely ravenous.

They called Jeff, who whisked them off to the local grocery. They bought fresh meat and cheese, salt, flour, oatmeal, cereal, and all the staples they would need to cook nutritious meals that they hoped would tempt Meely's appetite. They returned and filled the freshly cleaned cupboards and refrigerator.

They toasted bagels in the toaster, cooked thick sausage patties, and melted Swiss cheese all over them. They scrambled eggs and built huge breakfast sandwiches with ketchup slathered liberally in the middle.

They drank cold orange juice, talked with their mouths full, licked their fingers, and then Sadie jumped up for a roll of paper towels.

"No napkins. Mark, we forgot."

"Sit down, Sadie."

His voice was low and very serious, so she slid carefully into the heavy oak kitchen chair and watched his face as she wiped her hands on the paper towels.

The air was heavy with unspoken words and feelings too deep to be brought to the surface easily. The only sound was water dripping from the newly polished faucet at the kitchen sink.

"Do you...?"

His voice was drowned out by a piercing scream from the living room, propelling Mark out of his chair so swiftly, it fell over backward. He hurried through the arched doorway and into the living room to find Meely with her head pressed into the pillow, her body arched as she strained to escape the pain assaulting her back.

Her lips drew back and released another cry of agony.

Instantly, Sadie slipped an arm beneath her and held her thin shoulders.

"Meely! Don't. It'll be all right. Don't cry. It's okay."

No amount of coaxing or massaging would soothe the poor woman. Finally, Mark suggested calling an ambulance, anything to still her cries and ease her pitiful suffering.

"No! No! No!" she cried.

The dogs rose, whimpering, until Mark let them outside.

After the initial wave of pain wore out, Meely calmed down and obediently swallowed the Tylenol they offered. Then she asked for hot tea.

"You should eat," Mark said.

"No."

"If Sadie makes chicken soup, would you eat that?"

"No."

She drank the tea, then asked for more pillows.

Sadie went to the kitchen and put some chicken breasts in water to make homemade chicken corn noodle soup. Then she asked Meely if she would like a warm bath and a shampoo.

"No."

"Meely, I think it would help you feel better."

"Nobody's going to bathe me. No."

"Would you do it yourself?"

"No."

Sadie sighed and looked at Mark. The sour odor from her unwashed hair and body was loathsome, but she was afraid to mention it, not wanting to offend Meely, or Mark for that matter.

The tea seemed to give her a measure of strength, and she patted the pillows with nerveless fingers, a sort of repercussion from the caffeine in the tea.

"I have to talk." She spoke loudly, the words coming in quick succession, as if she might never be able to say the necessary words if she didn't say them now.

Sadie quickly walked to the kitchen to turn down the burner on the stove. When she returned, Mark was sitting on the red-wing chair. Sadie stood beside it, a hand on the arm.

"Sit down," Meely barked, angrily.

Obediently Sadie brought a chair from the dining room and sat beside Mark.

"I have cancer. It's in my bones. It started in my breasts. Had that taken care of, or so they thought. You know…"

Her hands fluttered like white birds swept by a gale, seemingly propelled by forces beyond their control.

"The doctors don't know what happened. Told me to quit smoking. Couldn't do that. I always smoked. Well, not always, but…" A terrified glance at Mark.

"After I left, I smoked a lot. Helped my nerves. Evan smoked. The…you know, the man I left with."

Mark nodded.

Her black gaze adhered to Mark's eyes with a certain wildness.

"Say you don't remember," she ground out hoarsely.

Mark sat motionless, made of stone. Then he nodded again.

As if her soul were in Mark's hands, Meely searched his face, earnestly hoping he did not remember the past.

"No. You don't. You can't. You were too young."

Why didn't he speak? Was it pride that kept Mark so still?

The dripping faucet in the kitchen violated the dead silence as effectively as a hissing scream, until Sadie thought the very atmosphere would fly apart.

"I remember everything, Mother."

Sadie's heart slowed, then dropped, when she heard Mark's words, spoken in Pennsylvania Dutch.

"*Ich mind allus.*"

"Oh, God!" The sick woman understood. The words, spoken in the language of her past, sealed her fate, and it was a thousand times worse than she feared.

Out of the depths of her ravaged soul came the words, "*Nay! Nay!*"

Her response in Dutch made Sadie shudder. If ever there was a time when she felt helpless in the face of these horribly buried pasts, this was surely it. She breathed a prayer to God to stay here, in this room, with his power and strength.

Meely became defensive then.

"It wasn't my fault. Atlee should have done something. He was so set in his ways. The farm was going downhill all the time. He ... was so unconcerned. All he wanted to do was ... lay around the house.

"He loved me too much. It drove me insane. I couldn't deal with it. When you were born, it was okay, but they just kept coming. The babies. Crying, wanting food, there weren't enough diapers. The washer was broken. Atlee... None of it was my fault. A person can only take so much. Not my fault."

She turned her face away, the subject closed. The past was smoothed over by adjusting the blame to someone else.

Mark's eyes blared with black fire, disgust, and fury leaping out of them. His mouth opened and then closed. He gulped like a dying fish receiving no oxygen but still floundering.

When he finally spoke, the words were cased in searing heat from anger pushed deep inside for much too long.

"No, Meely. Huh-uh. You're not going to get out of this so easily. I don't care if you are sick, you're going to hear what I have to say. I was only eight years old, but I knew. I knew what you and that...that Evan were doing. I can still see him, that cringing lizard at the front door, coming to mislead my Mam. I can still see you leaving in his red car, the babies crying. No, Meely, it was not my Dat's fault.

"He's dead, you know. Dat. Atlee."

She turned her head to face Mark, checking his face for any untruth.

"No!"

"Yes. Atlee killed himself after you left. He drowned. I found him."

There was a snort of derision from the sofa.

"Guess you had a shock, huh?"

Mark stood up, towered over her. She shrank into the cushions of the couch, afraid he might strike her.

With a hoarse, nameless cry, he turned on his heel and stalked out through the front door, slamming it so hard the windows rattled.

Sadie looked at Meely, who looked back with a blank, cold stare. The dark glare withered any sense of goodwill Sadie may have had.

✿ ✡ ✿

The smell of chicken soup floated through the house, creating a homey warmth. Mark had disappeared, and Sadie hoped she could get his mother fed and bathed by the time he returned. They might resume talking then, opening old Pandora's boxes, battling the spirits that spewed forth.

Sadie wheedled, coaxed, even joked, to get Meely to eat the soup. No amount of coaxing could persuade her. Finally, Sadie told her she needed some sort of sustenance to withstand another attack of pain. Nothing could persuade her to try a single spoonful.

"I hate that Amish stuff."

The words were shoved violently at Sadie and made her flinch. She stood her ground.

"English people make chicken noodle soup. Not just Amish."

"Don't want it. You're Amish."

"Okay. Then starve. We're going home."

"No. No. Don't." she cried pathetically. "I'll taste it."

"It's made with ingredients from your grocery store, so it's English soup," Sadie teased.

That brought a weak semblance of a smile, and she reached for the soup bowl. She tried some, then raised the black eyebrows.

"It's good."

She ate every drop, then asked for water with ice in it, which Sadie brought quickly. Meely drank half of it.

"You don't mean it," Meely said, her shoulders drooping. Then, "Why do you want me to live?"

"I want you to live long enough to reconcile your feelings with Mark. I care for Mark. I love him very much, and you're his mother, so I care about you, of course. You're his mother."

"You don't love me."

"I would if you'd let me bathe you," Sadie said smiling. A small twinkle flickered in her deep brown eyes.

"I'm a disgusting person, aren't I? Sick and dirty and weak. I wasn't always like this, you know."

Sadie nodded.

"I'll bathe myself. You can help me shampoo."

Sadie could hardly believe her good fortune. While Meely bathed, Sadie vacuumed the sofa and tucked clean sheets along the cushions. When that was finished, she glided noiselessly across the carpet and pressed her ear to the bathroom door. Meely was not yet ready for her shampoo, so Sadie hurried away to put the soiled sheets and quilt in the washer.

She was thankful for her experience of working at the ranch. She was accustomed to toasters, microwaves, washers, and dryers even though the appliances were not a part of her life at home.

Meely called from the bathroom, and Sadie braced herself, knowing it would take courage to enter.

When she quietly opened the door, Meely was submerged in water up to her shoulders. Her face was turned away, and she refused to meet Sadie's eye.

"Don't hurt me now." The voice was soft, like a child's, and it enveloped Sadie's heart.

Poor, frightened woman. Was she any different than Nevaeh, that sick beautiful horse, so pitiful in her weakness?

As Sadie gently massaged Meely's grimy scalp, work-ing the shampoo into it, Meely closed her eyes. Sadie could see the beauty that had been ravaged by disease and malnutrition. Her eyebrows were like dark wings, once plucked to perfection, now beautiful in their fullness. Her eyes were wide half-moons fringed with black lashes. Her cheeks were sallow and mottled, but the bone structure was perfect, just like Mark's.

As Sadie washed the matted mass of hair loosening under her hands, the water turned gray and then brown. She rinsed, shampooed again, then worked the condi-tioner in before the final rinse.

"There, Meely. Do you need help to finish?"

The "no" was quick and emphatic. But she had to call Sadie to help her dress in clean pajamas, warm socks, and another robe, a white one this time, which improved the stark outline of her figure.

Sadie led her to the red wing-chair and gently brushed her hair until all the tangles were smoothed. Sadie was amazed at the amount of black hair Meely still had, despite her illness. She was only graying a bit at the temples.

"I lost all of it before, you know. Chemo kills you," Meely said wryly.

"I've heard people talk of chemotherapy."

"It's as horrible as they say."

That was all she said. Her body was limp with exhaus-tion, so Sadie helped her to the sofa, pulling the quilt around her thin shoulders. Meely tried to speak, but her eyes, those beautiful half moons of light, fell. Her breath-ing deepened, and she was asleep.

Sadie stood, then reached out and tentatively smoothed the hair away from her pearly brow.

Dear God. *Unser Himmlischer Vater.*

As she prayed in Dutch, a wave of homesickness rushed over her. She missed her family. Reuben especially. She missed Paris and hoped Anna was riding her with Reuben and Moon. She missed Dorothy, too. She would call tomorrow.

She washed dishes, fed the dogs, ate some of the chicken soup. She was still hungry and decided to make *toast brot, milch und an oy*. It was an old satisfying dish when the stomach was not quite right or the body needed a bit of comfort within the next 15 minutes.

She put a small amount of milk in a little saucepan and broke an egg into it. Then she put a slice of bread in the toaster. When the egg and toast were ready, she dumped the egg and milk on the toast, salting and peppering it liberally.

She took a bite and closed her eyes, savoring this dish straight from Mam's kitchen.

Where was Mark?

She couldn't blame him for leaving. She couldn't imagine how difficult it would be to face those memories again, especially from his own Mam. It was almost beyond her comprehension.

When Mark returned a short time later, they sat in the neglected garden and talked. At first Mark was curt, defiant even, but as the late afternoon turned to evening, the dusty sunlight filtering through the trees, he spoke of his pain. He desperately longed to forgive his mother, but he didn't have the strength to do it.

Sadie could only slip her hand in his, lay her head on his shoulder, and listen. His pain was as raw as the day his mother had left so many years ago. Sadie knew then that he would always be bound by the fetters of his past, even if he reached a measure of forgiveness.

Perhaps forgiveness was like love. It came in small portions, but it was the exact amount you needed, poured out by a loving Father above.

Life is imperfect. To believe that painful things could be completely washed away, never to return, was wishful thinking.

The painful things of the past remained, but with forgiveness and love, you could lock them away if the key to that lock could be maintained by love. It was God who supplied the key of love yet again. He was always there.

So was love.

Chapter 21

THE FOLLOWING MORNING THERE WAS A RESOUNDING knock from the rusted knocker on the front door, followed closely by two insistent peals from the doorbell. Instinctively Meely clutched her robe with one hand and grasped at her quilts with the other, her eyes wide with terror as the dogs began their ear-splitting cacophony.

"They're coming to get me, aren't they?" she hissed, her dark hair flying about her head as she searched for a way of escape.

Before Sadie could stop her, Meely lifted the quilt, flung her legs over the side of the sofa, raised herself up, and with a frightened cry, fell headlong onto the carpet.

As the doorbell repeated its insistent peals, Mark and Sadie rushed to Meely's side, hoarse sobs escaping the pitifully thin body. Choking and crying, clawing the air with her thin, white fingers, she was clearly horrified now.

"Get the door," Mark said curtly.

Sadie went to the door, hushing the dogs as best she could before pulling it open tentatively, peeping out to see a large African-American man. Instinctively, she was reluctant to ask him in.

She stepped outside and kept her hand on the door handle in case she needed a quick escape back inside.

"How ya doin', honey? I'm Tom!" He extended his large hand and crushed Sadie's in an all-encompassing grip.

Then, rushing on, giving Sadie no space to introduce herself, he filled the air around him with a steady stream of words spoken loudly but in a rich, lovely baritone that sent shivers down Sadie's spine.

"I'm Tom, the preacher man. I've been tellin' the Lord that he needs to let me know if there's anything I can do for this lady. She never comes out of the house, but I'm trusting him to let me know if she needs help. Last night I saw someone walking around here as I was comin' home, an' sure enough, I knew right then that the Lord needed me here. How's she doin'?"

Sadie shook her head.

"I figgered. I figgered. Honey, she in a bad way?"

"She doesn't have long."

"Aw, honey!"

With that, Sadie was enveloped in what she could only describe as a bear hug, from which he released her just as quickly.

"You relation?"

"My ... boyfriend's mother."

"Aw, honey!"

There was a sweet lilt to his words, a butterfly perched on a question, a dove of peace on every endearment.

His words always came with a smile. His eyes were a constant glow of good humor, his white teeth a flash of goodwill. All this was apparent in these first few moments.

"She needs saved, right?"

Sadie nodded, hesitantly. The English used the word *saved*, but Sadie, like most Amish, was wary of the term.

Amish teaching instilled the fear of God as a strict master who demands that the faithful stay within the rules of the church and adhere to the keeping of good works. It was the Amish way, and it made them stumble at using the word saved to describe a believer.

"You think I'd be eaten alive if I walked through that door?" Tom asked.

Sadie smiled. "Oh, no," she said. "Follow me."

Sadie led Tom through the foyer. She did her best to keep the dogs at bay. Meely was lying on the sofa, still crying, her head moving constantly from side to side.

"Mark, this is Tom, a minister."

Mark looked up as Sadie caught her breath. How would he react?

Mark straightened, standing as tall as Tom. Then he extended his hand, a curious welcome in his brown eyes. Sadie breathed out, grateful now.

"Tom Dockers," he said, grasping Mark's hand with a firm grip. His white, white teeth and his eyes with their never-ceasing good humor won him immediately.

"Mark Peight. How do you do?"

"Fine. Your mother?"

"Yes."

Tom nodded. His eyes softened, then filled with warm tears of mercy. Slowly the massive form moved toward the frail woman. He stood over her, his head bent, his lips moving. He was clearly a powerhouse of prayer, faith, and love so great that Sadie felt sure she had never met anyone quite like this man.

Slowly, Tom placed his hand on Meely's restless shoulder. He closed his eyes. Tears squeezed between the lids.

Meely ceased her restless movement and breathed peacefully. Slowly she opened her eyes, then drew in a sharp breath. Her eyes popped as she screamed, high and desperate now.

"No! No! No!" she wailed. "Don't! Oh, don't. Don't torment me before my time!"

Her torment was visible and audible. The dogs whined in response, the large white shepherd beginning a howl of sorts.

Sadie moved quickly to let the dogs out before a situation arose that would have dire consequences.

Tom did not remove his hand. Instead he gently moved it back and forth, as if to calm the flailing woman on the sofa.

"Now listen, honey child. Nobody's gonna hurt you. I'm just here to talk awhile. Nobody's gettin' you."

His voice was drowned out by a piercing scream of agony. Still he kept talking. Half-reassurances, half-prayers. He talked on and on while Meely railed against him, cursing, crying, begging Mark to take this awful man away from her.

They felt the time had come for professional help, when they could no longer control the pain. Meely's lucid thoughts and words were fewer. The strain of trying to keep her comfortable was showing in Mark's eyes.

The local hospital had been extremely helpful, giving them telephone numbers, explaining various services, until they found an organization they were comfortable with.

At first Mark had resisted, until Sadie reasoned with him. His memories of foster care made him suspicious of anyone coming to help professionally. They were all part of "the system" in his words. Only the moans of intense discomfort from his mother's bed finally convinced him. He nodded, a sort of pitiful caving in of his resolve, when Sadie said she would make the call.

When a heavy-set nurse from Hospice showed up at the front door, Meely's screaming only increased. Undaunted, the blond-haired woman waved them all aside, telling them to "git," which they obeyed. Mark led Sadie and Tom to the kitchen, leaving the nurse to administer professional care.

They sat around the kitchen table with mugs of coffee and a blue packet of Oreo cookies. Tom took the time to introduce himself fully, explaining his life's mission as a small town "preacher man," counselor, mentor, cook, husband, and father of three: Levi, Jeptha, and Samuel.

"They my men, they my men," he chortled, swallowing yet another Oreo.

Sadie sipped coffee, quietly absorbing this man and his larger-than-life personality. She had never talked to a black man before. So she listened and became increasingly amazed by this man and his speech. He was completely and totally devoted to his Lord, his God. "My Man," as Tom called him.

Just how close could a person actually get to God? Was it possible to have a personal connection? It was a bit scary. Completely unnerving, really.

"We gotta pray us through this," Tom said. "Prayer is what my Man wants from us, y' know? He got the power. We don't, even though sometimes we think we do, y' know?"

That lilting "y' know?" served to include you fully into his outlook in a way that was not forceful or intimidating. Certainly, this man was not *fer-fearish*, the Pennsylvania Dutch term for being misled. The Amish were always alert for anyone with beliefs strange to them. They exhorted on this subject quite regularly.

Somehow, Tom was not to be feared, Sadie could tell. He just lived his faith in complete fullness. Nothing stood in his way. The way people dressed, their skin color, their way of life, their beliefs, their doctrine, it was all the same to him. He was amazed at the Amish way and glad of it.

"We all people. We all lose sight of the Glory. We sin, slip away. We come back when the Man chastens. He's the God of Glory, y' know?"

Is that how God worked? That would settle a lot of things, Sadie thought.

Tom nodded toward Mark. "Tell me about you and your mother."

So Mark told him his story. His voice was gruff, his eyes hooded sometimes, his manner brusque. But he spoke simply, leaving nothing out.

While they talked, Sadie refilled their coffee cups. She glanced at the clock, then set about grilling sandwiches and heating the chicken corn soup.

All the dishes and utensils in the kitchen were of the highest quality, bought in stores Sadie was sure she never heard of. She loved the feel of the heavy silverware, the weight of the pots and pans, and the china that was so smooth when she ran her hands across it.

"Noritake," it said on the back. Never heard of it, she thought.

Tom's hand was on Mark's now as tears dropped on the leg of his trousers. His head was bent so far, his dark bangs hiding his eyes safely from Tom's gaze.

Tom was praying, his lips moving to the words. Mark looked up and wiped his face.

With tears now in his eyes, Tom said, "We'll pray us through this, my man. You my man, Mark. You my man."

What absolute beauty in those words. Tom spoke as if every prayer went directly to God, who was so glad to have his power acknowledged that he, in turn, made all things possible. What a new and unbelievable thought.

No, unbelievable was not the right word. It was believable. It was just different. Tom had a large, hopeful perspective on God's promises.

After inhaling his lunch, Tom left with a promise to return the following day.

The Hospice nurse also left, but not before giving Mark and Sadie clear instructions. She was professional and precise, giving only the necessary information. She was friendly but firm. Hospice would send over a hospital bed. The morphine would have to be administered in regular doses with no let-up. Once the pain threshold got out of control, there was no bringing it back down easily. They were to give her any food she could keep down, but no caffeine.

The nurse said she'd return each day on a regular basis, and with that she was gone.

✿ ✡ ✿

Tom and the Hospice nurses from Lutheran Home Care became a grounding regularity, especially as Meely's condition deteriorated.

There were also phone calls now. Long, emotional calls from Sadie's Mam and sisters begging her to come home. Reuben told her that Paris wasn't eating her oats. He said it jubilantly, as if that fact alone would bring Sadie flying back as fast as Amtrak could carry her. He also informed her that Anna could finally ride now that she was as thin as a rail. Sadie stiffened with fear and insisted he put Anna on the line right now and get out of the phone shanty while they talked.

He turned the phone over to Anna, but not before he told Sadie about the latest horse shooting. They shot a palomino, but it survived. The police traced the caliber of the rifle. Many detectives were now on the case, according to the local paper.

"It's Paris they're after," Reuben concluded sagely.

Anna said she was not as thin as a rail. No, she was not throwing up. Neither was she forcing herself to purge the food she ate. Yes, she was eating healthily.

The rasping note in her voice set off an alarm in Sadie's mind, but she said nothing. She would deal with troubles back home when she returned. She had more than enough concerns here with Mark and Meely.

Mam was wonderfully supportive and sympathetic. She even cried tears of joy when Sadie told her about Tom. Mam told Sadie that, as she went through life, she would meet people from all walks of faith. Her view of God would widen and deepen. But no matter where her life led her, Mam told her to never lose sight of her wonderful heritage. She was privileged to be born and raised in an Amish home.

"We're people same as everyone else, Sadie, but hang on to your background. It is worth something."

✡ ✡ ✡

When possible, Meely would have a bowl of soup or some oatmeal. Sometimes she asked for a soft-boiled egg or a piece of dry toast. Most of the time, she didn't eat at all, just drifted in and out of sleep.

Once, when the sun was unusually hot and the dry prairie winds began to blow, she asked to have her bed raised. She asked Sadie to come sit with her and Mark, and she began to talk.

She asked about Tom first in her hoarse, weak voice.

"Who is that big, black guy that's in here? He walks through my dreams. He's always calling me, and I'm tied to the bed by my ankles. So I can't go. I can't reach him."

"He's a preacher," Sadie said.

"I figured," she whispered.

Then her tone changed, and she spoke forthrightly. "Yeah, well... I'm not stupid. My time is almost here, and I want to talk. I'm done, now. What I mean is, I'm done blaming everyone else for my life. You know I've always done that?"

Mark nodded in response to Meely's question.

"You don't know if I did or not, Mark, so why are you nodding?"

She was sharp, Sadie thought. She was surprised to see Meely let go of the pitiful thrust of defiance. There was a new expression in her eyes.

Mark said nothing, kept his eyes hidden.

"It's okay. I blamed Atlee. Then I blamed my father. Even my mother. God rest her soul."

She said the last few word in the softest whisper possible, but Sadie heard.

"To blame other people is how you do it, you know. You justify leaving a devoted husband and six beautiful children only by the power of blaming others. It's the easiest way. As long as you can do that, you can convince yourself that you're okay; you're a good person. It's the others, the bad people, who made you this way."

She stopped to cough. She was so weak that it raked

against Sadie's heart and brought tears to her eyes.

"So you do what you want," Meely continued. "You don't do what you know is right. You … you … *recht fertich*—justify yourself—by your own way of thinking. It starts to grow like a parasitic vine that eventually kills the tree that hosts it. The vine is your attitude—killing the truth. Soon you don't know what's right or wrong anymore. And you don't care."

Meely bowed her head, her black hair hiding her tortured eyes.

"I'm so afraid of the truth," she whispered.

Neither Mark nor Sadie knew how to respond. They remained quiet. The clock in the corner supplied the only sound for several minutes.

"What if I say it was all my own fault? Then what? My sins are so … monstrous, there's absolutely no way I can even hope of getting to… Ach, you know. I can't even say the word. I'm too dirty and wretched and lost."

The dogs whined at the door. The clock kept up its rhythmic sound. The refrigerator hummed in the kitchen.

"Mam, at least you admit that what you did was wrong," Mark said quietly. "That's a start, isn't it? I'm no saint either, Mam. But it seems to me, you'd be on the right track."

Mark was suddenly embarrassed by his halting speech in front of Sadie, not sure how she felt about his mother to begin with.

"Well, no doubt about it, if I die, I will go to hell. The devil made me believe I was this pitiful person all my life. Well … not all of it. I have six beautiful children. I see their faces every night before I go to sleep."

A sob tore at the ravaged throat, but she lifted her head and pressed on.

"Beulah. How happy I was to have a daughter! Oh, she was so cute. Even the midwives fussed about her when she was born. Eyes like half moons, a little button for a nose. I kissed her little face constantly. We named Beulah out of great joy. *Beulah* sounds almost like 'bugle.'"

The happy glow that spread across her face was replaced by a look of despair as she described Timothy's birth the following year.

"I wasn't ready. I resisted this little boy growing in my stomach. Oh, where is Timothy now? I pity him so *veesht*.

"He was so thin when he was born. I didn't eat right, I... Oh! Do I have to confess everything? Tell the whole truth?" she groaned. "Well, I have nothing to lose.

"I didn't want Timothy or any of the others after that. I tried to starve myself... I was selfish and mean and thought of no one but myself.

"Diana was as cute as Beulah, but so colicky. Atlee rocked her at night or carried her around on a pillow while I slept. He was always good with the babies. He wanted to name her Elizabeth. Lissie!"

Meely spit the word out with all the force she could muster.

"Lissie! His fat, vile mother. How I hated her! She accused me of so many things. How was I possibly supposed to keep all the laundry clean and white and have the meals ready on time with a colicky baby? That's when I..."

She lowered her head yet again, then asked for a drink of tea. She took a tiny swallow of the icy liquid before she resumed her story.

"When Rachel Mae was born, I knew there was no way I was going to make it. I had no interest in my children anymore. I just wanted out. I planned my exit secretly. Atlee felt it. He became steadily more despairing.

"Because I clung to tradition, I continued my wifely duties, at least for a while. Atlee was very conservative, too. He said the wife is subject to her husband in all things, and I believed him, although I rebelled inside. So horribly.

"I had already started seeing Evan when Jackson was born."

Suddenly Mark burst out, "Mother! Why? Why did you have all these children? It wasn't our fault that you couldn't stand your own life, but you blamed us all the time? That's all you did! Why did you bring innocent souls into this world only to raise them like some stinking... *vermin*!"

He spat the last word into her face, and she cringed beneath his hot wrath. He clenched his fists to his side.

Sadie rose partially, her hand outstretched as if to stop the flow of seething lava from the volcanic crater that was Mark's past.

"Don't, Mark," Meely whispered, weaker now.

"I will if I want to!" he seethed. "In your wildest imagination, Mam, you will never fully realize what you did."

Mark was panting now, his eyes terrible in their anger.

Sadie then broke in calmly in what she hoped was a quieting tone. She talked about Dorothy and Jim and how they couldn't have children and how they felt that God had finally answered their prayers by sending Marcellus and Louis into their lives.

"Perhaps," Sadie concluded, "God is answering your prayers. Perhaps things are not as bad as they looked."

Meely raised her eyes to Mark's. His fell first.

"Mark, I know that I've done a lot of wrong. But will you promise me one thing? I won't live long enough to find my children. Will you find them for me? I can die easier if I know that somehow, you will know where they are and … what they're doing. It might help for you to forgive me, too. Can you promise me that?"

"I'm not made of money."

Sadie could not believe her ears. How could he deny his mother's dying wish? How could he be so cold, so … uncaring?

She opened her mouth to tell him, then decided against it. She could never know what he'd been through or what it was like when he struggled to keep his little siblings from starving.

Who was to be pitied most? It was unanswerable. The past hung over them like a black shroud of misery.

Was Meely the only one at fault, or did Mark do wrong, too? Perhaps he hadn't as a child, but how long would it be until he came to grips with his past? Did those wrongs condone his festering grudges? How long was long enough?

Forgive us our debts as we forgive our debtors. How often do we say that? Sadie wondered. How often do we do it?

Was Mark's unforgiving spirit as bad as his mother's sins in God's eyes? Sadie shrank before the truth. Then she thought of Tom. We'll pray our way through this, she thought.

"Mark, listen. I want to contact my lawyer. You will get all this: the house, the farm, such as it is. I have no one else. Before you showed up, I considered leaving it to the dogs, but that's just nasty. And it is my wish that somewhere, somehow, you can find my … little ones, especially Timothy. Oh, he was so skinny. Please find Timothy someday."

Mark said nothing.

Meely sighed, a long, shaking sound. Then she let her head fall back onto the pillows. Her long dark lashes, so peculiarly thick in spite of the cancer treatments, brushed her cheeks as she closed them.

"I need to rest now."

There was nothing for Mark and Sadie to do but go to the kitchen. When they sat down at the table, Mark wouldn't even look at Sadie. His face stony, the features closed as tightly as a prison door.

Sadie was more than grateful when the phone rang. She grabbed the receiver like a drowning person grabs a life preserver. She smiled when she heard Dorothy's nasally voice say much too loudly, "Whatcha doin', Sadie?" followed by a lengthy list of all the wrongs Erma Keim performed every day, turning that whole ranch upside down.

She glanced out the window and saw Mark whacking furiously at weeds in the garden with an old sickle. She laughed out loud and let Dorothy think it was because of her.

Chapter 22

SHE CALLED LATE AT NIGHT. HER VOICE WAS STRONG, laced with the force of her terror. Her hands fluttered furiously as she kept repeating, "I'm lost. I'm so lost. I have no idea where I am."

Sadie panicked. Her forgotten robe fell open as she grasped Mark by the sleeves and pulled him away, whispering, "Mark! What if she's going? What if her mind is going before she's saved? We have to call Tom!"

Mark turned away from her as she grabbed the strings of her robe and tied them about her waist.

He snapped on the bedside lamp before sitting on the side of Meely's bed. His hair was tousled, his clothes thrown on hurriedly, his shirttail hanging over his trousers, his feet bare.

"Mam," he called softly. Then again, "Mam."

He reached for her moving hands, held them firmly, then released them when Meely thrashed her head about.

"Mam."

Suddenly she sat straight up and glared at him. "Don't 'Mam' me. You're as lost as I am." That was all.

Mark watched her face. Sadie slipped out of the room and went to the kitchen. She found the slip of paper with Tom's number on it beneath a magnet on the refrigerator. She dialed the number.

Tom arrived quickly, just as Sadie knew he would. He hugged her at the door and Sadie clung to him unashamedly. She led him inside. He clapped his hand on Mark's shoulder, called him "My man," then bent to look into Meely's face.

"What's up, honey?" he asked softly.

At the sound of his voice, Meely cried, softly at first, then with increasing force, until Sadie was afraid Meely's thin body would not hold up beneath the powerful sobs that ravaged her.

Tom placed his huge hand on her shoulder to soothe her and began to pray.

Mark and Sadie, unaccustomed to anyone praying verbally except for the prayers read from the German prayer book during church, felt a bit uncomfortable. Sadie was glad for the shadows in the room as she lowered her head and Tom prayed on.

Tom put a hand on Meely's head and prayed for the Lord to visit this woman now, to make known his presence. But she gave no notice that she heard Tom at all, or was beyond caring. Finally she turned her face away.

"Go away," she told Tom.

"I ain't goin' anywhere, honey."

And he didn't. He stayed right there by her side and read to her from the Bible. He read verses of encouragement and hope until Meely slowly quieted.

When she looked up a short time later, they noticed a change in her. The storm had passed and left behind it a woman who was completely void of anything. Her eyes were quiet pools of emptiness in the light of the bedside lamp: no defiance, no despair, but no hope either. There was simply nothing.

Then she lowered her head and spoke to Tom.

"Tom, what would you do in my shoes?"

She asked the question so softly, so pitifully, that it broke Sadie's heart.

"I'd ask Jesus to save my soul," Tom answered quietly in his magical voice.

"He can't anymore."

"And why not?"

"You know why. I'm too wicked. I've been too bad. I've had three other men. I killed Atlee."

"Now wait a minute. You what?"

"My first husband. The father of my children."

"You killed him?"

"Yes."

"How'd you do that?"

"Well, he drowned himself. But it was because I left him."

"I see."

Tom sat quietly for a long time until Meely began weeping violently again.

Then Tom said quietly, "Why don't you look the other way?"

Meely stopped crying. "Which way?"

"Look to Jesus."

"I can't find him. Besides, he won't forgive me."

"You'd be surprised, Meely."

Tom talked about salvation in minute detail. Every word was a caress, the love of God so evident with his "y' knows?" and "my Mans." He assured her that she had already taken the most important step: admitting her sinful past. Now she had to move on and ask for mercy.

"Just accept it."

"I can't. They excommunicated me. I'm given over to the devil."

Tom raised his eyebrows, then looked to Mark, seeking his help.

Mark explained the Amish way of excommunication that occurs when a member is disobedient or breaks their vows to the church.

"It is actually a form of love, Mam," Mark said, speaking softly. "It's a reminder of your wrongdoing so that your spirit may be redeemed."

Suddenly, Meely understood.

"Aah!" The cry was long and drawn out.

"Yes! Oh, how I do understand that, Mark! My guilt went with me everywhere I went. Especially when I lay in bed at night. My children's faces. Atlee's face. The fact that I had been disobedient. The shunning. The ban. It bothered me every day of my life. But…"

Here her eyes opened wide as she seemed to grasp a solid fact.

"Do you suppose… Could it be…? Now I'm sorry. Can I still be saved?"

"No doubt about it, honey. You messed up badly. But Jesus is still your only hope of salvation. He's the light that will get you safely to the other side."

Still she wavered. Still she doubted.

Tom prayed again, then began humming the first bars of "Amazing Grace." He asked Mark and Sadie to join him, which they did gladly, though sometimes they stumbled over the words.

Meely fell asleep, then, and Tom stood up, shaking his head.

"We're gonna have to pray our way through this," he said. "Stay with me."

✥ ✡ ✥

The cancer soon began invading Meely's nerve endings and tissue, causing excruciating pain. The morphine did little against the constant waves of torment, so the Hospice nurses adjusted the dosage.

The medication caused Meely to slide in and out of consciousness. Sometimes she spoke lucidly; other times she was completely bewildered.

During one particularly good afternoon, she asked Mark to sing the *Lob Song*, an old song in the German hymnbook that was sung at every Amish service. It was a song from her childhood, her past, even the years of overwhelming responsibility as a mother.

Sadie joined him, self-consciously at first, but their voices gathered strength as they sang. It proved to be a healing balm, a salve of love, that opened the way for Tom to minister to Meely.

When Tom spoke this time, she couldn't speak. She just nodded. Soon warm tears ran down her cheeks as she kept nodding, understanding, taking it all in.

Tom's words were like a warm summer rain that fell from kind skies, nurturing tiny, hard seeds in a cold, dry earth. The seeds cracked, broke, and new life crept upward. Finally, in the spring, the plant burst through the soil into the marvelous sunlight.

Tom's words finally produced light in her eyes.

"I do accept Jesus Christ."

She spoke quietly, the words illuminated by a first light of grace, and the angels sang.

Mark's face reflected the light in his mother's. Sadie had never seen such soft, broken, mellow light emanating from his eyes. It was almost holy. None of the old brashness was there.

Meely was quiet after that, and Tom respected her silence. He simply sat by her bedside, his hand on hers.

Sadie couldn't help but think how Amish it was. So quiet, with little fanfare. It was still Meely's way after all these years. Tom recognized this, and later called it right.

They left her then, and went to the kitchen, talking in low tones.

✿ ☆ ✿

They often sang for her now. Sometimes in German, other times in English, they sang any hymn they could remember.

One day when Sadie thought Meely was asleep, she chuckled quietly. Sadie thought nothing of it, thinking Meely may have been laughing in her sleep.

"Remember '*Schlofc, buppli, Schlofc*' ('Sleep baby sleep')"? Meely asked Sadie.

"Yes."

"I sang that little song at least a thousand times."

She opened her eyes, and in a pathetic, reedy whisper, she began:

> *Schlofc, buppli, Schlofc,*
> *Da doddy hüt die schofe,*
> *Die mommy melked die rote kie*
> *Kommt net hame bis mya frie*
> *Schlofc, buppli, Schlofc.*

Meely sighed. A tear trembled on her eyelid.

"Poor little Timothy. I sang that to him all the time." She turned to Sadie with an earnest look in her eyes. "If you ever see Timothy, promise me you'll tell him how I wish I'd been nicer to him. Please?"

Sadie nodded solemnly.

Meely lingered longer than anyone anticipated. The shroud of approaching death cast a dark pall over each day. Sadie's sense of homesickness grew.

One day Tom unexpectedly offered to stay with Meely and sent Mark and Sadie out for the afternoon.

"Pack a lunch. Go somewhere and have a picnic."

So they did. They packed ham sandwiches, fruit, and some of the chocolate cake Tom's wife, Malinda, had sent along over. They put ice in an old, plastic, two-quart jug and filled it with iced tea. Then they started out as the sun was climbing to noontime.

It was a warm spring day. Butterflies flapped and fluttered, hovering over wildflowers in the overgrown garden. Birds dipped and trilled their endless songs.

Mark was attentive, helping her over the broken board fence, holding her hand, teasing her, slipping a lean, brown arm around her waist. For a few hours they would forget. For a few hours they would remember they were young and in love with a bright future.

Mark did not mention his mother's account of her will, and neither did Sadie. It seemed too unreal, like a mirage. The delusional words of a dying woman. Better not approach the subject with any real amount of hope.

The lawyer had come and done all the necessary work

to fulfill Meely's dying wishes. Mark was the sole heir. If any of his siblings were found, they would be given their share.

It was quite a large sum of money, making the 20,000-dollar reward for rescuing the wild horses seem paltry. The sale of the farm would make the sum even larger.

They came to a creek of sorts. It was really only a trickle winding through a ditch and snaking along the prairie grasses and sagebrush. A few old willow trees grew along its banks, their roots reaching down into the water as if to sustain life by the small trickle the creek offered. The grass was thick and lush, however, especially beneath the dancing willow leaves, the long green fronds whispering as they moved gently in the breeze.

Mark threw himself on his back, his hands behind his head, his knees bent in a V-shape. He sighed contentedly and closed his eyes.

Sadie sat beside him, her arms wrapped around her knees. She watched the rise and fall of his broad chest beneath the blue denim of his shirt. He was so unbelievably handsome, the way his dark hair fell over his eyes. And that perfect mouth. Was it enough to base her love on that face?

She knew it wasn't, but she knew just as clearly that this was where God wanted her, beside this man and all his baggage. Yes, his past would return again and again to torment him. He would always battle between darkness and light. Even so, she knew she was right where she was supposed to be, directly in the center of God's will.

So she sat quietly as Mark feigned sleep. She pulled a few grasses, fingered that tender yellow part that rises from the earth, and thought of home.

She smiled to herself as she thought of Dorothy's last phone call. She had ranted on in the most erratic manner about Erma Keim, claiming she was in love with Lothario Bean, poor man. He was a good Catholic husband to his beautiful wife, and here was that red-haired giraffe after him with no shame.

Sadie had laughed out loud and told Dorothy it was just Erma's way. She was extremely outgoing, exuberant, and a bit overboard, but she was certainly not a man-chaser.

Dorothy huffed indignantly.

"Sadie, you can try and be the peacemaker all you want. But I know when I see a girl settin' her hat for someone. She's out of line. And you should see how Lothario acts about her fruit pies. It's unreal! He goes on and on about that Dutch apple she makes. You know, the one with the crumb topping? With streusel? Now if that ain't out-and-out flirting, I don't know what is. She even straightens her apron when my Jim walks through that kitchen door, so she does."

"It's just her way," Sadie repeated.

"Well, them fruit pies? She's gonna make 'em for all the men now. To take home. They're not *that* good. If you ask me, she's a bit stingy on the sugar. Now my blueberry pies, on the other hand, can't be beat."

Sadie assured Dorothy that her pies were the best, but she liked the idea of Erma pleasing those ranch hands with her apple pies. Erma needed a little praise and affirmation.

"Dorothy, you know as well as I do that an old maid like her needs love and attention, too. We all do."

"That's exactly right, Sadie. I ain't dumb. That's why she's after all them men, even Richard Caldwell. Why, when those two get together, I have to take my hearing aids out, so I do. The other day they was havin' a slice o' pie in my kitchen, mind you, both of 'em roaring like hyenas. That old Erma was a-slappin' her knee when she laughed. The boss, he eats it all up, same as her apple pie. Now that pie, Sadie, could do with at least another cup of sugar."

Suddenly Mark turned his head to look at her, his intense gaze interrupting her thoughts.

"Sadie."

She couldn't answer. There was a tone of endearment in the way he said her name that drove away her power to speak at all. Her limbs turned to water when he sat up, his gaze never wavering.

"Sadie."

He said her name again, a caress this time. She could not answer.

"Will you marry me?"

The words were spoken softly, then hung in the air between them, veiled in cascades of white roses and lilies of the valley. She heard lovely music from somewhere deep within, the sound of love starting in her mind and seeping into her heart and soul.

"Oh, Mark!"

The wonder of his question flowed through her being, through her hands. They fluttered to his as he sought them, laced her fingers together with his. She breathed the scent of the flowers into her answer.

"Oh, Mark! Yes! Yes, I will marry you!"

He crushed her to him, his lips finding her willing ones. Breathless now, they broke apart. Tears came to Mark's eyes.

"I wanted to find a perfect time and place, but... I'm not real good with words and romantic stuff... you know? Like getting down on my knees with a ring the way English people do."

Sadie laughed and kissed him again, never wanting to let him go.

"Mark, you don't need to. But I do want a clock," she teased.

A clock was the traditional Amish engagement gift. Once a young girl received her clock, whether a grand-father or a pendulum clock for the wall, the union was sealed for coming nuptials.

"I will let you have my mother's."

Suddenly, after that, he became shy, sensitive to the fact that this may be bad timing with his mother dying. Was it all too dark and foreboding for her? How could she say yes? There was no way her life would ever be easy. Perhaps she had no idea how hard.

"I probably have a pretty good idea what I'm in for. I mean, our dating has been a bit complex at times. To put it politely."

"All my fault. Every time."

"No, of course not. I just have to remember that you are…well, not like other people."

They laughed together, Mark held her and murmured his love. The fact that she would marry him put him in a state of disbelief.

"But why? Why would you marry me?"

"It's so simple, Mark. I love you. I know we'll have many dark valleys to go through, but this love will sustain us. I want to be with you. I want to make your breakfast, pack your lunch, wash your clothes, fold them and put them away…"

"Hopefully sleep in the same bed with me."

Sadie felt the color warm her face.

"That, too, of course."

"Sadie."

Suddenly, there was a different tone in his voice. Again she became quiet.

"I have been with other women. I'm not..." He couldn't go on.

Sadie nodded.

"Mark, it's okay. I figured as much. But..."

She needed to know, even if it was a question that would be old-fashioned and maybe even offensive.

"That was before you gave your heart to Jesus? Before you were baptized into the Amish faith?"

"Of course, Sadie."

"I'm so glad," she whispered.

And she was. His sins were forgiven, washed away by the blood of the Lamb. Thanksgiving welled up in her heart as that realization settled in, brighter and more real than ever before. For without the love of God, what would their union become?

Sadie's nature was not perfect either. She was full of selfishness, jealousy, and other weaknesses that would not serve his insecurities well.

Search my heart, O God, and show me my weaknesses. That was all she could think until it became a sort of benediction.

They sat together for a long time, talking of their future and making plans for the wedding. At last Mark spoke of his longing to find Timothy.

"It breaks my heart, to think of Mam's sadness for Timothy. I remember him well. He was so thin, whining and crying. I honestly think he drove her nuts. I'll do anything to honor her wish to find him."

"But Mark, why were you so cold when she asked you to find him?"

"Sadie, listen. There's one thing you will need to understand. Every single time I'm confronted with my past, I want to lash out, hurt someone, blame someone, make it all go away by the power of my own anger. Do you have any idea how horrible it is to remember the things I am forced to remember? Did you ever hear a child crying steadily all night long because of an empty stomach? The Jell-o... I can still smell it, feel the sticky, sugary powder against my hand as I shook a portion into the stinking, plastic, milk-stained bottle. I can't eat strawberry Jell-o to this day. I did what I had to do, but the gigantic despair I lived with is like a coiled snake, ready to strike. I can't really explain it... fully, I guess."

Sadie closed her eyes as tears leaked between her lashes and made wet trails down both her cheeks. Mark held her closer and kissed her forehead.

"Timothy wasn't very healthy to begin with. And Mam... Well, she wasn't really abusive, but she took out a lot of her frustrations on Timothy. That... in a way, is why I'm almost afraid to find him. How could he possibly have turned out to be a normal human being? He sure didn't have much to go on those first few years. His little bottom got so sore from his constant diarrhea. I feel so bad about that. I did the best I could, but there weren't always clean diapers. I..."

Sadie cut him off.

"All while I was in Ohio, eating my mother's good cooking, wearing her well-washed laundry, playing on the manicured lawn, living with the love of two good parents. I had no clue I had something special going on in my life."

Suddenly she sat up and turned to meet his brown eyes.

"And, Mark, I guarantee, if I would have been able to, I would have brought you a whole bunch of groceries. Better yet, I would have packed all of you in a car and brought you home."

"But..." Here Mark threw back his head and laughed, a free and beautiful sound.

"You probably weren't even born yet!"

Chapter 23

Meely's pain was the demon they all battled, but Tom's dark face and wondrous smile had a way of brightening even the most trying hour.

Hospice provided more pain-killers. They also brought the best mattress available, with a large gel-filled overlay. The gel moved through the well-built tubes of the mattress to relieve the pressure on her thin body.

Even so, no one could touch her. The softest, most gentle touch evoked shrill cries of alarm, pain, and horror.

She cried, begged, then finally, when her newfound faith found its footing, she prayed.

The hardness in her eyes was gone. They were now clear pools of love. She spoke of it, she whispered of it, and she sang songs of God's love. She sang "Shall We Gather at the River?," "How Great is Our God," and "Beulah Land," then lapsed into a soft conversation about her darling baby Beulah.

"You know, I must not have been all bad. I loved her. If I could only tell her that. You will someday, right, Mark? Tell her how cute she was, how I kissed her. I did love her.

"But you know, the love I have for her is such a tiny drop compared to the love we receive from heaven. The angels love me now, Well, I guess they did before, but I just didn't accept it. They're waiting for me. Not me. My soul. It'll fly away when I stop breathing.

"You know, I loved Atlee at one time. I love him now. I can't wait to see him. And I don't have to tell him I'm sorry. He already knows. Isn't that wonderful?

"Praise his name! Praise his goodness!"

And she was singing softly, humming under her breath. Then she slept, her thin chest heaving, then rising and falling slowly.

Her lips were so dry, so painfully cracked and brittle. Ever so gently, Sadie wet a sponge and moistened the once-beautiful mouth. Meely moaned with pain in her sleep.

Tom sat with his head bent. He held Meely's hand, whispering his prayers, still praying her through this.

Sadie sat wrapped in her robe, her dark hair pulled back in a ponytail, her head resting on the back of the red wing-chair, her legs drawn up and curled beside her.

Mark sat on the carpet, his head resting against the arm of the chair. They could barely stay apart from each other now. Their engagement opened a whole new world of love, dispelling any insecurities or doubts about each other's feelings that they may have felt before. They often discussed their plans to spend the rest of their lives together.

Tom had cried openly when they told him about their engagement. He cried, laughed, rejoiced, even danced around the kitchen, singing an English wedding song. Mark recognized it, but Sadie was completely perplexed.

He brought a cake, served it with ice cream. Malinda and his three "men" came, too.

Malinda was at least 250 pounds and had the most beautiful face Sadie had ever seen. She wore a multi-colored silk head wrap. Her beautiful eyes were pools of liquid amber, and perfect black eyebrows accentuated her golden brown complexion. Her full, soft lips were always drawn into a half-smile. Her clothes made her look like an African queen in swaying, brilliant skirts. A smartly-cut top made her silhouette appear well formed. A person of unquestionable presence, her movements sort of sailed through the rooms.

Their three boys, whom Tom called his "men," were polite, well-spoken, and seemed completely happy and well adjusted. Teasing their parents, — "Jus' jivin' wid ya," they'd say—their handsome faces were wreathed in smiles almost all the time, their laughter quick and easy.

Sadie wondered what kept those loose jeans from falling down, the only saving grace being the looser T-shirts that nearly reached their knees. Their odd shoes were either orange, green, or purple. Jeptha wore what looked like black pantyhose on his head, while Levi wore his hair in long coiled cornrows.

The family was full of an endless stream of laughter, love, and a generous helping of goodwill toward everyone in the room and outside of it.

Sadie asked Malinda if the family always got along in this manner and was astounded to hear an adamant, "No! Oh, no. Huh-uh, man. Who you think we are, huh? We people."

After they all left, Sadie and Mark looked at each other and laughed.

"What a great family!" Mark said, shaking his head.

The Hospice nurse left a short while later, so they went to the bedroom to sit with Meely while she slept. They didn't try to touch her at all, knowing it would only bring pain rather than comfort.

They took their seats and made themselves comfortable, ready to keep the vigil once more. They noticed something different. There was a quiet aura about Meely —too quiet.

Mark looked at Sadie, a question in her eyes. She responded with raised eyebrows.

Had she passed away so suddenly? When she was all alone? But, no. She was still breathing, though it was shallow and erratic, almost imperceptible. Then she stirred.

Mark reached her first. He put out his hands to guide her as she slowly sat up, but surprisingly, she needed no assistance.

Sadie was at Mark's side, astounded.

"We can't..." she began.

But Mark held a finger to his lips. They watched in disbelief as she turned her body and moved to put her feet on the floor. Their hands were outstretched, ready to catch her, but there was no need.

Was the setting sun casting this golden glow throughout the room? Or was it the glow of hovering angels?

Slowly, Meely's thin white feet touched the carpet. As if in a dream, she lifted her thin arms and walked to Mark. She smiled, and her dark eyes filled with a light beyond earthly comprehension.

With a soft cry, Mark enfolded her in his strong brown arms. Then they swayed, back and forth, in soft, undulating movements.

"Goodbye," she whispered, her dance of love complete.

Mark bent his head and kissed his mother's cheek, then led her back to the bed. He laid her down quietly and gently. He held Sadie in one arm, his dying mother in the other, while cleansing tears of healing rained down his cheeks.

"Goodbye, Mam," he choked.

And then Sadie knew she was gone. Her soul had taken its flight.

It seemed she had been partly in heaven and partly here on earth when she danced with Mark. She only needed to give away this great love before she left to be with Jesus.

Mark knelt by his mother's bed, sobs coming hoarsely at first, until the power of them sent him to the floor, where his grief turned to tormented keening that could not be stopped.

Wisely, Sadie stayed back. This was not ordinary grief.

This, she supposed, is what happens when a person takes her own way. She is like a barge propelled by a huge diesel engine of self-will, leaving disappointment and all-consuming sadness in its wake. When the end comes, when the barge runs aground and spills toxic oil into the pristine sea, it is those left behind who deal with the slick, poisonous hatred of unforgiveness for the rest of their lives.

But there was Jesus' forgiveness, yes. And there was closure for those damaged in the wake, oh, yes!

Sadie would never forget this moment. Sadie would never forget the sweetness of that whispered, "Goodbye." But to see Mark in the throes of this disappointment was almost more than she could bear. The disappointment of a wasted life. The anger of every hardship he had ever endured. The desperate, endless, life-draining swimming to get out of the toxic oil.

Now he had partially saved himself. He had to try and save his siblings. At least find them.

The future looked daunting and dangerous. All Sadie could see was a black dragon breathing fire, and she had no sword to slay it.

But she suddenly remembered, neither did David when he went up against the giant and slew him. How often had she heard that story? As a child she always sat up and paid attention when the preacher spoke of David and Goliath. Perhaps Mark's past and the deep grief of his mother's death, perhaps all that was their Goliath, a giant they must face together.

Then slowly the storm ceased, leaving Mark in a fetal position, his hands tucked between his knees. He shuddered, relaxed, then slowly rose to his feet. He stood silently with his back toward Sadie, looking at the still form of his mother.

Suddenly he turned on his heel. "Call Tom. I'm going out," he said brusquely, refusing to meet her eyes.

"But…" Sadie began to protest, then closed her mouth, wincing as Mark slammed the door on his way out.

Feeling more alone than she ever had, she walked over to the bed and gently pulled the sheet up over Meely's still body.

Mark's mother. May God rest her soul.

Sadie had loved her sincerely. She had.

✿ ✡ ✿

The following days were a blur of activity. Tom knew what to do and helped with the funeral arrangements. Samuel and Levi worked the computer, desperately trying to find Mark's missing siblings, coming up with nothing. Malinda cooked up a storm, delivering great casserole dishes of southern cooking, huge coconut cakes with slivers of pecans all over the top.

Neighboring farm wives came. These well-meaning women dressed in clean cotton frocks brought Pyrex dishes of homemade scalloped potatoes, lasagna, burritos, fried chicken, and green-bean casserole. The quantity of food was endless.

The kindness of ordinary people is a wondrous thing, Sadie thought. She wished Meely could see how these simple country folk turned out in droves to deliver their condolences in the form of warm food.

Tom's great laugh rang out while he and Mark sampled all the food. He spent a great deal of time with Mark, beginning that first evening after Meely's death. They spent hours outside under the trees, Mark sitting in the hammock, Tom on a rusted bench.

Sadie wondered if Mark would ever tell her what they talked about.

The viewing at the local funeral home was pitifully small. There was no long line of friends and acquaintances waiting to sign their names at the entrance. There were only a few people from the Hospice service, the man who brought salt for the water softener, and the fuel-truck driver. Mark was the only family.

Meely was still lovely, laid in a bed of white satin. Great banks of flowers surrounded the coffin, as she had wanted.

A soft, early, summer rain fell on the heads of the small group of mourners at the burial. A few well-wishers from Tom's congregation shook their heads at the sadness of it all. Their faces were a haven of kindness for Mark and Sadie now.

Tom spoke a eulogy of love. He read the Twenty-Third Psalm, called Meely "sister," and led the group in a hopeful hymn. Mark and Sadie bowed their heads and cried tears of cleansing. The past was partially settled, or at least as much as it could be in a matter of a few days.

They went back to the house, where Malinda served up a banquet of delicious food, urging everyone to take heaping servings of everything.

"Y'all tried this here chicken? Y' need more Coke?"

Mark ate hungrily. He smiled at Sadie, who sat across from him at the dining room table.

"You look amazing in your black dress," he whispered, sending her pulse racing.

✿ ☆ ✿

They finally made arrangements to return home. They said many tearful farewells to Tom and his family, who promised to visit. Then they climbed into the Amtrak train, that speeding wonder that would deliver Sadie once again to her family. Her heart pumped with excitement.

Going home!

Mark watched Sadie's face before commenting on it.

"Your eyes are just shining, Sadie."

"Yes, Mark, I am so happy to return home. It seems like a long time since I've seen everyone."

"Yeah, well, you're lucky."

That was all he said before turning his face away.

Oh, boy, she thought. Here we go again.

Anger bubbled out of a seething cauldron of hurt. A part of her wanted to sit up and actually hit him, yelling, *"Bupp! Grosse Bupp!"*

Would he always hold up that daunting shield of his past? Would he always make excuses and ask for pity? Or when he was jealous, would he take the role of a martyr?

Then Sadie sighed and fluctuated between self-blame and anger.

I know I'm lucky. I have a wonderful family. Maybe I shouldn't show how happy I am. It's my fault.

The steady rhythm of the train put her to sleep. It must have been a deep sleep, because she didn't remember letting her head fall on Mark's chest. She awoke completely confused, with Mark's arm around her securely.

He was in a jovial mood. He teased her and bantered incessantly about their wedding. He acted as if he had never been unkind, never left her out of his thoughts.

Complicated person, for sure, was her only rational thought.

✡ ✡ ✡

Arriving home was everything Sadie knew it would be. There were hugs and tears of welcome. Reuben hovered self-consciously in the background, wearing a brand-new shirt for the occasion. Sadie squealed and ran after him, giving him a very warm hug. He shrugged it off, but his wide grin gave away his true feelings.

Anna was alarmingly thin, just as Sadie suspected she would be. Her thin face made her eyes look abnormally large. All the loose fabric of her pretty teal-colored dress was tucked into her apron.

Sadie had to work hard to hide her fear, mentally shelving the talk she would have to have with Mam and Dat later.

It was Saturday, so no one had to go to work. Everyone piled into the kitchen and chatted over each other. There was so much to say.

Mam had prepared a wonderful brunch. There was

a breakfast pizza, made with a homemade crust, fried potatoes, sausage, eggs, tomatoes, and cheese. There were golden biscuits and sausage gravy, fresh fruit, orange juice, homemade yogurt, and granola. The coffeepot was never empty for long, but no one had room for any of the doughnuts available in great variety.

Not even Reuben's eyes were dry when Sadie spoke of Meely's death. Dat marveled over the whole thing and said he never heard anything like it. What would the ministers say about something like that?

What about the Bible story of the woman at the well? Mam asked. Wasn't that woman a sinner? Five husbands she had, and the man she was with that day was not her husband. Yet she recognized Jesus when those self-righteous scribes and Pharisees had no clue.

"Jesus offered much forgiveness and great love," she concluded. Her nostrils flared a bit. She got up to refill her coffee. It wasn't really necessary, but she was worked up by Dat questioning whether Meely was saved.

Mark listened closely. He had never heard Sadie's mam talk like that.

Dat quickly agreed, patting his wife's shoulder with a soft touch of contrition. Mam lifted her face to his, a soft smile spreading across her features. Dat returned it with one of his own.

That beautiful exchange was what came after 30 years of marriage, Sadie thought. Their own Goliath definitely had dwindled in size in the face of this long-practiced trust between them.

What a foundation! Surely it was worth more than gold. Surely she and Mark could make it, too.

After the long, drawn-out brunch, Mark followed Dat outside. Sadie knew he would tell Dat about their engagement. She decided to wait to tell Mam, anticipating the surprised expressions of her sisters and Reuben.

Her room was a welcoming haven. She had forgotten the tasteful simplicity of it, the calming white curtains and sand-colored comforter, the off-white walls, the candles and greenery blending so perfectly. She loved her room all over again.

She went to the bathroom to straighten her covering and check on the condition of her hair. She paused to sniff the familiar scent of Dove soap in the holder and to take in the border of seashells on the wall.

She raised her eyebrows when she saw the black plastic bottle of men's body wash. Was it Reuben's? Oh, my goodness.

Before long, Reuben would be going with the youth. *Rumspringa.* That was the time of "running around," when youth first experience the world and are forced to make some of their own choices. Some would be good, others bad. And yet, he would still be within the Amish arc of friends and under the scrutiny of a close community where things of a disobedient nature traveled through the grapevine at the speed of lightning. He would still have to pay the consequences once his poor behavior reached Dat's ears.

Anna was a far greater concern. Dat's frightened smile told her everything.

Sadie pushed the problems aside. She would wait to talk to Dat after Mark announced their happy news.

Mam's face actually turned a different shade and her eyes darkened, when Mark said they wanted to get married in September. She mentally calculated the months.

"June, July, August," she breathed shakily.

"Congratulations!" all her sisters yelled, in their "Happy Birthday" voices.

"Who's going to *huck nâva*?

"I will."

"I want to!"

"I'm the oldest!"

Reuben said nothing at all but just kept eating dough-nuts and washing them down with milk. Sadie watched him, then noticed him blinking his eyes and twitching the corners of his mouth into a downward tilt. It was the way he looked when he was not going to cry, no matter what.

For a moment, it erased Sadie's joy as clearly as a wet rag erased words on the schoolhouse blackboard.

Would that special bond with Reuben disappear when she married?

"I want Reuben to *huck nâva*," she said clearly.

He looked up, mid-chew, a slow smile starting in his eyes.

Nâva hucking was a high honor. He was young, but easily tall enough to escort one of Mark's family, whom-ever he chose, to the bridal table. He would even hold her hand.

"You want to?" Sadie asked.

"Of course," Reuben answered, his chin tucked in to make his voice sound much more masculine then it actu-ally was.

They decided on Leah, Sadie's next oldest sister, to be the second attendant, along with Kevin, her steady boyfriend.

Mam was in a state of happy panic; it was honestly the only way to describe her. Dat was gruff and businesslike, but he snapped his suspenders too often and drank way too much coffee.

Mark offered to pay for the wedding, telling them about the inheritance from his mother.

There was so much to say, so much to plan, that they quickly grew tired. Dat flopped on the recliner and reached for the *Botschaft*. Mam frantically washed dishes, no doubt mentally counting all the relations on both sides of the family and calculating how much food it would take to feed them all two meals.

Sadie stole away, then, to greet Paris. She entered the barn eagerly, slipping into Paris' stall, and flinging her arms around the horse's neck, noticing the condition of her honey-colored coat, the well-rounded stomach, the muscles well developed in her deep chest.

"Oh, Paris, I missed you so much! How I wish I could take you for a ride. But I can't yet. Dat said I can't even leave you out in the pasture because of those evil men. Well, they're not going to get you."

She kept caressing the silky coat, murmuring her words of love, when she looked up to find Reuben hanging on the gate.

"Why do you have to go and get married?" he asked, his voice cracking in mid-sentence.

"Reuben, I know..." she broke off, her emotions catching her off-guard.

She gave Paris one last pat, letting the horse nuzzle the palm of her hand with that wiggling, velvety nose. Then she turned to Reuben, desperately willing herself to stay happy and lighthearted.

Why did this bother him so much?

Before she could speak, he wailed, "You'll never ride with me again! You'll have a whole bunch of babies the way everyone does, and you won't ride at all."

Sadie opened the gate and put her hands on his arms, looking squarely into his innocent eyes.

"Reuben. I will always ride Paris, married or not.

And if I have babies, I guess Mark is just going to have to stay home and watch them so we can go riding together."

Before he could respond, she pulled him into her arms and squeezed him tightly.

Chapter 24

THERE WAS NO USE TRYING TO KEEP ORDER THE remainder of the summer. Dorothy and Erma were every bit as bad as Mam. Between the three of them planning the menu for the wedding, Sadie's mind was full of at least 30 different dishes, none of them even close to what she really wanted.

Erma, of course, insisted on Dutch apple pie. When Sadie told her that Mark's favorite was coconut cream, Erma wouldn't speak to her for two weeks. This bit of news escalated Dorothy to a state of glee, saying she was an expert at cooking homemade, cream-pie filling. Then Mam said there was no way anyone was going to cook coconut pie filling except herself. Dorothy pouted for a week after that, saying no Amish cook could outdo the pies she always made for the fire hall.

Sadie ended up having a serious heart-to-heart talk with Mam about the importance of give-and-take. Why couldn't Dorothy have the honor of making the pies? Especially if they decided to bread the chicken with Mam's recipe rather than Dorothy's?

The weather grew stifling hot. The heat rolled off the sun and pressed down on them with its force, like a steamroller made of hot air.

Sadie worked only three days a week at the ranch now because of all the work to do at home. She looked forward to the times she spent in the air-conditioning, though it did little to cool Dorothy's and Erma's hot tempers. Dorothy was always in a dither these days, with Erma wielding her red-haired power. Sadie flung back and forth between them like a tennis ball, until one day when she had less patience than usual.

She had just fought with Mam about the sleeves for her wedding dress. So when Dorothy and Erma started their bickering, Sadie stood in the middle of the kitchen, balled her fists, squeezed her eyes shut, and demanded some peace and quiet. Couldn't they both stop bellowing as if they were two-year-olds? She told Erma she did not want the seven-layer salad for her wedding. She didn't like all that mayonnaise spread on top of the lettuce. Dorothy could forget about making biscuits. Amish people ate dinner rolls. She wanted all whole wheat, and she was going to order them at a bakery.

That outburst brought an end to the competition, at least temporarily. Dorothy muttered under her breath for a long time afterward, and Erma took to helping Lothario Bean in the office at the stables whenever possible. Dorothy lifted a hand to her mouth and whispered in Sadie's ear that she didn't trust that Erma, and if she didn't stay away from that "little Mexican," she was going to contact his wife, sure as shootin'.

Sadie told Dorothy she was being overly suspicious. With Lothario being the staunch Catholic he was and Erma the Amish member she was, there was absolutely nothing to worry about. They just enjoyed each other's company.

Dorothy swiped viciously at a roaster, then held the sponge aloft like a judge's gavel, water dripping off her round elbows. She told Sadie to get off her high horse right this minute. She didn't care how religious they were, those two were human beings and were spending entirely too much time alone.

So Sadie approached Erma in church the following Sunday, telling her about Dorothy's concern. Erma's eyes opened wide, then wider, before a horrified shriek broke forth from between her open lips. Then she quickly clapped two hands across her mouth as three overweight matriarchs gave her a disapproving glare.

"Oh, my word!" she hissed with a disgruntled look on her face.

Sadie burst out laughing, then clapped her own hand to her mouth.

"He's … half my size! He's married! He's … he's Catholic! I'm just his friend! Oh, Sadie! To think Dorothy… Even bringing up that subject is enough to … to …"

"It's okay, Erma. Dorothy means well. She's just being careful. I think sometimes we Amish girls are a bit naïve. In our culture, married men are so off-limits, it's like they don't exist. But it's different in the English world."

Erma chewed on a thumbnail, then shook her head in frustration.

"That is just the plight of old maids. We're always being watched, talked about, matched up with someone … Ach, Sadie, it goes on and on."

Erma gazed unseeingly out the window, her eyes darkening with emotion, a cloud of sorrow passing over her usual animated glow. She continued, "It would be entirely different if we could…do something about our… Oh, whatever."

Sadie watched her, saying nothing. What could she say? Erma shrugged her slouching shoulders and went back to biting the thumbnail. She slumped down farther against the wash-house cupboard.

"It would be different if we…well."

She stopped. Suddenly she straightened, took a deep breath, and self-consciously tugged at her waistband. "See, you're one of the lucky ones. Mark loves you. You're getting married. Mine married someone pretty. He was mine, Sadie. We dated for a year. In the end, I wasn't enough."

She put up a hand to her coarse red hair. "My skin looks like…the Sahara. Nose like a crow's beak. I'm nothing to look at. But, Sadie, he loved me once."

"Who?"

Erma shook her head, closing the conversation.

"But.." Sadie began.

Erma closed her eyes and held up a hand to stop Sadie. She didn't want to discuss it anymore.

✩ ☆ ✩

That was how Sadie got the idea of asking Erma to *nâva huck* with Reuben. Mark had been unable to come up with any distant cousin as Reuben's partner in the wedding party. They had been racking their brains over whom to ask ever since.

When Sadie approached Reuben, he all but stood on his head in refusal. He shook his head back and forth so violently, his hair swung in his eyes, and he said no so many times, it became a sort of chant.

No amount of coaxing would help. Sadie even offered to buy him a new saddle, a brown one, brand new, from the tack shop in Critchfield.

"Nope. I'm not *nâva hucking* with her. She's twice my age. She's taller than me. She's too loud. No."

As time went on, the thought of a new saddle weighed heavily on his mind, slowly tipping the scales away from the avowed no. The turning point came about a week later. Surely he could do that for his best sister. For Mark.

Mark was not nearly as hard to deal with as Reuben. He smiled constantly, shrugged his shoulders, and said anything they planned was fine with him. All he wanted was Sadie. She was so happy, so completely in love with him, and so glad she had made this choice to marry him in spite of their rocky courtship.

He worked tirelessly on his house. He gutted the interior and replaced the old plaster with pine boards. He replaced the flooring and built all kinds of furniture. He hoped to have most of it finished by the day of the wedding for his new bride.

Sadie spent many evenings with him, sanding and varnishing. He laid the stones of the fireplace himself, working so late that Sadie fell asleep on the dusty old chair in the corner. Wolf laid at her feet, his head resting on his paws, his blue eyes watching Mark's every move.

He was as loyal to Sadie as he was to Mark, never barking or showing any hostility. He faithfully followed both of them around the property, keeping an eye out for any intruders.

Sadie was glad to have Wolf. Mark's place was so secluded. The road was about a quarter of a mile below the house, without much traffic. There were certainly no neighbors to run to if she needed help.

The house was surrounded by woods, although there was enough space for a nice lawn in the front. Mark had cut down quite a few trees to make the lawn larger. Then he chopped the trees into firewood and stacked it neatly in a shed for many winters to come.

Originally Mark had made plans to raze the house. Then he decided to preserve it by keeping the structure, the western character, the odd corners, and the dormers built into the front of the roof.

The house was brown, covered with stained oak boards. The new windows were a dark brown color as well. The door was made from heavy oak boards with narrow windows on each side. A deep porch ran along the front and left side of the house. There were no steps or sidewalks yet, only a few boards that led up to the porch.

Sadie didn't mind. She knew everything would take time. She often wondered if it was right to love a house so much. She adored the looks of it. She loved the way the house blended with the surrounding trees and how the large, old barn complemented the whole area.

She couldn't wait to put her brand-new furniture in the house, decorate the interior, keep it clean, do laundry, make meals, and do all the other everyday things married women did in their homes. It was a joy to think about and imagine.

Then one Sunday in church, the deacon announced Mark's and Sadie's upcoming nuptials. Mark had gone to speak to the deacon previously, who came to visit Sadie and confirm her desire for marriage. It was an age-old tradition and one that Sadie fully appreciated.

After the services, members of the church approached the Miller family wearing wide smiles of anticipation. Women offered to make food for Mam. Men shook Dat's hand, clapping his shoulder with work-gnarled hands. It was their way of saying, "We're here, we're happy for you, we're looking forward to a wedding. What can we do to help?"

Dat grinned and grinned, then he batted away his tears when Sadie's uncle came to tell him he had raised a remarkable daughter. The way she had placed her love and trust in this Mark Peight was commendable.

"They'll be blessed," he said wisely, shaking his head.

"I think that boy's come a long way, from what I've heard about his family."

Dat nodded, unable to speak.

On the other side of the room, poor Mam threw up her hands with laughter. So many people offered to make food that Mam asked Leroy Betty for a notepad to write everything down.

Betty would bring bars the day before the wedding for the relatives to eat while they gathered to prepare the food, the shop, the tables, or whatever else was to be done.

Leroy Betty – Banana Nut Bars.

Leroy Betty was the traditional way of identifying Betty. She was not referred to as Leroy Troyer's wife, Betty, but just Leroy Betty.

Simon Mary – Oatmeal Cookies.

Dave Lavina – Molasses Cremes.

Lod-veig Andy Sarah – Macaroni Salad.

The name *Lod-veig* is Dutch for apple butter. Who knew how Apple-Butter Andy got his nickname? He likely came from a long line of men who cooked apple butter and sold it, or made it exceptionally well. At any rate, once a nickname like that was applied, it stuck for generations.

Sometimes, there were simply too many Andy's within a 20-mile radius, and that was a sure way of knowing which Andy was being mentioned. There were also Pepper Bens and Cheese Haus Sams, and on and on.

Later that day, Mark went to the Miller home for supper. Mam had made fried chicken with the breading recipe they would use for the wedding. She wanted everyone's opinion of it so she could perfect it before the wedding. She also cooked potatoes mixed with an onion sauce and cheddar cheese. There was a roaster of homemade baked beans that had bubbled all afternoon, the bacon and tomato sauce sending up a heady fragrance.

Right before they ate, Rebekah tossed a salad, Leah made the dressing, and they all sat down to a table of happy laughter and endless chatter about the coming wedding. It was less than three weeks away.

Dat said the shop was ready, but everyone protested loud and long, contesting his statement that it was "ready."

The shop was a sort of large garage. It served as Dat's workshop and was where he kept the carriage and spring wagon. Bikes, extra picnic tables, folding chairs, express wagons, and pony carts were also stored there. So was anything else Dat bought or found or thought he needed.

Amish weddings are mostly held in the shop instead of the house because it is a huge areas of unfettered space and 200 or 300 people can be seated there. Tables are set up the day before with white tablecloths and dishes. A neighbor usually offers to host the service, where the actual ceremony is performed during a church service of three to four hours.

David Detweilers agreed to hold the service for Mark's and Sadie's wedding in their shop. Then the wedding guests would walk or drive the half mile or so to the Millers' home for the remainder of the day.

"You've only power-washed the shop," Mam gasped.

"The windows! All those windows!" Leah shrieked.

"The fly-dirt on them!" Anna joined in.

"What did you do with that old picnic table? Surely you're not going to leave it in there?" Mam asked.

"What picnic table?" Dat asked defensively.

Mam laughed and waved a hand, assuring everyone that they had plenty of time. Then she promptly sat down, took off her glasses, and began rubbing them so vigorously that a lens popped out. She quickly got to her knees, scrambling furiously for the missing necessity.

The pandemonium continued when Dat couldn't find the kit to fix Mam's glasses. Sadie upset her glass of water, soaking the clean tablecloth. Leah shrieked and jumped to get a clean tea towel, spilling another glass of ice water with her elbow. Reuben threw up his hands, declared everybody nuts, and went to the refrigerator for more ice.

Mark laughed more than Sadie had ever seen him laugh before. He seemed relaxed, his eyes calm, his smile quick and broad as he reveled in the joy of "his" family.

"Everybody needs to keep calm," he observed, laughing yet again.

"I agree!" Dat called from the living room, followed by a frantic question as to the whereabouts of the eyeglass kit in a tight voice about two octaves higher than normal.

It was a happy time of joy and anticipation, but also of quick, loud responses fueled by worn and edgy nerves. That was what an upcoming wedding did to a family, and you simply couldn't help it. At least that was Sadie's conclusion.

The girls pressed their dresses and hung them neatly

in the closet. They had made a dress for Erma, too, planning and scheming how best to help her with her hair without hurting her feelings. Between sewing projects, they cleaned the house.

Dorothy smirked all week long, batting her eyelashes coquettishly, baiting Sadie with little remarks.

"I went to the Dollar General store, Sadie. Gittin' close to wedding time, now ain't it?"

Sadie nodded happily, her eyes sparkling as she carefully extracted an English muffin from the toaster. She spread a liberal amount of butter all over both halves, took a big bite, and closed her eyes in contentment, her lips glossy with butter.

Dorothy watched her, then sniffed. "Y'know, that's an awful lot of butter on there, young lady. You gonna turn into one of those women that double their weight after they git married?"

"Dorothy!"

"Well, I'm jus' sayin' is all.

"Yep. I went to the Dollar General."

When that bought no response, she cleared her throat loudly.

"Yeah, just thought I should go. Don't really need new shoes but had other stuff on my mind that I needed to get."

Sadie munched her English muffin, saying nothing. Dorothy cleared her throat loudly.

"They got some awful nice wedding wrap."

Sadie's thoughts were far away, thinking of Leroy Betty helping Mark with his wedding suit. She had generously offered to order the suit and all.

"Didn't know if I should get the bag shaped like a gold bell, or the pink with gold polka dots. I told myself that a purple bow would look awful nice on a package like that."

Leroy Betty had even hemmed the sleeves and trouser legs for him and pressed the whole suit afterward. She certainly was the salt of the earth.

"You listenin' ta me?" Dorothy stood over Sadie, hands on hips, her head tilted like a little robin waiting for the earthworm to emerge from the dirt below.

Sadie stuffed the last of the buttered muffin into her mouth. Then she looked up wide-eyed and startled.

"What? What?" she stammered, thoroughly confused.

"Well, I ain't repeatin' myself."

Sadie shrugged her shoulders, gathered up the cleaning supplies she needed for the morning, and headed to the bedrooms.

While dusting the dresser in the master bedroom, a movement in the yard below caught her eye, so she laid down the dust cloth and went to the window.

There was little Sadie Elizabeth, toddling toward the bent form of Bertie, shrieking with glee when he scooped her up in his arms. The regal form of Barbara Caldwell moved across the lawn toward them. She was dressed in the latest fall fashion, her hair coiffed to perfection. Sadie watched the sweet-mannered way she patted Bernie's arm.

It hadn't always been like that. The darling baby girl had done wonders, completely changing Richard and Barbara Caldwell. These two wealthy landowners had it all, but their one real source of happiness was their cherished daughter.

Sadie sighed, then turned back to her dusting, polishing the top of the dresser to a rich sheen as she contemplated the people and her work at the ranch.

Did she really, for sure, want to give up this to become Mark Peight's wife? She knew she'd no longer be able to keep her job at the ranch when the first baby arrived.

It was the Amish way. Women stayed home and took care of the children and their husbands. For generations, mothers prepared their daughters for this important role by teaching them the art of running a home smoothly.

Yes, she was eager. She was prepared to be Mark's wife. She looked forward to her new life with him. But she would miss these people so much. She would come back, yes, but it would never be the same. She wouldn't know the same camaraderie she had known from working among these people day in and day out.

She set the heavy brass candleholders back on the dresser, then frowned as the taper candle wobbled in its socket. Grabbing a tissue, she tore it in half, folded it a few times again, wrapped it around the bottom of the candle, then put it firmly back in the brass holder. It stood straight and strong.

Sadie smiled to herself. What they don't know won't hurt them.

She would miss this house. She loved just being in it, even if it meant cleaning. She enjoyed the work, lifting and replacing and touching objects so far above anything she would ever own.

A muffled screech broke through her absentminded reverie, and she turned to look out the window once again.

She put her hand to her mouth when a shrieking Erma Keim came barreling out of the tack room, her legs churning, her skirt flying above her white knees. A grinning Lothario Bean followed quickly on her heals, both hands holding the pressure nozzle at the end of a long green hose and the water following Erma's yelling form.

Oh, dear.

Sadie laughed as some of the water connected with the retreating back and laughed again at Lothario's obvious glee.

But still. She had pooh-poohed Dorothy's idea of Erma overstepping her bounds with Lothario. She still felt that way. But the scene in the yard was a bit unsettling, nevertheless.

Sadie knew Erma's behavior would be looked at disapprovingly among their people. The scene playing out in the yard below was why some Amish mothers frowned on their girls working "out."

Sadie winced as Barbara Caldwell turned to watch, then relaxed as she saw her laugh with Bertie. As long as Erma knew her place, it would be all right, although Lord knew she had sorely overstepped her designated "place" in Dorothy's kitchen.

As she ran the vacuum cleaner, she thought again about her decision to have her in the bridal party with Reuben. What if she became noisy and, well, like she was today? She was just so overboard.

Back in the kitchen, she spoke to Dorothy about it, which was a big mistake. Sadie wound up defending Erma's reputation and desperately trying to hush up Dorothy before poor Erma returned.

Dorothy said she would have thought better of Sadie. How could she even think Erma would keep that mouth shut long enough to be in a bridal party? And how did she think that red hair would ever lie flat long enough to be in a wedding?

Sadie spent the rest of the day in a sour mood. When she got home that evening, everything got worse. Anna was throwing up again out behind Paris' stall, just one easy retch and she emptied her stomach of the food from supper. She was wiping her mouth when an angry Sadie appeared. All Anna could do was sink to the floor of the barn and deny everything.

Sadie confided in Mark, who said she couldn't expect to fix everyone's problems. Anna was just passing through a phase. This, too, would pass.

As far as Erma Keim was concerned, he wouldn't worry about that either. She was a delight. He was glad she was going to be *nâva hucking*, and he planned on finding a husband for her as soon as Sadie helped her tame that red hair.

Chapter 25

THE DAY OF THE WEDDING DAWNED.

Actually, the day began in the pitch-black hour of four o'clock in the morning when the battery-operated digital alarm went off and woke Jacob Miller from a sound sleep. He found his wife getting dressed in the bathroom. Unlike her husband, she had been wide awake since two-thirty, her mind tossing at the thought of all the disasters that could occur.

He bent to kiss her good morning but was brushed aside like an overgrown housefly.

Aah...well. Mam had a lot on her mind.

Mam woke the whole household, sparing no one, not even relatives in the basement, or Eva and Sadie, who had rejuvenated an old, old bond, by talking until midnight.

Mam popped breakfast casseroles into the oven and got out cups for water and coffee. There was no juice or toast this morning. Cranky little cousins yelled as mothers wet their hair, pulling fine-toothed combs through the long tresses. Mam helped pin capes and adjust coverings.

Erma arrived at five-thirty with a driver and was whisked upstairs with the speed of lightning, though she looked back at the breakfast casserole with genuine longing.

Leah produced all her best hair products and explained the need for neat hair. Rebekah nodded in agreement, exclaiming the wonder of the gels and sprays. They sprayed and pulled and pinned until they finally stepped back and smiled.

"Look at you!" Rebekah cried. "You're gorgeous!"

Erma bent her head to look in the mirror, then put her hands to her cheeks in dramatic fashion.

"Well, you may as well have ironed my hair and been done with it."

They put a new covering on Erma's glossy, now-subdued, red hair and were astounded at the results. What a difference it made!

Sadie combed her hair at least five times before it suited her. She needed both Leah's and Rebekah's help in pinning the white organdy cape and apron.

Mark appeared in his new black suit, his shirt as white as white could possibly be. His hair cut to perfection. Sadie took one look and knew she had never seen him look better.

Was it really true? Was this striking man about to become her husband?

Sadie glanced toward Reuben and winced when Erma linked her arm through his. She smiled gamely at him, bolstering his courage with a quick whisper of, "Remember the saddle."

Poor Reuben.

Sadie hung on to Mark's arm in sheer alarm when a whole army of buggies, vans, buses, and vehicles of every description wound their way up the rural road toward the Detweiler home. When their own ride was at the door,

Sadie gulped down a few swallows of black coffee before following Mark to the waiting carriage that would take them to the Detweilers for the service.

The glossy pine benches in the Detweilers' spotlessly clean shop were set in neat rows. The wedding guests took their seats. Mark and Sadie sat beside each other with Reuben and Erma on one side, Kevin and Leah on the other. They greeted the wedding guests: family, friends, and members of the community.

There was only a handful of Mark's relatives from Pennsylvania, but Sadie was grateful for every single one that came, for Mark's sake.

The family belonged to a sect of the Old Order Amish who dressed a bit different from Sadie's community. They greeted Mark with a sort of curious fascination, as if he was an ancient relic that had survived a remarkable amount of excavation.

He had been given up as a bad sort, a black sheep. Was it any wonder, coming from that sort of family? And here he was, looking normal. It was a miracle. Atlee and Meely's oldest. My, my.

The single boys filed in and were seated on the men's side of the shop, the girls on the women's side. The service began when the first song was announced, a wave of slow, undulating tunes from the German hymnbook enveloping them in the familiar way.

The ministers rose to go to an adjacent room for a conference with Mark and Sadie. This was when the ministers explained the rules and value of Christian marriage and asked if they wished to become man and wife. The ministers wished them many blessings, as was the custom.

When they were dismissed, Mark and Sadie were joined by their *nâva huckers*. Blond-haired Kevin was so striking alongside Leah; Reuben's face was white and tense, while Erma averted her eyes in the greatest show of humility she had ever managed.

Slowly, they walked among the congregation and sat in six special chairs in the ministers' row. The three women sat facing their men, their heads bent, their eyes downcast in the proper way.

The singing ended when the ministers came back from their conference. Then the first speaker stood up and spoke. When he finished, they prayed. Then the second minister stood up and told the story of Tobias, a touching tale of a youth and his bride.

When he came to a certain part in the story, he announced to the wedding guests that Mark and Sadie wished to be united as well.

Very solemnly, their eyes downcast, Mark and Sadie rose. The minister asked them if this was their wish, and they promised it was with a subdued "*Ya.*" The minister joined their hands, pronounced a blessing, the congregation stood in prayer, and they returned to their seats.

Never once did they raise their eyes while the remaining ministers gave testimony. Only when they rose from the last prayer, and the final, rousing, German hymn had begun, did Sadie dare raise her eyes to Mark's own.

He met her eyes. One fleeting look.

How could a lifetime of love be poured forth from those dark eyes in a few seconds? It took her breath away.

She loved him so. With all her heart and soul. Even the fear of the tough times ahead diminished in the face of this love. She was so secure now. His love to her was real. She could never doubt that.

When the song ended, he looked at her again and smiled, a slow easy smile that warmed her the whole way through.

"My wife," he whispered for her ears alone. Her eyes shone into his.

The remainder of the day was a movement of color, warmth, smells, hands shaken, hugs accepted, senses awed by light and sounds.

Their wedding table was a corner. Mark sat on one side, Sadie on the other, their attendants on either side.

There were candles, chinaware, stem glasses, and silverware on white tablecloths of Sadie's choice. The cloth napkins were an off-white color, as were the placemats and accessories.

The mashed potatoes and fried chicken were cooked to perfection, although Sadie hardly remembered what she ate or how it tasted. The women slaved over ovens and stove-tops, getting everything just right.

Sadie loved how the butter was molded in a perfect butterfly-shape on the butter plate. She exclaimed over the perfection of the whole wheat dinner rolls, sadly disturbing the butterfly to spread a small amount of butter on her roll.

Would she ever forget Dorothy's remark about doubling her weight?

Jim and Dorothy dressed in their wedding finery. Dorothy wore a blazing-pink polyester suit with a large corsage from the Dollar General firmly imbedded in the lapel. Her hair looked really good, for Dorothy. Jim smiled and beamed beside his portly, brightly-colored wife.

Richard and Barbara Caldwell were seated at the English table, the one that had special servers for important guests. They were as resplendent as Sadie had imagined, and little Sadie Elizabeth was a vision in yellow.

Beside them, Bertie Orthman and Lothario Bean and his lovely little wife, followed by their beautiful daughters, were all laughing and seemed to be enjoying their first Amish wedding.

Then Marcellus and Louis came back from wherever they had gone and Sadie leaned over. "Mark!"

He looked to where Sadie pointed, and his eyes became soft with emotion as he looked at the two lovely children, their dark faces alight with interest. He watched as Jim bent to tie a shoe and brush off a bit of dust. Dorothy hovered and filled their plates like a pink mother hen.

"They're definitely two of the lucky ones," Mark said meaningfully.

Sadie nodded, found his hand, and squeezed it reassuringly.

After dinner, they opened a towering mound of gifts. Richard and Barbara Caldwell came to talk to them, and Sadie found herself choking up, unable to speak. Richard Caldwell quickly gathered Sadie into a bear hug while Barbara patted her white organdy cape.

The Caldwells' present was a painting of horses, the kind Sadie never thought she would own. It took her breath away. A band of horses running against the wind, with a thunderstorm in a background of gray, beige, blue, and green clouds.

Dorothy's gift was encased in the gold, bell-shaped gift bag. Inside were the two ceramic crosses with pink flowers that she had promised Sadie a long time ago.

"One for each side o' yer hutch cupboard," Dorothy beamed.

There were so many gifts. A gas grill. A pair of Adirondack chairs. Dishes, cookware, towels, blankets, shovels, brushes, utensils, wooden racks, clothespins, tea towels, bakeware, lanterns, batteries. Would they need to buy anything at all?

Rebekah wrote it all down in a notebook, listing the gift and the giver.

The rest of the afternoon was filled with hymn-singing.

They served a supper of scalloped potatoes, home-cured ham, lima beans and corn, and a tossed salad. There was also more wedding cake and Dorothy's coconut cream pies, which even Erma pronounced the best she had ever tasted.

Sadie was feeling a bit wilted now, ready for the day to come to a close and be alone with her new husband.

Evidently Erma still had energy to spare. She was having an animated conversation with Reuben. When she flicked a spoonful of meringue at Reuben, hitting him squarely on the nose, they both fell into a fit of convulsive giggles that they were powerless to stop.

"Whooo!" Erma said in the most unladylike voice Sadie had ever heard.

Reuben, however, was thoroughly impressed. He eyed Erma with a newfound respect. Anyone who could flick a spoon and hit the target directly was pretty awesome. So she showed him how to do it.

Mark grinned, then laughed outright when a glob of meringue landed squarely in Kevin's lap, barely missing Sadie.

Mam frowned in the direction of the wedding tables, her eyes looking completely exhausted. Somehow Dat was still going strong, although he had a look about him like a hot-air balloon getting ready for its descent.

Sadie caught sight of Rebekah seated beside Benjamin Nissley, their heads bent as they sang in unison. It was only a matter of time for those two.

Sadie sat back and let her eyes roam the room. She thought of weddings she had been to in the past, sitting beside boys she barely knew, eating food that tasted like sawdust, gamely making attempts at conversation, relieved beyond words to be finished with the singing.

Her eyes landed on Anna, who was seated much, much too close to Leon Hershberger. Leon seemed to be leaning in close to her, his auburn hair cut in the English style, the disobedience glaring from his bold eyes. Anna had a spot of color on each cheek, her smile wide, her eyes never leaving his face.

Sadie's heart sank. Would Anna ever understand the fullness of her self-worth and the beauty of her character?

Sadie silently grieved for Anna, if only for a moment. She could not solve the problem today, not on her wedding day.

After the last guest finally bade them a goodnight, Mam and Dat kicked off their shoes and sat down with fresh mugs of coffee. Rebekah and Leah wearily sagged in kitchen chairs, Anna seated on the bench.

Reuben went straight to bed, but only after eating another slice of wedding cake and calling Mark "brother" with a toothy grin.

Mark asked Sadie if they should ride Paris and Bruno, Mark's new horse, over to their house for their first night together.

It was a wonderful idea!

Sadie raced up the stairs to change clothes and pack a bag. Then she hugged her parents, telling them they'd ride back in the morning to help clean up.

"But…" Mam started protesting.

"She'll be okay," Dat broke in, looking at her meaningfully.

Mam closed her mouth, then smiled as Sadie dashed out the door, her duffel bag swinging.

When Sadie reached the barn, Mark had Paris ready, the saddle securely in place. Bruno pranced beside her.

"Oh, Paris!" Sadie burst out, then swung up while Mark secured her duffel bag behind his saddle.

The moon was not completely full, but almost. Sadie couldn't really tell, except that one side seemed a little lopsided. It outlined the ridges, the trees, even the winding road in front of them.

Bruno pranced, wanting to run. He hopped sideways, then bucked lightly.

Paris walked slowly down the drive, her head up, her ears pricked forward, alive to every movement around her. Her mane rippled and flowed, the moonlight catching the white highlights. She picked her way carefully, as if she thought she was carrying royalty.

Was it only Sadie's childish imagination, or did it seem like Paris knew this was a special evening?

No, Paris would know.

After Bruno settled down, Mark rode very close to Sadie. He extended his hand, his white shirt sleeve silver in the moonlight. Sadie met his hand halfway and grasped it.

The saddles creaked, the horses hooves made a dull thunking sound. Far away, a coyote barked, then wailed eerily. The pine trees stood tall and straight on either side of them while the stars twinkled above.

"This whole day has been unbelievable," Mark said. "I feel like I'm in a dream."

His voice was gruff, the emotion he felt making it sound ragged.

Sadie smiled at him. "Why?"

"I simply do not deserve you. How did you ever agree to become my wife?"

"It's so easy, Mark. I love you. This is all I ever wanted."

Then they galloped their horses up the side of Atkin's Ridge. The cool breeze fanned their faces; the stars disappeared when they rode beneath the trees. Rounding the corner of the ridge, they slowed the horses for the downhill ride to their home, their start to a life lived as one, for better or for worse, in sickness and in health, until death parted them.

The End

Glossary

Ausbund—The *Ausbund* is the hymnbook that the Amish sing from during church services. The old, German book was written by their forefathers during a time of persecution and imprisonment.

Bann and meidung—A Pennsylvania Dutch dialect phrase meaning, "ban and shunning."

Barmherzikeit—A Pennsylvania Dutch dialect word meaning, "mercy."

Blottchich—A Pennsylvania Dutch dialect word meaning, "clumsy."

Botschaft—A Pennsylvania Dutch dialect word meaning, "message." Also the name of an Amish newspaper.

Broadfall pants—Pants worn by Amish men and fastened with buttons rather than a zipper.

Bupp! Grosse Bupp!—A sentence in the Pennsylvania Dutch dialect meaning, "Baby! Big Baby!"

Bupplich—A Pennsylvania Dutch dialect word meaning, "childish."

Covering—A fine mesh headpiece worn by Amish females in an effort to follow the Amish interpretation of a New Testament teaching in 1 Corinthians 11.

Cuts—A Pennsylvania Dutch dialect word meaning, "throw up."

Dat—A Pennsylvania Dutch dialect word used to address or to refer to one's father.

Dichly—A Pennsylvania Dutch dialect word meaning "head scarf" or "bandanna." A *dichly* is a triangle of cotton fabric, usually a men's handkerchief cut in half and hemmed, worn by Amish women and girls when they do yard work or anything strenuous.

Driver—When the Amish need to go somewhere, and it's too distant to travel by horse and buggy, they may hire someone to drive them in a car or van.

Eck—One corner of the room reserved for the wedding party during the wedding reception.

English—The Amish term for anyone who is not Amish.

Excommunicated—A practice performed when a member of the Amish church breaks his/her vows to the church and refuses to repent. The former member is *excommunicated* and not permitted to participate in church activities or interact with the Amish community.

Fer-fearish—A phrase in the Pennsylvania Dutch dialect meaning, "misled."

Frieda—A Pennsylvania Dutch word meaning, "peace."

Ga-mach—A phrase in the Pennsylvania Dutch dialect meaning, "chaos."

Gehorsam—A Pennsylvania Dutch dialect word meaning, "obedient."

Goot-manich—A phrase in the Pennsylvania Dutch dialect meaning, "kind."

Huck nâva—A phrase in the Pennsylvania Dutch dialect meaning, to be an attendant in a bridal party at a wedding.

Ich mind allus. —A sentence in the Pennsylvania Dutch dialect meaning, "I remember everything."

Im bann—A phrase in the Pennsylvania Dutch dialect meaning, "In the ban" or "shunned."

In-between Sundays—Old Order Amish have church every other Sunday. This is an old custom that allows ministers to visit other church districts. An *in-between* Sunday is the day that a district does not hold church services.

Kessle-haus: The part of the house that Amish families use as a catchall for coats, boots, umbrellas, and laundry, also for tasks such as mixing calf starter, warming baby chicks, and canning garden vegetables.

Komm—A Pennsylvania Dutch dialect word meaning, "come."

Lob Song—This hymn is sung at every Amish church service. It comes from the *Ausbund* and is Pennsylvania Dutch for "Song of Praise."

Lod-veig—A Pennsylvania Dutch dialect word meaning, "apple butter."

Mam—A Pennsylvania Dutch dialect word used to address or to refer to one's mother.

Mennonite—Another Anabaptist group which shares common beliefs with the Amish. The differences between the two groups lie in their practices. Mennonites tend to be more open to higher education and to mission activity and less distinctly different from the rest of the world in their dress, transportation, and use of technology.

Mommy—A Pennsylvania Dutch dialect word used to address or to refer to one's grandmother.

Maud—A Pennsylvania Dutch dialect word meaning a live-in female helper, usually hired by a family for a week or two at a time. *Mauds* often help to do house-, lawn-, and garden-work after the birth of a baby.

Nay! Nay!—Words in the Pennsylvania Dutch dialect meaning, "No! No!"

Ordnung—The Amish community's agreed-upon rules for living, based upon their understanding of the Bible, particularly the New Testament. The *Ordnung* varies some from community to community, often reflecting the leaders' preferences and the local traditions and historical practices.

Poosing—A word in the Pennsylvania Dutch dialect meaning, "pouting."

Phone Shanty—Most Old Order Amish do not have telephone landlines in their homes so that incoming calls do not overtake their lives and so that they are not physically connected to the larger world. Many, however, build a small, fully enclosed structure, much like a commercial telephone booth, somewhere outside their house where they can make phone calls and retrieve phone messages.

Putting patties down—Putting one's hands on one's lap before praying, as a sign of respect. Usually includes bowing one's head and closing one's eyes. A phrase spoken to children who are learning the practice.

Recht fertich—A phrase in the Pennsylvania Dutch dialect meaning, "justify yourself."

Rumspringa—The time in an Amish young person's life between the age of 16 and marriage. Includes structured social activities for groups, as well as dating. Usually takes place on the weekend.

Schlofc, buppli, Schlofc,
Da doddy hüt die schofe,
Die mommy melked die rote kie
Kommt net hame bis mya frie
Schlofc, buppli, Schlofc.

A lullaby in the Pennsylvania Dutch dialect meaning:
Sleep, Baby, sleep,
Grandfather watches the sheep,
Grandmother milks the red cows,
Won't return till early morning,
Sleep baby sleep.

Schnitza—A word in the Pennsylvania Dutch dialect meaning, "lie."

S'hut kenn dragons—A sentence in the Pennsylvania Dutch dialect meaning, "There are no dragons."

So veesht—A phrase in Pennsylvania Dutch meaning "so much."

Toast brot, milch und an oy—A phrase in the Pennsylvania Dutch dialect meaning, "toast, hot milk, and a soft boiled egg."

Ungehorsam—A word in the Pennsylvania Dutch dialect meaning, "disobedient."

Upp—A Pennsylvania Dutch equivalent of "Hey!"
Unser Himmlischer Vater—A phrase in the Pennsylvania Dutch dialect meaning, "Our Heavenly Father."

Vass geht au? —A sentence in the Pennsylvania Dutch dialect meaning, "What's going on?"

veesht—A word in the Pennsylvania Dutch dialect meaning, "so badly."

Verboten—A word in the Pennsylvania Dutch dialect meaning, "forbidden."

Working Out—To *work out* means to work outside of the home. Amish children usually work at a job away from home during their teen years.

Ya—Pennsylvania Dutch for "Yes."

Youngie—A word in the Pennsylvania Dutch dialect meaning "youth."

Other Books by Linda Byler

LIZZIE SEARCHES FOR LOVE SERIES

BOOK ONE

LINDA BYLER

When Strawberries Bloom

BOOK TWO

BOOK THREE

TRILOGY

COOKBOOK

SADIE'S MONTANA SERIES

BOOK ONE

BOOK TWO

BOOK THREE

TRILOGY

BOOK ONE

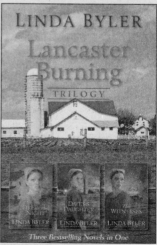

BOOK TWO

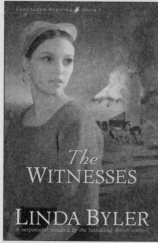

BOOK THREE

TRILOGY

HESTER'S HUNT FOR HOME SERIES

BOOK ONE

BOOK TWO

BOOK THREE

TRILOGY

The Dakota Series

BOOK ONE

BOOK TWO

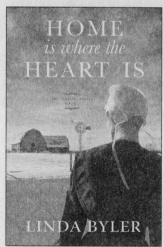

BOOK THREE

TRILOGY

THE HEALING

A SECOND CHANCE

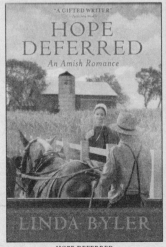

HOPE DEFERRED

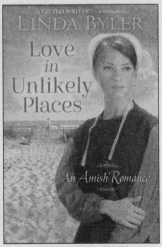

LOVE IN UNLIKELY PLACES

THE
Christmas
VISITOR

AN AMISH ROMANCE

LINDA BYLER

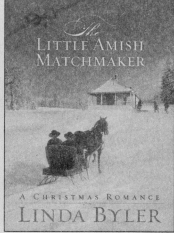

The
LITTLE AMISH
MATCHMAKER

A CHRISTMAS ROMANCE

LINDA BYLER

LINDA BYLER

Mary's
Christmas
Goodbye

AN AMISH ROMANCE

LINDA BYLER

BECKY
Meets Her
MATCH

*Is Daniel Stoltzfus
really ready for Becky?*

A Dog for CHRISTMAS

AN AMISH CHRISTMAS ROMANCE

LINDA BYLER

A Horse For ELSIE

AN AMISH CHRISTMAS ROMANCE

LINDA BYLER

LINDA BYLER

The More the Merrier

AN AMISH CHRISTMAS ROMANCE

A gifted writer. —Publishers Weekly

LINDA BYLER

Amish Christmas ROMANCE COLLECTION

Three Novellas in One

LINDA BYLER

BUGGY SPOKE SERIES FOR YOUNG READERS

BOOK ONE

BOOK TWO

BOOK THREE

The Author

LINDA BYLER WAS RAISED IN AN AMISH FAMILY AND IS AN ACTIVE member of the Amish church today. Growing up, Linda loved to read and write. In fact, she still does. Linda is well-known within the Amish community as a columnist for a weekly Amish newspaper. She writes all her novels by hand in notebooks.

Linda is the author of six series of novels, all set among the Amish communities of North America: Lizzie Searches for Love, Sadie's Montana, Lancaster Burning, Hester's Hunt for Home, The Dakota Series, and the Buggy Spoke Series for younger readers. Her stand-alone novels include *The Healing*, *A Second Chance*, and *Hope Deferred*. Linda has also written several Christmas romances set among the Amish: *Mary's Christmas Goodbye*, *The Christmas Visitor*, *The Little Amish Matchmaker*, *Becky Meets Her Match*, *A Dog for Christmas*, *A Horse for Elsie*, and *The More the Merrier*. Linda has coauthored *Lizzie's Amish Cookbook: Favorite Recipes from Three Generations of Amish Cooks!*